DEAD REGULAR

ALSO BY HARRY COLFER

Number 01: Abdominal Pain
Number 03: Animal Bite
Number 04: Assault
Number 05: Back Pain
Number 06: Breathing Problems
Number 08: Carbon Monoxide
Number 09: Cardiac Arrest
Number 10: Chest Pain
Number 11: Choking
Number 12: Convulsions
Number 15: Electrocution
Number 16: Eye Problem
Number 17: Fall
Number 21: Haemorrhage
Number 23: Overdose
Number 24: Pregnancy
Number 25: Psychiatric
Number 29: Traffic Accident
Number 31: Unconscious
Number 32: Unknown Problem

And

Collection 1: The First Twelve Tales

DEAD REGULAR

HARRY COLFER

Dead Regular

Published by Harry Colfer Books

Copyright © 2020 Harry Colfer

All rights reserved.

ISBN: 978-0-6489735-1-5 (Paperback Edition)

ISBN: 978-0-6489735-2-2 (eBook Edition)

No part of this book may be reproduced in any form or by any electronic or mechanical means, including information storage and retrieval systems, without written permission from the author, except for the use of brief quotations in a book review.

❀ Created with Vellum

DISCLAIMER

This story is set in Brisbane and takes place in 2012. Although the described medical procedures and techniques are authentic for that year and references are made to some real places and organisations, it is a work of fiction created for entertainment purposes only.

The paramedic characters portrayed in this story work for the Brisbane City Ambulance Service (B-CAS), which does not exist and is in no way meant to portray, or depict any existing, or former ambulance service, or organisation. The names, characters, or incidents mentioned herein are also completely fictitious. Any similarity to the name, character, or history of any person is entirely coincidental and unintentional.

This book is dedicated to all paramedics working the frontline, especially Gareth Miller, a family friend who lost his fight against cancer in 2014, the year I completed the first draft of this story.

PROLOGUE

A young man sits on a bench, his arms outstretched along the wooden back support. He is directing his face up towards the warmth of the summer sun. His eyes closed behind his aviator Ray-Bans as a smile plays at the corners of his mouth.

He is wearing shiny black shoes and a light grey suit, jacket draped on the seat. A blue patterned tie and crisp white shirt complete his ensemble. He looks like a shopfront mannequin. His head rolls forward and he appears to watch a raucous squabble that breaks out among a small flock of noisy miners. They squawk and fight in a three-dimensional tussle that only birds can manage. He watches their progress within the line of palm trees arranged in front of him until they disappear into the sprawling canopy of a weeping fig.

His focus turns to the Treasury Casino across the road. The grand sandstone facade reminds him of the imposing Forgan Smith building and he smiles. His third year of studying Law at the University of Queensland is now over with excellent results. But he expected that. He worked hard and deserves his grades.

He raises his wrist and looks at his watch. Just past noon. His parents are meeting him opposite the Casino at 12:30 PM. An easy place for them to find if they take the right off-ramp. They insisted on driving all the way up from Sydney, instead of him jumping on a plane. Silly old fools. They called from a hotel in Coffs Harbour last night.

The young man returns to basking in the sun. He thinks of the freedom a summer at the family beach house might bring. At the very least he can have a few months break from his own cooking. He wonders if his brother will be back from Melbourne. Their university choices had finally separated them. It was a deliberate decision. A lifetime of being dressed in the same clothes makes you yearn for individuality. A personal identity. But they both missed each other. He misses him now.

He looks at his watch again. They will be here soon, they are never late.

After a while he gets up from the park bench and swings his suit jacket over his shoulder, hooking his finger through the loop in the collar. He adjusts his Ray-Bans with his free hand as he casts an admiring glance to the girls sunbathing on the grass. He saunters down the walkway towards the Conrad Hotel, like a peacock wearing sunnies. One girl leans to the other and they giggle. He shrugs and pretends to study the plaque below the bronze statue of Queen Victoria.

He eyes his watch and frowns, walking down the adjacent paved area to the road. He dials a number on his mobile, slowing his walk as he waits for the line to connect.

"Hey Dad, you got yourself lost?" The background noise on the call was unfamiliar to him.

"Afternoon, son. We'll be with you in a second. We were held up by traffic near the Gold Coast."

"Excuses, excuses. Thought you were never late."

"C'mon, cut your old man some slack. Two days drive and I'm less than ten minutes behind schedule."

"You're the one who set the standard so high."

"Touché. It's the Elizabeth Street turn-off we want, isn't it?"

"Yes, that's it."

"Just taking the off-ramp now."

"See you in a minute, I'm on the pavement to your right, next to the park."

The young man hangs up and drops the phone back in his pocket. His attention on the intersection, the sunbathing girls forgotten. Then he sees his father driving a brand new silver BMW 3 series convertible round the gentle slope towards him. No wonder he wanted to drive. The top is down, his mother beside him and someone else is in the rear seat. It's his brother!

His face breaks into a beaming smile and he waves as they approach the junction. His family all wave back as the car sails through the red light and into the path of an oncoming garbage truck.

The scene plays out like a slow motion crash-test video. But where there should be dummies wearing black and yellow calibration marks, he can see his parents and brother. The truck driver has no time to apply his brakes and the wide expanse of the cab hits square on to the passenger cell of the BMW. Tonnes of steel and household waste travelling at sixty kilometres an hour transfer their kinetic energy via the impassive laws of physics into the gleaming new German bodywork.

Metal crumples.

Glass shatters.

Seats buckle.

Bones break.

Organs fail.

Bodies burst.

The collision is over in a heartbeat and before the sound reaches him, his mother is already dead. Her head collides with the truck's grill and explodes. The outstretched arm she waved in welcome limply follows the arc of blood and brain matter that sprays from her body.

His father is the next to die, killed by his own wife. The impact of the truck crushes the car's structure so much that the two front seats slam together. Despite the seat belt, her torso and arms fly into contact with her husband's chest, transferring the truck's deadly energy. His heart flings to the right, its own weight tearing a hole in his aorta. He lives just long enough to realise what his mistake has wrought. Blood floods into his thoracic cavity, his breathing falters as his consciousness fades.

His brother is the only survivor of the initial crash. Sitting on the driver's side spares him from the onslaught of folding metal and plastic, but with his right arm raised, his chest is thrown against the door. Ribs crack, the broken ends puncture his lung. The ligament supporting his liver acts like a cheese wire and lacerates the organ. His pelvis succumbs to the shearing forces and breaks in two places as his femur snaps and dislocates from its socket.

Another heartbeat passes. The young man is standing transfixed. His arm raised. Mouth open.

His lungs finally work and he sucks in a huge breath that he uses to scream a single plaintive word, "Noooo!"

The garbage truck screeches to a halt, but the driver remains sitting, clutching the steering wheel. Knuckles white, eyes wide, staring at the devastation.

The young man can finally move and runs to the mangled BMW, now an integral part of the truck.

His mother's upper body lies in his father's lap. He has seen them sitting that way so many times before. Curled up in front of the TV, each with a glass of wine. But it is not claret spilt over their clothes.

Her head is deformed, like a deflated soccer ball, and blood mats her long blonde hair. The muscles of her upper arm twitch, involuntary movements from tissues still functioning, despite the body's demise. But her hips and legs lie lifeless, crushed and twisted among the buckled remains of the car.

His father sits upright, head resting on the restraint. Mouth and eyes open, the sightless pupils fixed and dilated even in the glare of the bright sunshine. His skin as white as snow, his chest as still as a tombstone.

The young man takes a second to view the carnage and moves on to the back seat. He can do nothing for his parents now. Behind them, his brother's body hangs outside the car. He reaches for him and holds his trunk and head, lifting him up to free the door. With that released, he drags him out onto the road, stumbling backwards so he ends with his brother lying on his legs.

Concern etches the young man's face, as his brother's eyes flicker open and he coughs. Blood dribbles from the corner of his mouth as he tries to smile and says in a weak voice, "Surprise."

Cars have stopped.

People run over.

Onlookers stand and gawp.

The air is heavy with gasoline fumes.

The young man turns and yells out, "Someone call an ambulance! Now!"

He cradles his brother's head in his arms, stroking his hair. "Don't worry, Bro. Help's on its way."

His brother gives him a weak smile. He is looking pale.

"I thought you had too much studying to do to leave Melbourne."

He licks his lower lip. His mouth feels dry. "Mum and Dad said I could do with the break... Didn't think they'd be so literal."

"Ha! Always the comedian."

He nods towards the car. "How are they?"

The young man shakes his head.

"Fuck... What a mess."

His brother coughs again, his chest makes a gurgling sound, and then he cries out in pain. The young man looks around and sees a woman holding a phone to her ear. He shouts at her, "Where's the ambulance?"

She is in her late twenties, wearing a dusty pink chiffon blouse, a black pencil skirt and stilettos. Her face appears paler than his brother's, if that is possible. "I'm talking to them now. They said they're on their way."

"Tell them to hurry!"

She turns away as she speaks into the phone.

He goes back to stroking his sibling's hair. "C'mon, Bro. You're a medical student, what should I do?"

"Physician heal thyself, eh?" *He grimaces.* "OK… what's my pulse doing?"

The young man reaches to his wrist and feels for the familiar beat, but can't find anything.

"Try my neck… if there's nothing there."

He does as instructed.

"Got it. It's weak and fast."

"Shit." *He licks his lips again.* "I'm going into shock… Must have an internal bleed… Christ, my leg hurts."

"What can I do?"

"Don't suppose you have… a few bags of blood… and a surgical team handy?"

A distant wail of a siren grows louder.

"Hang on in there, Bro, here comes the cavalry."

The noise is soon deafening, bouncing off the high-sided buildings as the vehicle approaches through the traffic. But as the source of the cacophony arrives, all that appears is the red front of a fire truck.

Four firefighters decamp from the tender and rush to the wreck and the young man's confusion turns to anger. "Where's the ambulance? He doesn't need firies, he needs medical help!"

Two of the firemen approach him. "Sorry mate, they'll be here soon. We need to move you out of here. The fuel could ignite any minute."

"I'm not leaving my brother!"

"I'm not asking you to leave him, we just need to move you a safe distance from the car."

His brother agrees. "Listen to them, Bro… You can't help anyone… if we're both… flame-grilled."

The young man slides from beneath his brother and lowers him to the ground, then assists the firemen with the lift. As they relocate his injured body, at first he screams, but then stifles his anguish to a series of whimpers.

More sirens wail and the young man twists in their direction, but all he can see are two police cars approaching the scene. He looks about wildly, shouting at no one in particular, "Where's the ambulance? Where's the fucking ambulance?"

1
―――――
GOGGLES

He sat in the driver's seat with the headlights off, a motionless silhouette in a vehicle parked some way down from the alley he was watching. The gap between the buildings was dark and foreboding with two large industrial bins obscuring half the entrance. They created a blockade that meant that once in the alley you were unlikely to be seen. The stench from the overflowing garbage provided further seclusion, making the venue uninviting for drunken couples looking for a quick grope while staggering back from their latest nightclub conquest. Parking lots and office blocks lined the road, the steep sides of which prevented any view down into the alley from the tall high-rises of the Brisbane skyline. Street-lamps were either broken or non-existent. The only light filtered through from the main drag of Leichhardt Street, a few turns away.

It was the perfect spot for the homeless to enjoy an undisturbed sleep and he had learnt it was a regular haunt for his latest target. From his research, he knew there were no CCTV cameras and at this hour most of the revellers and potential witnesses had left the city. After all, it was Thursday morning and most had to wake for work in a few hours.

There was movement in the alley, but it was just the brush-tail possum he had seen earlier, slinking in to pick up a tasty morsel from the bins. The cat-sized marsupial was now carrying a half-eaten apple in its mouth. It stopped in the middle of the road and dropped the prize to sniff the air. A wild animal juxtaposed on an urban street scene. As if detecting the nearby brooding menace, it turned its head and seemed to stare straight into his eyes. A moment passed and then it snatched the apple and scampered off, disappearing among the branches of the nearest tree.

Time ticked by. Through the slight gap at the top of the window, he heard a siren wailing in the distance, probably an ambulance plying its trade. He tried to keep himself calm, but the wait was starting to affect his already tense body. He rubbed the tips of his fingers together and felt the moistness of his skin. Sweating, dilated pupils, increased heart rate, increased breathing rate. He mused over the neurological and chemical pathways of the sympathetic nervous system that caused these signs and symptoms and found composure within his medical knowledge.

He looked down at the syringe in his lap. He preferred to keep changing his modus operandi to make his actions less easily traced, always using the guise of a non-suspicious death to hide his killing spree. But no one looked for elevated levels of insulin in homeless corpses. Death on the streets was just a consequence of that lifestyle choice and these scum rarely, if ever, worried about their health.

Movement in the shadows up ahead interrupted his thoughts. Although his vision had grown accustomed to the dark, he still had to strain his eyes to make out the figure stumbling along the pavement, bumping off the walls. The man clutched the cause of his unsteady gait, a four-litre sack of cheap wine that was now almost empty. On finding the opening between the dumpsters, the drunk stopped, swayed and for a moment it looked like a backwards fall onto the concrete was imminent. A head injury sustained like that and there might be no need to leave his car. But somehow the man stayed vertical and then dragged himself past the bins and out of sight.

The watcher waited, but now there was an added intensity. Was this his prey? Had Brian Briggs just staggered into his trap? BB was an urban outdoorsman who spent half his life in the Emergency Departments of either the Princess Alexandra or Royal Brisbane hospitals. Sometimes he was ill, but mostly he just wanted a free meal and a warm bed for the night. BB had figured out that claiming chest pain gave him at least six hours under cover and that was when there were no delays. His latest visit to the Royal had been for pneumonia, but he self-discharged after two days, desperate for a drink.

The watcher passed the time by thinking about the effects of chronic alcohol abuse. Most people have heard of liver cirrhosis, but he mulled over the more insidious sequelae. How the organ's impaired function increases the blood pressure in the portal system causing ascites, all the accumulating tissue fluid distending the abdomen like a balloon. But worse still was the development of oesophageal varices, or varicose veins of the gullet. Once one of those vessels ruptures an alcoholic often bleeds to death through their mouth, vomiting their life blood like the countless times they spewed their drinks.

He looked at his watch. Twenty minutes had elapsed and it was time for action. He once again checked the street, using the rear-view and wing mirrors to search behind him. Nothing moved. Nothing stirred. He slipped on some vinyl gloves and picked up the syringe, dropping it in his pocket. With the wait now over, a calm befell his body and he exited the car in a single fluid motion. Crossing the road, he walked to the alley, moving more quietly than the possum, not stopping until he too had ducked out of sight.

The darkness enveloped him like a pall and he paused, listening. The reek of rotting refuse was almost tangible, but he focused on the rasping breaths that were coming from deeper in the passageway. As he suspected, he could have located his victim just by sound in the cave-like conditions, but checking for other inhabitants and finding a vein would have been impossible. He reached into his jacket and brought out a set of night-vision goggles, donning and switching them on with practised precision. An artificial green light bathed the squalid scene.

Brian Briggs lay propped up in a corner amongst a pile of soiled blankets, wheezing with every snoring breath. From the labels on the linen, there was quite a collection amassed from several hospitals. Although his actual age was fifty-two, most would have put him in his seventies. A life strewn with disappointments, failures and alcohol abuse, along with years of exposure to the Queensland sun, had taken its toll on his appearance and demeanour. Various blemishes, sores and infections scattered his tanned craggy skin. His limp greasy grey hair was far beyond redemption, despite the advertising claims on any shampoo bottle. The unkempt beard that adorned his chin had been trimmed, no doubt by a well-meaning nurse, but any improvement was spoilt by the build-up of sputum at the corners of his mouth. BB was someone who felt that life owed him a favour and one of his many burdens was the monumental chip he carried on his shoulder. As such, he had never been someone who spawned friends easily and most of the other street people avoided him like the plague.

With his quarry confirmed, a visual sweep of the alley revealed no other low-lifes, so the watcher approached the sleeping man and squatted down beside him. He reached over and gave him a shake. Nothing. No reaction. Just more snoring. He nodded to himself then slipped a tourniquet around BB's grubby bare arm and retrieved the syringe from his pocket. Removing the cover, he looked for a vein passing beneath one of the many sores on the old wino's skin. Choosing the best option, he pushed the needle through the wound, concealing the track mark from any over-diligent pathologist.

Suddenly, BB let out a groan and his eyes blinked open, staring right into the watcher's eyes. "Wha' the fuck?"

For a moment, he thought there was a flicker of recognition. Then he realised it was pitch dark. He was the only one who could see. He responded in a soothing voice. "Just some more antibiotics for your chest infection, BB. Go back to sleep."

"Oh aye, no worries." With that his lids drooped and his head lolled onto the wall, the snore resuming.

The watcher flipped off the tourniquet and pushed the plunger, then withdrew the needle and applied pressure to the site. As he waited for the blood to clot, he recapped the syringe and dropped it and the tourniquet back in his pocket. Then he stood, surveying his handiwork and searched the scene for anything out of place. Anything to alert the authorities. Anything that may raise suspicion.

Satisfied, he turned and walked away, slipping off his

goggles before leaving the seclusion of the alleyway. All up, he had spent less than five minutes out of his car. As his footsteps receded, the loud rasping breaths of the homeless man began to slow, the pause between each getting longer and longer until the alley eventually fell silent.

2

A GOOD JOB

The last remaining embers of a fading sunset were yielding in the darkening night's sky. It was 6:30 PM, towards the end of a twelve-hour day shift, due to finish in thirty minutes. And I was shattered. So far, we'd completed nine jobs without a break and were now facing overtime as Comms had just dispatched us to a road traffic collision in Carseldine. What I needed was a triple-shot of coffee, either that or a good job. And this call sounded like a good job.

Non-paramedics always have difficulty grasping the concept of a good job. What they don't understand is that emergency work is filled with so many time-wasting call-outs. A good job is when the patient needs saving. Not some bullshit saving from their dreary existence. Nor saving from some self-induced calamity that could have been solved by opening a can of 'Toughen-Up'. But someone who is actually near to death. It's a common misconception that ambulances only go to emergencies. Ironically, real emergency situations are not routine for most paramedics in Brisbane. Countless jobs boil down to an expensive taxi ride, so when you get to use your expertise and training, that's a good job.

This frustration is doubly true for me being an Intensive Care Paramedic rostered on a two-man truck. Most ambos working for the Brisbane City Ambulance Service are Advanced Care Paramedics, but there is a smattering of ICPs who have added skills and experience. As a result, we're allowed to play with a lot more toys and drugs. We get to wear gold epaulettes instead of the usual red ones and a few of the lucky ICPs work on dedicated single-manned rapid response vehicles. These cars are dispatched to high acuity cases and so skill wastage is less of an issue. Not so for the truck ICP. We have to hold out for the good jobs and hope we can remember what to do. After all, the buck stops with the ICP when one arrives on scene.

We were hammering along Gympie Road, Brisbane Northside, weaving through the rush-hour traffic at breakneck pace, not due to the severity of the case, nor the compassion of the driver, but because it was Scotty behind the wheel. When asked why they do their job, some paramedics will say they do it to make a difference. Others, perhaps more jaded ones, say it's to pay the bills. Scotty is a rev head. He does it because he can ignore the speed limit. In a colourful three-tonne truck. With flashing lights, sirens and a very loud horn.

It makes for an interesting passenger experience. A good deal of which is the physical control needed to prevent yourself from flinching or grabbing at the armrest. Because that's part of the game for Scotty. He takes great joy from generating fear in his crewmate while flying through traffic or screeching round a blind bend. Especially if you're an ICP.

But I would not whimper. Even if he wrapped the ambulance around the nearest telegraph pole, or smashed us into an unsuspecting B-Double truck, I'd give him my pre-rehearsed unimpressed look. I'd worked with many other ambos, all had their foibles. You have to take the rough with the smooth. And some were rougher than smooth. I've always tried to learn from the different ways people work. The ones with questionable practice I'd either try to educate or placate, but the good operators I'd observe and assimilate their knowledge and techniques. Now, a decade in the job, I was less tolerant of incompetence. However, Scotty was far from incompetent. He just liked to drive fast.

Although he looked a lot older, Scotty was only twenty-nine and qualified as an ACP five years ago. His premature ageing was in part due to his receding hairline that was making a rapid two-pronged attack from both temples. As a result, he kept his dark hair cut short, but compensated by maintaining an almost permanent layer of stubble that helped to frame his infectious grin. He had a thin wiry build and boundless energy, fuelled by a voracious appetite for junk food.

Triple J was filling the cab with some light-mood music, but our ears focused on the VHF radio. It's weird, when a good job goes down an experienced ambo is suddenly alert, like Spider-Man. What we refer to as our 'Spidey' senses. Despite a composed and nonchalant exterior, we were both listening to the different resources being attached and keeping an ear open for the arrival of the primary crew.

I had just thrown Scotty a pair of gloves on the dash when the radio crackled into life. "Comms, 831 on scene. Windscreen sitrep. Three-car RTC, very high mechanism. Several patients involved and one's been ejaculated from the vehicle. Will call again with a clinical sitrep. Confirming need for ICP backup and the doctor truck."

Scotty looked at me with eyebrows raised. "Did he just say what I think he said?"

"Yep, I certainly heard e-jac-u-la-ted."

I grabbed the mic and pressed the transmit button. "Comms, 965. Please inform the crew we're coming."

Scotty gave me a stunned look, perhaps the one he'd been trying to elicit from me with all his unbridled driving. Then I realised that the Head Medical Officer was probably listening to my last comment.

"Shit, Scotty! You need to take better control of the mic."

Before he could reply Comms responded. "Sorry Alpha 965, your transmission was broken. Can you repeat?"

I pursed my lips and blew out my cheeks. "965, just saying we're on our way." I turned to Scotty. "D'you think that covered my arse?"

"Doubt it. And if they review the tapes, they'll be kicking yours."

"Hey, the tapes'll only be reviewed if there's a fuckup, so you'd better stay away from any sick patients."

So much of ambulance work revolves around the aftermath. Such 'reflective practice' can be a positive process, but the inevitable auditing and scrutiny often degenerates into a witch-hunt when things go wrong. Most hospital consultants would hate to work in our uncontrolled environment, making the odd critical decision with little to no background information and only one crewmate to assist. Treating patients in this prehospital field requires thinking outside the box, acting on your feet and working in shades of grey. But the investigations that ensue are always in black and white, focusing on taped conversations, written documentation and any video footage. The moral of the story: be careful what you say on the radio, watch out for bystanders holding up smartphones and make sure your paperwork's as watertight as a fish's butt hole.

As we neared the turnoff for Graham Road, the traffic became thicker. Not only in numbers, but also in the response of the drivers. The stupidity of the modern motorist never ceases to amaze me. People so often commute home in their own little post-work bubble, having the windows and stereo up with the aircon settings down. All that exists is what they can see through their windscreens; the rear-view and wing mirrors are optional extras. Sometimes vehicles would pull over to let us pass, but then some inconsiderate tosser would fill the gap, speeding their journey by a few precious seconds. Scotty would reprimand any indiscretion by holding down the horn way longer than necessary, just so everyone knew who had screwed up.

We eventually screeched round the corner into Graham and, after heading up the hill, could see the flashing lights of the primary crew, along with two fire trucks and three towies.

"Hey, d'you think it's up there where all the pretty lights are?"

"Nah, don't be silly, they've just got their Christmas decorations up early. It must be further down."

Despite the voiced levity, we were now both wearing our game faces. The adrenaline was pumping and I could feel the familiar rush that always accompanied a good job. And this had all the hallmarks of one. The promised clinical 'sitrep' or situation report hadn't arrived. That was a red flag for city work where backup was never too far away. If the crew had time to get on the radio, it probably wasn't serious. But when the shit goes down, working on patients takes priority.

As we approached, we could see in our headlights the remains of a new Holden Cruze. Most of the front end was destroyed and the car was on the wrong side of the road. Debris and wreckage were strewn across the bitumen. A second vehicle, an old white Toyota ute, was to our right, lying in the garden of an adjacent house. The bonnet and wing were a tangled mass of twisted metal and the driver's-side front wheel was missing.

Fire crews were busy making each vehicle safe, disconnecting the batteries and blocking the wheels. The light masts that sprung from their trucks were illuminating most of the road area. However, there was just faint street lighting over where the primary crew had focused their attention. Lying on the lawn of a house was a body, a good fifteen metres from both cars.

The collision had occurred at a suburban crossroad that was often used as a rat-run to avoid the traffic on Gympie Road. A few occupants of the nearby homes had come out to investigate the commotion. They were now standing in small huddles as if watching a local footy match.

I hit the 'on-scene' button on the Mobile Data Terminal as Scotty came to a halt and we both jumped out of the cab. My partner was already wearing his fluoro vest, but as the traffic was blocked in both directions, I couldn't be bothered retrieving mine. I opened the side door of the ambulance and grabbed the monitor as Scotty pulled out the response kit.

"Oxygen, boss?"

"Best. Don't know what we've got."

As we walked over to the scene, I inspected both cars remembering my old mentor's words: always check out the vehicle damage first, it'll point to the most injured patient. In this case, it seemed obvious: it was the one who'd been 'ejaculated'.

The primary crew were from north of Brisbane, probably on their way back from hospital when they copped the job. A stocky man in his fifties was on his knees next to the battered figure of a woman, who I could see was still breathing. A young female paramedic student, distinguished by her epaulettes, was attaching monitoring equipment. I recognised the crew's faces, but as per usual recalling any names was far beyond me. I covered my ignorance by using my standard phrase. "Hi guys, what've we got?"

The unconscious patient before us was about twenty-five, lying face up with her head supported between the knees of the male paramedic. There was a large swelling to her forehead and blood trickled from both nostrils. She was wearing shorts and a T-shirt, which meant I could see her chest moving in the correct rhythmical fashion. Both her forearms were broken just behind the wrists and her right shoulder looked dislocated.

The older paramedic responded first, he seemed flustered and I wasn't sure why, until he spoke. "G'day Jono, we've got a dead one in the Cruze, you have to see it to believe it. Other than that, there's a guy covered in blood who's walking around over there and another trapped in the ute. He's shouting out in pain, so his airway's fine. This girl here's GCS 3 with an obvious head injury and a blown left pupil, so she's taken our priority. Sorry, didn't get a chance to give a proper sitrep."

"No worries, mate, you just gave it."

I looked at the monitor and saw her vital signs were within normal limits. "Keep working on her, obviously spinal precautions, IV and prep to extricate. This one'll be the Doc's when she arrives. I'll go check the rest."

I gripped his shoulder for a moment and nodded to Scotty to follow me. We moved over to the ute first. When you see a look like that in the eyes of an experienced paramedic you know the man in the Cruze was beyond saving.

As we approached the ute, we could hear the moans and expletives from inside. A firie was at the window trying to calm the occupant. The car had taken a massive frontal impact to the driver's side, which not only removed the front wheel, but also crushed the engine and chassis into the passenger cell. Crumple zones only work to a point. The posted road speed here was sixty, so if both opposing cars were travelling at the limit, it was the same as driving into a brick wall at 120 kph. Physics can really screw you up.

I nodded to the firie who moved back to allow me access to the patient. The man looked in his early thirties with a shaven head and dark brown goatee. He was wearing a singlet that seemed chosen to display his collection of skull tattoos. I reached in through the broken side window and held the man's wrist.

"Hi, I'm Jon and this is Scotty. What can we call you?"

Although pleasantries may seem ridiculous in the circumstances, with this one question I was checking his conscious level, respiratory status and cardiovascular system.

"Declan. What's happened to Amy? She wasn't wearin' her seatbelt. Where the fuck is she, man? Is she OK?"

"Mate, we're working on her over there. Scotty will ask you lots of questions. I need you to keep your head as still as possible and focus on him, OK?"

He agreed and from that twenty-second interaction, I knew his conscious level, breathing, blood pressure and heart rate were all as would be expected. When holding his wrist, my fingers had palpated a good radial pulse. There were no obvious signs of a head injury and he'd been moving his head in such a way to suggest no damage to his neck. Despite that, he'd still need a collar due to the mechanism of the crash. I'd also looked down into what remained of the footwell and could see that his shattered lower legs were twisted amongst the ute's dashboard and pedals. At least he'd worn his seatbelt and both of his thighs appeared intact. You can bleed out from a femur fracture.

Scotty launched into his patter while attaching the monitoring to Declan as I withdrew from the ute and continued my sweep. Part of making an initial triage when dealing with multiple casualties is to maintain your momentum. This is so you can deploy the available resources in the most appropriate manner as they arrive on scene. You have to try to keep your emotions in check. That said, even I wasn't prepared for what greeted me when I ducked my head inside the mangled Cruze.

In my line of work, you get to see things that give you flashbacks: fleeting but vivid mental pictures that pop into your mind like an involuntary slide show, sometimes when you least expect them. For the most part, they fade over a few days. It's probably some form of post-traumatic stress, but I guess, only if you let the images stress you. Every so often, a gory tableau will stay for much longer. From one look, I knew this would haunt me for some time.

The body of a man in his twenties was sitting in the passenger seat of the car. His face was as pale as alabaster with eyes wide open in a thousand-yard stare; his lips parted, giving him an expression of astonished disbelief. Both of the car's airbags had deployed during the collision and they now hung deflated, still attached to the dashboard and steering wheel. However, a congealing layer of blood hid their usual white colour. In fact, blood was everywhere. On the windows and windscreen, the inside of the doors, all over his clothes and up on the ceiling. There was even blood hanging like mini stalactites from the sun visor, the act of dripping frozen by the coagulative process.

The source of the blood was easy to see. A wide gaping slit ran across the front of his neck, just below the larynx. His trachea and both his carotid arteries had been sliced through and the inadvertent blade lay before him. Amongst all the carnage sat a MacBook Air laptop, a screen saver projecting swirling coloured lights through the numerous splatters on the glass. His hands were still gripping the edges of the keyboard. The crafted thin aluminium border of the open computer must have acted like a guillotine when flung forward by the explosive force of the airbag. Talk about cutting-edge technology.

I shook my head. "I don't get paid enough for this shit."

Straightening up, I walked to the other side of the road where a group of people were standing, on the way calling for a firie to put a tarp over the Cruze. There are some things the rubber-neckers shouldn't see.

As I approached I called out in a loud voice, "Anyone else involved in this collision?"

A woman in her forties dressed in a tailored skirt suit was leaning against a black Audi TT Coupe. The pulsing lights of the gathered emergency vehicles reflected in its immaculate paintwork, marred only by a dent to the rear passenger side. She had bleach-blonde short hair and harsh features that even her makeup failed to soften. She interrupted her phone conversation to wave a hand at me, which caused the jewellery around her wrist to jingle.

"Hey, ambulance driver. Some idiot clipped my car as I drove across from over there."

She pointed to where I could see the road joined Graham at a stop sign. "I'm fine, but I need to get to an address as I'm meeting a client. So, be a nice man and pass on my details to the police and I'll be on my way."

As she talked, she walked towards me and thrust her real-estate business card into my hand with what she must have thought to be an engaging smile. She then turned to carry on her phone conversation. As she had no obvious injuries, she was not a significant part of my triage sweep and so further interaction was to some extent a waste of time. But I couldn't let it go. Not only had she just admitted to causing the collision by running a stop sign, she had made the cardinal sin of calling me an ambulance driver. I'm not sure why the term winds me up so much. Probably because it fails to recognise that paramedics do a lot more than drive a truck. I guess it's the equivalent of referring to a nurse as a bum-wiper.

Reaching forward, I plucked the phone from her grasp and spoke into it, "She'll get back to you", before pressing the disconnect button.

Her mouth dropped open like one of those fairground clowns you throw balls at to win prizes. Then she glared at me. "You may have just cost me a million dollar sale!"

I silenced any further complaint by leaning my face close to hers. "Listen here lady, one person is dead, another critically injured and one more is entrapped by his legs. You are going nowhere until the police arrive. So be quiet and sit down in your car. We'll get to you when we've dealt with the wounded."

Her eyes bulged and her mouth snapped shut. Despite the dim lighting and layers of makeup I could see the blood drain from her face. Reality had just broken through her business-based bravado. I handed back her phone and stomped away, looking for the driver of the Cruze.

He wasn't hard to find. A thin man in his thirties sat on the kerbside near a tow truck, leaning forward with his arms folded on his knees. He looked as if a firie had hosed him down with blood. The congealing liquid matted together his brown hair and his face had red smears where he'd tried to clean himself. I crouched down next to him. "Hi, my name's Jon. I guess you were in the Cruze. Any injuries?"

He stared at me, confusion and bewilderment in his eyes. "Me? Injured? No, not at all, but Andy... He's... he's dead. His neck... We were driving back from work and he lifted his laptop up to show me something. There was this almighty bang. All I remember was being hit in the face with the airbag.

Then I was being sprayed with liquid. It was blood. It was everywhere. But it wasn't my blood…"

His voice trailed off as he put his head in his hands and sobbed. Although it sounds callous, I didn't have time for this. Whenever there's a grieving patient or relative, I always try to find a female ambo to deal with them. I would like to say it's because women have an innate ability to console, their mothering instinct as it were. That's true, they do, but that's not the real reason. The reality is, I'm no grief counsellor. In fact, I'm crap at it.

But tonight I had a further excuse: I was on a triage sweep and needed to report my findings. I reached out and touched his knee for reassurance, picking a spot where there was less blood.

"There'll be someone along in a minute to look after you, I've got to go."

I stood up, turned away and walked straight towards the primary crew, depressing the transmit button on my handheld radio.

"Comms, 965. Sitrep."

"Go ahead Alpha 965."

"Do you know if the Doc's travelling with an ICP?"

There was a pause. "That's affirmative 965."

"Great. In that case we could do with one more transport crew, Code One, and we need the cops here pronto. We have one dead, one multi-system trauma, one entrapped and one walker."

"Roger that 965."

My triage sweep and sitrep had taken less than five minutes and I was now back with the original crew. They had fitted a collar around the young woman's neck, inserted an intravenous line and were sliding a scoop under her broken body.

"Hi guys, how're her numbers looking?"

"All good, Jono, blood pressure's holding and she's only just tachy at 110. Still GCS 3 though."

"Can we get a pelvic binder on the stretcher?"

"Already there."

"Brilliant, you guys are cooking on gas."

"It's Emma, she's been playing a blinder. I've been stuck supporting the head."

The female student beamed at the compliment and not for the first time I was struck by how young the new recruits were looking. I smiled back. "Great work. The guy in the ute called your patient Amy. I'll try to get more details for you before you leave. I'll hazard a guess the Doc'll want to RSI this one."

The sound of an approaching siren punctuated the end of my sentence. "Speak of the devil. Let's look lively, the Big O'll be here any second."

Having the Head Medical Officer of the ambulance service arrive on scene was both a blessing and a curse, reserved just for Brisbane crews. Dr Sarah O'Driscoll brought with her valuable experience and knowledge, as well as extra drugs and techniques. But there was a downside. Stress. Imagine that your mind is spinning; you're at the end of your shift; you have to make a snap decision that could mean life or death for some poor schmuck; you're in the limelight with every orifice puckering, and that's when the head honcho turns up. Their presence is unlikely to steady any jangling nerves and Dr O'Driscoll didn't suffer fools gladly. If you weren't at the top of your game, you'd soon know about it, often with the bluntest of critiques.

The doctor's marked-up dark blue Subaru Impreza screeched to a halt behind my ambulance and I stood up and strode over towards the smashed ute. As I approached, I called to my crewmate. "Hey Scotty, everything OK with your guy?"

"Yes, boss. His figures haven't changed and I've started him on morphine. The firies are getting geared up to cut the cab."

"Cheers, I'll be back with you soon, just have to deal with the Doc."

"Good luck!"

I returned his smirk and walked over to Dr O'Driscoll as she climbed out of the driver's side. The HMO was wearing a green paramedic jumpsuit with 'Doctor' emblazoned across the back. She was a big lady, not fat, just up-scaled. She was in her late forties and wore her red hair short with little styling. Most of her features were rather bland, almost androgynous, apart from a pair of piercing blue eyes that never failed to unnerve anyone caught in their glare. I can't remember ever seeing her with even a hint of makeup and a single woman of her age and appearance inevitably spawned rumours concerning her sexuality. But the likelihood was that she had no time for physical love affairs. She had spent so much of her career trying to beat the men who formed the medical boys club her femininity had been lost as collateral damage. Now she was just married to her job.

The passenger door opened and Liam Fraser stepped out, an ICP who worked within the HMO's office. Being in charge of clinical oversight, he was renowned for his pedantic nature regarding documentation and protocols. He was not someone I gelled with and we had locked horns several times in the past, but we somehow maintained a cordial relationship. He was tall and around ten years my junior, having shot through the ranks with questionable speed. Blonde, tanned, toned and good-looking, he was the archetypal Aussie. Everything any man could want to be and I tried very hard not to hate him.

Liam nodded and walked to the back of the Subaru, opening the boot to retrieve Dr O'Driscoll's kit. I stifled the urge to call him the doctor's bag bitch, but the owner of the bag interrupted my thoughts. As per usual, she was straight down to business.

"So what have we got, Jon?"

"Hi Sarah. Liam. We have five people involved in this three-car collision. The Audi over there blew the stop sign and clipped the Cruze into the path of the ute. The latter two crashed head-on throwing the girl over there and trapping the driver by his legs."

As I talked, we walked to the girl who was now on the stretcher. I pointed to the patient. "She's a candidate for an RSI as she has a head injury with unequal pupils. If you and Liam want to work on her, I can deal with the guy in the ute. It'll allow me to stay on scene to talk with the cops when they arrive. They'll be most interested in the driver of the Audi, who's unharmed and sitting in her car. I've got a crew coming to treat the driver of the Cruze, who also appears uninjured, but he'll require a collar as his passenger died."

Until now Dr O'Driscoll had been looking down, listening. Her eyes shot up and I was speared by one of her unwavering blue glares.

"Nice of you to save the best until last. I heard you mention a death in your sitrep, I presume you have a good reason for not attempting a resus on a traumatic arrest?"

I was prepared for this salvo and returned fire. "Yep. Exsanguination. The guy bled out when both his carotids were severed. The lid of his laptop was embedded into his neck when the airbags deployed."

Her face was impassive, but I could tell she was surprised because her stare was broken by a series of rapid blinks. "Right. OK, sounds like we have a plan. Liam, you're on airway and I'll get the drugs prepped. Which truck are we using?"

I pointed to the other ambulance. "That one, it's 831. I'll be at the ute if you need me."

"OK, thank you Jon."

With that she strode off to 831, with Liam following along in her wake. I returned to the ute to find a fire truck was now bathing the scene in light. A team of firies had already removed the door and were debating the best way to free the driver's legs.

"Hi Scotty, how's Declan doing?"

"All his numbers are good, but the morphine has only taken the edge off the pain. I've given two 5 mg doses so far, along with four of ondanz, but I think he'll need your services before we can extricate him."

"Right, thought as much. Have we any idea what's the state of his legs?"

"From what I can see, his right appears to be a fracture dislocation of his ankle, but both of the pedals are wrapped around his left leg, which looks pretty twisted. The problem is that the firies are having difficulty getting the cutting equipment to the pedals."

"OK. I'll sort out the ketamine and midaz if you can put a line up, oxygen on and have another morphine drawn. Any chance you could hook him up to the end tidal as well?"

"No worries."

I beckoned to a firie. "Are you able to get the stretcher from that ambulance?"

"Sure. Need anything else?"

"Don't suppose you'd know where we keep our splint bag?"

"Is that the big orange one in the side door?"

"That's it, cheers!"

We all set about our tasks when Scotty grinned. "Hey, when you have a mo, check out the back of the ute."

While drawing up my drugs, I wandered to the rear of the vehicle and saw a dark shape hanging from the tailgate. Closer inspection revealed the body of a cattle dog suspended by a leash, its neck broken. The girl was not the only one who'd been thrown from the ute. Something on its collar glinted in the spotlights. A shiny chrome tag was embossed with the name 'Lucky'.

I walked back towards the cab. "Thanks Scotty, I really needed that."

"You see the tag?"

"Yes. The irony wasn't lost."

Just then the firie returned with the splint bag. "Sorry, but some cockhead's boxed in your ambulance. I can't get the stretcher out without denting their Subaru."

"Ah, right. That cockhead will be our Head Medical Officer. I think I better go get the keys." I turned to Scotty, who was once again grinning. "Oh well, I said I'd find some details on their patient. No time like the present."

I stepped over to the ute and knelt down beside Declan. "How's it going mate?"

"Fuckin' painful. Can't you guys get a move on?"

"Sorry, but there's a few things we need to get sorted before we can move you. The firies have got to cut the pedals to free your legs. But I'll use a powerful drug called ketamine to knock you out while they do that. It'll take us a little time, but most of the delay is accessing your legs. On the bright side once you're sedated you won't remember any of this."

"Whatever. How's Amy doin'?"

"The doctor is working on her as we speak. You'll both be going to the same hospital, so the staff there'll be able to tell you more when you get there. What I need right now is some info about you and Amy."

I took out a notepad and between winces, he gave his full

name, date of birth and address. Then the same for his girlfriend. As far as he was aware, they were both fit, well and had no allergies. I thanked him and stood turning to Scotty. "I'll go get the keys if you could get another set of obs and give five more of morphine."

"Yes, boss. And once again, good luck."

I walked over to 831 where there was a hive of activity. The back doors were open and the older paramedic was holding the stretcher out from the vehicle to give more room to intubate the patient. Other than Amy, there were three crammed in the ambulance. The student, Emma, was supporting the patient's neck, while Liam used a laryngoscope to view Amy's glottis, the hole between her vocal cords. Once visualised, he inserted a clear plastic endotracheal tube through the opening and into her trachea. Dr O'Driscoll had been overseeing the Rapid Sequence Induction and had provided the drugs necessary to sedate and paralyse the patient. She was now almost cheek-to-cheek with Liam as she leant over his shoulder to watch the procedure. I smiled to myself: nothing like a bit of pressure, eh Liam? But I knew better than to voice my thoughts. I'd been where he was sitting enough times and the proximity of the HMO never eased the difficult operation. On the flip side, Brisbane was the only place in Queensland that paramedics could perform an RSI and it was all done on O'Driscoll's ticket, so I could understand her concern. After those meds are given, if you can't secure the airway and breathe for the patient, they'll die from a lack of oxygen.

While I watched, Liam withdrew the laryngoscope, attached a bag-valve mask to the tube and then ran checks to ensure all was well and that the plastic was in the right hole. His shoulders relaxed a little and I heard him confirm the placement, so I moved to the side door.

"Excuse me Sarah, can I borrow your keys, we can't access our stretcher."

Without taking her eyes off the patient and monitor, she reached into her pocket and passed me a set of keys. As I took them, I placed the page from my notebook in her hand. "Got your patient's details."

I received a fleeting glance. "Oh, thanks." Then her focus was back on Amy.

"No worries."

I returned to the ute where the firie was still standing and tossed him the keys. "Cheers."

He nodded and left.

Scotty was grinning. "So how was it? Did the Big 'O' spit the dummy?"

"Nah, I picked my moment. Painless really. On that subject, how's Declan?"

"OK, but morphine's not enough."

"Right, let's get cracking with the ketamine."

More sirens heralded the third ambulance, followed by a police car.

"Great. Apologies Scotty, can you hold the fort while I give those guys a quick handover?"

"Man, you're earning your extra two dollars tonight."

Although often joked about, this supplement to our hourly rate was the stark truth. All the added training, techniques and responsibilities amounted to a pitiful pay rise when an ACP graduated as an ICP. Needless to say, we don't do it for the money.

I didn't recognise the crew as they climbed from the cab, a lanky man in his thirties and a woman in her twenties. A glance at the vehicle number explained why. They were from the Southside. Often the closest resource can be some distance away when nearby ambulances are stuck at hospital or on other jobs. Plus it was getting close to shift changeover, which always ties up crews. A fact that explains why the police were just turning up now. At least we had fresh cops on scene.

I went to the ambulance crew first as the cops were putting on their fluoro vests. "Hi guys, your patient is the one covered in blood over there. He'll need a collar as his passenger died in the collision, but it's only a precaution. You should be fine to walk him to the stretcher. It's a bit weird as his friend was holding a laptop up when the airbags went off. The lid sliced his neck open."

The tall paramedic's jaw dropped. "You're shitting me?"

"I shit you not. All that blood on him is not his. He appears OK, so Charlies should be able to deal with him, which'll ease the pressure on the Royal."

Even though the Prince Charles was by far the closest hospital, it was not a trauma centre so the other patients would have to bypass Charlies and go to the Royal Brisbane.

"Sorry to dash, but I've got to brief the cops and get back to my patient."

"Right, we're on it."

With that they were off and I turned to find two uniformed police officers had walked up behind me. The shorter one was a very attractive blonde woman in her late twenties. I had to stop myself from scoping her out and put aside any random thoughts involving handcuffs. I'm sure she'd heard all the jokes and I was spoken for, but there's no harm in looking.

With a smile I spoke to the female copper. "Evenin' officers. Glad you could join us. What we have for you is a three-car RTC…"

I gave them a brief description of the events. "The Audi driver's a real piece of work. I only wish I could be there when you caution her. Please, do me a favour and don't hold back, you'll understand when you look in the Cruze. Anyway, I've got to dash, the driver of that car's off to Charlies, but the other two are going to the Royal. Might see you there?"

The policewoman gave a beautiful smile and I fantasised it was reserved just for me. "You never know. Thanks for the info…"

Her partner interrupted. "We need the names of all the ambos here."

"I'm Jonothan Byrne…"

I glanced back at the police woman. "… but the rest of the names'll have to wait until later. I really have to go."

I nodded to them both and marched off to the ute. Scotty had everything prepared, the stretcher was in position, a spinal board had appeared and the firies were set to cut the pedals. "Sorry 'bout that, can't imagine why I'm so popular this evening."

"Only in your dreams if you're referring to that blonde copper."

"What, there was a blonde police officer? Can't say I noticed. Right, enough of that, let's get Declan out."

I knelt beside him and in a calm quiet voice explained the procedure. "Now close your eyes and imagine yourself lying on a beach somewhere. It'll make the trip smoother."

Although he looked sceptical, he obliged and I began administering doses of ketamine. At 60 mg he stopped responding to my muted questions and I opened his eyelids revealing sightless eyes. It's known as the 'ketamine stare'. I turned to the firies and spoke in a hushed voice. "OK guys, you're good to go."

Without even a groan from Declan, they cut the metal that was pinning his mangled left leg and, using the spinal board, helped Scotty and I slide his limp body out onto the stretcher. Scotty took over control of his head, murmuring to him, while I went to inspect his legs. The left looked as if he had sustained multiple fractures to both the tibia and fibula. There were several deep lacerations, but none of the bones were projecting through the skin and the foot had a good pulse. The right foot however was pale, cool with poor perfusion. It was angulated inwards at ninety degrees with an obvious fracture dislocation. As the injury was impairing the blood supply, I gripped his foot. "I'm going to reduce the right one, Scotty, he might react. OK?"

"Go for it."

I pulled and the ankle slotted back into place with a slight 'pop'. Declan gave out a faint moan, but remained still. The colour returned to his foot and with the help of Scotty I fitted a vac splint on each of his legs.

I left Scotty to load the stretcher with the firies as I'd seen Dr O'Driscoll return to her car. The other two ambulances had already gone. As I neared, I could hear the Doc was on the phone to the Royal giving them a heads-up on her intubated patient. Liam must have accompanied Amy to the hospital. I waved a page from my notebook at her, the one with Declan's details, and she took the sheet of paper. She nodded and included his information in her conversation, pausing and raising her eyebrows at me after saying, "And he has sustained…"

I picked up the cue. "Lower leg fractures, all vitals within normal limits. I've sedated him with ketamine for extrication and fracture reduction of his right ankle."

She repeated this and gave an ETA before hanging up. I handed her the keys I'd retrieved from the firie. "I think you might need these."

"Oh. Thanks for that. And Jon, good work. I'll see you at the Royal."

With that she closed the door and drove off. After all my years in the Service that was about as high praise as you could expect. I stood there for a moment surveying the scene and basking in the minor glory. But my bubble was burst a few seconds later when another marked-up sedan arrived and the Senior Operations Manager stepped out. He took one look at me and barked, "Where's your fluoro vest?"

"In my vehicle, I'll just go get it."

I climbed in the back of the ambulance. "Quick, Scotty, the brass has arrived. Let's go."

He laughed, jumped out and slammed the side door before getting in the cab and heading off for the Royal with a slight screech of the tyres.

3
___

BREATHE

The park bench was the perfect vantage point to watch the evening's sunset as the sky glowed like molten lava, fuelled by the dust from a distant bushfire. But the lone woman huddled on the seat had missed the whole display. The only fires Rosie Brennan knew about were the flames burning within her own body.

It had been over twelve hours since her last hit and she needed one now. It consumed her consciousness, digested her dignity, fed on her frailty. She wasn't craving a high; she hadn't cared about that for a long time. It was the withdrawal symptoms she had to stave off.

The old familiar drowning sensation had started to build, like the need for air when you're underwater. She would kick out to reach the surface, but something was always holding her down. Her chest burned, the panic intensified and she knew there was only one solution.

She rubbed her upper arms with bitten-down fingernails, knowing the crawling bugs were only in her mind, but unable to stop scratching. Where could she get some money?

She turned her head to look over at the shithole that was the current squat she shared with five others. None of them had any cash. What's more, those fuckers wouldn't share their stash with her, not even for a shag. All those junkies cared about was their next hit.

She looked around the darkening park and discovered she was alone with the silhouettes of the gum trees. Finding a punter this early was unlikely, but she guessed it was her only option. She couldn't face the suffocation, the burning, the agony, the need to breathe…

A man approached from off in the distance. He was walking along the path, being led by a small dog, straining at its lead. He appeared disinterested in the mutt, a bored husband forced to exercise a pet he never wanted.

She decided to try her luck. As he came towards her, she relaxed back on the bench, sliding her bottom down and easing her legs apart. She then used one hand to stroke her inner thigh. In the dim light she saw he was in his fifties, bald head and beer gut with a dissatisfied look on his flabby face. His pace hadn't changed, so she called out as he passed. "Got a light?"

He stumbled to a stop and turned her way, as if noticing her for the first time. The dog whimpered and pulled on its lead. "Eh, what?"

"You got a light?"

"Er, no. I don't smoke."

Using her thigh-stroking hand, she lifted her short skirt to reveal a skimpy pair of red panties. "Fancy a good time?"

The man's eyes bulged and he looked around, before leaning towards her. "Fuck off, you junkie whore." He then strode off into the darkness, dragging the little dog behind him.

She flopped forwards, resting her head in her hands. The

air seeped out of her lungs as the weight of shame compressed her body, crushing her soul against the wooden bench. She gave a short mirthless laugh. What soul? She'd cashed that in many years ago, along with every vestige of self-respect. Who could have known a broken leg would lead to this? Once hooked on pain killers, she'd been sucked down into a never-ending vortex of addiction. Could she stoop any lower?

But then the burning suffocating need for a heroin hit replaced the guilt and depression. It was then she realised there was no depth to her depravity. The pain was too much.

Just then the bench creaked and she jumped as a man sat down next to her. He was wearing dark trousers and a black hoodie that hid most of his face. When he spoke, the sound hissed between closed teeth. "You looking for a good time?"

She couldn't believe her luck, but somewhere, deep inside, a tiny voice cried, "Run!"

Unfortunately for Rosie, the clamouring scream of her opiate receptors drowned out the warning. She sidled up close to the stranger and put a hand on his thigh. "Depends how much you've got to spend, lover boy."

He shook his head within the hood, while reaching out to remove her hand. "No, you misunderstand. I'm interested in selling you a good time."

Her shoulders sagged and she let out a sigh. "Guess we're both shit out of luck then. Unless you'll sell a hit for a fuck, I'm out of cash."

"No need. First one's on the house. Call it a gesture of good will. I take care of my clients. Here, this one's already drawn up, ready to go." He reached into the pocket of his hoodie and passed her a syringe. "Best gear in Brisbane, guaranteed."

She grabbed the narrow plastic tube and removed the protective cap with her teeth. Leaning forward, she held her ankle with one hand and waited for the vein in her foot to puff up. Even in the twilight she knew where it was. She'd spotted it when her last score had her folded up as he pounded her from behind. A good junkie always remembers a decent vein.

The speed of her action surprised the man in the hoodie. "Christ, not here!"

But it was too late, Rosie had inserted the needle and pushed the plunger. She sucked in a lungful of beautiful clean air as her head broke the surface of her liquid torment. The burning was gone, the craving satisfied, her skin felt fresh and new. She lay back on the bench and savoured the release.

Her new supplier pulled her up by her arm and thrust her toward the squat. "You can't stay here, you need to go inside."

She staggered forwards, her mind floating to her bed, her legs struggling to walk. She climbed the stairs of the dilapidated house and crashed through the front door, bouncing off the mouldy corridor walls with their peeling wallpaper, until she fell into her room. Swaying back and forth, she somehow shed her clothes, all bar the crimson G-string, and collapsed onto the stained lumpy mattress.

In her mind she was relaxing on a comfy lounger having just enjoyed a long swim in the crystal clear waters of a luxury hotel pool. The tropical sun caressed her body as she breathed a contented sigh. All of her problems had faded away. She was filled with love and everything was right with the world.

In reality, her chest had stopped moving and her skin was turning blue.

The man in the hoodie stood next to the park bench. He had picked up the syringe and recapped the needle, concealing the evidence within his pocket. That was the first time he'd seen a junkie shoot up with one of his lethal doses. Her ability to find a vein was impressive. At least she'd go out on a decent high; a gram of pure uncut heroin would see to that.

He wandered off through the park, looking back every so often at the house. There were no shouts of alarm, no raucous activity, no life-saving sirens. Taking out junkies and homeless losers was proving easier than he thought. Perhaps now was the time to turn things up a notch.

4

CASCADE

The trip to hospital had been uneventful. I'd topped up Declan's pain relief with further doses of morphine and a thorough secondary survey revealed only minor lacerations and abrasions. He had been getting more talkative en route and we were about to offload when he let out a long moaning wail. My immediate thought was it might be due to the ketamine, so I leant over and spoke in a reassuring voice. "It's OK Declan you've been in a car crash."

Between sobs he said, "… Lucky…

"Yes, your legs are pretty broken, but you were very lucky."

He glared at me and yelled, "Not me you cockhead, my fuckin' dog."

"Oh right. He wasn't so…" I stopped myself just in time. "… Er, he didn't make it."

This brought on a fresh bout of tears and sobbing, which I hoped was caused by the drugs. He'd seemed nowhere near as upset about his girlfriend's plight. I nodded to a smirking Scotty, who was holding open the back door of the ambulance and we unloaded the stretcher from the truck. As we traipsed into triage with our weeping macho man, I called over to the nurse behind the glass. "This is the second one from the RTC in Carseldine."

On the way in, I'd phoned through to the emergency department to make sure they were aware of our impending arrival. She nodded and pointed to the high acuity 'resus' corridor. "Straight through, they're expecting you."

There were two other crews waiting to be triaged and they moved their stretchers to one side so we could pass. A paramedic I knew from Roma Street piped up. "Hey Jono, aren't you supposed to give 'em some pain relief?"

"I did. I just broke the news about his dog."

My last comment elicited fresh wailing from Declan and I mouthed 'ketamine' to the quizzical looks. Nods of understanding greeted my non-verbal explanation as we pushed the stretcher through to resus.

A nurse directed us to Trauma Room 2 as the other one was bustling with staff looking after Amy. After transferring Declan to the hospital bed, I gave my handover and made a hasty retreat. I know some could accuse me of being insensitive, but his weeping was getting on my nerves. Never having had a pet, I wasn't able to relate to the loss of his dog. However, the disparity between his expressed emotions for Lucky and those for his girlfriend jarred with my sensibilities. The ketamine may have been a convenient excuse, but I wasn't so sure. I walked out to where Scotty was cleaning the stretcher and we looked at each other, then both shook our heads.

Scotty grinned. "Love me, love my dog, eh?"

"I'm glad the pooch was dead. Can't imagine the Doc being too chuffed if I'd lined her up for an RSI on Lucky rather than Amy."

He laughed. "On that subject, where is the Doc? Her car's not here."

"Dunno, I'll go check."

I walked over to the write-up room and punched in the code to open the door. Numerous paramedics populated the small area, some writing up jobs and others just chilling. Our role has its stresses and one way we unwind is to talk about cases, often with a warped sense of humour. Several years ago this used to happen at station, but these days we spend so little time there. Instead, the hospital write-up rooms have become the default de-stress venue, much to management's frustration.

The Ambulance Liaison Officer, Mike Dobson, greeted me as I walked in. It was his task to reduce our time at hospital. "Hi Jono. George and Emma were telling us you all had a good job."

The crew first on scene turned to greet me. At least I now knew both their names.

"G'day Mike. Get this, that muscle-bound bogan we dragged out of the ute arrived blubbing his eyes out over the death of his dog, but there were no tears for his girlfriend. How's she doing?"

George responded. "Not too good. They've sent her for a CT scan, but the Doc wasn't too optimistic. You missed them, her and Liam had to dash off to the Southside. Any chance you can help us with their paperwork?"

"Will do, once I've had a brew."

Another paramedic grumbled without looking up from his Toughbook. "Don't fancy your chances. There're no more cups; it's a new cost-cutting measure."

"Cost-cutting my arse, they just don't want us hanging around here any longer than we have to. Ain't that right, Mike."

Mike responded with a smile; he didn't take his role too seriously. "Don't know what you're talking about, Jono. Hey, haven't you finished your paperwork yet? You've been here for over five minutes."

"Give me a chance, mate, I haven't even opened my Toughbook. Must be the lack of caffeine."

I turned to Emma. "Did you see the guy in the Cruze?"

"Yes, but only for a second or two. I looked over George's shoulder as he checked for a pulse."

"You OK with it?"

"Yes, thanks, I'm fine. It was my first traumatic dead body. And an awesome one at that!"

Her bubbling enthusiasm was probably there to mask any signs of stress, but I let it go, turning to George. "Have you ever seen anything like that?"

"I've been to some weird stuff in my time, but that one was new to me. Twenty-five years in the job and few things faze me, but I'm not ashamed to say, that hit home. Shit there was blood everywhere."

"Death by laptop, what a way to go. The ultimate system crash. Mind you, that Mac was still working. Bit of a clean and you could sell it on eBay. One careless owner. Perhaps they'll rename it the MacBook Airbag?"

There were groans all around when a face I recognised appeared at the door. He looked straight at me. "Jon, isn't it? Detective Giallo. Any chance we can have a chat?"

He pronounced his name with a slight Italian flare, emphasising the Gee.

"Sure." I got up and followed him into the corridor.

We'd met before on previous jobs. One was a stabbing and the other a vicious assault with a baseball bat. My statements had meant I was cross-examined in the witness box during the subsequent trials. It was never a pleasant experience and was the reason most paramedics were reluctant to give the police their details. As an ICP, I always had to take the fall.

After we were some distance from the write-up room, the detective stopped and leant against the wall. "You'd all fled the scene by the time I arrived. Got your name from Officer Hadden."

I smiled. "Was that the gorgeous blonde lady?"

"I think you'll be referring to Sue and I can't possibly comment on a fellow officer's wonderful looks. But no, Officer Hadden is the less attractive of the two."

"Well, at least I know her name."

"Not that it'll do you much good, she's married to another copper."

"Oh, no worries there, I've got my own babe, but now I can wind up my crewmate."

With the initial pleasantries over, Giallo got out his notebook. "As you may have guessed, we need your account of what you saw and what was said."

I did this as he took notes, asking numerous questions. When I'd finished, twenty minutes later, the detective leaned in and I could smell the tobacco on his clothing. "Just so you've got a heads-up, the driver of the Audi is likely to file a complaint against you. She seems to think you were rude and aggressive."

I shrugged. "From her perspective I probably was, but she was intending to drive off and I'd just seen the guy in the Cruze. As I mentioned in my statement, she said she'd driven out of the road marked with the stop sign. So for her to collide with the Cruze meant she didn't give way. To be honest, I think she's got far more to worry about than my behaviour."

"I agree, but I thought you'd better know."

"Thanks. If we're done, I have to finish my paperwork. I'm on overtime, so they'll be hassling me soon."

"I think that's everything. Here's my details if you need to get in touch."

He handed me his QPS card, nodded a farewell and walked away.

Before returning to the write-up room, I ducked into the passageway between the trauma bays and asked the radiographer to bring up Declan's X-rays. She obliged and I was marvelling at how smashed his left leg was when someone tweaked my backside. Thinking it was the radiographer, I turned in surprise only to be greeted by nurse Amber Shaw.

"What's all this I hear about you and a blonde copper, hey?"

She was feigning anger and her trim shapely body was looking very sexy in her uniform. She had her jet-black straight hair tied back in a ponytail, exposing the full beauty of her features. Large dark brown eyes twinkled with amusement above her high cheekbones. The tiny laughter lines in the corner of each eye were the only hint to her thirty-one years of age. But then again, I was biased.

"Who's been spreading such an outrageous rumour? You know I only have eyes for you, my dear."

"You're full of shit, I heard you talking to the detective."

"So you also heard me say I've got my own babe?"

"Nope. Anyway, what girl would be dumb enough to put up with all your crap?"

"Er, I think that may be you, Miss Shaw." I glanced up and down the corridor and seeing we were alone, I slipped my arm around her waist and planted a firm kiss on her lips.

As she pulled away from my grasp, she said with a broadening smile, "Unhand me you brute, I'm pretending to be pissed off with you."

"You know that never lasts. I can always come up with something that makes you laugh."

"Yes, usually when you strip naked. Anyway, weren't you supposed to finish your shift about an hour ago?"

"A last minute multi-cas and I've still got a shitload of paperwork to do. I'll tell you about it later, but I need to get back to writing. Don't suppose you have any plastic cups, I'm dying for a drink."

"I'd hate to see a grown man cry. Follow me. There'll be some in our break room."

I grabbed a stack and she gave me a peck on the cheek as she walked away. "Don't want to hear another thing about any more blonde coppers."

"Yes, dear."

I returned to the write-up room and was greeted with cheers when I produced the stack of cups. Scotty offered to make the round, so I could finally start my paperwork. I'd just begun typing when Mike interrupted. "Sorry Jono, but the powers that be are already hassling me."

"Did you mention I had to give a police statement?"

"Yep."

"And that I have to help the other crew with their write-up?"

"Yep."

"And they were both complicated cases?"

"Yep. They want to know when you'll be finished."

"As a wild stab in the dark, I guess that'll be when I pick up the mic and say: this is 965 we're clear at the Royal."

"Hey hey, don't shoot the messenger. I tell you what, I'll field one more call, then you get to talk to them, OK?"

"Just give me the phone next time. I'll put them straight."

Mike smiled. "Fine by me."

I started typing as my pager went off. Glancing at the message, I swore then read it out to the room. "Please advise of any delays at hospital. Do they have any idea how frustrating all this hassling is?"

Steve Roper who worked out of Ashgrove responded. "It's a cascade of shit, mate. Some bigwig decides what the latest issue is, usually from something published in the Courier Mail. They then shit on the rest of the brass, who shit on the next rung of managers, who then shit on the Comms staff. They then shit on us with dumb fucking pages like that one."

"Thanks Steve, that's very profound, although I'm now suffering from some rather disturbing mental images."

Undaunted, he continued. "Did you know there are managers who've nothing better to do than to log in at home to check on the current statistics. Knowing fuck all about the caseload, or what a crew has just been to, they phone up Comms and bitch about a vehicle that's been at hospital for over 30 minutes. As I said, it's a cascade of shit."

We all agreed, but Steve was someone who could flog a point to death if you encouraged him. Mike broke the uneasy silence before he could start up again. "Hey, did you hear they found BB dead as a pork chop in some alleyway? The shit's hit the fan here because he self-discharged only a few hours before he died."

"Who?"

Scotty reminded me. "You know, BB. Brian somethin' or other. The grey-haired old grumpy alco from Spring Hill. The one who'd claim he had chest pain so he could get a trip in and a free meal."

"Oh Christ, that one. Yes I know him. Smelt like a sewer in the sun with a matching personality."

Steve once again leapt on his soapbox. "That old fucker. Good riddance! Tell me where they found his rotten corpse and I'll dance on the spot. Oxygen thieves like him should get a lethal injection rather than lefty do-gooders pandering to their every whim. He was a drain on the limited resources of us honest taxpayers and the less of his kind the better."

Compassion fatigue is common among ambos who train for emergencies, but so often are tasked with social work when care in the community fails, or just doesn't exist. However, Steve took things to another level. He was in a compassion coma. Although it might add fuel to his fire, I couldn't help myself. "Thanks for that Adolf, got any other thoughts on eugenics?"

Mike jumped in before Steve could reply. "Hey, the council workers called it in when they came to empty the bins. Would you believe, he'd been rotting there for a day or two, but the cops felt it necessary to call an ambulance."

There was general laughter, but it reminded me of one of my recent cases. "Don't laugh. I bet it's got something to do with a police job I went to a few weeks back. They called for a 'confirmation of death', but when we arrived the poor old chook was still breathing. She'd been there for hours and the place stank to high heaven. I think the cop had done a pulse check from the doorway. You should have seen their faces when we started working on her."

There was an air of disbelief and Steve grabbed the opportunity to seize the final word. "Anyway, all I'd like to say is bye-bye BB. One less fucking time-waster to deal with."

In response, we all returned to either typing or coffee drinking, hoping he wouldn't launch into another rant.

Half an hour later I'd helped George complete his paperwork, despite other crews arriving and insisting on an account of the latest 'good job'. On each occasion I gave a brief rendition with Scotty filling in the details while I returned to typing. George and Emma left to make their way back to Bribie and I was finishing my notes regarding Declan. It wasn't the descriptive text that took the time. There were hundreds of fields that required data entry and at the end of the day, the final document was the only thing that covered my arse. Type in something wrong and you might trigger an automatic audit that at the least would precipitate a 'please explain' email. Mind you, the Big 'O' reviewed most cases involving ICPs, so I had to be sure the information entered was correct.

Eventually Mike spun on his swivel chair and waved his mobile at me. "Hey Jon, I've fielded two calls, but now the Senior Operations Manager has insisted on talking to you."

I sighed. "Hand it over."

I held the mobile to my ear. "Express deliveries, can I take your order please?"

A rather grumpy male voice answered. "Are you on 965?"

"Last time I checked."

"What's going on, you've been at hospital for over ninety minutes."

"I think Mike has already explained the situation, what more do you want me to say? The longer we talk the more this conversation delays my departure."

"Look, I understand that ICPs may have to write more, but an hour and a half? And what's your crewmate doing? Sitting there twiddling his thumbs?"

"He's cleared up the vehicle and made at least two rounds of coffee. What can you expect when you put ICPs on a truck?"

"Right. Well, I'm going to escalate this. You'll be hearing from your Station Officer."

"I'll look forward to the chat. Can I go now?"

The line went dead and I handed the phone back to Mike. "Hey, he just hung up on me."

"Well, you do have that effect on people."

I shrugged. "True, but this time it wasn't just me, he also had a go at Scotty."

Scotty looked up from his mobile. "What've I done?"

"Nothing, which is why he was whinging, seeing as you're on overtime."

"I've been making coffees."

"Yes, but they've got Mike for that."

Mike laughed. "Up yours."

I finally completed my write-up and printed out the document for the hospital staff. As always, I was hit by the irony of standing next to the printer and waiting for the sheets to churn out. Here I was being given the bum's rush, while I turned a digital file into a hard copy, so that an admin clerk could scan the pages into the hospital's computer system. The process chafed against my IT background, but pointing out the futility had only labelled me as a whinger. I guess that's government work for you.

When I walked back into the ED to hand in the paperwork, I discovered they'd moved Declan to a resus bay and he was sleeping off a sedative. However, Amy was up in theatre and destined for an intensive care bed.

Scotty and I said our farewells and as I jumped back in the cab I picked up the mic. "Comms, this is 965. Please inform the brass we're now clear at the Royal."

"Roger."

"You can never resist needling them can you?"

"It's all part of swimming against that cascade of shit. Christ I'm knackered, let's go home. Warp factor ten Scotty."

"Aye, aye, Cap'n."

And with that, we were belting our way back to station.

5

PEA POD

The woman lay on her back with her arms by her side, naked except for a fine crimson G-string that barely covered enough anatomy to save her blushes. But it had been several years since she had blushed. Flowing auburn locks gathered around the nape of her neck cushioning her head from the hard metal surface on which she rested. Long eyelashes caressed her high cheekbones while the closed lids protected her deep hazel eyes from the stark glare of the fluorescent strip lights above. Her full lips pouted as if savouring a loving kiss. The gentle line of her jaw jutted upwards at what appeared to be a vain attempt at defiance. Her exposed ample breasts sagged outwards over her shapely form, revealing the lack of any silicone enhancements. But the colour of her bare nipples was as drained as her lips, making them only a shade darker than the surrounding pale skin.

In response to a harsh metallic click, a bright white light bathed her cold near-naked body. A faint whining sound intensified as the flashgun prepared for another onslaught.

Harry Meyham, the Scene of Crimes Officer entrusted with

photo-documenting the autopsy, looked up from his camera. "I'll just get a few more frontals then you can flip her over." He was wearing white gumboots, purple gloves and a white disposable suit with an attached hood. A duck-billed paper mask covered his mouth and nose, while clear plastic safety goggles protected the rest of his face. The whole ensemble appeared somewhat ridiculous and Harry's generous girth meant he resembled a huge foie-gras goose ready for market. He even had the liver to match the look.

Harry adjusted various settings on his rather battered-looking Nikon digital camera and rattled off four more shots. After a quick glance at the images on the rear display, he nodded to the mortuary assistant, Dave Nesbit, who manhandled her stiff body. The task proved more difficult than he thought and after a while he paused. "Come on guys, stop gawping and give me a hand."

The only female present in the main mortuary room of the John Tonge Centre on Brisbane's Southside was the dead woman on the slab. The two SOCOs, three police officers and one mortuary assistant were all male. Even the other corpses lying on the adjacent examination tables were all men. The genitals they had kept so well hidden for most of their lives now exposed for all to see, like an identity parade in a nudist camp.

As Harry was the only other one wearing protective clothing, he put down his camera and assisted Dave. Once face down, her new position revealed the postmortem staining, etched on her skin like a red tide mark. When the lifelong pumping of her heart ceased, her blood was free to drain under the influence of gravity into the lowest vessels and capillaries. There it thickened and congealed. This 'lividity' resembled a patchy severe sunburn. White areas on her shoulders, buttocks and calves showed where her body's weight had impeded the flow. Even the light pressure of the G-string had left a pale impression. It was this two-tone colouration alone that flagged her death as suspicious, as the pattern established she died on her back, but the police found her lying on her side.

The officer leading the investigation, Detective Frank Giallo, was leaning against a large fridge kept for the mortuary's over-sized customers. He struck a nonchalant pose with his arms folded against his chest and one leg in front of the other. He was in his late forties, with a tanned clean-shaven face that was not unpleasant, but not good looking. Grease slicked back his black hair that some would say was too dark for his age. But his green polyester shirt and ill-fitting blue jeans, both suggested his physical appearance was far from the focal point of his life. He tipped his head to the side and said to no one in particular, "So, did you hear the story of our lovely Rosemary Brennan, aka Rosie?"

Harry was preparing to take another shot and replied through his mask. "Yep. They found her dumped outside her current squat with the rubbish bags. It would appear her public-spirited flatmates didn't want her body stinking out their living room."

A wry smile grew across Giallo's face. "Ah, but did you know last summer she was feeding her heroin addiction by selling her wares around the Gold Coast for just ten bucks a go?"

"Ten bucks! Christ, I wonder how many punters in Bris Vegas now have Hep C?"

The fact that she was likely to have contracted this disease from either sharing needles, or unprotected rough sex was an occupational hazard for a junkie prostitute. Most intravenous drug users fail to live long enough for the Hepatitis C virus to bother them. They would be hard pushed to distinguish its early symptoms from a few day's withdrawal from their choice of addiction. But the implications for the upcoming procedure were significant. As her virus-contaminated tissues would still be infectious for at least two weeks, the high-risk suite was the mandatory venue for the autopsy. Here the powerful ventilation system maintained a negative pressure within the room. Once the work begun, movement back and forth was restricted and there was even a trough of disinfectant at the door that acted like a sheep dip for the gumboots.

Dave joined in the banter. "Ten bucks? She's been undercutting me! I charge more than that to have a go on the dead ones."

He was wearing the same attire as Harry, but was yet to pull up his hood and don the goggles. He wore his long dank hair tied back in a ponytail, revealing a face that even his mother must have struggled to love. Wide-spaced brown eyes sat either side of a huge beak-like nose that was further accentuated by a tiny receding chin. Yellow buckteeth and a large bobbing Adam's apple completed the facial mêlée. His unfortunate appearance and lecherous grin gave an air of credibility to his quip.

Harry smiled beneath his mask. "You're totally sick, Dave."

"Funny you should mention that. I put that exact phrase on my résumé and look where it got me."

He laughed at his own joke and stepped aside to allow Harry to take more photographs. As he waited, he studied the three Chinese characters tattooed across the small of Rosie's back. After a while he pointed them out with a flick of his hand. "Anyone know what those mean?"

In a deadpan voice, Giallo drawled out, "Turn me over."

The morgue erupted into laughter and even Harry had to stop working as his chuckling was causing the camera to shake. Once he regained his composure, he flashed a couple more frames. "OK, Dave, I'll take a few shots of her totally naked before the Doc starts slicing and dicing."

Understanding the instruction, he attempted to remove her G-string, but the rigor mortis once again hampered the task. After struggling for a few seconds, he produced a pair of scissors and cut the lacy garment from the corpse, depositing it in an evidence bag.

Giallo smirked. "That's got to be the most trouble anyone's ever had getting her knickers off."

Once again laughter boomed out and was echoing around the morgue when the pathologist, Dr Hilary Beecham, walked in the room. She wore the standard protective garb over every inch of her body, but despite her concealed stern features she still projected a sense of authority. "I hope you gentlemen are not laughing at the expense of this morning's unfortunate subject. I'm warning you, I'm not in the mood for any mortuary humour. I was called to a job early this morning and haven't slept since."

The laughter ceased as she scanned the room. "Dave, you know we're dealing with an infected cadaver, so could you at least follow policy by wearing your hood and goggles? And Detective Giallo, if you wish to be in here for the duration you'll need to suit up."

Giallo nodded and retreated to the viewing area where the other officers were working. She then addressed the SOCO. "Harry, I thought you were aware this autopsy was for the high-risk suite?"

Harry had worked with Dr Beecham for many years and had become used to her sleep-deprived sharpness. "Yes, Hil, I know, I was getting the external shots out here where we've got more space. I'll get Dave to move the body over in a few minutes."

She nodded and strode off to the side room. "Make sure

that table's thoroughly disinfected afterwards." And without turning round, she entered the high-risk suite to prepare her equipment. Harry rolled his eyes at Dave, but the gesture was lost behind his plastic goggles.

Once everything was in place, the autopsy began. Speaking in a loud monotone voice so the recording system would pick up her every word, Dr Beecham started by describing Rosie and commenting on her external features. "The subject is a 26-year-old female Caucasian. She appears to be in good health despite her documented extensive history of recreational IV drug use."

As Rosie had received a coronial investigation only because of the lividity, the pathologist described the feature in detail. She also mentioned the slight greenish colouration to her upper abdomen, one of the first signs of decomposition. As they are full of digestive enzymes, the intestines are quick to decay, giving off hydrogen sulphide gas that reacts with the iron in the blood to turn the skin green. The extent of the shading can act as an aid to estimate time of death. Another point of interest was the sheer number of track marks along her arms, legs and around her groin. The most recent one on her foot was no more suspicious than any of the others. Rosie was a junkie running out of usable veins.

With the external descriptions complete, the internal exam could start. The pathologist used a large scalpel to cut a Y-shaped incision starting from each shoulder and joining at the base of Rosie's sternum. She then sliced down towards the pubic bone of the pelvis. Only a small amount of dark red blood oozed out of the wound despite cutting deep into the tissue. Most of the fluids had drained away from the upper surfaces, or had congealed. Dr Beecham peeled back the skin and musculature to expose the rib cage and abdominal cavity, flipping the triangle of tissue at the top onto Rosie's impassive face.

Until now, the atmosphere of the mortuary had been characterised by a general odour of disinfectant. But with the puncturing of her skin, the putrefaction of Rosie's internal organs began its true assault on the forensic team. Harry had already plastered Vick's VapoRub on his top lip and was oblivious to the initial reek, but by some twisted logic, Dave considered the practice wimping out. However, his large nose meant he was at a disadvantage and he coughed, turning his head away. "God, I hate this bit."

A consummate professional, Dr Beecham carried on without the merest flinch. With a set of large shears, she cut along the outer margin of Rosie's ribs. Each bone snapped with a sound like a pair of garden secateurs slicing through a stubborn twig. As in life, the hollowness of her chest amplified the sound and each "thunk" resonated around the small room. After making the cuts, the doctor lifted up the whole bony breastplate and put it to one side, revealing the organs of the thoracic cavity. All the banter had ceased, in part because of the recording, and the only voice was that of Dr Beecham. "On initial viewing, the pericardium and lungs appear in good order."

She continued her narrative while removing, weighing and dissecting her heart, which had pumped tirelessly despite years of abuse. Next she processed Rosie's lungs that only failed due to the sedative effects of heroin on the central nervous system. All the time, Dave and Harry bottled, recorded and categorised the collected blood and tissue samples.

Then the viscera of Rosie's abdominal cavity received the

same treatment. Dr Beecham examined her stomach contents to establish her last meal. Although not definitive, the passage of food within the gut can help determine time of death. But Rosie was someone who never ate more than a few bites. Satisfying the hunger that was her addiction was far more important.

In a departure from her dispassionate verbal account, the pathologist veered off-piste. "Such a waste of life. How does a young thing like this become a slave to the needle? Would you believe she ticked the organ donor option on her driving licence?"

Dave paused while transferring Rosie's spleen to the nearby bench, not sure if she expected him to respond, but Dr Beecham continued her musing. "So ironic that the way she mistreated her own body prevented any posthumous use of her organs."

She shook her head and broke the awkward silence. "Wow, sorry about that. I must need some sleep."

One by one she removed the remaining abdominal viscera. Eventually Rosie's body became an empty husk resembling a bloody pea pod, shelled of all its contents.

The primary aim of this autopsy was to determine the likely cause of death, which appeared to be another opiate overdose. As with most aspects of government work, time is money and therefore there was no need to dissect Rosie's arms or legs. So the pathologist moved her focus to the head. She had already examined the oral cavity when she removed Rosie's tongue through her neck during the evisceration of her larynx and trachea. But the brain remained within its cranial vault.

Dr Beecham made an incision behind Rosie's left ear and scored the scalpel below the hairline, round to the other side. She then lifted the freed edge of the scalp away from the skull and pulled the skin forward over itself. As a result, Rosie's auburn locks disappeared under her inverted scalp. With some effort, the skin was dragged down over her face like a gory rubber mask, until she had exposed the skull as far as the brow ridges.

Armed with a Stryker saw, Dave shattered the mortuary's quiet with the power tool's whizzing screech. He gave a couple of presses on the trigger like a do-it-yourself enthusiast about to drill a hole in a wall, then used the oscillating blade to carve a slit around Rosie's cranium. The design of the tool meant that it vibrated soft tissues such as the brain whereas it wore through the dense immobile bone. An attached vac collector sucked up skull fragments and contaminated fluid to reduce the infection risk for those still able to breathe. Once the cut was circumferential, he lay down the saw and with both hands pulled away the resulting skull cap. An audible "shh-luck" accompanied the action.

After observing Rosie's brain in situ and making verbal notes, Dr Beecham severed the connection with the spinal cord and detached the cranial nerves and blood vessels. That done, she lifted the entire brain out and placed it on the side bench. The organ that governed everything that Rosie did during her short life—her thoughts, her passions, her dreams, her failings and, indeed, her cravings, essentially the entity that had been Rosemary Brennan—was then sliced like a loaf of bread with a large knife and a few samples preserved in formaldehyde.

With the examination over, Dr Beecham left the high-risk suite, while Harry met to confer with his colleagues outside. Only Dave stayed behind to clear up the remains. He sealed the removed organs in a bright yellow medical waste bag, including her brain, and dumped them into her abdominal cavity. The empty corpse acting as a convenient waste bin. He replaced the breast plate and skull cap and returned the skin to its former position. To join the cut edges he used a disposable staple gun rather than a needle and thread, to avoid the chance of a needlestick injury. Despite Rosie's body now being intact, the putrid fetor still lingered in the room, though Dave's olfactory sense had long since adapted to the stench. He even hummed a tune to himself as he started cleaning all the equipment.

The postmortem procedure has developed over many centuries, with the incisions placed in such a way to rebuild the corpse so that relatives can view the deceased without being aware of the body's desecration. Of course, the reconstruction was only superficial. The cut to the back of her scalp was now hidden beneath her hair while clothing could mask the Y-shaped stapled scar that extended the length of her torso. But poor Rosie's fate need not have warranted the effort. No open casket with grieving mourners would be at her send off. Her sole surviving relative was an unwanted offspring, a two-year-old girl she had not seen since her birth. A child rescued from the inevitable self-perpetuating poverty cycle by the adoption system. No. The only thing that awaited Rosie was a cold black plastic body bag and the scorching hot burners of a communal crematorium. She was the unwitting accomplice in her own murder and not even the spotlight of a coronial investigation could make her silent body cry out for justice.

Dr Beecham had shed her protective shroud and was now seated at her desk wearing light green theatre scrubs. She was reviewing the digital recordings of the autopsy through white earbuds and tapped the keyboard of a rather old-looking desktop computer with her long slender fingers. She was in her mid-forties with straight grey hair cut in a bob that came down to her shoulders. Her narrow nose and down-turned mouth gave her face an austere look, but when she smiled her features melted into an attractive combination. Unfortunately, Dr Beecham rarely smiled.

She had picked up a steaming cup of coffee and was enjoying a rejuvenating sip when Giallo leant his head around the door of her office. "So Doc, what're your preliminary thoughts on our young Rosie then?"

He sauntered into the room and sat on a vacant table, awaiting her reply.

Looking tired, she pulled her earphones out. "Well, as you can see, I'm only a few minutes into my report and I'm sure you're aware that the blood tests and sample processing take weeks. So I guess you'll have to wait until my findings arrive in your in-tray."

She took another sip of coffee.

"Come on Doc, cut me some slack here. We all know this case is bullshit. Let's face it, the only reason we're here is because her body was moved. It's just another junkie who was so high she forgot to breathe."

He instantly regretted his last statement as he could see the hackles rise on the pathologist before she delivered her rebuke.

"Detective Giallo! She may be just another junkie to you, but she's someone's daughter and from her file and my examination I can see she's also someone's mother. Don't think I'll cut any corners or otherwise be less than thorough because of your prejudices. We all have our addictions, Detective, and from your smell and discoloured fingers I'm guessing yours is nicotine. In my opinion, that's just as lethal as heroin, it simply works on a different time frame."

Giallo was suitably cowed. "I'm sorry, Dr Beecham, that came out wrong. What I meant to say is that from the case description there seemed to be nothing too suspicious regarding this death. You know how it is, I've got several other investigations I need to work on. I was hoping I could at least get an idea whether I should treat this as foul play and focus resources accordingly. If not, is it appropriate to place it on the back-burner while awaiting the lab results?"

Dr Beecham sighed. "I think I mentioned earlier, I've only had a few hours sleep and I'm a little… irritable." The near apology seemed to remind her of her tiredness and she sipped her coffee. "OK, the best I can give you is that from my examination of the body I've not seen anything that was…" She paused to choose the most appropriate word. "Untoward. But the tox screen and blood results may paint a different picture."

"Thanks Doc. Looks like a back-burner will do." He slid off the desk and gave her a wink. "Enjoy your caffeine, I'm guessing that's your addiction." And with that, he was out the door before she could reply.

She shook her head as she stared into the dark fluid within her cup. "Cheeky son of a bi…"

She was interrupted by Giallo popping his head round the door with an impudent grin. "Do you really think I smell, Doc?"

6
BEE

A gentle breeze caressed the secluded garden causing the fern-like leaves of an overhanging jacaranda to sway. A few of the colourful petals floated down to the well-tended flower bed below, where a diligent bee searched for sustenance. The insect hovered before alighting on a nearby inflorescence. Using its forelegs, it held on to the bloom and beat its wings with such rapidity it created a loud buzzing noise. The resulting vibrations precipitated a shower of pollen that it collected before flying on.

A man was kneeling on the adjacent manicured lawn, a smile played on his lips as he watched the behaviour, which confirmed his identification: *Amegilla cingulata* or the blue-banded bee. From his research he knew it was an Australian endemic, which was of no interest to him. Although it could inject toxins, it was far too placid for his needs. He was looking for a species that would defend itself with little provocation. Compared to the native bees, the one he wanted was a feral animal. A relative newcomer to Australia's natural fauna, introduced along with the British convicts.

The man looked around his oasis of tranquillity, a verdant sanctuary where he sought refuge from the hectic stresses of his work life. Despite being just a few kilometres from Brisbane's central business district, his home was the only building he could see from within the garden. Located in the affluent suburb of Ashgrove, he had spent much of his spare time restoring the ornate traditional Queenslander to its former glory.

He turned his attention to a humming noise coming from a lavender bush. A larger bee was working the purplish-blue flowers of the shrub. It seemed to pick a bloom at random, scurrying its way through the aromatic flower clusters then moving on to another stem. It was certainly not buzz-pollinating. The pollen released by its biting mouthparts and bustling movements was collected in a brisk and efficient manner. It then transfer the protein-rich food to the pouches on its hind legs. Fine hairs covered both its stocky thorax and the black and yellow stripes on its abdomen. For the watcher these facts verified its identity: *Apis mellifera* or the European honey bee.

He knew that worker bees like this one were sterile and lived for mere weeks. Therefore, they were only too happy to lay down their lives in defence of the colony. As soon as the barbed sting entered the skin of an aggressor, the bee would seal its own fate. A hand may swat the insect off, or the animal may disembowel itself in an effort to fly away. But the embedded mechanism left behind would continue to dig deeper into the dermis of the victim. Evolution even provided an integrated pump to ensure the sustained delivery of venom for at least a few minutes. Not that he would need any more than the tiniest drop to enter a capillary. Anaphylaxis would achieve his goal.

He let his mind wander to the pathophysiology of this most severe allergic reaction and thought about the way an often-innocuous allergen causes the body's defences to over-react. How the subsequent antibodies incite the immune system into sabotaging the very organs that support life itself. He could visualise the text book diagrams of the cellular interactions; inflammatory mediators causing capillaries to leak and smooth muscles to constrict. Simple processes essential in the fight against disease, but catastrophic when misdirected towards the narrow passageways in the lungs. Swollen tissues here block the flow of air leading to death within minutes from asphyxiation.

He regained his focus and in a deft flick of his wrist removed the yellow top from the clear plastic tub he was holding. It was a small cylindrical pot, like the ones used for urine samples. Reaching out with slow but steady movements, he placed the inverted container around the lavender stalk. The oblivious bee continued to collect pollen, but by the time it detected the danger it was too late. Its natural response of flying up and away only trapped it against the transparent base. It was then a simple task to cut off the bee's retreat by replacing the lid.

The man brought the container up to his eyeline and shook it with a slight movement of his hand. He watched the reaction of the insect with amusement. Incarcerated in its perspex cell, the bee buzzed its frustration and indignation. After all, it would be an innocent party in the watcher's latest murder.

7
___

COFFEE

The sun had risen about an hour ago and was warming up the city as I freewheeled my bike down Hamilton Road towards the station. It took me about thirty minutes to cycle the twelve kilometres from my home in Sandgate and I'd made good time today. I stuck to the quieter back streets and cycle ways, often having to navigate through the suburbs in the dark. Although my line of work meant I was all too familiar with how cars and cyclists are incompatible, I used the ride as a regular form of exercise. The return journey was also a simple way to de-stress after a tiring shift.

I glanced at my watch as I slowed to a stop at the gate before punching in the entry code. There was still half an hour before log on. Today was a seven to nineteen and as per usual I didn't know who was my crewmate. I was a bit of a station whore, often crewed with someone different each week. It was perhaps because my Station Officer wanted to share the experience of working with an ICP, or he felt no one could put up with me for too long. Knowing Boardie, it was probably the latter. Either way, I kept the surprise for when I arrived, seeing as there was little I could do to change the roster.

I left my bike against the wall in the plant-room, where we housed ten or so ambulances, and used my swipe card to access the station. Maxine greeted me as soon as I opened the door. She was an enthusiastic but needy mature-aged student, whose sole focus was herself. From my experience she was struggling with the basics, though she tended to concentrate on the less relevant 'nice to knows'.

"Oh, hi Jon. Just the person I wanted to see. I was called to this job yesterday and the patient had an unusual 12 lead, which I thought might be a bifasicular block, but the qualified I was working with was unsure and so here it is for you to check."

She thrust an ECG strip in my face and I had a sinking feeling I'd been rostered with her. I thought about turning around and going home. She was well meaning enough, but she took talking to a new level. Even one of the station's most positive paramedics, Little Sophie, has been known to switch off her hearing aids when working with her.

I held up my hand in a stop gesture and closed my eyes. "Max, you know the rules. No questions until I've had a coffee."

Jan Reid was seated on a nearby wheelie chair, checking her emails. She was around thirty, slim and with short black stylish hair that made her attractive in a Tomboy sort of way, but she had a sense of humour as dry as the Nullarbor.

She pushed herself away from the desk. "Jesus Max, let the guy get changed. Spare us all from seeing him in those Lycras."

"You know I only wear them for you, Jan."

"Remind me to lodge that Cease and Desist Order with the cops."

With Max stumped for words, I dove into the changing rooms. After standing under a piping hot shower for about ten minutes, all I needed was a coffee and then I'd be ready for whatever the day threw at me.

Once dressed, I peered around the door to the corridor, but Max was nowhere to be seen. Breathing a sigh of relief, I made a dash for the drug room. It was my first shift of the month, so I had to check the expiry dates on the thirty-odd drugs in my response bag. We were supposed to have twenty minutes at the start of each shift to sign out kits and ensure the vehicle was ready, but these days Comms often dispatched us as soon as we logged on. As a result, many ambos would come in early, preparing for the day in their own time. But I objected to this on two counts. First, I'd have to get up earlier for no reward and second, it exploited our good will.

Jan walked in the room and proffered a pager. "Looks like you're on with me for the next few days."

Relief must have shown in my face.

"Don't worry, I had Max write a list of questions for you. I think there were about twenty before she left on a call."

"Ah, Jan, it won't be the same coming from you. You'll have to ask all of them without taking a breath."

"We know you love her really. Anyway, here's hoping we get some ICP work."

"Ha! You've got the wrong guy for that. I had my good job for the month last week."

"I heard. They've dubbed it 'Death by PowerPoint'. By all accounts it was pretty messy."

As expected, I retold the events of the case. The mental image of 'laptop man' was still haunting me, but reciting the story numerous times was part of the healing process. For me, of course, not the patient; he'd be pushing up the daisies by now.

I was in mid-flow of my verbal catharsis when our pagers started beeping. A glance at the screen revealed a 2C, the lowest acuity case for an emergency ambulance. Jobs starting with '1' require lights and sirens. Therefore, the '2' meant we'd be stuck in rush hour traffic, driving under normal road conditions.

I groaned. "Have you logged us on already?"

"Of course, it is ten past seven. I'm not copping flack because of your slack arse."

"Well, Jan, seeing as you're raring to go, you can attend first. It's for a sick person, no priority symptoms."

"Great. My specialty."

"What car are we on?"

"962's all ready. We just need your ICP stuff."

I locked the drug safe, threw my kit in the ambulance and we were off on the first job of the day, B.C.

Before Coffee.

The address was in Zillmere. It's strange how certain suburbs become synonymous with poor quality call-outs and Zillmere rarely bucked the trend.

We pulled up outside a dilapidated low-set fibro house that had seen better days: I'd guess about fifty years ago, just after it was built. And the garden looked like it had been festering ever since. We both jumped out and I grabbed the monitor while Jan shouldered the response bag. I walked over to a small wooden gate that spanned a gap between the untidy thickets either side. Unclipping the rusted latch, I held open the barrier with a low bow. "After you, my dear."

As I spoke the gate's hinges collapsed and I was left holding the rotten frame. "Ah, shit."

"Smooth. Real smooth."

Jan walked past and picked a path through the undergrowth as I propped the gate against a bush and followed her to the front door. She rattled the aluminium security screen with her fist. "Ambulance."

There was a shuffling noise from inside, accompanied by a prolonged hacking cough before the door opened. In front of us stood a woman in her late fifties. She looked as if she'd been decaying at the same rate as the house. Her pale face was like a bleached prune framed by a frizzy mop of brown hair. What was left of her teeth would have caused an orthodontist to break out in a cold sweat. The fingers on her right hand mirrored the dark yellow staining of her battered enamel.

"Where you been? I called hours ago."

Hearing her croaking voice, I could imagine her vocal cords were like two ancient kippers, smoked to thin frazzled crisps.

"Yes, well, we're here now. Are you the patient?"

"Yes, missy. Course I am. C'mon in. It's a bit embarassin'."

She beckoned us to follow and shuffled ahead into a dingy untidy living room. No surface seemed free from piles of clutter, all coated with thick layers of dust. At about one-metre intervals in every direction was a network of overflowing ashtrays. The walls and ceilings that may once have been white were now stained a yellowish hue. What a paint manufacturer might call 'hint of nicotine'.

She slumped into a threadbare armchair and paused to catch her breath. We both stood and waited for her to give us some clue as to our presence. My money was on breathing problems.

"Well. As I said, it's a bit embarassin'."

Jan offered some encouragement. "Don't worry, darl. Believe me, we've heard it all before."

"Well... Y'see, I've got a whole load of blackheads 'round me anus."

"What?"

"Y'know. Spots near me bum hole."

Jan stared at her for a few seconds. "OK. Correction. Now we've heard it all. You called an ambulance for that?"

"Well... I thought you'd take a look for me."

"How long have they been there?"

"Bout six months."

Standing on the sideline watching the interaction, my efforts were shared between suppressing laughter and trying not to think how this woman had discovered the blackheads.

Jan continued. "In that case, no. I'm not looking. There are people who are paid far more than me that'll do that for you. They're called doctors and your local one will open in the next..." She looked at her watch, "... ten minutes. May I suggest you call them?"

"D'you know how long it takes to get to see one?"

"No. But if it's an issue, try a different doctor. You don't need an ambulance."

I gave Jan a wide grin. "Would you like me to take a set of obs?"

"I don't think that'll be necessary."

She turned back to the woman. "Now can we have your details for our paperwork. Name, date of birth, medication list and any allergies?"

It was her answer to the last question that had us both stumped. Jan was the first to find her voice. "You're allergic to cigarettes?"

"Yes. They sometimes make me breathless. And I get a cough."

We both stared at her for a while, not sure if she was taking the piss or just stupid. We both decided it was the latter.

Jan picked up the response bag. "I'd mention that allergy when you go see your doctor."

She then turned and walked out the house. The woman looked at me as if expecting a pearl of wisdom. I was fresh out. All I could muster was a mumbled goodbye, but as I left, I turned back and spoke over my shoulder. "Oh, by the way, did you know your gate's broken?"

Jumping in the cab, I found Jan staring out the windscreen shaking her head. "Why would you call an ambulance for that? What the fuck's wrong with these people?"

I grinned and fired up the engine. "Well, she's got a zitty arsehole, but the general term you're looking for is urban acopia." I drove into the next street to avoid our patient calling us back and pulled up under the shade of a gum tree. "You know, I've come to the conclusion that city folk seem to think there's an ambulance on every corner. So, whatever your medical problem, call triple zero and you'll get a blue-light taxi. No worries."

Jan grabbed the Toughbook to document the job. "Although I hate to agree with you, I think you're right. I just don't know how to write that up."

"Well, while you have a think, I'll do the sitrep." I scooped the mic off the dash. "Comms, this is 962."

"Go ahead Alpha 962."

"Yes, well, this 58-year-old lady has, for the past six months, been concerned about the appearance of blackheads around her anus. We declined the offer of a personal viewing and have suggested she gets her doctor to look into it. That's the spots, not her anus. We're clear pending paperwork."

There was a long pause before the dispatcher responded and when she did, we could hear the amusement in her voice. "Thanks 962. Sure you don't want to go back for a better look?"

"That'll be a negative, Comms. I could do without that sort of PTSD."

"Roger, 962."

Jan shook her head while typing. "You always have to play to your audience, don't you? If I made comments like that I'd be hauled over the coals. Guess us ACPs are easier prey than a golden child like you."

"Ha! The shine's long worn off my epaulettes. I think they've given up on my misdemeanours and are hunting for bigger transgressions."

"Well, you keep giving them ammo."

I sat back and smiled to myself. She had a point, but I couldn't help bucking the system. It was the irony that was galling. B-CAS had spent so much time and money training me to be a critical thinker, making judgement calls on the fly, but then would get upset when I questioned orders and wouldn't do as I was told. If they wanted 'yes men' then they should have stuck with stretcher bearers.

Jan looked up from the laptop. "C'mon, give me a condition I can use in this writeup."

I thought for a moment and dredged something from a distant memory. "How's about perianal comedones."

"Comedones?"

"It's the technical term for blackheads, the singular is comedo."

"How the hell d'you remember crap like that? You're such a smart-arse."

I shrugged. "Better than a zitty arse." We both laughed. "Hey, make sure you type that term in, though."

"Why?"

"Well, if anyone audits the case, it'll give them something to look up. With any luck, they'll do a Google image search. It's about as close as I'll get to giving management a brown-eye."

"Now there's more of that ammo I was talking about."

The first job set the tone for the day and the hope of a decent coffee receded as the hours progressed. A patient from Northgate with a two week old chest infection that had not responded to antibiotics. A trip to a doctor's surgery in Strathpine to transport an old man to hospital with a sore elbow. A 30-year-old in Albany Creek with non-traumatic back pain unable to stand. The list went on and so did the kilometres.

We'd just cleared at the Royal when Comms called us up. "Apologies Alpha 962, we understand you're due a break, but you're the only available resource and this job's been on the board for some time."

I picked up the mic. "Send it down, we know how important a clear board is to you guys."

I paused then added, "Doesn't matter you'll have no other ambulances to respond to real emergencies should they arise. I guess we're just a small cog in the grand design and you have that infamous 'Big Picture'."

Jan turned to me with an unimpressed look. "So, how much did you say with the transmit button held in?"

"Not much more than 'Send it down'. You're no fun. Maxine would have lost her shit."

"I think Max would have caused you to lose your shit about four hours ago."

"True."

The Mobile Data Terminal beeped and I pressed the buttons to read the details of the job. It was gone 1:00 PM and so I was now in the attendant's seat. Most crews split shifts half-and-half like this to break up the day. However, as an ICP, I was the clinical lead on every job, regardless of where I sat.

"Wonderful. A 64-year-old man in Stafford is suffering a bout of diarrhoea."

Jan laughed as I noticed something in the coding from the Advanced Medical Priority Dispatch System. "Hey, check this out. AMPDS has a code for the shits. It's a 26A11: defecation / diarrhoea. Do you think anyone ever thought of questioning why an emergency ambulance dispatch system needs a code for a dribbly bottom?"

"Hey, would you want a rellie in your car if they're likely to shit on your seats? I'd call that an emergency."

"You haven't seen my car. No one would notice. Hold on a minute. How old's Wally Dickens? Hasn't he moved to Stafford?"

"I reckon he's sixty-four, or thereabouts. Sounds like this job is just made for your ICP skills."

"Ah shit!"

"Precisely."

"Drive slow, we might get diverted."

"Not a chance. This'll be priceless."

Wally Dickens was one of our regulars. A frequent flier with the Brisbane City Ambulance Service. If we awarded our customers loyalty points, he would be a platinum member. His ailments were numerous and varied, but none were life-threatening. However, he knew how the ambulance system worked and would often quote protocols at paramedics if they diverted from a particular treatment pathway. What's more, he would write a complaint at the drop of his Akubra, so most crews just took him in. It avoided the hassle of an investigation and the local hospitals had action plans to deal with him. This meant you were spared the delight of nursemaiding him while waiting for a bed as he would go straight to 'fast track' and be booted out of the department at the earliest opportunity.

I sighed before pressing the on-scene button as Jan pulled up in the car park that served a small complex of warden-controlled units. Before getting out she gave me a grin. "I heard he once called triple zero to get his pillow fluffed up."

"You're joking. You're just trying to wind me up. Aren't you?"

"It's true! The crew said they hadn't received adequate training in pillow fluffing and left."

"Well, if I do anything with his pillow it'll be to hold it over his face."

As we walked towards the units, a man came out of an office and greeted us. "Hi, I'm the warden here. How can I help?"

"G'day, we've just had a call from one of your residents. He's in number 24."

"Oh God, not again. What's wrong with him this time? He's been here less than two weeks and this is the ninth ambulance I know about."

"By any chance does he go by the name Wally?"

"Yes. Do you know him then?"

I could see Jan's smirking face out the corner of my eye. "Oh yes. There aren't many Brisbane ambos who don't know Wally. Anyway, not to worry, we'll deal with it from here, but thanks."

"Bloody waste of your time if you ask me."

"I hear you, mate. Believe me, I do."

We made our way to number 24 and knocked on the door.

A prim, nasal voice replied. "Come on in, it's unlocked."

Everyone knew he had a habit of welcoming crews having just mislaid his pants, so I called through the closed door. "Hey Wally, it's Jon from the Ambulance. Make yourself decent or I'll lodge a sexual harassment claim and get you kicked out of your new digs."

There were scuffling noises from inside. "Whoever you are, Jon, you must have me mistaken with someone else."

"You know me, Wally. I took you to Charlies only a few weeks back."

I threw open the door to find a tall thin man standing in the middle of a small living room tucking in his shirt and buckling up his belt. He was almost bald save for a few wisps of hair, but he sported a wonderful pure white handlebar moustache. He was sporting a baggy old grey suit with a red tie, complete with the Australian Defence Force insignia.

"Gotcha, Wally!"

"I... I don't know what you mean. I've just been to the toilet and didn't realise my shirt was out.

"Right. Nice tie, did you get it from Vinnies?"

"I don't like your attitude, sonny. I'll have you know I fought for this nation in World War II. Show me some respect, young man!"

"Wow, that's impressive, Wally. Did you mount an assault from within your father's scrotum?"

His eyes bulged and his mouth fell open. Jan even let out a muted splutter.

I qualified my last statement. "Wally, you're sixty-four. You weren't born when the war ended, don't be ridiculous. We had a similar discussion the last time we met."

"I've never been so insulted in all my life."

"Somehow I doubt that. Now, what are we here for today?"

He sat himself down in an armchair and tried to regain control of the situation. He gave a sigh and patted his tummy. "I've had this pain in my epigastric region for the past few days and I've been suffering some rather severe bouts of diarrhoea."

"What did the doctor say?"

"I haven't seen my doctor."

"Wally, you visit the Prince Charles more than I do and I work from within the hospital grounds. What did they say about this pain?"

"You must have the wrong person, that's not me. Now how's about you let this nice young girl take a set of obs? You need at least two sets to make sure you're not audited."

"Right, Wally, let's cut to the chase. Get your bag and hat and walk out to the ambulance. Sit in the seat, not on the stretcher, and only talk if I ask you a question. If you feel you must write a letter of complaint, only mention my name, Jonothan Byrne. Leave my crewmate out of it. Your blue-light taxi will be departing in five minutes, with or without you. So you better hurry."

He opened his mouth to say something, but I turned around and left, followed by Jan. We walked in silence to the ambulance and loaded up the kit. She finally spoke. "Well, that's one way of dealing with him. I'm surprised you offered a lift."

"That's because if I didn't, as soon as we left he'd call triple zero again. This way he gets what he wants and I keep management off my back."

"You realise he's just a lonely old man?"

"Yes, but why can't he go to an RSL like the rest of them? All these ambulance calls must cost the tax payer a fortune."

"If he went to an RSL they'd pick him out as a phoney. D'you think he'll come?"

I nodded over her shoulder as Wally approached carrying a green shopping bag of belongings. He was wearing his battered old Akubra at a jaunty angle as he swaggered towards us with a polished wooden cane held under his left armpit.

"Never doubted it for a second."

After we dropped Wally off at Charlies, Comms sent us back to station for our first break. As neither of us had anything to eat, we returned via pickup, driving to a nearby Subway.

I looked at my watch. "I suppose three-forty's too late for that coffee."

"Mmm. I think you've missed the coffee-bean window. You could settle for a coke and chocolate if you still need your caffeine fix?"

"Now there's a plan. A twelve inch sub, a bucket of coke and at least four double-choc cookies."

"Pig. You realise that cycle ride of yours'll only burn off one of those cookies."

"Give me a break, you sound like Amber. A man needs to eat and I'm hungry."

She raised her eyebrows. "Oh, so you're talking about Amber now. Things must be getting serious."

For a brief second I thought there was a flash of annoyance in her eyes, but I could've been mistaken. As per usual, I relied on humour to cover my confusion. "You know any dates I have with others are only practice for the real thing with you, hey Jan."

She turned her back on me to order her food. "Ha! In your dreams smart-arse." And the moment was gone.

We paid for our meals and then Jan drove to the station to start our break. As the roller door opened the sight of a few ambulances still parked in their bays came as some relief. At least they'd give us cover while we ate our food.

Three crews greeted us as we walked into the main room, all were from other stations. As we were based on the grounds of the hospital and in a central location, our station was often used as a break venue. Today was no exception. I knew most of those present, even some of their names, and there was the usual banter as Jan and I sat down at the table.

Gerry Seabrook, a mate from Roma Street called out from a La-Z-Boy. "Heard you had a good job last week, Jono."

"You heard right." And so, in-between mouthfuls of Subway, I once again indulged in the mental cleansing process of storytelling. That is, until our pagers went off. "Ah for fuck's sake! I didn't get to eat my cookies. What've we got Jan?"

"Oh crap, it's a 1A. We'd better go."

As we got up to leave Gerry leant over from his horizontal position on the recliner. "Guess they must need an ICP. Sucks to be you, Jono. Go earn the big bucks, I'll keep your seat warm for you."

On the way out I passed behind him and couldn't resist the temptation. I grabbed a handful of ice out of my empty coke cup and dumped it in his lap. "Here, Gerry, warm this."

I ran for the door and was out the station in one of my fastest response times. I was still chuckling to myself as Jan pulled out onto Hamilton Road and flipped on the sirens. She gave me one of her looks. "How old are you?"

"Hey, you're only young once, but you can be immature for the whole of your life."

"That figures."

"So, what're we going to?"

"We're backing up 912. A neighbour can see an unconscious woman lying on the floor of her house, but the place is all locked up."

"Great, we get to break in!"

"The firies are on their way."

"Bummer."

"Are you always like this after a bucket of coke?"

"Pretty much. Where we going?"

"Aspley. You may be high, but you can still read. I have to drive."

I scrolled through the info on the MDT and stopped when I recognised the address. "Hey, isn't that where Shirley lives?"

Jan paused. "I think you might be right. Looks like you're getting all the classy jobs today."

Shirley was another regular. Not in the same league as Wally, but still a gold member of our loyalty scheme. Her usual calls were for depression, suicidal thoughts and breathlessness. But seeing as she lived on her own, drank like a fish and smoked like a chimney, her ailments were pretty much predictable. What was different on this occasion was that Shirley hadn't made the call.

Jan eased our way through the traffic building up at the lights near Maccas and turned right. "Smile for the camera."

A white flash lit up the intersection capturing our progress on film. I grabbed the mic. "Comms, 962. Red light camera activation on Gympie Road, Aspley."

The radio crackled back. "Roger 962. The other vehicle should be just ahead of you."

True enough, a few hundred metres away we could see the flashing lights of 912 turning into a side road. "Hey, they do have a big picture."

We made a couple more turns and pulled up behind the first ambulance, now parked on the verge with their lights still flashing.

The crew was talking to an elderly woman by the front door of a low-set unrendered brick house. The building sat within a large block devoid of flowerbeds and the only tree was a single tall palm that somehow accentuated the heat of the afternoon. There was no fence nor wall separating the property from the road and the yard looked about as empty as what I imagined Shirley's life to be.

I hit the on-scene button and Jan flipped off the lights. "What do you need?"

"Just my airway kit and drugs that'd be great. They haven't got in yet, so I'll go find out what the story is."

I left the cab and walked over to the small gathering, nodding to both the ambos who were from Eatons Hill. "Hi guys. What've we got?"

The woman prevented them from replying. "It's Shirl. I'm her neighbour from across the road. I knew something was wrong as there hasn't been an ambulance here for a few days. I thought I'd check in on her and when there was no response I had a look around..."

The older ambo, who was wearing a name badge 'Alan', jumped in at that point. "You can make out someone's legs from a window down the side. But I reckon they've been there a while. The place is pretty well locked up with the windows all closed, so I thought we'd wait for the firies."

"Mind if I have a go at breaking in, I always like to get one over the water fairies."

"Be my guest."

I walked up to the door and grabbed hold of the security screen, giving it a pull to see how strong it was. To my surprise the entire mesh pulled out of the frame and as I turned, I ended up holding the screen between me and the others.

"Guess it wasn't Crimsafe."

Jan walked up behind me. "You've got a thing about gates today."

"Guess I don't know my own strength; must have been that coke."

I threw the mesh to one side and used my multitool to cut through the fly screen. I was disappointed to find the door unlocked - kicking in doors can be quite satisfying. As soon as I stepped inside the smell of decomposition engulfed me like an invisible fog. I turned back to look at Jan. "You might want to move the neighbour away."

She seemed confused until tendrils of the stench gripped her. "Sounds good to me."

I walked through the house holding my nose, with Alan and his student following, more out of morbid curiosity rather than a need for extra hands. The smell of death is quite distinct and Shirley had been dead for a while.

We soon found her body in a bedroom, sitting on the floor with her back propped against a wall. Shirley was in her early sixties and it was unlikely that anyone would have described her as pretty, but what remained of her was grotesque in the extreme. Her head and shoulders were dark purple and her face was swollen beyond recognition. Fat toad-like lips surrounded her open mouth, as if she was coming up to breathe. And her sightless glazed eyes were so wide and bulging they looked fit to burst. Her right hand was still clutching her throat, while the left lay draped down, less than a metre from a phone, knocked off a bedside locker.

Trapped inside her brick tomb, the heat of a Queensland summer had only accelerated her putrefaction. Her skin looked like a delicate parchment straining to contain the darkening soup within and, where her body was in contact with the floor, she appeared to be melting into the carpet. All around the edges of her legs, dark tissue fluid was oozing out into a widening pool, like black coffee overflowing from a trainee barista's cup.

The local insect life was having a field day. Lines of ants were crawling up and down the wall, transporting our regular patient piece by piece. Although the screens had limited the number of flies, some had joined the party as maggots wriggled at the corner of her eyes and several swam in the surrounding coffee pool.

I turned to my colleagues. "Anyone for CPR?"

Alan smiled. "Well, I was hoping we would see some ICP interventions. Do you have any drugs that'll bring this one back?"

"Let me check my bag. Nah. I guess we've got to look on the bright side."

"What's that?"

"With all these bugs around, at least she didn't die alone."

Alan smirked. "Jono, that's so wrong on so many counts."

The student was looking pale and attempted to speak. "I think I'm going to be..." He then made a retching sound and ran from the house with a hand to his mouth.

Alan and I looked at one another and grinned. He shook his head. "The kids today, eh? They don't breed 'em like they used to."

"I guess this means no more calls from Shirley."

Alan pointed to her outstretched left arm. "Looks like all we needed to do was keep her phone out of reach. Hey, what's that on her hand?"

I leant closer to see what he was pointing at. Although the skin was discoloured, there was a swollen area on the back of her left hand. And right in the centre, still attached by its stinger, was the black and yellow body of a honey bee.

8

HUEY

The next night, Jan and I started our twelve-hour shift at 7:00 PM and were straight out the door. We were now on our sixth job and it was being dragged out because there were no beds available in the emergency department. We were standing around in the triage area of the Prince Charles Hospital next to our latest patient, having been ramped like this for over an hour. So far, it'd been another shift of bunions, boils and bullshit. The sort of ailments that out-of-hours doctors should've dealt with, if only they bulk-billed. For many patients it came down to a simple matter of maths. Two hundred dollars for a GP you've never seen before, and then the hassle of trying to claim it back; or call triple zero and get an ambulance to drive you to hospital and see a doctor for free.

A bed became available and we handed over our patient to the staff at Charlies. Returning to the ambulance, I kicked my feet up on the dashboard and yawned as I looked at my watch. "Five past three. What's the chances they'll say: Alpha 967, we're sooo sorry for running you ragged all night, you can go back to station and sleep for the rest of your shift".

Jan gave me a tired, but withering look. "You do realise that you've just screwed any chance of that happening." Like most ambos, she had a healthy disdain for any comment that could tempt fate.

"Let's roll the dice then." I reached over and pressed the relevant button on the Mobile Data Terminal, which beeped an acknowledgement and the screen displayed 'Cleared by Dispatch'. "Ah shit, that was way too fast."

As if in response to my expletive the radio crackled a reply. "Apologies Alpha 967, we've got a 2A for you in Aspley, details on your MDT."

"Many thanks Comms, I was just remarking to my colleague how we could squeeze in another job before our first break."

Jan winced as she typed the address into the satnav and after a long pause Comms replied with a curt "Roger." I was never sure if the all-too-frequent pause related to the dispatcher's lack of wit, or if they were reviewing the tape to decipher my sarcastic tone. On the other hand, it could be due to a supervisor leaning over their shoulder to stifle any budding repartee.

"So, Jan, wanna guess what we're going to?"

"No." She pulled out of the parking bay and followed the directions on the satnav.

"You're no fun." I leant forward to read the screen, pressing buttons to scroll through the sparse information. "Hey, at least we can be certain it won't be Shirley."

"True. Unless her ghost's found a phone."

"Wouldn't that be typical? Still getting two call-outs a week to respond to her in the crematorium." My comment conjured up an image of Shirley's rotting corpse and I shook my head to clear the memory. "D'you hear we've also lost BB?"

"Yes. News like that travels fast on the grapevine. His

death'll sure reduce the workload of the city crews. Come to think of it, you didn't have anything to do with BB and Shirley, did you?"

"Me?"

"Wouldn't put it past your jaded arse to bump off our regulars to get more downtime on a night shift."

"I'm shocked you'd think I'd stoop so low."

She nodded to herself. "Yes, you're right. If murder was on your mind, you'd start with our management."

I laughed. "Jan, you know me too well."

"Anyway, what are we going to?"

"Oh, some pissed-up 24-year-old tosser who's been kicked out of a taxi 'cos his scalp wound was getting blood on the seats."

"Great. Another quality job."

We travelled in a comfortable silence that often befalls the cab in the early hours of the morning. I watched the familiar scenes drift by in a half-comatose stupor, my body yearning for sleep while my mind ticked over, fed by the toxic amount of caffeine I'd consumed throughout the shift. The roads were deserted, except for the odd taxi and it reminded me of a line from the Dire Straits song 'Your Latest Trick': ...*most of the taxis, most of the whores are only taking calls for cash*.

Approaching the location, I reached up to the row of glove boxes and pulled out a pair of large and another of small. I received a grunt of acknowledgment as I threw the latter on the dash. Up ahead, I could see two people in the beam of the headlights.

Despite being the only living souls we'd witnessed the entire length of Kirby Road, one of them thought it necessary to wave his arms like a windmill and step out onto the bitumen. I yawned as I watched the performance. "Don't suppose I can tempt you into running him over and creating a real patient?"

"See, there you go. You do have murderous intent. But better not, it'll create too much paperwork."

She flipped some switches on the dash and bathed the scene in white light from the halogen lamps mounted on the roof. As we came to a standstill, we were greeted by two drunk men in their mid-twenties. The one who had flagged us down opened my door with some difficulty and beckoned me out, pointing to his friend. "It's me mate, he's cut his fuckin' head."

"Thanks, I can see that."

The other man was naked from the waist up, holding a crumpled T-shirt. Numerous dark brown rivulets snaked down his back and chest, made only more striking by the contrast with his pasty white skin that shone in the glare of the scene lights. At the back of his head, congealed blood matted his shock of orange hair, but the wound must have happened some time ago because there was no active bleeding.

"I'm Clark and this is Lois, what's your name?"

Jan rolled her eyes, but said nothing.

"Ian, but they call me Ranga, or Bluey."

"No shit. OK, let me check your head."

He turned around and I combed my gloved fingers through his hair looking for the blood's origin. I soon found a two-centimetre laceration towards the top of his head, which was being held together by a combination of hair and clotted blood. There was only a small amount of blood oozing from the wound and the bump it sat on suggested a minor haematoma, or a slight bleed under the skin.

"So, tell me what happened."

Ranga turned back to face me. "Well, after having a few beers at Gilhooleys we were waitin' for a taxi when some dopey twat started fuckin' about. He was jumpin' up and down and pushin' people in the queue. Cockhead. Anyway, security turned up and for no fuckin' reason one of them jumped me, grabbin' me round the neck. He was this huge big black Kiwi fucker and he began crushin' me neck until everythin' started goin' blurry and I could see lights an' fuckin' stars an' all. But before I lost me shit, he lifted me up and threw me to the ground. Head first! I guess that's when me head got cut, 'cos after I felt something dribbling down me back, which was all this fuckin' blood."

He used his free hand to wave around his upper body to point out the blood, just in case we'd missed it.

While he'd been talking, I reached out and, without thinking, wiped the blood off my gloves on the T-shirt he was holding. "So did you lose consciousness?"

"No, mate, no."

His friend chimed in. "Na, he didn't get knocked out, or nuffin', he was shoutin' an' yellin' all the way through."

Jan gave her opinion on the situation. "I'll go fetch a collar."

I took the hint though I was a little reluctant to be too invasive with treatment.

"OK, from what you've told us you received a pile-drive from some irate Maori body builder. Therefore, we need to work on a worse-case scenario by making sure we protect your spine, the most delicate bit being your neck. So, what's going to happen is we'll lie you on our stretcher and support your neck with a collar…"

The patient interrupted my spiel by rolling his head around and flexing his neck. "No man, look, me neck's fine."

He then bobbed and weaved like a demented meerkat, breaking into a full-blown dance routine, only encouraged by his friend who marked out an accompaniment with a rapper-style vocal drum beat. After waiting a short while for the gyrating display to wind down, I reached round the back of his neck to palpate his upper spine.

"You should audition for the next intake of 'Australia's Got No Talent'. Keep still while I check your neck. Any pain when I press here, here, or here?"

I pressed my thumb along the bony protuberances that mark the ridge of the cervical spine.

"No man, I told ya, my neck's fuckin' fine."

He again wobbled his head about and it was difficult to suppress the thought that any significant spinal injury may prevent him siring a new generation. "OK mate, you're within your rights to refuse my treatment, but I can only recommend you get your injuries checked out by a doctor."

"Well, you'll have to take me to hospital. No fuckin' taxi's gonna drive me nowhere and I ain't walkin' all the fuckin' way home to Kallangur."

Although it was an obvious abuse of an emergency ambulance he had a point. Who else other than ambos or the police would transport a blood-encrusted abusive drunk at three thirty in the morning? And if we called the cops, we'd have to hang tight for an hour or so until they arrived and that was no way of getting back for some long-needed La-Z-Boy shut-eye.

It was an easy decision to make. "OK, in you get. Mind your head and sit there."

As I pointed to the captain's chair I grabbed a sheet from the stretcher and threw it over the seat to minimise the subsequent clean-up of the ambulance.

He climbed in and sat down, placing his T-shirt on the shelf by his left side. "What 'bout me mate?"

"He can get in the front, if he promises to behave."

I looked over to Jan and she gave a slight nod, opening the door so he could get in. His mate grinned, mumbled his thanks and stumbled aboard. I sat down on the top end of the stretcher and collected an obligatory set of obs. His heart rate, oxygen saturation, blood pressure and respiratory rate were all normal, as expected.

Jan had already slammed the side door, installed herself in the driver's seat and was plugging the data into the MDT. "Back to Charlies I guess?"

"Where else?"

"Good to go?"

"Yep."

As I retrieved the Toughbook I looked at my bare-chested patient. "Aren't you cold?"

"Am a bit."

"Might be an idea to put your T-shirt on."

"This?" He said the word while holding up his discarded item of clothing with an incredulous look. "This? This is my best T-shirt. I've only had it a few days and it cost me over a hundred bucks. Why d'ya think I took it off, I've got to stop me blood from trashin' it."

I remembered the point when I'd used his precious garment to wipe the blood off my gloved hands and I had a slight pang of guilt. "They must've seen you coming, mate. I've got loads of T-shirts I could sell you for a similar price."

He gave me a drunken look of confusion, not sure if I was being serious or winding him up. Just in case, I defused the situation by grabbing a blanket, which I unfurled and draped round his shoulders. "Here, wear this, it's free and someone else will wash it, but you need to put your seatbelt on."

I sat down in the attendant's chair and we trundled back to Charlies, making idle conversation with Ranga while collecting pertinent information to type into the Toughbook.

"Normally fit and well? No medical conditions like asthma, epilepsy, diabetes? Any medications or allergies? Taken anything other than alcohol? Do you have any idea how much you've had to drink tonight? So, that'll be somewhere between a shitload and a skinful?"

I've had hundreds of such conversations with inebriated patients over the years, some more entertaining than others. It was only the aggressive ones that were an issue.

Or so I thought.

An abrupt commotion from the cab caused my drooping eyelids to spring open. Ranga's mate had appeared to pass out against the passenger's side window when he made an unexpected noise. Something ominous. Something guttural.

Then Jan screamed. "Sick bag! NOW!"

But it was too late. The tsunami had started and nothing would stop the tidal wave. We screeched to a halt, but this only served to splatter vomit on the inside of the windscreen as our human geyser sprayed his stomach contents wherever his head was thrown. Jan leapt out of the cab and ran round to the passenger's side to open the door, dodging a spray of body fluid. It was one of the worst cases of projectile vomiting I'd seen in a long time and to be honest, from the safety of the back, it was rather entertaining. Every time Jan approached him, he would clutch at his face and another fountain of puke would shoot out at a random angle, to which Jan would scream and leap to avoid.

Entertaining that is until the smell hit me.

At that point, I reached through to the cab and released his seat belt, giving his right shoulder a slight push of encouragement. As a result, he slid out of the vehicle and fell to his knees, pebble-dashing the kerbside with last night's alcohol, burger and chips. I joined Jan outside the ambulance and we both stared dumbstruck at the aftermath as our newfound patient continued to dry retch at our feet.

It was an unwritten rule that whoever attends the patient has to complete the write-up while their crewmate gets to sort out the ambulance. With this in mind, I was the first to speak. "Christ, two patients. That's a lot of paperwork."

Jan fixed me with a steely glare. "If you think you're leaving me to clean up all this crap while you swan around chatting with the nurses you've another thing coming. Anyway, it's your seat he spewed on, so whoever does the clean-up, you're gonna have to sit in it."

She paused as she turned her head to one side to get a better view. "Is that your bag?"

I looked with dismay at what used to be my lunch bag and realised that it and whatever remained of its contents were now destined for the dumpster.

"Ah shit, I had my double-choc cookies in there."

Vomit dripped from the dashboard, and small pieces of half-digested food slid down the windscreen or were stuck between the slats of the air vents. My gaze rested on the source of our misfortune, who was lying on his side with his face resting in his own pavement pizza.

There was a slight flash of light and I turned to find Ranga leaning out of the ambulance and using his phone to take a photo of his mate.

"Wow, man, he sure can hurl."

I was not in the mood for digital evidence of our situation. "Get back in your seat!"

A sheepish Ranga disappeared inside. Looking around, I realised we were on Rode Road just metres from the entrance to the hospital grounds. "Have you seen where we are?"

"I was driving, dumbarse. Three more minutes and he'd have been puking on the nurses."

"Shit, shit, shit."

I put my hands on my hips and looked up to the heavens, seeking divine intervention. As expected, I only saw the starry night's sky, so I closed my eyes and exhaled.

"OK, let's load him up."

The time of the morning somehow emphasised our rotten luck. I strode around to the rear doors, flung them open and dragged the stretcher out, clattering it over the kerb and bashing it down next to the patient.

"Hey, mate, wakey-wakey."

I gave his hip a gentle shove with my boot, wanting to avoid the vomit. There was no response. I squatted down and shook his shoulder. "Come on, get on the stretcher."

Nothing. I reached under his arm and used the knuckles of my fist to press the centre of his chest, a technique known as a sternal rub. He showed more signs of life, but other than a few groans and half-pronounced expletives he just mopped up more vomit with his hair.

"Ah Christ, I haven't got time for this."

I stood up and reached for the folded sheet we keep on the stretcher, only to realise I'd used it earlier for Ranga's chair. I let out another curse and once again stomped around to the back of the ambulance for a spare sheet. On return, I unfolded it on the ground and Jan and I rolled vomit-boy away from the mess and onto the clean sheet.

"You want the foot end?"

She nodded. "I wouldn't say no. I hurt my back last week when some pisshead fell on me."

She walked round to his feet and grabbed the sheet, while I moved to the heavier end, avoiding the vomit. I took a good grip. "On three. One, two, three."

We swung him up onto the stretcher where he landed with a thump and then rolled him into the recovery position.

Jan sighed and shook her head. "Don't suppose you know his name?"

"Haven't a clue. Maybe it's Spew?"

"Could be Chuck."

"Don't forget Huey."

"Or is it Ralph?"

We said each name with the appropriate onomatopoeic sound effects and despite all the vomit and the pervading smell we both started laughing. A subdued voice drifted out from the ambulance interrupting our levity. "It's Simmo."

Jan and I looked at each other and stifled a giggle. "Oops, I forgot about him."

Regaining our professional composure, we lifted the stretcher to its full height and slotted it in the ambulance. Jumping in the back, I slammed the side door and a cautious Jan climbed into the cab, searching for any errant splashes of vomit. She opened both windows and shifted the transmission into drive. "Good to go… again?"

"Good as I'll ever be."

Simmo grunted something unintelligible and retched twice, but produced nothing more. I looked at the less cocky Ranga. "Is Simmo short for Simon, then?"

"Yes, his name's Simon Fuller."

I paused for a moment at the irony of his name, but decided not to make a quip. After all, we'd already been pinged for joking at his expense. I was able to get his basic details written on the back of my glove when I felt the ambulance reversing into the parking bay at Charlies.

"Well, here we are folks, the Prince Charles Hospital. Ranga, follow me. I'll let you out first."

I squeezed past the monitor and opened the side door. "Mind your head". I spoke as Ranga stood and bumped his head on the air-conditioning unit.

"Shit."

"I did warn you. See this big hole in the side of the ambulance? Try and get out of that without any further injuries."

He staggered as he climbed out. "You're a right smart-arse, aren't you?"

"Some say it's my most endearing quality."

I walked round to the back to help Jan with the stretcher as our pagers went off relaying all the times we'd entered into the MDT. We both reached down and pressed the button to stop the annoying alarms, then wheeled Simmo over to the entrance doors, beckoning Ranga to follow. As Jan plugged in the door code, I caught sight of the triage nurse through the glass.

"Oh God, Kath's on triage. Can this job get any worse?"

There has always been a certain amount of rivalry between nurses and paramedics, but for a small proportion of ED staff, this can manifest as open hostility. Kath Howler was one such 'ambo-hater'. A morbidly obese one at that. She projected the likely hatred she had for herself as a loathing for all wearing green. We are often unruly, undisciplined and cheeky, but our worst flaw in her eyes was that we brought her more work.

I led our little procession into the triage area and told Ranga to sit on the first available seat, which he did, wrapping his blanket around him to ward off the cold of the air-conditioning. Kath looked up from her computer as I plonked the Toughbook down on the end of the bench, but she went back to typing, ignoring our arrival. This was her usual welcome.

As I stood there, fatigue spread through my body like a virulent disease and I had to lean on the wall for support. Moving my head would have sapped more energy, so I watched Kath as she typed away. With every movement of her fingers, her chins jiggled in time with the vibrating rolls of fat under her arms. It became mesmerising and I couldn't help wonder why a clinician who's exposed to so much health advice and often berates patients for not following their doctor's orders, can let themselves get to the size of a wildebeest.

OK, so that's not fair. Wildebeests have thin legs. I think a hippo is a far more appropriate comparison. As my eyes fell on her enormous buttocks that were overflowing her straining wheelie-chair, a vivid picture of a natural history documentary sprang to mind. The one where the camera zoomed in on the backside of a hippo as it sprayed dung about with its tail to mark its territory. I had to shake my head to clear the image and when I looked back, Kath was staring at me over the top of her horn-rimmed glasses. I had a moment of panic; had I been thinking out loud?

"Rough night?"

Her apparent empathy took me off guard. "Not the best."

Then she pounced with a more typical acid comment. "The walls are to keep the roof up, not for ambos to lean on."

I leant forward onto my feet, but knew better than to take the bait. "Are you ready for a handover?"

"Not yet."

With that she returned to her fat-wobbling typing and I stood and waited. Time. Was it Einstein who said it was relative? He must have been a shift worker. At this hour of the morning, time travels slowly and what was only a minute or two could seem like an age.

It's often this stage in a night shift where soul-searching and self-reflection come easy. Or at least you think they do. The inclination towards introspection no doubt results from a sleep-deprived brain. Mind you, being dispatched to some tosser who calls an ambulance at three in the morning for their month-old sore knee is bound to beg the question: why am I here?

Why was I here? What led me to this point in time? Why

did I loath this typing woman so much? Was it because she was so fat? I had to admit to a limited tolerance for obesity. Like a reformed smoker, I was a fatist nazi. Unless you have a high metabolism, any sedentary IT job where you stare at a screen while shovelling in Tim Tams with every cup of coffee can pile on the kilos. And I was no exception. I was that fat gross computer nerd from Jurassic Park until I turned things around. But that sea change had taken the death of my brother.

I felt myself teetering on the brink of a familiar mental precipice and deflected my consciousness towards dissecting one of my personality flaws. Addiction. I'd somehow swapped eating for exercise, driving for cycling, but what would satisfy my cravings now I was a reformed fatty? The adrenaline rush of this job had sufficed for so many years as you never know what the next case would bring. But like any addict, the effect of your chosen drug always fades and you either need larger doses or more frequent hits. And working on a truck would never suffice. Perhaps that's why I was so angry with management. It was a manifestation of my own withdrawal symptoms.

Kath finished what I hoped was an email to Weight Watchers and looked up. "OK, what've you got?"

I let out a breath, speaking just loud enough for her to hear. "… ninety-nine, one hundred." Then launched into my handover. "Well, we have a two-for-one deal for you this morning. Our first patient is the 24-year-old gentleman seated over there with the obvious head laceration."

I pointed at Ranga. "He was the injured party in an altercation with a pub bouncer, who took it upon himself to throw our patient to the floor after he had 'done nuffin', apart from drinking alcohol for several hours…"

Kath interrupted me. "Why hasn't he got a collar on? He's

been drinking and has a head injury. Don't you guys know anything?"

I ignored her and continued. "The patient's vital signs are all within normal limits; he's usually fit and well, with no allergies nor meds and the two-centimetre laceration on his occipital region has no active bleeding…"

"Didn't you hear me, why haven't you collared your patient?"

"… and I deemed that the patient had enough capacity to understand the implications of his decision when he refused to let us collar him, which, I may add, was against our advice."

This verbal slam-dunk caused her mouth to pucker and I was again subjected to an involuntary mental image of a hippo's bottom. As she had lost this bout of the recurring ambo-versus-triage-nurse-collar debate, she changed tack. "What's wrong with the other one? He looks in a worse shape."

"Ah, Simmo. Well, he only became a patient a minute or two before our arrival here. We revoked his passenger status when he voided what would appear to be most of his alimentary canal into the cab of our ambulance."

"In the cab?"

"Yep, not my smartest move, but as we speak his vomit is congealing on the inside of our windscreen."

She gave me a disbelieving look. "What's his GCS?"

The Glasgow Coma Scale was developed many years ago to assess the degree of coma in an ICU patient and to reveal any trends in their condition. Since then, it has been adopted by emergency practitioners as a measure of consciousness, assigning numerical values for eye opening, verbal response and limb movement, so that a score of 3 equates to unresponsive, which rises to 15 for a fully conscious patient. It has its limitations in the prehospital field and I was too tired to bother calculating one. "Well, I'd say, eyes are blurry, verbal's slurred and motor response is impaired. So I guess it's GCS pissed."

She skewered me with another puckered-mouth stare and peeled her immense bulk off her relieved chair, waddling around the desk to the patient. "Hey, matey, wake up."

Simmo didn't respond, perhaps exhausted after all his vomiting. "Come on, wake up."

Still nothing. She took a pen from her uniform pocket and used the long edge to crush the nail bed of his index finger on his uppermost hand. This, like the sternal rub, is a standard way to administer a painful stimulus to assess whether a patient is unconscious.

However, Simmo was unaware of that. He let out a yelp and launched himself up onto his elbow. "Wha' the fuck!" He blinked a few times, focussed on Kath and then slurred the immortal words, "Jesus, girlfriend, you're fuckin' enormous."

Before she could respond, he collapsed down and began dry retching. When she turned back towards her seat, her reddening face was one of fury and without looking at me she hissed, "Not… a… word."

I decided discretion was the better part of valour and, using a monumental amount of self-control, somehow maintained a deadpan face.

Wedging herself back in front of her computer, Kath hit the keyboard with added fervour that caused tiny shock waves to ripple through her arm fat. "Did you give him anything?"

"Nope, it all happened less than a K away."

She gave a nod and I thought I spotted a faint smile. "The first one can stay where he is, while the one on the stretcher can go to resus."

I was a little surprised that she triaged Simmo to a resus bay, which is where high-acuity patients are treated, but sometimes that's done when there aren't beds in the acute area. However, her plan became transparent when she bustled past us as we pulled the stretcher towards the waiting resus staff. She spoke in a loud voice so that all present could hear, including those patients sleeping upstairs. "Info is sketchy on this one, the ambos weren't able to ask his friend for any of his details, there's no line in, no anti-emetic given and no fluids administered. Shoddy work in my opinion."

She dropped the paperwork on a table and barged her way out of the cubicle. As she shuffled off down the corridor I called out, "Thanks. *Girlfriend*."

She stopped in her tracks, tensed for a second, then continued without looking back.

I turned to face a rather stunned resus team. "Don't worry, a lover's tiff. I'll give you a real handover once we've got him on your bed."

As I walked out of the emergency department, a small group of paramedics were there to greet me. They were standing around the open passenger door of our vehicle admiring the cab's new-look interior.

Scotty led a round of applause. "Love your work, Jono. To err is human, but it takes an ICP to really fuck things up. Has all that driving about in a sedan caused you to forget that the patient goes in the back?"

He knew full well I spent most of my shifts working on a truck, but couldn't resist the opportunity of a friendly jibe. I stood with both my hands out, palms up. "As an ICP I take full responsibility for this situation and I delegate all the subsequent clean-up to Jan."

There was a collective "Ooooo" as Jan jumped down from

the ambulance and walked into view. She folded her arms and cocked her hips to one side. "Oh. Really?"

"Er… I was just saying that this ambulance won't be cleaned until Jan, or maybe Feb, so I'll call Comms and put us out of service." There was a general groan. "D'you like that save?"

Jan shook her head. "You're full of shit, Jono. Mine's a coffee, white with none, what d'you guys want, the round's on him."

Everyone ordered a drink, which I suspect was even if they didn't want one, and I made the order before getting my phone out to call the Metropolitan Ambulance Coordinator. He answered after about three attempts and I explained the situation. "We're out of service until the vehicle's cleaned and it really needs a professional valet to steam the front seat. As we're out of Charlies, we could swap to another vehicle to be operational sooner and leave the clean-up for my Station Officer to sort out."

He paused, mulling over my proposal, but saw through my attempt to avoid shovelling vomit. "I think you'd better clean up your own ambulance, let me know when you're available."

"Oh well, your decision. Guess you're happy putting an ICP crew out of service. Just so you're aware, I've also got two write-ups to do for this job."

"Noted." And the line went dead.

I relayed the conversation to Jan and she smiled. "Perhaps the MAC could be the first on your hit list."

"Sounds like you're keen on the idea. You realise that incitement is also an offence."

She turned to the other ambos in the room. "Anyone hear me incite Jono?"

Scotty choked on his tea. "Is that rude? Better not let

Amber catch you inciting him, never know what she might do."

Jan shook her head and looked at me. "See. D'you think anyone here would make a credible witness?"

"You've got a point. Anyway, hold fire on any clean-up until we get back to station. At least there's a mop and bucket there, as well as other cleaning stuff. I'll get on with the write-ups."

"Sounds good."

Despite the phone call to the MAC, thirty minutes after arriving at hospital the MDT beeped to notify that Comms had made us available. A fact that neither Jan nor I knew until our pagers began beeping. I picked the annoying gadget out of its holder. "What the fuck? Don't those guys in the Ivory Tower talk to one another? It's a 1C in The Valley, this is bullshit!"

An Eatons Hill crew had completed their paperwork. "We can do that job for you, Jono. To be honest, I don't want to spend too long here anyway, I'm catching a whiff of your truck."

"Cheers for that, I'd better go call them up though."

I walked out to the ambulance, slipped a glove on and reached through to pull the mic out. Standing outside the cab, I flicked a piece of vomit off the grill before depressing the transmit button. "Comms this is 967."

"Go ahead Alpha 967."

"Er, you appear to have dropped a job on us, but we're out of service, as per my conversation with the MAC. We do have 912 here who are willing to take one for the team, so could you please send it to their MDT."

"Apologies Alpha 967, but we require an ICP backup for a Bravo crew already going to an unconscious male in the city."

I shook my head. "Right, gotcha. How would you suggest I get there as my vehicle is not serviceable? It's at least a couple of hours walk there with all my kit."

There was the obligatory pause while I presumed they went to ask a grown-up. Then they came back with the nuclear response. "Are you refusing to go on a Code One?"

This phrase was Comms-speak for 'Do you want to face a disciplinary?' A verbal big stick to beat stroppy crews back into line and it was something to avoid agreeing to at all costs. "No Comms, I'm not refusing, simply questioning my mode of transport. Perhaps 912 could give me a lift?"

After another pause. "Roger that, details on their MDT."

"Err Comms, out of interest, has anyone checked if the patient is taking a nap?"

"The caller is not with the patient."

Mobile phones have brought many positive changes to the way we live, but good Samaritans calling triple zero as they drive by what they perceive to be an emergency is not one of them. All too often Comms dispatches an ambulance to some poor bastard who's trying to sleep off too much grog.

I grabbed my drug bag and airway kit and jumped in the back of 912 just as the Northgate crew reported their findings on scene in The Valley.

"Comms 923, sitrep. After we woke him up, this rather drunk patient is GCS 15. He's now wandering off down the road and has declined our services. You can stand down the ICP and we'll be clear once we've completed our paperwork."

"Roger 923. Alpha 912 did you copy?"

"Copied and predicted. I'll go back to my out-of-service vehicle, shall I?"

"Affirmative, 912. Let us know when you're available."

I ignored the last comment, seeing as, available or not, they seemed determined to flog us for the rest of the shift. I turned to the crew of 912. "Well gentlemen, it's always a pleasure. We must do this again some time. I'll jump out and you can make a run for home."

"Cheers. And good luck with that clean-up. We'd offer to help, but... beep, beep, beep, I think that's another job."

"Totally understand. Catch ya later."

I threw my bags back into my ambulance and walked to the write-up room as a marked-up Forrester pulled into the parking bay.

Jan looked up as I entered. "That was quick, d'you use your extra clinical skills to heal them from afar?"

"My mere involvement was enough to cure them. By the way, someone with shit on his shoulders has just arrived. D'you think they're here to help us with the clean-up, or should I get my balls ready for a bruising?"

"I'm surprised you have any nuts left you've had so many roastings."

"Didn't you know, I've got massive kahunas?"

I uttered these words as Andrew Mitchell, the Senior Operations Manager, stuck his head round the door.

"Er, Jon, can I have a word?"

"Oh, hi Mitchy. We were just talking about you. How can I help?"

He gave me a confused look and the creases on his leathery face suggested it wasn't an uncommon expression. There is a widespread belief in ambulance services worldwide that incompetent staff who risk the health of patients are promoted into managerial roles as a litigation-mitigation exercise. However, the downside of safer streets is that operational paramedics often have to deal with managers who are not the sharpest cannula in the kit bag.

Mitchy was no exception.

He beckoned me outside and I obliged, having to follow him until he had walked out of earshot of Jan before he spoke. "Couldn't help but hear on the radio what sounded like you refusing a Code One. As you're an ICP, I feel that your attitude is becoming an issue and you should be setting a more appropriate example for your Advanced Care colleagues, not to mention the impressionable younger students who may be listening."

I looked at him hoping for a smirk to reveal he was winding me up, but I should've known better. He was serious. I bit my tongue. "Come, take a look at this."

I walked over to our ambulance and opened the passenger door, revealing the full extent of the vomit bomb that had detonated earlier. "Does this resemble an operational vehicle? Care to take a seat and drive to the next job?"

"How the hell did you let this happen?"

The lack of sleep and unnecessary bureaucracy was taking its toll. "I squeezed the guy like a giant tube of toothpaste until he spewed everywhere."

"See? That's the attitude I'm talking about."

"OK, please explain this. As it was a passenger who vomited and not our patient why is it that when the same thing happens in a taxi the culprit cops a fine? Yet, because he puked in an ambulance, we can't charge him, can't afford to have the cab valeted and it's the paramedics who have to clear up the mess."

He looked as if he was giving my observation some consideration, but I misread his expression. "Look, smart-arse, we represent a government SERVICE. It was your 'passenger', your poor judgement, your ambulance, so your responsibility. Now get it cleaned up so you can provide that SERVICE as soon as possible."

He turned his back and strode off to his car, presuming he had put me in my place. Mission accomplished.

In response, I snapped my heels together with a loud thud and gave a goofy salute. "Yessir!"

He glared at me as he swung into the driver's seat, gunned his engine and drove off.

Jan frowned when I sat back down in front of the Toughbook. "What was that all about?"

"Mitchy just knocked the MAC off the number one spot on my management hit list. The fuckwit wants us to clean the cab ASAP, so when I've done here we're off to the station."

From my expression and body language Jan guessed I had something planned, something she wouldn't like. "I think I might make myself scarce when we get back, if you don't mind."

"Probably for the best."

I printed out both write-ups, handed them in to the relevant staff and grabbed a disposable plastic apron before leaving the hospital. Once outside, I climbed into the driver's seat and Jan jumped in the back, guessing that my mood did not call for idle chatter. I drove the short distance over to the station and typed the code into the keypad to open the roller door. I didn't want to go searching through the vomit for the remote control. Once inside, I parked the ambulance in the wash-bay and opened all the doors. "Can you see if you can find a couple of plastic bags before you disappear?"

"Sure."

She gave me a quizzical look, but said nothing. I dragged over a yellow medical waste bin, donned the plastic apron and threw everything in the bin that wasn't bolted down. When Jan returned with two plastic carrier bags, she watched as I tied them around the MDT and the radio. I then stepped out and picked up the spray gun of the Gerni.

Jan's eyes opened wide. "You're not serious are you?"

"He told me to clean it as soon as possible. Got any better ideas?"

She shrugged, shook her head in resigned disbelief and left

before she could witness me jet-washing the inside of the cab. As I pressed the Gerni's trigger, water fired through the driver's side door and I got some minor satisfaction from seeing the vomit blast out the open passenger side and onto the wash-bay floor.

9

THE VOICE

A man, thin as a rake, dragged away an old rotten wooden pallet that covered a hole in a chain-link fence and slipped inside. After pulling his tattered bag of belongings through the wire barrier, he crouched down low in the long grass and checked for any movement. This was the point where the railway security might spot him, but tonight the clouds were in his favour. They had dimmed the moonlight to a muted glow.

His eyes scanned the expanse in front of him. Nothing stirred. Nothing moved. The only noise was from the cars passing along the Inner City Bypass. The next train wasn't due for at least ten minutes. He waited a little longer, then scampered across the open ground and darted beneath the bridge. Once again, he crouched in the shadows, catching his breath as he surveyed the railway sidings for any hint of trouble. Any sign he'd been spotted. Nothing. He was all alone with the wildlife.

He slunk deeper inside the overpass to reach his preferred hiding place and pulled out a grimy dark green sleeping bag.

Climbing inside, he leant against the cold concrete wall and waited for the 10:30 PM to Roma Street Station.

After what seemed like an age, he could feel the rumble through the ground, well before the distinctive sound of the clattering rails. Then, with an ear-popping thump, it flew past. Tonnes of thudding shaking screaming metal accompanied by the strobe-like lights from the passing carriages. Seconds passed and it was gone. His bedroom returned to its semi-tranquil state and he rested his head on the layers of cardboard, intending to get some sleep.

But then the voice spoke.

"Marcus?"

All his muscles froze as he held his breath. Straining his ears for a footfall, the crunch of gravel, the sigh of breathing. But there was nothing, other than the drip of water from a cracked overflow pipe, the rumble of traffic on the road above and the scurrying squeak of a distant rodent.

"Marcus?"

He sat up and pulled his legs to his chest, his eyes darting around, looking for anything out of place in the gloom. The voice had an amorphous quality, hushed but strong, pleasant but intimidating.

"Marcus. Are you not talking to me, you fucking lowlife?"

He hugged his legs in closer to his body and hit his forehead on his knees, rocking back and forth. When he finally spoke it was a shrill sound. "What d'you want?"

"I want what I always want."

His head swung around looking in all directions. "You... you sound different."

"It's those drugs you've been taking, you little shit. Thought you could get rid of me, eh? Not likely, you're useless at everything, why d'you think you could win against me?"

"They said they would stop you!"

"Marcus, I'm part of you. Why would you want me to stop?"

His response came as a whisper. "'Cos you scare me."

"Scare you? Scare you! If you would only listen to me I'd give you strength. I'd give your life meaning. Empower you. Make you invincible! But no, you're too chicken shit for that."

"They said you're part of my schizophrenia."

"Well they would do, wouldn't they, Marcus? They're part of the system. They want everyone to conform. They want to control you, so you can't control them."

The rocking became more rapid. "You wanted me to kill my parents."

"Only so you could resurrect them. You have the power over life and death, Marcus. You are the son of God. Listen to me and you can assume your rightful place, instead of living like this. Like a fucking leper!"

"I live like this so no one gets hurt."

"This isn't living, Marcus."

The night returned to the comparative silence of the dripping pipe, rumbling traffic and foraging rats. His rocking slowed and he raised his head to look around. With eyes now accustomed to the darkness, the exit of the overpass appeared like a dim oblong of night, the lights of the city's high-rises twinkling in the distance. The rail lines disappearing off towards them, like they were the promised land.

His shoulders relaxed as he eased the embrace on his legs. Would the voice ever stop? He'd spent most of his life in and out of hospitals. He'd tried drugs, he'd tried alcohol, he'd tried mixtures of both. He sometimes listened to the doctors, sometimes ignored them. Nothing seemed to help. He had thought the new medications were working, he'd even had a few days respite. But now the voice was back. He should have known nothing worked for long. It was hard to leave your mind at home and go out for a walk, get some time alone. The voice was always there.

"Marcus?"

His whole body tensed again and he pushed his back against the concrete wall. "What?"

"Do you want to be rid of me?"

"Yes."

"My only role is to prove to you who you are."

He rolled his head back onto the cold surface and looked at the dark ceiling. "So, let me guess. You want me to kill someone so I can revive them?"

"No. You've shown that you don't believe me enough to risk someone else's life. So how about yours?"

"Mine? How?"

"You have the power over life and death. You can't die."

"Jesus died."

"He wasn't the son of God, you are. I'll prove it to you."

"How?"

"Step in front of the next train."

"What? No!"

"What have you got to lose? If I'm right, you'll discover your true potential."

"And if you're wrong?"

There was a low chuckling laugh that seemed to echo off the walls and caused his hair to stand on end. "If I'm wrong, Marcus, you'll be free of me forever."

The ground beneath him shuddered as the train approached. "Here comes your destiny, Marcus. Show me you're not the loser everyone thinks you are."

He stood, letting the sleeping bag fall to the floor and then stumbled back against the tunnel wall.

"What, you going to do it, Marcus, or just run away again, you little shit?"

The rails sang as the headlights swept into the short tunnel. Sparks cracked and spat from the overhead cables as the sound of the train thundered in the confined space.

Loud enough to drown out the voice.

Loud enough so Marcus couldn't even hear himself think.

Then he let out a scream and launched himself off the wall.

His thin body shattered on impact.

His cheap tattered clothes were turned inside out as his bones splintered, muscles tore and tissues were crushed under the wheels. The driver only realised what had happened when he heard the thud and applied the brakes. It was an occupational hazard for an inner-city train driver and his main concern was the inevitable late finish. Why did the mad bastards always pick his train?

Back in the overpass a figure dressed in dark clothes stepped out of the shadows. He picked his way along the wall, adjusting his night vision goggles and stopped when he found the discarded sleeping bag lying on the pile of cardboard. Crouching down, he retrieved the remote speakers and microphone hidden in the gravel and dropped them in his pocket. Then, checking nothing was amiss, he retraced his steps and melted into the darkness as the wail of sirens wafted on the night's air.

10

FLATHEAD

I woke feeling like I hadn't slept, but a glance at my watch told me otherwise. It was 4:20 PM, late Saturday afternoon, when everyone else would be thinking of the night ahead. I just wanted to roll over and close my eyes. Give in to the fatigue. Sink into oblivion. But I knew if I did, I'd wake at some ungodly hour and be watching crap TV until sunup.

Working rolling shifts was the problem, they're like playing thrash metal with the body's circadian rhythms. Years ago, when I started ambulance work, some of the old hands assured me I'd get used to nights. It was all bullshit, I never have.

I rolled on my back and forced my eyes open, staring at the ceiling. Working through the night was something I'd done before as a programmer. I'd get lost in the code, working late trying to squash bugs before an overdue beta release. But sitting in front of a computer, engaging only my brain, was nothing compared to the physical nature of my current role.

Outside I could hear the last strains of the whipper-snippers, mowers and leaf blowers that had punctuated my sleep.

If Sunday is supposed to be the day of rest and religion, then Saturdays are for sports and mowing. I could understand why people like to keep their gardens tidy, but why the fuck couldn't my neighbours at least coordinated their lawn-based laments? It was like a chain reaction, one firing up their two stroke reminded another, who would wait for silence before launching into their own solo performance. I was sure any half-competent gardener could have tidied up the Brisbane Botanical Garden in a fraction of the time.

I let out a groan then grimaced when I remembered the water-soaked cab. At least we hadn't had another job and it might have dried out enough for a day crew to use. No doubt I'd cop flack, but I had my cover story worked out.

Sleep was once again clouding my consciousness when my ringtone dragged me back from the brink. I sighed and rolled over to pick up my phone, but smiled when I saw the photo on the screen. "Hi babe, what ya up to?"

"Oh, sorry Jon I thought you'd be awake by now. You still sound half asleep."

"I am, but no worries, I need to get up. It's nice to hear you though. You still good for Monday night?"

"Of course, I've been looking forward to it."

I smiled and closed my eyes, wrapping her voice around my mind like a warm doona. "How's your shift going?"

"Busy. Look, I've got to keep this short as I had to duck outside, but I overheard Gerry saying you were in trouble. What've you done now?"

I was awake in an instant and sat up on the edge of my bed. "Er… Trouble? What did he say?"

"Oh, nothing much. Just the small matter of you jet-washing the cab of an ambulance."

"And Gerry Seabrook said that?"

"Yep."

"How the hell would he have heard? He's from Roma Street."

"So it's true?"

"Maybe, but there were extenuating circumstances."

"Shit, Jon. You sure know how to piss off your management."

"Don't worry, babe, I've got it covered. I'm just amazed that Gerry knows. How did the story get on the rumour mill so fast?"

"Well, I guess someone's got it in for you. Mark my word, Jon. You need to watch your back."

Water lapped on my tinnie with a relaxing rhythmical tapping sound as I took a rest from throwing a line. It was early Monday morning and I'd been casting toward the shore, allowing my lure to drift with the tide. So far, I was out of luck. I'd anchored at one of my favourite sites in the mouth of the Pine River, near the middle of the channel just downstream from Bald Hills Creek. Out to sea, the sun glinted off the impressive span that was the dual bridges of the Houghton Highway. Over in the shallows, some sand banks were rising from the water and a few waders worked the exposed sediment, probing their beaks in search of tasty morsels.

I lent back on the padded stern bench with my feet resting on the gunwale and tipped the brim of my fishing hat down low over my eyes. Although I was in the canopy's shade, the sun felt warm on my skin, providing a pleasant soothing effect. I was still tired from Friday's night shift, despite waking this morning from a decent rum-induced sleep.

Whizzzz!

I must have dozed off because I woke to hear my reel whining as a fish took the lure. I didn't even remember leaving the line in the water. Grabbing the rod from its holder, I slowed the fish's run and then reeled it in. The animal fought hard, turning and darting and I was glad I had backed off on the drag setting. With every ounce of my patience, I wound in the line, excitement building as I realised this was no ordinary catch. A large shape appeared, circling near the boat; somehow I'd snagged a decent-sized flathead. Recognising what it was, I was careful not to lift its head above the water; given half a chance, flaties will thrash their heads and sure as shit I didn't want the line to snap.

I reached down and felt for the handle of my landing net and with my heart in my mouth, drew the fish closer to the boat until I could scoop it in. Letting out a whoop of joy, I tipped the large dusky flathead onto the deck. It was huge. "You little beauty!"

My intention had been to catch a couple of fish for a recipe I'd planned for tonight. But from the fillets I could cut from this beast, it would last me the rest of the week. "Well, looks like my day's fishing done."

It was 9:30 AM on a beautiful morning; not a cloud in sight. So on a whim, I started the engine, hauled anchor and went for a spin. The 75 hp outboard meant getting my 16 foot Easyrider up on the plane was a breeze and I soon had it zipping across the flat-calm waters. I shot like a rocket between the numerous supports of the bridges before heading out into Bramble Bay and then Moreton Bay proper.

In the distance, I spotted a squadron of five pelicans flying low over the sea. Pointing the bow in their direction I gave chase. Beyond the influence of the mainland a slight swell caused my boat to lift and crash in an explosion of foam, like a flat stone skimming across a lake. With the wind whistling through my shirt and spray splashing my face, any remaining mental cobwebs of night-shift fatigue were blown from my mind like the leaves from my neighbours' gardens.

The magnificent seabirds appeared unconcerned by my approach and as I drew near I could see how graceful and effortless they remained aloft. Cruising along, harnessing the layer of air close to the water; conserving energy by gliding in their search of food. Without warning, the lead bird banked upwards in a wide arc over my boat, followed by the other four. They all seemed to falter, hang in the sky, and then each one folded in their wings and plummeted into the sea on either side of my wake.

I laughed aloud like a crazy man, amazed at the natural spectacle I'd just witnessed and revelled in the freedom of the open water. I've always had a love of the sea, ever since growing up on Magnetic Island, Townsville. Most of my childhood memories revolved around boats or beaches, with my brother and I having spent all our free time either snorkelling, swimming, or fishing.

Having grown up with such an outdoors lifestyle, my initial chosen career in IT must have been such a shock to my system. In hindsight, spending years sitting for days on end in a pocky cubicle lit only by artificial light was a sure-fire recipe for obesity. The only positive thing to come from my brother's death was that it triggered a rebirth in me, a mental kick to carve out a healthier future. But the same event had left my parents broken. Dad had walked out when it became obvious Mum was intent on drinking herself into oblivion and I hadn't seen him since. I still hadn't forgiven him for being a no show at her funeral. It was little wonder I was left struggling with my own addictions.

I guess, a part of me will always yearn for that youthful simplicity; a chance to relive those memories spent with my lost sibling. And so, for me, the sea represents a way of turning back the clock, a time machine to my childhood.

After about an hour of unbridled liberation, the engine spluttered and I switched tanks. Accepting the need to return to reality, I headed inland with a heavy heart, navigating along the Pine River as far as the boat ramp where I'd left my ute and trailer.

I dropped the boat off down the side of my house on Flinders Parade and carried the flathead-filled esky inside. Although the building was little more than a large beach chalet, I'd bought my seafront property before Brisbane's housing boom and it sat on a decent plot of land compared to many other houses along the strand. My intention was to sell to a developer, or start a new build at some point, but I was in no rush to do either. I'd renovated the wooden structure as best I could, maximising its only drawcard by installing glass doors at the front. This modification provided the open-plan kitchen and living area with uninterrupted views of the bay, especially when I folded the doors back.

A few hours later, I was appreciating my twilight bayside vista, standing in the kitchen with an ice-cold glass of Sav Blanc in my hand. Powderfinger was beating out a ballad from the stereo and I'd managed to reach an inner calm after reading the expected email from my Station Officer. The table was set for two with my best unchipped crockery and the cutlery kept for special occasions. In pride of place on the workbench was the monster flathead, hanging over the sides of my maple cutting board. Now I was ready to cook.

Putting down my glass, I took my Sujihiki from its stand, holding it with the care and reverence it deserved. I had a set of three Japanese chef's knives, each built for a specific purpose and this one's job was slicing. The polished metal shimmered in the kitchen's downlights, with the name of the master craftsman appearing in delicate Kanji script along the upper half of the blade. Actual silver rings and jet-black ebony formed the handle, with a small fish motif carved from abalone shell adorning each side. Although functional, it truly was a work of art.

As the music blared, I set about preparing the flathead. With knife skills that would have impressed Zorro, I soon had two prepared fillets and packed the rest away in the fridge. Moving on to the crusting, I burled together some pistachios, olive oil, garlic and cayenne salt and spread the green paste onto each fillet, before placing them in the oven.

As I started on the accompaniments, I only just heard the doorbell ring over the music. Turning the stereo down, I opened the main entrance I'd relocated to the side of the house. Amber stood there like a vision in the doorway. She had her black hair down, flowing past her shoulders and was wearing a white strapless dress that accentuated her long slender neck. A streetlight shone behind her, creating a halo around her body, which made her look stunning.

"Hi babe, you're looking ravishing tonight."

"Why thank you, kind sir."

I reached forward and gave her a kiss while holding the nape of her neck and my heart did its familiar flip. As our lips separated, we both smiled at each other. "Any reason you didn't let yourself in?"

"Thought I'd like to make an entrance."

"Well, you did that. Come on in. How was your shift?"

"Crap. Where's the wine?"

We walked into the kitchen. "There's an open Sav Blanc in

the fridge, or plenty of red in the rack. White'll be better as we're having fish, but help yourself while I finish here."

I picked up my knife and resumed the veggie preparation. Amber filled her glass and wandered around the living room, bending over to inspect the large aquarium along one wall. I paused to appreciate the spectacle and found myself wondering what I'd done to deserve this woman.

She spoke without taking her gaze from the brightly lit water. "Anything new?"

"Not that I can see. Your arse still looks great."

She reached a hand back and gave me the bird. "I meant in the tank."

"Nah. I think you've seen the last addition, you know, the mantis shrimp."

"Arnie?"

"That's him. He's working his way through most of the other crustaceans, so it's looking a bit bare."

"You need to get some more stuff."

"I was going to organise a collecting trip over to Moreton Island in the next week or so. D'you want to come?"

"Sounds great."

She wandered over to the other side of the kitchen bench and sat down on one of the tall stools. Her hand played with the condensation on the glass while she watched me prepare the food. "I realise I've seen them before, but those sure are fancy knives."

I stopped my chopping and looked up. "Fancy knives?" I gave her a look of mock indignation. "These are mirror-finished Mizu-Honyaki blades. Each one hand-crafted in Japan from a single piece of high-carbon steel, employing centuries old techniques once used to forge the katanas of the Samurai."

She was unimpressed. "As I said, fancy knives. Where did you get them from?"

"Would you believe, Japan?"

"You haven't been there, have you?"

"Er, no. I usually tell people they're a family heirloom passed down from my great-grandfather, but the truth is rather embarrassing."

"Embarrassing, how come?"

"Well, I'd been wanting to buy myself some decent knives for a while and one night I indulged in too much rum and somehow bought this set on the internet. I woke the next morning feeling I'd done something stupid, but couldn't remember what it was. Until, of course, when the package arrived a few weeks later. It took me about six months to pay off the credit card bill."

She laughed at me. "You idiot! Why didn't you return them?" It was a beautiful, easy laugh and I made a mental note not to screw-up this relationship.

"Well, it was an option, but they were the ones I'd been drooling over for ages. Prior to my drinking session, I decided I couldn't justify the expense. But once they were in my possession, it proved more difficult to let them go. Hey, some people write-off their cars when they're pissed, or get themselves arrested, or worse. At least after my drunken episode I ended up with a magnificent set of 'fancy knives'."

She laughed again. "Have you ever considered putting them to good use and training as a chef? You're always whinging about being a paramedic."

"Huh, so says the one who just described her working day as 'crap'."

"True. But seriously, have you thought of doing anything else?"

"After the email I received today, I might have to."

"Email? Is that about you jet-washing the ambulance?"

"Could be. Plus two letters of complaint. My Station Officer's summoned me to a meeting on Wednesday."

"Two letters? Jon, you worry me."

"Don't, it's all bullshit."

"And the jet wash? Is that bullshit too, or are you going to tell me what happened?"

"It's a long story."

"I'm not in any rush."

While continuing to prepare the meal, I regaled her with the tale of Ranga and Mr not-so-Fuller, along with the resultant managerial interventions. At the end she nodded with a wry smile. "And you wonder why you're in trouble?"

"I know, I know. After ten years in the job I may have become a little… disaffected. Some may even describe me as a troublemaker."

"Heaven forbid, I find that hard to believe."

"No, really, it's true. But I'm sure I'll manage to blag my way through this latest disciplinary."

Amber grimaced and shook her head. "I'm not so sure, Jon. I've got an uneasy feeling about this. The way other ambo's talk about you, it's like you're a modern-day Spartacus leading a revolt against an oppressive regime. But we all know how that ended."

"You reckon they'd crucify me just to make a point?"

"Well, the hospital's laying off nurses left, right and centre at the moment. I'm sure B-CAS could get rid of one problem paramedic without too many hassles. You need to pull your neck in, Jon."

I laughed. "Funny you should say that. I think Jan used that exact phrase after I finished cleaning the ambulance."

She took a sip of wine. "Mmm… She seems a wise woman. Well, if you won't listen to me, listen to her. And come to think of it, you seem to talk a lot about Jan. Is there anything I should know?"

I smiled and leant across the bench, giving her another long kiss. "I only have eyes for you, my dear. And anyway, I could never date a paramedic, we all whinge too much."

"Now that's the truth! Which brings me back to my original question: why not look for something else to do?"

I paused my food preparation to ponder my answer. "You know, there are many things I love about being a paramedic and I'm not sure I could return to a regular job." I shrugged my shoulders. "I just have a problem with the way management treats us and, of course, the pay's a joke."

"You should try working in a hospital. The hierarchy is so rigid, we have to ask permission before we do anything."

"And that's why I couldn't be a nurse. At least we've got free rein to treat patients as we see fit, as long as we stick within the guidelines. The other great advantage is being able to dump off the annoying ones with you guys and then do a runner."

"Yes, I've noticed. Especially when they're covered in shit."

I held up my hands in defence. "Not me, Amber. I'd never do that." Just then the timer buzzed on the cooker. "Hey, saved by the bell."

I grabbed the wine from the fridge and topped up our glasses. "Would you like to take your seat, I'll only be a few minutes plating up."

"It'd be my pleasure."

I began constructing the meal on each plate. "By the way, talking of annoying patients, do you remember Shirley? She'd either present as breathless or suicidal?"

"Is she the one who always comes in with self-harm marks that barely scratch the skin?"

"That's her. She prefers the Royal 'cos Charlies got sick of her and often kicked her out before we'd completed our paperwork."

"Perhaps we should stop being nice to her? We could start by refusing to make her cups of tea."

"Ain't an issue for you anymore. I found her dead a few days back."

"Really? Oh my God! Did she finally top herself?"

"No. Would you believe a bee managed to dispatch her? Looks like she died from anaphylaxis."

"No way!"

"I know this may sound a little less than caring, but I guess it's a win for us. With her and that old guy BB gone, there'll soon be no more ramping."

Amber laughed. "Guess you could include Mad Marcus in that category."

"Mad Marcus?"

"You know, the skinny schizophrenic dude with the God complex. Always in and out of the mental health unit."

"Yes, I know him, but… what happened to him?"

"Oh, you wouldn't have heard. A crew was talking about him today. He jumped in front of a train last night. Bit messy by all accounts."

"Christ, he finally listened to that voice of his." I shook my head in disbelief and then laughed. "Y'know, perhaps the government's missing a trick here. Just think of the cost savings if we started euthanising all the regulars. They could make it a public health policy."

"I wouldn't put anything past the current lot. Mind you, with ideas like that, you should talk to our new consultant in the ED. You'd get along like a house on fire. He's always bitching about the regulars and saying how he wishes he could deny them treatment."

"Sounds like a wonderful chap, what's his name?"

"Oh, far from it. Dr Martin Cansfield-Clarke. Would you believe, he likes to refer to himself as MC-squared? We all know him as Eeeee equals MC-squared. He's a loathsome stuck-up prick, if you ask me. Gives me the creeps."

"Oh, and I'd get on with him? Thanks."

"Well, if you kept your conversation to bumping off regulars you might."

"Great, I'll keep that in mind. Anyway, dinner is served."

I carried both plates round to the table and placed one in front of her with a flourish. "Pistachio crusted flathead with sweet potato fries and roast pumpkin salad. Bon appetite."

"Wow. That looks fantastic."

"Well, here's hoping it tastes as good as it looks."

We both tucked into the meal and I have to say the fish was divine. Over dinner we chatted about Amber's day and I described how I'd caught the fish. When the night was drawing in, I felt I should at least offer to drive her home.

She gave me a knowing smile. "Don't you want me to stay?"

I smiled back. "I didn't want to be too presumptuous."

"Always the gentleman."

She held up her glass. "Pour me another. I guess I've brought dessert."

It looked like today would go down as a good one and all thoughts of the email had long since left my mind.

11

SPEECHLESS

I stood in the kitchen area of the crew room with a cup of tea in my hand, watching the humorous to and fro between Mel and Koshie on the big plasma TV. On any other day I would be taking advantage of the slow start by either checking emails, or catching up on sleep, dozing in one of the La-Z-Boy recliners. But today was different. Today I was meeting with my Station Officer, Darren Boardman. He'd set no actual time, just whenever we were both around. If I was out and about I could delay the inevitable. So why wasn't today like any other day? Straight out the door, never to see the station for at least twelve hours. Murphy's law, I guess.

I picked my pager out of its holder for the third time and once again checked it was working. The only message on the screen was the random flavour-of-the-week pager-check sent by Comms when we logged on, about an hour ago. 'Remember to bend your knees when you lift'. I snorted and muttered, "Remember to bend over and take it up the arse, more like."

My crewmate for today, Ed Roberts, woke from his slumber. "You say somethin'?"

"Nah, go back to sleep."

I envied Ed. He'd been in the game for thirty-odd years and had turned sleeping into an art form. Within a few minutes of sitting down, he would be snoring away. At station. At hospital. In the back with a non-acute patient. In the passenger seat of the ambulance, even while I drove Code One. Some thought he should be pensioned-off on health grounds: diagnosis narcolepsy. But I believed Ed to be a master of the power nap. From what I could see, he chose his moments to sleep. After all, being paid to slumber makes you well rested for your days off. Only once do I recall witnessing Ed have an unplanned sleep. I remember being half comatose in the early hours of the morning, staring out the windscreen and wondering why my view was drifting over towards the dirt on the side of the highway. Looking over at Ed, I discover his eyes closed and his chin on his chest. I reached over to hold the steering wheel and then flipped the sirens on. At least I thought it was funny.

Ed was approaching retirement, but still had a full head of silver hair and matching moustache that George Negus would have been proud to sport. He had a weathered complexion and a large belly restrained within a shirt three sizes too small. I guess by not ordering larger clothes he could pretend to himself he wasn't getting fatter. However, someone had once joked that his buttons were under such pressure they represented a Work Place Health and Safety risk. I think the quote was 'One day he'll have someone's eye out with those bloody buttons.'

Darren usually got here about 8:00 AM, so I only had a few minutes left for a reprieve. Ed returned to his snoring and I sipped my tea. I much preferred coffee, especially in the morning, but we only had crappy instant at station. I could've driven out for an espresso, but that would've been too obvious. No, I had to wait for an actual job if I was going to avoid this meeting.

Then my pager went off. I did a mental air punch, put down my cup and was striding out to the vehicle when I discovered it was just an update. 'Due to current workload at Redcliffe Hospital, please consider all other alternatives'.

"Damn."

I walked back to the crew room where Ed greeted me, eyes still closed, body still horizontal. "Always check if it's a job before bothering to move your arse."

"Thanks for your words of wisdom, oh enlightened one. Can I rub your belly for good luck?"

"Try and you'll discover who they based Kung Fu Panda on."

"OK Po, I won't mess with ya."

"So why are you so wired? Too much coffee this morning?"

"Nah. Got a meeting with Boardie regarding some… issues."

"Who you been pissing off this time?"

"It'd be quicker to list those I haven't."

"Good point, 'nough said."

He finally opened his eyes and turned his head to look at me. "You didn't have anything to do with 967 going to workshops due to water damage, did you?"

For Ed to have heard about 967 meant that my meeting with Boardie may be more significant than I thought. "Don't know what you're talking about."

"Word from the wise. When Boardie asks that question try to answer it without smiling."

"Thanks Po."

"Up yours."

He went back to his sleeping and I finished my tea.

At 8:00 AM sharp, Boardie walked into the crew room and

got straight to the point. "Morning gentlemen, can we have that meeting now, Jon?"

"No time like the present."

I followed him into his office and he closed the door, which was never a good sign. He sat on the large leather wheelie chair in front of his computer and gestured towards the other more modest one without wheels. "Take a seat."

Boardie was in his late thirties with short brown hair and dark browline glasses. He reminded me of a young version of Mr Bennet from the TV show 'Heroes'. Like the fictional character, he was dedicated to his job and his employer. I believed that if you snapped him in half you could read 'Brisbane City Ambulance Service' from head to toe. I'm guessing he assumed the role of Station Officer with a plan to climb the management ladder. However, working from the station with his own response car meant that as a fellow ICP he could assist with any call-outs whenever he was available. And he was always available for good jobs. He wore a radio on his belt and had a VHF base station installed in his office, so he was never out of range of the radio chatter. He lived for the job and we were like chalk and cheese. But unfortunately for me, he was my line manager.

I moved the chair further away from his, as much as the cramped room would allow, and sat down. Placing my hands on my lap, I stopped myself from crossing my legs, trying to maintain an open demeanour and bided my time.

He focused on his computer, as he fiddled about with the mouse, bringing up his email list. I looked out the window at the blue sky and remembered the view of the pelicans flying free over the ocean. I could almost feel the sea breeze on my face.

After a minute or two, he spun round to look at me. Reaching his hands behind his head, he lent back in his chair with a big sigh. He paused, as if he was thinking things over. "So Jon. What are we going to do with you?"

"You could give me a pay rise."

He glared at me with an expression that lay somewhere between anger and incredulity. "You don't get it, do you? This week alone I've received two written complaints from patients, two verbal complaints from the Senior Operations Manager and now there's a question of you causing deliberate damage to an ambulance."

I looked at him with as calm and affable a countenance as I could muster and waited for him to continue. It was an intentional ploy. I used it when I wanted to hear what someone had on me, before I launched any defence.

He stared back. "Do you have anything to say for yourself?" He held up his right hand with a tiny gap between his thumb and forefinger. "Do you realise you're this far from a request to show reasonable cause?"

Exasperated by my silence he grabbed some papers off his desk and waved them at me. "A well-respected real-estate agent was 'shocked and dismayed' by your aggressive attitude. An elderly war veteran was 'appalled by your lack of respect' and, what's more, you were the last to use 967 when it failed to start due to…" He referred to one of the pages, "… significant water damage to the electrical circuitry."

As I suspected, he didn't have much. I leant forward, hunching my shoulders and gripping both arm rests so that my hands appeared to look like fists. After spending many years watching the non-verbal communication of patients for those telltale signs of potential violence, I had become fluent in body language. I adopted this aggressive posture to prevent any interruptions, but in contrast, I spoke in a flat calm voice.

"OK, point one. The well-respected real-estate agent in question was arrested after our altercation and is likely to be charged with manslaughter, or reckless driving causing death. I admit to having a verbal confrontation with her, but that was when she attempted to leave the scene of the collision. Point two. Most on-road ambulance staff who have spent more than a few months working in central Brisbane have received at least one letter of complaint from Wally Dickens. Correct me if I'm wrong, but I think that includes you."

I didn't wait for a response as I was on a roll and I could see that Boardie was looking far less comfortable.

"Furthermore, Wally is not a war veteran and every time he poses as a digger he displays a complete lack of respect for those who have fought for this country. And finally, point three, I'm guessing the main reason for this meeting. On the night shift in question, a man accompanying a patient had a massive vomit in the front passenger seat. Despite suggesting that a professional valet service deal with the mess, both the MAC and the SOM instructed me to clean the vehicle as soon as possible. While doing so, I slipped with a bucket of water as I climbed into the cab. The water went everywhere, over the dash and probably the fuse box. I carried on cleaning as best I could and left a note on the steering wheel to explain the situation."

I sat back and once again relaxed my hands into my lap. During my diatribe, Boardie had folded his arms and crossed his legs. Either signifying a defensive posture, or a closed mind.

"So that's your story? A bucket of water?"

"I take it you didn't get my note?"

"No."

He leant towards his desk and rested an elbow there, cradling the side of his head in his hand. He then looked at me out the corner of his eye. "It's just that the mechanic reported that the water got into so many places within the cab it must have been under pressure."

I maintained an impassive face. "Pressure? What can I say? I guess I scrubbed too hard."

"So, you didn't use the jet wash then?"

"That would've been irresponsible."

He stared at me for a good thirty seconds before letting out another sigh. "Whatever. In future, Jon, if anything like this happens again could you please contact me immediately so I can arrange for the appropriate servicing."

The radio interrupted my response as a voice called up requesting ICP backup. We both looked at each other and I was the first to speak. "Are you logged on?"

Boardie's shoulders sank. "No, not yet. I had to attend a meeting."

I could hear the disappointment in his voice. Right on cue, my pager beeped and I stood up as I read the message. "Guess I'm the closest ICP. Must dash. What do you want to do about the complaints?"

He swivelled to face his computer. "I'll file them with all the rest."

The ICP backup turned out to be a none event, just a crew requiring a second set of eyes on an ECG. After that, Ed and I attended a series of mediocre jobs, ending up at the Royal around 2:00 PM. As we were overdue a break, Comms sent us up to the cafeteria to get a meal.

Not being that hungry I grabbed a sandwich and sat down at a table to wait for Ed. He arrived about ten minutes later with a huge plate of soggy fries topped with a massive piece of pepperoni pizza, dripping orange-coloured grease into a pool of fat accumulating under the chips.

"Christ, my arteries are hardening just looking at that. You ever heard of a balanced diet?"

"Do I look like someone who's worried about healthy options? My motto is: why have a six-pack when you can have the whole keg?"

He patted his rotund belly and my eyes made an involuntary flinch. The danger posed by those buttons was a threat my subconscious couldn't ignore.

I called Comms to inform them we were starting our break and, as I'd finished my sandwich, I had to suffer the delight of watching Ed engulf his meal. He shovelled each oily mouthful into his maw well before swallowing the previous one. There was no time allowed for talking and hardly enough for breathing. This was a man in a feeding frenzy, but it was a learnt behaviour not isolated to Ed. It's common amongst ambos who often have their meals broken by jobs.

"So, how much Nexium are you on Ed?" I was referring to his gastric reflux, or what I liked to call the 'Ambo's Disease'. It's the inevitable result of years of wolfing down food and eating during the night.

He looked up and between swallows managed a mumble. "Forty milligrams a day."

Ed had almost finished when our pagers began beeping.

I stood with a grin. "Ka-ching! Another broken meal payment. C'mon, I think you've had enough."

A small piece of half-chewed pizza flew from his mouth as he spoke. "You go, I'll catch you up."

I left him scoffing the last of his cholesterol overload and made my way down to the ambulance. The job was a Code One in The Valley, Centenary Place. A man had fallen from standing and was now unconscious. The case description had a strong whiff of bullshit, but at least I was driving.

We were on scene in a matter of minutes and I parked the ambulance off-road to avoid snarling the traffic. After all, this tree-covered park area was little more than a large roundabout near the central business district.

A concerned-looking Asian man waved and beckoned us down one of the paved walkways. Grabbing our bags, we followed. He ran back and forth to speed us along, but paramedics don't run. We are the calming influence, adding an air of normality to what are often hectic situations. So, if we turn up running, panic can spread like a bush fire.

The sounds of the traffic receded as the foliage muffled the constant drone and a honeyeater twittered from a high vantage point. The sweet scent of an early flowering frangipani drifting on the breeze was a welcome replacement for the acrid smell of petrol fumes. Up ahead I could see a dishevelled and diminutive Aboriginal man lying on his back next to an empty bag of goon. As we approached, I recognised his craggy wrinkled face and wispy white beard. "Oh crap. It's Mr Wendal."

Mr Wendal was another regular. I'm guessing it wasn't his real name, but in the words of the Arrested Development song, 'No one ever knew his name 'cause he's a no-one'. However, unlike the character depicted in the lyrics, I was yet to receive any knowledge from him. All I got was a whole heap of verbal abuse. When he needed a feed, he would often feign an injury or unconsciousness to get an unsuspecting tourist to call for an ambulance.

Ed put down the response bag. "G'day Mr Wendal. Are you hurt or just wanting a lift to the hospital?"

His rheumy eyes snapped open and he fixed Ed with a glare. "I've hit me fuckin' 'ed, ya Cap'n Cook cunt! Ain't a black fella's pain important enough for ya? Ya big fat prick."

I jumped to Ed's defence. "Oh come on Mr Wendal. You know you can't use names like that. Cook was only a lieutenant when he arrived in Australia."

He looked me up and down and appeared to consider my comment. "Hey, smart-arse Captain Cook cunt, shut ya fuckin' mouth. I was talkin' to the fat fella 'ere."

Ed turned with a smile. "Yes, shut up smart-arse. I'm attending."

"Fine by me."

"So, did you get knocked out?"

In a swift flowing motion, Mr Wendal swung himself up into a seated position with his legs crossed. He then waved in the ambulance's direction. "Ah, ya can shut the fuck up as well. Just go get ya fuckin' stretcher. An' I ain't wearing' one o' dem fuckin' neck t'ings."

The Asian man tapped me on the shoulder. "I go now, OK?"

"Sure mate, thanks. I think we can handle things from here."

He gave a deep gracious bow and made a rapid exit.

I walked back to the ambulance, offloaded the stretcher and wheeled it over to our patient. "OK, on you get. Let's go."

He hopped onto the lowered stretcher and the frangipani scent gave up the battle against his body odour. It was a concoction of sweat, urine, faeces and alcohol, for Mr Wendal never washed. But then again, when you're on your own living rough in a city, where can you wash? And would you make it a priority? As with all alcoholics, his fundamental focus was on finding his next drink.

He sat cross-legged on the stretcher, arched over his head low. I raised the back so I could attach the seat belts and in this proximity had to hold my breath. "Would you like a sheet?"

"Nah, fuck off smart-arse."

It was worth a try. I pitied Ed being in the back even though it was only a five-minute journey to the Royal. We lifted up the stretcher and trundled our way to the ambulance. I'd positioned myself at the front to avoid the stench wake that flowed behind.

Once loaded with the vent on full bore and both windows open, I called back to Ed. "Want me to take the scenic route?"

"The most direct, please. And don't worry about getting there in one piece."

As we left, Ed tried to assess Mr Wendal. "So, do you mind if I measure your blood pressure?"

"Touch me, fella, an' I'll punch ya fuckin' lights out."

"You know you can't speak like that to the nurses."

"Ya not a fuckin' nurse."

"Good point." He picked up the Toughbook and began typing.

As soon as I stopped at the Royal, Ed launched himself out the side door. He took several theatrical gulps of air before helping me offload our patient. Wanting to avoid the risk of ramping I turned to Ed. "I'll go get a wheelchair."

"Good idea."

"Yer. Fuck off smart-arse."

I smiled and walked away. It wasn't worth the hassle of responding, not when we were minutes from parting company.

Entering the triage area, I was surprised to find it empty. The nurse behind the desk was one of Amber's friends and she greeted me with a delightful smile. "Hi Jono, how's your day going?"

"G'day Bell. Not as bad as yours is about to get."

"Oh no. Who've you got?"

"Mr Wendal."

Her shoulders dropped and she looked to the ceiling.

Exhaling, she let out a sigh. "Shit." Her loss of composure was brief and her smile returned. "How bad's the smell?"

"Bad. You can't put him in acute unless you want to clear out the department."

"That's an idea, but I doubt the consultant will go for it. OK, I'll get someone to prep the isolation room."

I grabbed one of the waiting wheelchairs and called back, "I am sorry."

"Can't you take him somewhere else?"

"I'm not that sorry."

We transferred him to the wheelchair and then pushed him into the triage area where a large frumpy nurse was now standing wearing a plastic apron. She may have been selected for the job as she appeared to have no sense of smell. She squatted down in front of him and patted his hand. "Hi there Mr Wendal, what's wrong with you today?"

He smiled at her revealing four or five crooked yellow teeth. "G'day nurse. A've 'it me 'ed. It 'urts so much, an' these fellas 'ere 'ave done nuttin' for me."

She glared at us as if we were wearing fascist insignia and then addressed our newly reformed patient. "Come on through and we'll sort you out."

Without a word, she took over control of the wheelchair and bustled away. As she disappeared down the corridor Mr Wendal looked over his shoulder and gave us a wink and a sly grin.

Both Ed and I were speechless. We turned to look at each other and I shook my head. "You get the paperwork done, I can't imagine it'll take too long. I'll go fumigate the ambulance. Gotta love Glen 20."

After using half a can of the spray disinfectant over every internal surface, I left the doors open and the stretcher out to help tame the lingering smell. I then wandered through the emergency department to see if I could find Amber, but was met by a rather intense-looking doctor, shadowed by a young female intern.

He was tall and slim with thinning fair hair combed across his head from a side parting and his pockmarked face suggested years of schoolyard bullying. Perhaps studying had been his teenage escape. I hadn't seen him before and I was guessing he was the new consultant Amber had mentioned the other night. What did she call him? MC-squared?

"Did you bring in Mr Wendal?"

His condescending manner irritated me and I took an instant dislike to the man. I gave him a one-word answer. "Yes."

"Why? There's nothing wrong with him, other than the need for a good scrub. His stench has impacted the whole of resus."

"Well, you must know that the Brisbane City Ambulance Service has a 'you call, we haul' policy. I can't leave a patient behind who claims to have sustained a head injury, unless you're able to supply me with a pair of X-ray specs, or a mobile CT scanner."

He gave me a look of surprise, as if he was unaccustomed to someone having the audacity to challenge him. "Have you seen the size of his file?" He pointed to the huge folder packed with dog-eared pages that the intern was carrying. "He's had over three hundred admissions to this hospital alone!"

"And what do you want me to do about it?"

He sighed and the exhaled breath seemed to deflate him like a punctured inner tube. He stared at the ground for a moment and when he looked up, he was facing the intern. "Something needs to be done about these time-wasting patients."

I nodded. "You're preaching to the converted there, Doc.

People like him have a need, it's just not for an emergency service. I realise we're part of the problem, but if I leave a caller on scene and anything goes wrong, my arse is in a sling."

He paused while I was talking, but didn't glance at me and when he spoke again, it was to the intern. "There has to be some legislation enacted to deal with this issue, they're such a drain on our resources. If someone ignores repeated warnings to stop wasting our time, they should lose their right to an ambulance and an emergency bed."

He rubbed his chin. "I think society has to face up to the fact that although some lives may be lost, in the long run, it would be for the greater good. How many people with a real need have to wait longer for ambulances because closer ones are dealing with serial abusers?"

"Well I'll vote for anyone who tries to get that through parliament."

He looked at his watch. "Just three more hours to go."

His dropped his head so that his chin touched his chest and then brushed past me on his way to Mr Wendal, as if I was nothing more than a drip stand. I stood in the corridor watching him stride away as the intern trotted along behind. Once again, I was lost for words.

12

CRAVINGS

Ivy Watson was sitting up in bed holding a polystyrene cup of tea and watching the hustle and bustle of the emergency department. A nurse had told her that there were changes on her 'Easy-G' and so they moved her to one of the Cadillac beds. She didn't know why they called them that, they didn't look like cars. But there were a few more machines around her, which made her feel important. She also liked the position as she now had a good view of the fishbowl. She heard the staff use that name for the area where all the nurses and doctors would stand and chat. But despite the huge glass walls that surrounded the room, she was yet to spot any fish. And she didn't quite understand why they would have fish in a hospital. Perhaps they provided a calming influence. Ivy liked fish. She had two goldfish of her own and had named them both Bob. That way they could mouth their names to each other.

Ivy was sixty-three with grey hair permed into tight curls. She had a kind face, but not one that was ever in danger of being attractive. Not unless wrinkles, jowls and dewlaps came into fashion.

She took a sip of her tea. Ivy liked coming here. It was the only time that anyone seemed to give a damn about her. People talked to her without mocking and she was often the centre of attention. The only problem was she wasn't allowed to smoke. She could do with a tab right now. Really do with one. She still remembered when you could light up in the hospital, but nowadays it was banned. She didn't understand why. OK, so smoking might be bad for you, but her neighbour was 92 and she smoked all her life. It hadn't done her no harm.

She watched as an ambo pushed an empty bright yellow stretcher across in front of her. He glanced her way. "Oh, hi Ivy, in again I see. You'll have to give up those smokes one day, you know."

She recognised him, he was a cocky one she didn't like. He always refused to treat her unless she stubbed out her cigarette. And she wasn't doing that for no one. Smokes are expensive, it's not like they grow on trees!

She tapped her free hand against her chest. "Nuffin' to do with me smokes. It's me heart, chest pain again. Me Easy-G was not right this time, though."

The paramedic kept walking, not allowing the interaction to break his stride. "Mmm… OK Ivy, gotta go. Catch ya later."

"Oh right, bye now." She was then back to her near-cold cup of tea and gnawing nicotine cravings.

About twenty minutes passed before the pretty, dark-haired nurse returned. "Hi, Ivy. It's all good news. Your blood tests are negative, so everything's normal."

"That's good. Does that mean I can go?" She had already swung her legs over the side of the bed in anticipation of her next tobacco hit.

"Well, you should wait a little while, so you can take a letter with you."

"No need, it'll only go on the stack at home. I'll be off then..." She frowned as she struggled to read the nurse's name badge. At least it was short and there was a smiley-face sticker covering her surname. Someone once told Ivy she had dyslexia, but most just thought she was thick. "... Am-ber. Thank you so much, I'll find my own way out."

She hopped off the bed, picked up her handbag and went bustling off to the nearest exit.

Another nurse joined Amber as she watched Ivy leave. "I'm impressed. Pity you couldn't have done that a few hours ago."

"Nothing to do with me. She's just in need of another cancer stick. I'm surprised she's lasted this long. Usually an hour in fast track is too much for her."

"Hey, was that your ambo boyfriend I saw you with earlier?"

"Maybe. What of it?"

"Oh... let me know if you tire of him. I wouldn't mind giving him a spin."

Amber laughed and leant towards her. "You're such a slut, Deb. You keep your hands off him. Anyway, I thought you were trying to snag a doctor."

"That's the long-term plan, but there's no harm in practising."

Ivy was rummaging in her bag for her smokes and lighter as she exited the hospital through the glass doors of the front entrance. It was now dark, gone midnight and there were only a few people wandering around outside. She doubted security would bother chasing her over smoking a durrie or two and she didn't care if they did. She wouldn't pay the fine either way.

In a well-practised move, she flipped the lid of the box and had a lit cigarette between her lips in a matter of seconds. With an intent expression, she took a long hard drag, causing the tip to flare and crackle as oxygen enriched the burn. She inhaled the fumes deep into her lungs and felt a wave of relief spread through her body. Holding her breath, she turned her face to the night's sky and exhaled, billowing smoke upwards like a deep-sea vent.

After a few drags, she exhausted the cigarette and flicked the remains onto the pavement, lighting the second before the butt had even stopped bouncing. This one she smoked at a more leisurely rate, having satisfied her initial needs. She looked around and saw a couple kissing their goodbyes. The woman got in a taxi and the man waved as it drove away. He stood there in his dressing gown, his hand still raised for a while after the car had gone, looking downcast, or perhaps reluctant to return to the hospital. Eventually he walked back through the doors.

Despite his obvious dejection, Ivy envied him. At least he had someone in his life even if he was sick. Ivy was on her own, apart from both Bobs, but they weren't much company. She wasn't allowed to keep a dog or cat in her apartment and she had no one she'd call a friend. Her family had disowned her, either by choice or demise. She sighed, flicked another smouldering butt into the air and walked over to the last remaining taxi.

As she reached for the car door, a man tapped her on the shoulder. She turned in surprise, not having heard or sensed his approach. The hospital lights framed his head like a solar eclipse, but squinting she made out a smile. "Jesus! You scared the living shit out of me."

"Sorry Ivy, you left in such a rush you forgot to take your new tablets."

He handed over a white tub of medications that bore the label Sildenafil Citrate 100 mg. She screwed up her face, unable to read the writing.

"You need to take one every morning and another at night. And any time you get chest pain you must take two. Remember that, two for chest pain. Here's the letter for your doctor. Have a safe trip home."

He was walking away before she had time to reply and so she just blurted out her thanks. He checked his step and spoke without turning. "You know those cigarettes will be the death of you, don't you Ivy?"

She opened the door and spun herself down onto the back seat of the cab. "Ha, so they keep telling me."

The taxi driver craned his neck back. "Sorry, love, what was that?"

"Oh, I was just talking to that guy." But when she looked the man had gone.

"What guy?"

She peered at the tub of pills and envelope in her hand, then put them in her bag. "Oh, don't worry. Doesn't matter."

13

MAGNET

We were hurtling along Kingsford Smith Drive with the stereo thumping out 'Boom, boom, pow' by The Black Eyed Peas. As we weaved our way through the morning traffic our heads bobbed to the music. Scotty yelled over the heavy bass. "Look at this dickhead, he hasn't a clue we're behind him."

Despite our flashing headlights, blaring siren and deafening musical accompaniment, a beat up old Holden Commodore was crawling along at about forty in a sixty zone determined to act as a roadblock.

"I'll show him what his mirrors are for."

Scotty closed to within polishing distance of the back bumper, held down the horn to let out an ear-piercing blast and when the car began the inevitable 'what-the-fuck-wobble', swerved round the offside close enough to brush off flakes of rust. "Do the stare, do the stare."

I obliged with a standard ambo passing stare, delivered to all wayward drivers who impede the progress of a Code One ambulance. I looked out the passenger window, tilted my head down and stared with a stern face at the driver. As per usual, the focus of my attention stared out of his own windscreen and tried not to acknowledge the three tonnes of light-flashing Mercedes edging past his side window.

As we sped away, Scotty reached forward and turned down the music. "Did I ever tell you about the time some tosser put in a complaint about my driving?"

"You'll have to be more specific. Was it from the public or a shit-scared crewmate?"

"It was someone like that last cockhead. We'd taken ages to get round him, so as we overtook I lowered my window and flipped him the bird."

"Go on, this one's new."

"Well, the prick lodged a formal complaint and I was hauled in for a disciplinary. When they asked me to explain my actions, I said the driver must've been mistaken. I didn't raise my middle finger, it was my index finger. I was trying to point out our flashing lights."

"And they bought it?"

"Got away Scotty free! Guess they couldn't prove otherwise. Told me I should keep my hand signals down to a minimum to avoid any confusion. Bunch of…"

He finished his sentence with a one-handed gesture and we both laughed.

I reached forward to crank up the stereo as the bass beat kicked in. "I love this bit!" And we returned to our head bobbing.

When the track ended Scotty switched off the music. "So what we going to?"

"A 28-year-old chick who's short of breath, query asthma."

"Could be good. But my money's on a panic attack."

"We'll soon see. It's number sixty-one."

We had turned off the main road, passed the entrance to the Eagle Farm Racecourse and were now flying down a wealthy avenue in Ascot. Spotting the address, we screeched to a halt outside a rather grand red brick residence. Two wings of the double-storey property formed a central courtyard separated from the street by a white trellis fence. The woodwork was thick with a trailing vine and the canopy of a huge old Poinciana provided shade and seclusion.

On seeing the house Scotty gawped. "Christ! Don't fuck this one up Jono, you know they'll be lawyered up."

"Well do me a favour and keep quiet. And that applies to both your voice and your screaming body language."

Grabbing the kit bags and monitor, we approached the doorway in the fence that had an intercom built into the brick support. I pressed the button. "Ambulance."

There was no response, but a few seconds later the lock buzzed and the door opened. I looked at Scotty with raised eyebrows. Was this a security measure, or someone who needed to allow remote access? As we walked across the courtyard the two front doors did the same buzz-open trick and both my feet and pulse picked up the pace.

We entered a large foyer that was complete with a marble-tiled floor and sweeping staircase. I called out 'ambulance' again, but the sound of wheezing breaths coming from down a hallway to the left was enough of a response. Trying not to knock the beautiful furnishings with our bags, we made our way into a kitchen that was bigger than my entire house. Our patient was seated on a stool near the central island. She was leaning forward with her hands on her knees in the classic tripod position that asthmatics adopt when they're struggling to breathe. Sweat was dripping off her face and her eyes had the wide stare of someone fearing for their life.

Scotty attached the monitoring while I knelt in front of her. "Can you talk?"

She shook her head. A bad sign.

"Ever had an ICU admission?"

She nodded and held up three fingers. Another bad sign. While asking the questions, I snatched out my stethoscope from my belt pouch and listened to her chest. Although there was an audible wheeze, she was moving little air. Bad sign number three. This was no panic attack.

As the diagnosis of asthma has become so widespread, non-sufferers often think the disease is simply a bit of breathing difficulty. After all, you can always treat it with a puffer. That may be true for many, but this patient was an example of how dire things can get. She was experiencing a life-threatening attack and would die in front of us if we weren't quick with her treatment.

Scotty was grabbing out a neb mask from the oxygen kit. "Atrovent and ventolin, boss?"

"Roger that, I'll give her a shot of adrenaline first and prep the rest of my drugs. Can you get a line in as soon as the neb's running?"

"On it, boss."

We busied ourselves preparing our respective treatments and checking the vials. At all times I kept an eye on the patient looking for signs of exhaustion. "Sharp scratch, then you'll get another needle in your lower arm, OK?"

She nodded. Like us, she'd been through this before.

With the adrenaline on board and neb mask hissing, I drew up some intravenous salbutamol. After a check of her breathing, I gave the drug through the cannula Scotty had secured and prepared a dose of magnesium. Scotty saw what I was doing. "Need a second line for that?"

"Yes please, in the other arm if you can. And after that any chance of a bag of fluid on the first line?"

"Yessir!"

There was so much to do and it was a relief to be working

with someone as competent as Scotty. If I'd been rostered with a student my workload and stress levels would've been a lot higher.

While he cannulated her left arm, I drew up the magnesium and fished out the Springfusor from my bag. A simple device that delivers the drug over a ten-minute period, freeing us to look after the patient. After checking her latest blood pressure, I connected the line and taped the syringe-driver to her arm. There were two more drugs to draw up, diluted adrenaline for intravenous use, in case things went pear-shaped, and hydrocortisone, a nice-to-add steroid if time allowed.

Scotty had disappeared to get the stretcher and I realised I didn't know our patient's name. She was attractive with a slim, even athletic build, olive skin and long dark hair. If it wasn't for the current situation, she would've looked the picture of health. She still had the 'roo in the headlights' expression, but I could tell our meds were relieving her panic.

She reminded me of Amber and I had to stop myself from daydreaming. Shit, if a woman can distract my thoughts in the heat of battle, perhaps she is the one? I dragged my attention back to the patient with a question. "Getting any better?"

She nodded.

"Able to talk yet?"

She shook her head.

"How long has this been building, hours?"

A shake.

"Days?"

She held up two fingers.

Shit. From that answer I realised that whatever we did now we were unlikely to reverse her condition. There's a general rule of thumb that the longer an asthma attack takes to develop, the slower the patient responds to emergency medications. On a positive note, they tended to crash slower, but that depended on their level of exhaustion.

I looked at her with a comical frown and wagged a finger. "You should know better."

She gave a shrug. Despite the neb mask, I could still see her apologetic grin through the clear plastic and clouds of atomised drug. So many people with life-threatening illnesses just wanted to be normal. There's always the temptation to believe that if they struggle on, they'll get better. But, hey, that mentality keeps me in a job.

"Have you got identification to bring with you?"

She nodded and reached over to grab a small clutch bag.

"Mind if I see your name?"

She retrieved a business card from her bag: Michelle Ludkowski, Investigative Reporter.

"A reporter! Have I got stories I could tell you."

I tried to return the card, but she folded my hand around it, pointing to me and then sticking her thumb and little finger out. After making a phone sign near her ear she thumbed to herself.

I laughed. "A true journalist. Struggling to breathe, but still able to hunt for a story."

She shrugged and I pocketed the card to placate her.

"Anyway, let's get the introductions over with. Hi Michelle, I'm Jon and the stubbly one coming in with the stretcher is Scotty."

"Hey, I resemble that remark."

Although we sounded flippant, it was a deliberate ploy, a tool of our trade. By remaining calm and jovial, the patient is more likely to relax, which helps them and makes our job easier. What you're thinking and feeling, however, can be quite the opposite. I call it the swan philosophy: above the water is all serene and graceful, but below the surface your feet are paddling like hell.

She smiled at our banter, but her focus was still on breathing. After listening again to her lungs, I gave another dose of IV salbutamol and topped up her neb. We positioned our bed right next to her seat and with minimal effort from her, transferred our patient to the stretcher. The last thing an asthmatic in this condition needs is any form of exertion. They can drop off the perch as fast as a drunk kookaburra and then you're left pushing shit uphill.

We wheeled her out the house, across the courtyard and through the fence door. "Have you got your keys so Scotty can lock up?"

She waved a hand and reached in her bag, bringing out a small remote. With a push of a button the doors all closed and locked shut.

Scotty was impressed. "Wow. That's a new one on me."

"And I thought I was the gadget freak." I looked at Michelle. "You've done this before, haven't you?"

Again a shrug and a smile from behind the mask.

While I conducted another set of obs, Scotty loaded everything in the truck and jumped in the driver's seat.

"Le Royale, Code One boss?"

"Yes please, but make it smooth. Somewhere below warp factor two, I've still got to work in the back and Michelle's sitting bolt upright."

"You make it sound like I speed or something." He then caused the wheels to give their customary take-off screech.

"Behave!"

"Yu canna change the laws of physics."

But the trip in was as smooth as if we were in a Lear jet, even despite the Brisbane roads.

Michelle's condition didn't improve much. But she didn't

get any worse. I kept topping up her neb mask and gave her the hydrocortisone dose, though I held off on any more adrenaline. The hospital staff were expecting us as I called ahead and we took her straight to resus.

In the whole time we were with her, even after the prolonged write-up, her breathing was so bad she'd been unable to say a single word. We checked in on her as we left the emergency department and we still only got a wave and a thumbs up. It would be a long time and a world away before I found out what her voice sounded like.

It was now about 10:30 AM on what had become a glorious blue-sky day as we walked towards the ambulance. I jumped in the cab and slammed my door. "What is it with you, Scotty? I can go weeks and use nothing from my drug bag, but every shift with you it ends up needing a serious restock."

"I thought you knew I was a shit magnet. Always have been. My first few months on the road as a student I did so many resuses they called me the Grim Reaper. One day a few crews started taking the piss in the write-up room, so I walked outside to avoid them. There I was, looking at something on my phone, when a psych patient leapt off the top floor. I nearly crapped myself when he splattered in the industrial bin next to me."

"Now that's what I call a shit magnet! Not only do you go to the good jobs, but they start landing at your feet. I'm surprised I haven't heard that story."

"Oh well, it happened up in Townsville and it wouldn't have made the papers 'cos it was a suicide." He frowned. "I've always thought that's weird, y'know, the way the media doesn't report suicides. I guess it's to stop copycats, but without the coverage people still jump from high places, take overdoses, or throw themselves in front of trains."

"Seeing as you mentioned trains, d'you hear about Mad Marcus?"

"Yep, I was talking to Gerry, he went to it. Said one of the wheels went over his head. He was walking along the track looking for the body and something white shone in his flashlight. Turned out to be the top of Marcus' skull with a pile of brain matter inside. Said it looked like a bowl of pink blancmange, as only Gerry could describe it. Guess the mad bastard finally found a way of getting that voice out of his head."

We both laughed. "Brutal but fair. If they reported more suicides, people would discover how common they are and something might get done about it."

"I wonder if the public realise that 'an incident' on the Story Bridge means that some dickhead has put the city into gridlock because they haven't got the balls to jump."

I nodded. "True. As soon as they leap the roads are freed up and it's down to the water police to fish out their body. Come to think of it, I've never known why we park on the bridge for those jobs. If they don't jump, they're not injured and the cops can take them to hospital and if they do jump, we're in the wrong place. Anyway, shall we dance?"

"Go for it."

I hit the 'Request to Clear' button on the Mobile Data Terminal and picked up the mic. "963 clear at the Royal. Please be advised, we need to restock drugs after our last job."

Comms responded in the form of a husky female voice laced with a lilting Irish accent. "Alpha 963 you're clear to return. We'll try to get you back, but you are the only available resource."

We looked at each other and Scotty voiced our thoughts. "Wow, where did she come from?"

I couldn't resist the opportunity. "I'm always available for you."

Once again her voice filled the cab. "Guess that means I can dispatch you any time."

Scotty laughed. "Ooh, you just got burned, mate."

"Well, anything for a bit of banter on the radio. I like her, she must be new. I'm going to name her Dispatcher Love." Scotty gave me a blank look. "You know? Dispatcher Love. From the movie 'Bringing Out the Dead'?"

He shook his head.

"Oh, come on, surely you've seen that? It's ambo training 101."

"Nope."

"What were they teaching you up in Townsville? It's a classic film about an American paramedic who's lost the plot. Nicolas Cage is in it. I'm sure we've got a copy at station. If we get back, I'll see if I can find it."

I have to admit, I was a few years in the job before I saw the film, but had read the book first. I was having a drink with a new neighbour when he discovered my profession and insisted on lending me a copy. Working in that world the story drew me in, but I couldn't understand or relate to the level of empathy exuded by the main character. He kept seeing the ghosts of patients he failed to revive whereas I can hardly remember the patients I treated the previous shift. In my mind, empathy is the enemy of the paramedic. You do need some for the job to interest you in the first place, but too much and you'll burn out quicker than a prayer candle. I said that to my neighbour when I returned his book. He gave me a quizzical look and told me he thought the central character was barking mad. Perhaps he was. Perhaps I am. Still, my failures aren't haunting me, so there may be hope for me yet.

The MDT beeped as we pulled out of the Royal's car park onto Butterfield Street.

"Well, I guess we can scratch any idea of getting back to station."

The newly dubbed Dispatcher Love seemed to hear me. "Apologies Alpha 963, looks like the Southern Board has taken you for a Code One in Wynnum. Could you switch to voting group six please?"

I turned to Scotty. "The Southside! I'm going off her."

I spoke into the mic. "Roger that. I'll send up a flare if we get lost south of the river."

"I'll keep an eye out for you."

"Mmmm. She's got me again Scotty. It's that accent."

The engine revved as the Code One unleashed Scotty from normal road speeds. "I bet she's some big fat bushpig who just has a nice voice."

"Hey, don't burst my bubble. Anyway, if she's new to Comms she won't have had time to develop dispatcher arse. She might yet be saved."

"I thought you were going out with that hottie at the Royal."

"Amber? I'll tell her you're a fan. And yes, we're an item, but that doesn't stop me looking. Would you go into an art gallery blindfolded, just because you've got a Da Vinci at home?"

"No, but when you talk about adding a Picasso to your collection, things start getting dodgy."

"Point taken. Anyway, I wonder what's happening in Wynnum of all places."

I scrolled through the MDT info and my shoulders sagged.

Scotty took his eyes off the road. "What?"

"Paed."

"You hate paed jobs."

"I hate paed jobs. Too many bloody calculations and I've got to be nice to them. Give me a drunk or a psych patient any day. At least I can sedate them if I cop too much shit."

"What's wrong with this one?"

"Other than being too young? Seems like the little tyke bumped his head at a daycare centre."

"Code One 'cos of altered consciousness?"

"Yep. Sounds like bullshit, but it'll get us out of the city."

We'd been humming along at 110 kph through the Airport Link Tunnel with the light traffic behaving itself and moving over to the left lane. Anything over 30 Ks above the speed limit on a Code One can elicit a 'please explain' email from management. But they have to catch you first and Scotty was well aware that the tunnels are full of speed cameras, so he was sitting on the maximum.

Sunlight blasted into the cab as we launched out of the exit and onto the East West Arterial, heading over to the Gateway Bridge.

"Right, there's still at least 10 minutes until Wynnum, even with your driving. Time to play Last Patient Playlist."

I got out my iPhone, tuned the cab's radio into my FM transmitter's frequency and flipped through the music tracks. "So, any thoughts?"

"Asthma attack. Mmm. What about 'Breathless'?"

"Who by?

"The Corrs."

"Really?"

"OK, so it's a bit lame."

"A bit? How about 'Every breath you take' by The Police?"

"Too old school."

"'Breathe me' by Sia?"

"Mmm. Too slow for a Code One."

"OK, got it. Try this one for size."

I tapped the screen to select the track and the cab filled with the spine tingling electronic intro to 'Breathe' by Prodigy.

Scotty nodded his head in appreciation as the frenetic drumbeat began and the song blasted out as we hurtled south of the river.

We were now on suburban roads and the traffic was lighter, but Scotty was still pushing the envelope. He glanced over at the satnav. "Should be along this road somewhere."

"You know, you could slow down so the numbers are not just a blur."

"Where'd the fun be in that?"

As we talked, we flew past a woman leaning against a wall who raised her hand as we shot by.

"D'you think it'll be where she was waving back there?"

"Could be, let's check it out." The road ahead was clear, so Scotty threw the ambulance into a screeching 180-degree turn, leaving circles of rubber on the bitumen. I just had time to brace myself to avoid slamming into my door, but the glove boxes were not so quick to react. A deluge of blue vinyl flew off the overhead shelf and covered me like a rash. I looked at Scotty as we rolled towards the waving woman.

He was struggling not to laugh. "Sorry, boss."

"Would you like a pair of gloves? I've got every size."

I threw a few at him as he drove into the car park, following the woman who was now strolling ahead, forcing us to watch her huge backside as it swayed to and fro. I sighed. "Looks like she's not too stressed. Wanna bet it's company policy to call an ambulance if any of the kids get hurt?"

"SOB, boss, SOB: Standard Operational Bullshit."

Scotty parked in front of the entrance and I stepped out of

the cab. The woman came over, shielding her eyes in the bright sunlight. "That was an impressive turn."

"Well, we like to get here quick when it's an emergency, Ma'am."

She looked down at the gloves falling from the ambulance. "Well, I don't think it's a real emergency, he did only fall off a chair."

"Mmm."

I turned and paused before opening the side door, staring up for a moment at the big white fluorescent letters that spelt out the words EMERGENCY PARAMEDICS. I suspect the irony was lost on her.

We picked up the bags and followed her through several narrow corridors covered with colourful kindie creations. As she walked, she described the events that resulted in the injury. At one point she glanced over her shoulder. "You've got to carry an awful lot of stuff, haven't you?"

"Never know what we're going to, Ma'am. We must be prepared for any emergency."

I looked back at Scotty as he grinned and shook his head.

We finally walked into a large classroom full of yelling kids. "Here we are, there's your patient over there."

Her point was in the vague direction of about ten children, all of whom were involved in some boisterous game that required running around and screaming at one another. None appeared impaired in any way.

"I don't suppose you could be more specific."

"Oh. Er, it's the little blonde lad with red shorts, there."

The boy was imitating a kangaroo, bouncing after a girl with brown pigtails. When the woman called him over, he stopped and walked towards us with some reluctance.

I knelt down, so we were at eye-level. "Hi, my name's Jon and this is Scotty, what's your name?"

DEAD REGULAR

"My name is Troy Newton. I'm four and a half. Are you a policeman?"

"No Troy, I'm a paramedic."

He looked confused. "I work on an ambulance. Y'know, nee-nah, nee-nah. I'm here to check out your head."

He frowned. "I got a booboo on my head." He pointed to the bump on his forehead and winced as he touched it.

"I know, I can see that. Can you sit down here, so we can check you over?"

He shrugged and sat on a nearby chair. Scotty set about getting a set of obs while I checked his head and neurology.

"I'm going to shine a bright light in your eyes, look straight at me."

"Is that a radio?"

"What? Oh, yes."

"Why d'you need it?"

"So I can talk to people."

"Are you married?"

"What? Er, no."

Scotty butted in. "He may as well be."

"OK, so I've got a girlfriend."

"What's her name?"

"Amber."

"I've got a girlfriend. Her name is Jaden. I'm going to marry her."

"Good for you."

"Are you going to marry Amber?"

"Now there's a question."

Scotty chimed in again. "I would, given half a chance. She's a keeper."

Troy frowned. "What's a keeper?"

"Never mind."

I turned my attention to the woman who was hovering nearby. "Is he usually like this?"

"Oh, yes. Very chatty and straight to the point is young Troy."

Troy looked over to where the other kids were playing and stuck a finger up his nose, having a good delve around as he watched their antics. I stood and spoke to the woman. "So, just to recap. He fell forwards from one of these small chairs, which means less than half a metre, and bumped his head on a carpeted floor. He cried immediately, wasn't knocked out, remembers the event and hasn't been sick, or drowsy since. From your records, he has no previous medical history, has suffered no behavioural changes and the only pain he has is localised to the bump on his forehead."

"That's about it in a nutshell."

"I don't want to appear rude, but… why did you call an ambulance?"

She was taken aback. "Well, it's company policy to call an ambulance if any of the children suffer a head injury."

I looked to Scotty. "You were on the money with SOB." Turning back to the woman, I gave her my most affable smile. "So, which hospital are we taking him to?"

She raised her eyebrows above the thick-rimmed glasses she was wearing. "Hospital? Does he need to go? I thought you'd just check him over and be on your way."

"Well, it's our company policy to transport all paediatric patients. They don't supply us with X-ray specs and I'm fresh out of magic wands. I doubt he's sustained any significant injuries, but then again, if it was me I wouldn't have called an ambulance. However, we're here now and we're obliged to transport him to the nearest hospital. So, I guess you'd better get his stuff together."

She blew out her cheeks and was about to reply when a

rather flustered looking beach ball of a woman burst into the classroom. "Is he OK?"

Troy stopped rummaging for boogers and pulled his finger from his nose as his face broke into a huge smile. "Mummy!"

He ran the distance between them and launched himself at her legs. "Look! I got a booboo on my head."

She gave him a big hug, fussed over him and scooped him up as she stood. "Hi guys, how is he?"

"G'day, I guess you're Mum. I think Troy's nailed it, he's got a booboo on his head. All his vital signs are normal, he wasn't knocked out and he's not showing any signs of a head injury, other than that nice egg he's got on his forehead. I was explaining to the staff here that even though the injury seems minor, he should go up to hospital for further assessment, just in case."

"Well I can take him up to Redlands, it's near where we live and it'll save you guys the bother. I'm sure you've got more serious stuff to deal with."

"Does Redlands do kids? I haven't a clue. We're a Northside crew and I'm lost when it comes to Southside hospitals."

"Yes, I'm sure Redlands does. I've taken Troy and his brother there in the past."

"Well, we're happy to take him up there, but if you insist, we'll be on our way."

I jotted down some details, said my goodbyes and ducked out the classroom, following behind Scotty's hasty retreat. Back at the vehicle he was already in the driver's seat with the engine running. "Quick boss, let's go before she changes her mind."

"I'm with you on that."

I threw in the response bag, slammed the side door and jumped in the cab. "The seafront can't be too far from here.

See if you can find me a spot with a nice view to do the write-up."

"Will do. Wasn't that a load of crap? I drove over 20 Ks Code One for a booboo."

"Just think of all those lives you risked on that journey, especially mine."

"The problem is that people these days don't know what an emergency is. What ever happened to common sense?"

"It became so rare they renamed it 'seldom sense'."

"I like it. It might catch on."

We had driven about two blocks east and were now on Wynnum Esplanade. "Anywhere along here looks good, Scotty."

He pulled nose-in to a parking bay shaded by a large fig tree, offering some natural cool from the midday sun. Switching off the engine, we opened the windows, allowing the smell of the sea to waft into the cab. I closed my eyes and took a deep relaxing breath, filling my lungs with the scented air and my mind with childhood memories.

The sound of our pagers broke my mental reverie and I looked at the device with some disdain. "Shit, they must have seen us move locations. It's a welfare check. I wish they'd be more honest with their messages. They don't give a shit about our welfare. The page should read: what the hell are you up to?"

"It's that or: hurry up you've been too long."

"Or: can you clear so we can drop another job on you? The thing is, if our welfare was in question, wouldn't we have already called them? And if we couldn't, sending a page to ask if we're OK ain't going to help. The only time I've ever known them to follow-up on a welfare check is when we've gone into overtime."

Rant over with, I picked up the mic and smiled as I called up. "Comms, 963."

"Alpha 963, go ahead."

"Many thanks for the welfare check. I'm sure you'll be glad to know that we're both doing well, although my colleague is suffering from a bad case of haemorrhoids. As to our last patient, he sustained a minor bump to his head, with no priority symptoms and his mother insisted on taking him up to Redlands hospital in her own car. We are completing paperwork and will advise as soon as we're clear."

"Roger 963, we'll make you partially available pending paperwork… and sorry to hear about your crewmate."

I turned to find Scotty staring at me open-mouthed. "Haemorrhoids! Haemorrhoids? What the fuck? You bastard!"

"Hey, you didn't think you'd get away with that 180-degree turn with no comeback, did you?"

His indignation dissolved into a knowing grin and he nodded a few times. "Fair cop. You're still a bastard though."

I settled down to writing up the documentation while Scotty played a game on his phone. Although there was little to record, it's the patients we leave on scene that require the most thorough paperwork.

Scotty interrupted my thoughts. "Hey, boss. Can you see what I see? Fancy a cooked lunch?"

I looked where he was pointing through the driver's side window and saw a bustling fish and chip shop less than fifty metres away. "Sounds like a rippa idea."

As I finished my typing, he returned with two paper bags and we walked a short way to a covered picnic table near the beach. I stared out through my sunnies at the distant horizon. "Now this is the life. There're few jobs where you can do this while still on the clock."

"I guess we're available if they need us."

"You're working with an ICP, Scotty. They'll page us whatever we're doing, available or not."

"True."

The fish was excellent and the chips just right. I made a mental note to remember the shop, adding it to the list of places to take Amber. My thoughts skipped back to Troy and his questions. Was I going to marry her? More to the point, would she say yes? Mind you, commitment was something I'd always shied away from, ever since I lost my brother. Perhaps I didn't want to go through that pain again. After putting my life back on track, I'd gone through a string of short-term relationships, most of which I chose to leave. But Amber was different and I knew it. Even this early in the relationship, I couldn't imagine being without her.

I thought I'd broach the subject with Scotty. Although I considered him a good friend, most of the time we spent together was on shift and we rarely met on a social basis. But working alongside someone for twelve-hour shifts and being exposed to the things that are a part of this job can make you close. And what's more, I valued his opinion. "So you think Amber's a keeper?"

He almost choked on a chip. "Shit, that one came out of nowhere. But, yes. Hell yes! I'd be popping the question after I passed first base."

"Perhaps that's why you're single."

"D'you reckon that'd be too soon?"

"Well a proposal after a kiss screams of desperation."

"So how long have you two been an item?"

"Oh, I don't know, about five months. We've kept things on the down-low for quite a while to avoid the inevitable gossip."

"Five months? I thought it was longer. Never think of becoming a spy, boss. Both of you were pretty crap at hiding your feelings. It's been like watching two love birds trying to avoid the same perch." He grinned at me as I stared back. "But hey, I'd say you're as good as married anyway, so seal the deal, mate. Seal the fuckin' deal! Let's face it, you ain't gonna get any better than her... No offence."

I smiled at him, stunned by his insight. "None taken, mate. I was amazed when she agreed to the first date."

He laughed. "So was I!"

I shook my head, jabbing the few remaining chips onto my fork. Then the beeping pagers saved me from any further deliberations.

Scotty shovelled in his last piece of fish. "Perfect timing for a change. So what's the latest calamity?"

I glanced at the tiny screen and read the details. "What the hell? It's a 1B in Boondall for a chest pain, that's miles away! We'd better be backing someone up."

The job was an ICP backup, but I knew the crew and they were on the ball. They'd diagnosed an inferior infarct, a heart attack affecting the lower side of the heart, and had started the appropriate treatment. All I had to do was meet up with their ambulance and jump on board, leaving Scotty to follow behind.

After checking the ECG, I ran through my checklist and called the interventional cardiologist to activate the cath lab. Although my involvement was limited, it avoided the need to stop in the ED, which reduced the subsequent damage to his heart. For these patients there's an old adage, time is muscle.

On arrival at Charlies, we marched through triage with nothing but a wave to Kath, who scowled at being bypassed. We then wound our way through the maze of corridors to the cardiac catheter lab and I gave a handover to the gowned-up staff. By the time we arrived in the write-up room Scotty was sitting in a chair with his feet on the table. "Did I miss anything?"

"No. But you really are a shit magnet Scotty. Any chance the next patient can be a plain old nanna-down?"

"Hey, we went to Troy's booboo. You can't get much lower acuity than that. Fancy a cuppa?"

"Thought you'd never ask. I've my bit of the paperwork to do, but I've first got to call The Big 'O' as I activated the cath lab." I turned to one of the crew I'd backed up. "Can you start the write-up, Sam?"

"Just on it. Hey, are you on 963?"

I frowned. "Why?"

"Which one of you has piles? That was a classic!"

I laughed. "Scotty. I had to get back at him for his driving. Came up with that on the spur of the moment. Do you have any arse-grapes Scotty?"

"None of your fuckin' business, boss."

There was general laughter that almost drowned out the beeping of our pagers. "Oh for Chrissake, what now?"

I looked at the display. "Great, better go. It's a 1A in Nundah. Fill out the paperwork as best you can, Sam, and I'll try and add my bit later. Jesus, at this rate my drug bag will be empty before we get a chance to restock. The B-CAS education department should use you as a training resource, Scotty."

"Hey-hey, the shit magnet strikes again. Just call me Magneto."

"Magneto? Hey, if you're him who am I?"

"Well, you sure as fuck ain't Wolverine."

14

VIAGRA

Vic Morris was sick of working with students. It was one thing having to do a twelve-hour shift with another qualified paramedic, but he wasn't paid any more to nursemaid snotty-nosed school-leavers. He just seemed to keep being lumbered with them, no matter how many whinged about his attitude. His fucking attitude! He was the one with the reds on his shoulders and those epaulettes had been there for almost thirty years. Surely that counts for something? Not in their fucking minds. According to them and their stuck-up Uni lecturers, he was a dinosaur. A dinosaur! Not yet fifty and already labelled extinct. Well, his fossilised teeth could still fucking bite.

Vic looked older than his forty-eight years. Decades of rolling shifts will do that to the body, not to mention working under the Queensland sun. At least he'd avoided the expanding midriff that had afflicted so many others. It was probably the smokes that helped with that. He kept his grey hair cropped close to his scalp, like an ageing tennis ball, and his face was lined with more cracks than a dried up billabong.

He was driving along Gympie Road on the return to Sandgate station, but he didn't fancy their chances of getting back. The traffic was already building up and it was nowhere near rush hour. Ah well, more meal overtime. Best cash in now before the government takes it away. Ambos need to be more aggressive about their work conditions, like the firies, but there're too many whingers in the ranks and not enough militants. And that's only set to get worse with all these fucking Uni students. After forking out for a degree, they're just glad to get a job. They've no idea of what's been fought for over the years and as most are young, free and single, they think the crap wage is great.

He scoped out his crewmate from the corner of his eye. At least this one was a looker and knew when to shut up. Lizzy Ack-something. Fuck, he was working with a student a week or so back who couldn't stop talking. What was her name again? Maxine, that was it. Max volume more like. Shit, he even told her to shut the fuck up, but that only bought him about twenty minutes of peace.

Lizzy Ackman was nineteen and wore her straight blonde hair up in a ponytail, held by a green hairband to match her uniform. She was a second year university student and today was only her fourth shift as an actual crew member. She'd completed her pre-requisite prac weeks as a third officer, but now she'd put her name down for some relief work to get more experience. And to earn some needed cash. Her other shifts had been great, her crewmates so helpful, but not this one. Next time she'll ask rosters who she's working with. If it's Vic, they can shove it.

She could see the old pervert checking her out from behind his sunglasses, what a creep. OK, so she was still on her P plates and had trouble reversing the ambulance into the tight parking bays at Charlies, but that was no reason to 'ban' her from driving for the rest of the shift. He was just lazy and didn't want to do any write-ups. Plus, he could watch her arse while she bent down to assess the patients. How was she supposed to learn anything from this old fossil if he refused to talk to her?

The two of them travelled along in a brooding silence. They hadn't been able to agree on a radio station, so they were left staring out of the windscreen. Until the MDT and their pagers beeped. Even though he had predicted a job and was looking forward to the extra money, Vic still cursed. "Shit! What now?"

Lizzy attempted to scroll through the info, but he flicked her hand away and turned the unit towards him to read the display. "1C in Nundah, chest pain. Hold on. Ah fuck! That's Ivy's address."

"Who's Ivy?"

He ignored her question and flipped on the lights and sirens, easing out of the lane into a gap provided by the traffic. He did a U-turn at the intersection and headed for Nundah. "Course, you wouldn't know her. Ivy Watson. She's a pain-in-the-arse regular. She gets bored and calls triple zero like normal people call for a pizza. Just the sort of patient for someone like you to practise on."

"Right."

"Don't suppose you can cannulate yet, can you?"

"No."

"Fuck. Guess I'll be doing everything. You can at least try and assess her, then ask me what you think she needs. Don't do or give anything without clearing it with me first. Got that?"

"Yes."

OK, so she was new. She got it. But did he really need to rub her nose in it with every comment? She could feel her heart rate rising. As if driving Code One to an emergency wasn't stressful enough, she also had to put up with this jerk. She took a deep breath and tried to prepare herself. Blanking out Vic's presence, she deliberated over relevant questions and which drugs she might use. She went through the contraindications for aspirin and glycerin trinitrate in her head, but struggled with the sixth one for the latter. After a moment's concentration it came to her. Of course, Viagra!

Vic was also deep in thought. Great, fucking Ivy! She was always trying to bum a dart off him. She could no doubt smell the nicotine on his uniform. He reckoned the Uni should draw up a contract with a bunch of these regulars and give them a special phone. That way, when they call for an ambulance one manned with students arrives. The oxygen thieves get what they want, the rookies gain experience and the tossers wouldn't bother real paramedics.

They pulled up outside a block of units that screamed 'government housing' and Vic flipped off the lights. He got out and put on his gloves as he walked around to the side door. Lizzy was struggling to feed the monitor's shoulder strap over her head. When she had done, he grabbed the response bag with one hand. "You going to bring the oxygen kit?"

"I can't carry that and the monitor, it's too heavy."

He gave a pitying shake of his head. "You're pretty fucking useless, aren't you princess? Can't drive and can't lift. Ever thought you might be studying for the wrong job?"

She bunched up her fists and gritted her teeth, but somehow managed not to respond. She pushed past him and climbed the stairs to the unit, determined not to cry.

The door to number seven was open, but she still knocked. "Ambulance."

A croaky voice came from inside. "In 'ere."

She walked into a small flat that looked like it was

furnished from a skip. A woman with a sagging face and tight grey perm was sitting in a threadbare armchair, sucking on a cigarette while a daytime show played on the TV.

"Hello. My name's Lizzy, are you our patient?"

"See anyone else here? I got me chest pain again."

She tapped at her chest with her free hand and carried on watching her show. Lizzy heard Vic come in and dump the bags on the floor.

"OK, what can I call you?"

She laughed. "Ivy. Thought every paramedic knew me name."

"OK, Ivy, when did the pain start?"

"Dunno. Before lunch I think."

"And how would you describe the pain?"

She looked confused and took another drag on her cigarette. "Painful."

"No, I mean, what word would you use to explain the nature of your pain?"

She thought for a moment. "Hurting?"

Vic interrupted. "I haven't got time for this. Ivy, if you want a lift to hospital grab your fags and shift your arse."

"OK. Just let me finish me smoke, I've already got me stuff packed."

"Didn't doubt it."

He picked up the kit bags and turned to leave. "Come on, princess, let's go."

Lizzy stood in the room open-mouthed as Ivy stubbed out the remains of her cigarette and climbed out of her seat. He hadn't let her ask more than a few questions and they didn't have a set of obs.

Ivy bumbled past her. "Come on luv, if you want you can do me Easy-G in the ambulance."

Back in the truck, Vic threw the bags in and directed Ivy to the captain's chair. As she climbed in, Lizzy turned to Vic. "I wanted to do an ECG. Wouldn't it be better if she lay on the stretcher? She does have chest pain."

Vic rolled his eyes. "Ivy's always got chest pain. I'm not changing the linen, or rolling out the stretcher for her. If you want to dot her up, go ahead, but do it while she's in that seat."

Lizzy sighed and put the monitor into its cradle before sitting down on the top of the stretcher in front of Ivy. Vic slammed the side door, walked around the cab and installed himself in the driver's seat. As he fired up the engine Lizzy called out. "Do you mind if we stay here while I do a few things?"

"Fine by me, princess. Knock yourself out."

He rummaged through his lunch bag and found an apple, which he ate with loud crunches. Lizzy ignored him and collected her first set of obs. She then asked Ivy more questions while applying the dots for an ECG. Eventually, she lent through into the cab. "This is her three lead. I can't see anything, but she is still complaining of central chest pain. I'd like to give her an aspirin and GTN."

He glanced at the printout she proffered. "Whatever. Just go through your contraindications."

"Well, she's already prescribed both drugs, but here goes."

She sat back in front of Ivy. "So Ivy, I've got to ask you a few questions before I can give you some medications. Are you allergic to anything?"

"Don't think so."

"Have you had any psychostimulants recently?"

"What's that?"

"Drugs like cocaine."

She laughed. "Can't afford that stuff. I've enough problems paying for me fags."

"Do you have any bleeding disorders, or current stomach ulcers?"

"Don't think so."

"And you're over eighteen."

"Have been for a while, love."

Vic tutted from the cab and shook his head.

"OK. That's it for aspirin, now GTN. Your blood pressure is 135 over 82 and your heart rate is 76, so that's all good. You're not having a stroke and you haven't injured your head. That leaves one more question. Have you taken any erectile dysfunction medications in the last twenty-four hours?"

"Eh?"

"You know, Viagra or something like that."

Ivy laughed like a drain, while Lizzy sat and watched. After a while she tapped Lizzy's leg. "Sorry love, it always makes me laugh when you guys ask me that one."

"Right. Am I OK to give them, Vic?"

"I think if she was having a heart attack she'd be dead by now. Get on with it."

She closed her eyes for a second or two, then turned her attention to her patient. "OK Ivy. Open your mouth and raise your tongue to the roof. That's it, great."

Lizzy shook the pink bottle of glycerin trinitrate she had retrieved from the drug bag and gave a test spray into the air, then squirted a dose in Ivy's mouth. "Right Ivy, chew on this aspirin while I get you a drink of water to wash it down."

She reached over to open the lid of the fridge, but the catch was stuck. After a few goes she called to Vic. "Is there a trick to getting into this fridge?"

He sighed between mouthfuls of sandwich. "Press the button in and flip it up at the same time."

"Oh, thanks."

Reaching in, she pulled out a cold bottle of water and turned to Ivy. "Sorry about that, here you... Ivy?"

Ivy had slumped forward in the seat with her head on her knees, her arms hanging down like a rag doll. Lizzy pushed her back in the seat, lifting her head up to look at her face. Her eyes had rolled back in their sockets and drool mixed with crushed aspirin dribbled from her mouth. "Ivy!"

Just at that point, Ivy's body went rigid, then her limbs and head thrashed back and forth in a jerking motion. Once again, Lizzy called out her name, but this time there was panic in her voice.

The side door shot open and Vic jumped in. "What the fuck did you do?"

"I don't know! She just started seizing!"

"Right, I'll draw up some midaz. Get the stretcher sorted."

Vic drew up the drug for an intramuscular injection and jabbed the needle into Ivy's upper arm, giving her the full dose. Ivy's body soon stopped its twitching and she once again slumped forward.

He then barked at Lizzy. "Grab her legs, I'll get under her arms. When I say so, drag her onto the stretcher. Ready? Now!" They manhandled her limp body from the seat and arranged her in the recovery position. "So what the fuck kicked that off?"

Lizzy was stunned. "I don't know. She was chewing on the aspirin. I went to get some water and when I looked back she had slumped forward."

She looked down at Ivy. "Vic... Is she breathing?"

"She's possdictal."

"What?"

"God, don't they teach you anything? It's a drowsy state after someone has a fit."

With no malice intended, Lizzy corrected his pronunciation. "Oh, you mean post-ictal. Are you sure?"

He glared at her and tapped his shoulder. "Hey, princess, I'm the one wearing the reds. Don't fucking question me!"

The confined space of the ambulance took on an icy chill, the tension only disturbed by the trace of the monitor, which was now beeping at a rate of thirty. The silence from Ivy was complete, because she had indeed stopped breathing. In fact, she was dead. The dots were recording the failing electrical impulses of her heart, but the muscle ceased beating after her hypoxic seizure.

Lizzy gritted her teeth and picked up enough courage to reach out and touch Ivy's wrist. "Vic, please check she's breathing. I can't feel a pulse."

"Probably 'cos you're not doing it right." That said, he still reached to her neck and checked for a carotid.

His hand fumbled to the other side. "Shit! Quick roll her on her back."

As soon as she was lying flat, Vic started chest compressions. Lizzy was standing wide-eyed, her legs wedged between the stretcher and the attendant's chair. Her mouth open, body still.

"Don't just stand there. Get some scissors and cut her top off. She needs the pads on!"

Lizzy followed his instructions, as Vic grabbed an oropharyngeal airway from the kit on the wall and slotted it into Ivy's mouth. He then inflated her lungs twice using a bag-valve mask, before returning to pound on her chest. As Lizzy connected the pads, the trace told him nothing new. He couldn't shock that rhythm. "Right. Jump out the back and get on the radio. Call for ICP backup Code One, CPR in progress." Lizzy stared at him. "Now!"

His shout galvanised her into action and she flung open both the back doors and jumped onto the road behind the ambulance. As she ran to the cab, Vic yelled out, "Close the goddam doors!"

His CPR efforts on a half-naked Ivy were now visible to any of the passing motorists who cared to look. She rushed back to slam the doors, but in her haste got the order wrong, the second one closed with a grating crunch. She watched with dismay as the shiny chrome Mercedes logo flew into the air and skittered off across the road.

From inside she heard Vic. "What the fuck was that?"

She decided not to answer and just flipped the order before slamming them. Once in the cab, she grabbed the mic. "Comms, we need an ICP Code One. Our patient has arrested." Despite her intention, she failed to disguise the tremble in her voice.

"Last unit calling, can you give your call sign?"

"Er... 925. Oh no, that was yesterday. Er... 824."

"Please tell me you didn't have the button pressed for all that?"

"Bravo 824, we have you as departed. What is your current location?"

"Outside Ivy's flat... I mean, at the caller's address. We haven't left yet."

"Roger that, dispatching ICP Code One now. They'll be coming from Prince Charles."

"Great, thanks."

"Stop chatting, I need you in the back."

Lizzy dropped the mic and left the cab, returning to the back. Vic had worked up a sweat thumping on Ivy's chest and beads were dripping from his chin. "You need to do

CPR while I cannulate, but first draw up some adrenaline."

"How much?"

"Three in a ten mil syringe, but make it fast."

"OK."

She pulled out three ampoules from the drug kit and read off their labels, before breaking the tops and sucking the drug up into a syringe. She was quick for an inexperienced student, but not fast enough for Vic.

"Haven't you done that yet?"

"I'm taping a vial to the syringe now."

"Right, you need to do CPR from the head end. Stand there and when I say, lean over to do the compressions. After thirty, give two ventilations with the bag. Got it?"

"Yes."

"Right, it's time for another rhythm check."

He looked at the screen, while feeling for a carotid. The rate of pulseless electrical activity had dropped to about ten per minute. "Still PEA. You're up!"

Vic flopped back into the attendant's chair and threw a tourniquet around Ivy's arm. He then rummaged through the drawers for cannulation supplies. Glancing up he barked at Lizzy. "Make your compressions faster and deeper than that. Do you know the song Another One Bites the Dust?"

"Er, I think so."

"Well that's the rhythm you need to maintain."

She nodded and he looked for veins on Ivy's arm, but Lizzy interrupted his search. "Da-da-dum, dum, dum, dum, another one bites the dust…"

"Jesus! Keep it in your head!"

Vic returned to his task, but he didn't like cannulating. It was a skill he'd never got the hang of and as a result, his patients rarely received an IV line. Arrests were the one time he couldn't avoid it, so he would rely on his crewmate. But not today; Lizzy hadn't been signed off. Bloody students!

He was making his third attempt when the side door swung open to the sound of a familiar voice. "Hi guys, what've we got?"

After leaving the hospital, we shot down Rode and hung a screeching right into Sandgate Road. On the journey, I scrolled through the MDT while battling against the G-forces.

Scotty took a break from swearing at motorists. "So what's the story?"

"Seems like a crew has called in a resus after going to a chest pain. Weird thing is, I'm sure that's Ivy's place."

I read out the address to him. "I think you're right, boss. Perhaps she finally had an ailment worth calling triple zero. Either that, or she's bored a friend to death."

"I don't think she has any friends."

We ducked down a few back roads and soon saw the other ambulance parked on the side of the street. As we approached, there was a crunch as we drove over something on the road.

"What was that?"

"Dunno. Looked like a Mercedes logo. D'you want your drugs and airway kit, boss?"

"Yes please."

I jumped out the cab with my gloves already on and walked the short distance to the ambulance, flinging open the side door. "Hi guys, what've we got?"

The sight of a very young female paramedic greeted me, her blonde ponytail whipping back and forth each time she delivered a chest compression. She appeared to be head banging to a silent beat. As I looked inside, I recognised Ivy on the stretcher, whose skin now matched the colour of her grey perm. Then my heart sank. Sweat was dripping from Vic Morris' forehead as he lent over the patient while attempting to cannulate.

If I was ever in doubt Comms had sent me to a shit fight, seeing Vic on scene would confirm my suspicions. People often referred to him as a dinosaur, but I believed he was something more akin to an offshoot of the primordial soup. Some sort of basic organism that was pissed off because he'd missed out on evolution.

Out the corner of my eye, I noticed that the student had stopped compressions and was staring at me. "Hey, don't stop, keep going. What's the story, Vic?"

"Hi Jono. As you know, this is Ivy. She was up to her usual bullshit, calling for chest pain and then had a seizure after one dose of GTN and an aspirin. I gave her a shot of midaz for the seizure and we lay her in the recovery position, then she arrested. What the fuck! Anyway, I'm working on my own here 'cos this student's only a few days in."

He waved a dismissive hand at his colleague. "So we've done little more than CPR as Ivy's a bitch to cannulate."

"Right. Thanks, Vic, can you take over from… I'm sorry, what's your name?"

The student's flushed face looked up. "Lizzy."

"OK. As you two swap over, let's do a few checks. How long has she been down for?"

Vic looked at his watch, before taking over compressions. "'Bout fifteen minutes."

"And the rhythm has always been PEA?"

"Yep."

"What's her airway like?"

"She's been easy to bag, but there's only an OP in."

"OK, Scotty are you able to get an LMA in place while I look for a line."

"On it, boss."

"Do we have adrenaline drawn up?"

Lizzy handed me a syringe with a vial taped to it. "There's three doses in there, drug checks have been done."

I sat in the attendant's chair and grabbed a large bore cannula. "Right, Lizzy, can you prepare a bag of fluid?"

"I think so."

"Great. There should be one in the side pocket of the response kit."

I looked at Ivy's arm and inserted the cannula straight into a vein. It was like jabbing a witchetty grub with a cocktail stick. Vic was full of shit, a bitch to cannulate my arse. "OK, I'm in. First dose of adrenaline given. Can you be time keeper, Scotty?"

"No worries. LMA is in and working well. Good rise and fall of her chest and a normal end tidal waveform."

"Excellent. I'll take over the airway in a minute, if you bag for now. You still OK with the compressions Vic?"

Vic's face was red and his close-cropped silver hair glistened with sweat, but he nodded an affirmative. I drew up a dose of sodium bicarbonate. "How's that bag of fluid going, Lizzy?"

"I'm trying to get rid of the bubbles."

"That's fine, pass it here. Can you go to the cab and crank up the aircon, please?"

I connected and secured the line and hung up the bag from the hook on the wall. "Fluids up and the sodi bic's going in now."

I looked at the monitor, but all I could see was the waveform created by Vic's compressions. At least he wasn't totally useless. His perspiring body was blocking my way to the head end, so I climbed out the back and came in through the side door, intending to prepare my airway kit. As I stepped in, I stood on something and looked down. It was a large handbag, the contents of which were spilling out onto the floor. I was about to kick it aside, when a white medication pot rolled out. The label stopped me in my tracks. "Oh shit!"

Vic looked at me. "What's up?"

I pointed to the bag. "Is that Ivy's?

"Yer, why?"

I picked up the container and showed him the label. "Sildenafil Citrate. That's the generic name for Viagra."

"What, you don't think she's… Oh shit, that's a contraindication for GTN."

"Right."

"Shit, shit, shit, shit!"

"If she's been taking this, it'll explain her arrest."

"Oh fuck!"

He compressed her chest with renewed vigour. "That student definitely asked her if she'd taken Viagra. The fucking bitch just laughed!"

I took a deep breath. Oh God, what a cluster fuck!

"She's due the next adrenaline, boss."

"Thanks Scotty."

I gave another dose while my mind raced. "OK. Whatever happens, we're taking her into hospital. I'm not calling this on scene. So, I'll get her tubed and then we'll move."

I prepped for an intubation and when I was ready, Scotty made way for me in the captain's chair. After bagging Ivy a few times, I removed the laryngeal mask airway and slid the laryngoscope into her mouth, sliding the blade down past her tongue. Even with Vic continuing to pound her chest I had an unobstructed view of her vocal cords and she was an easy tube. With the plastic in place, I connected the bag and ran the checks. All was good and we were set to go.

"OK, Scotty can you draw up more adrenaline and let's run one more rhythm check." Vic paused compressions and I felt for a carotid. Despite the trace on the monitor showing a rate of around fifty, there was still no pulse. "Nothing. Back on the chest. OK, this is the plan. Scotty, you drive. We'll go to the Royal seeing as most of the way from here will be in the tunnel. Lizzy, you take over from Vic so he can have a rest. And Vic, can you drive our vehicle up to the hospital?"

Vic looked up from his compressions. "What, you want the student in the back with you?"

"You got a problem with that, Vic?"

"Whatever."

He stopped working Ivy's chest and stomped out of the ambulance.

"Right, Lizzy, looks like you're up."

Scotty threw Vic our keys. "Be gentle with her."

"Ha! Don't flog her like you do, you mean?"

"Something like that. See you at the Royal."

Scotty handed me a syringe with two more adrenaline doses, slammed the door and climbed in the driver's seat. "She's due another dose now. Ready to rock and roll?"

"Ready as I'll ever be."

"What vehicle are we on?"

Lizzy responded. "824."

"Thanks."

He picked up the mic. "Comms, 824."

"824 go ahead."

"Comms, we're departing Code One to the Royal with the ICP on board. 963 is following up Code Two."

"Roger that."

As Scotty pulled away, I looked back through the glass of

the rear doors and saw Vic leaning over the bonnet of the ambulance, his head in his hands.

While bagging, I called up the Royal and gave them a heads-up as to what we were bringing in. I kept the message brief and hung up. "Do me a favour, Scotty, can you pull over for a second?"

"Whatever you say, boss."

Lizzy gave me a strange look, but carried on pushing Ivy's chest. "Right Lizzy, swap with me. I'll do the compressions while you bag. Just keep at a rate of ten a minute. I want to ask you a few questions."

As soon as we changed rolls, Scotty drove off. "OK. Tell me exactly what happened and don't feel you need to cover for Vic. Everyone knows he's an arsehole."

She looked as if she was about to burst into tears, but then launched into a detailed account of the events prior to our arrival.

"So Ivy's blood pressure was fine before the GTN spray?"

"Yes, it should be on the code summary. I'm sure it was 135."

"And you definitely asked about Viagra?"

"Yes. Vic told me to go through all the contraindications for both GTN and aspirin."

"How long do you think it was from when she collapsed to CPR starting?"

She paused, staring at the bag as she pressed it to inflate Ivy's lungs. "At least five minutes, maybe longer. Vic said she was post-ictal, but I'm sure she wasn't breathing."

"Thanks for that, you did good. Don't worry, you'll be fine. Look on the bright side, you can put all this down to an immersive learning experience." I gave her an encouraging smile and she replied with a sheepish grin.

"Turning into the Royal now, boss."

"OK, Lizzy, let's swap back. They'll think it strange if they see an ICP doing compressions."

Scotty laughed. "Too fuckin' right. I reckon that's the first time I've ever seen you pushin' on a chest. Surprised you remembered what to do."

"Hey, it acts as a refresher every time I've got to correct your technique."

"Yeah, yeah. Looks like there's a welcoming committee."

Before Lizzy took over I did a pulse check, gave another adrenaline and moved the monitor onto the stretcher between Ivy's legs. I didn't believe anything we did would bring her back, but I had to go through the motions. This would be viewed as a death in care, so there would be the inevitable coronial enquiry and my management had to be spot on. I also wanted a doctor to make the final call. Doctors come coated in Teflon, shit never sticks to them. Paramedics, on the other hand, are made of Velcro and everything we touch is covered in little fluffy loops.

Between ventilations, I took down the remains of the bag of saline so we were ready to roll out. As Scotty reversed into the parking bay, three nurses wearing plastic disposable aprons opened the doors. "Do you need anything?"

"An O-two cylinder and someone tall enough to do CPR next to one of our stretchers."

"Got the oxygen and Ash here is pretty tall, he'll have to do."

"Righto. You get the oxygen connected then we can move."

I disconnected the hosing and threw the end to the nurse, who I didn't recognise. Whipping out my stethoscope, I check my tube was still inflating both lungs. "OK, everyone ready? Let's go."

Scotty dragged out the stretcher as Lizzy continued to do compressions. On reaching the back step, Ash took over and she jumped out of the way. I followed the stretcher, continuing to bag Ivy as I stepped down from the vehicle.

We bypassed triage and went straight into a resus bay, where around ten people were waiting for us. The only face in the crowd that caught my attention was the consultant, MC-Squared.

"I'll give a handover when she's on your bed."

I relinquished my hold on the endotracheal tube to a registrar, while two nurses wedged a large plastic Patslide under Ivy's body. They then slid her across onto the resus bed and another nurse, standing on a footstool, took over compressions. I stepped to one side and using a loud voice, delivered my handover.

"This is Ivy Watson, a 53-year-old woman that most of you know as a regular here in the ED. Today she called triple zero for chest pain and the crew treated her as per usual, conducting an ECG and giving her 300 mg aspirin and a 400 mcg spray of GTN. Ivy subsequently collapsed and had a seizure, for which she received 5 mg of midazolam, IM. The crew then realised she had suffered a PEA arrest and began CPR. I arrived a good 15 min post arrest. I gained IV access and inserted an ETT, 22 cm at the lips with a size 8 tube. She's had four 1 mg doses of adrenaline, 100 ml of sodium bicarbonate and has now sustained a PEA for at least half an hour, with fixed dilated pupils."

I turned to look at MC-Squared and said in a quieter voice, "The only reason I've brought her in is that I found these in her handbag."

He took the medications from me and raised his eyebrows. "I wonder who put her on these."

"Beats me. Perhaps it was deliberate. You've heard of death by cop? This could be death by ambo."

He ignored my comment and addressed the emergency

department staff. "Right. Let's run our checks. Any pulse? Pupils reacting? Heart or lung sounds? End tidal high?"

Every question was answered with a shake of the head from the relevant attendant. "OK. This woman had an extensive cardiac history, I don't think we need to do any more here. Let's wrap things up. Time of death recorded as…" He looked at the clock on the wall, "… 14:31."

And with that, he left the throng who switched from active resuscitation into clear-up mode, with most drifting away to other duties. I turned to Lizzy and Scotty who had followed the action into the cubicle and shrugged my shoulders. "Well that was short and sweet. Guess we'd better get on with our own clear up and paperwork."

We threw all our gear on the stretcher and wheeled it outside to the ambulance bay. There had been an unusual silence between us, with everyone absorbed in their own thoughts, but Scotty broke the mood. "Viagra? Ivy? What the fuck?"

"Takes all sorts."

"But she could only have been using them for a few days. I don't think she's ever lasted a week without calling an ambulance and most crews give her a shot of GTN."

"She was in here a few nights ago. I saw her in a bed in acute. She was going on about her Easy-G and I told her she needed to give up her smokes. Perhaps she thought Sildenafil was like Nicorette."

Scotty laughed. "She was pretty stupid."

Lizzy spoke for the first time since the resus stopped. "Do you think I killed her?"

I paused as I searched for the best response. "No, Lizzy, you didn't kill her. Ivy was taking Viagra, which reacts with the GTN you gave. Both drugs combine and enhance their effects, causing the smooth muscle of the blood vessels to relax. As a result, her blood pressure plummeted through her boots causing an arrest. The seizure you witnessed was because her brain wasn't getting enough oxygen. Although a dose of midaz is indicated, it wouldn't have helped the situation."

I shrugged my shoulders. "But don't worry. If there's anyone to blame, it's Ivy. You asked whether she was taking Viagra and she didn't tell you she was. She either didn't know, didn't understand, or didn't care. Whichever it was, you couldn't have known. You were just unlucky."

"So why was she taking Viagra, it's not like she'd have erectile dysfunction?"

"Now there's the million-dollar question. Some women take the drug because they think it improves their libido. But its other use is to reduce pulmonary hypertension, y'know, high blood pressure in the lungs. Her doctor may have put her on Viagra for that, given her inevitable lung disease, but he should have warned her about GTN. Of course, our contras only mention erectile dysfunction medications, so we never ask if someone's taking drugs for pulmonary hypertension. Go figure."

I realised what I'd said as Lizzy frowned. "So if I'd asked about pulmonary hypertension she might be alive?"

"I doubt it. Ivy couldn't pronounce ECG right, never mind understand the risks associated with her many medical conditions. I take it she didn't mention she was on any new tablets?"

"No."

"Well, you can't be expected to guess that, especially with a regular. At some point patients need to take responsibility for their own health. You didn't neglect anything and stayed within standard treatment protocols. You have nothing to worry about and you're certainly not to blame. Just stick to the truth and don't change your story."

I nodded to reassure her, then added, "Can you help Scotty with the clean-up, I must do the paperwork, but first I've got to call the Big 'O'. The smelly brown stuff'll hit the fan with this one, so I'd better forewarn the powers that be."

I walked away as I took out my phone. "Hey Scotty, that's the fourth regular who's died in the last week. At this rate we'll soon be out of a job."

15

LIFE LINE

He looked at his hands as they held onto the metal bar. It was almost as if he didn't recognise them. The hands of a stranger. What was that phrase, knowing something like the back of your hand? It never made much sense to him. How often did people look at their hands? Would anyone be able to describe their own in any detail?

He tried to raise his right arm, but nothing happened. It was as if his consciousness was a separate entity from his body, sitting somewhere up inside his head, pulling levers and turning dials, but nothing was working. He knew what he wanted to do, but his body didn't respond. As he was contemplating this dissociative state, his hand raised up towards his face, a delayed response that both amused and confused in equal measures. His palm seemed to float before him and he studied the craggy lines etched across the skin. Despite the dim light, they were easy to discern due to a mixture of grime and sweat that had collected in the recesses. He struggled to remember which crease was supposed to be the love line.

Which was the life line? He laughed. It really didn't matter, he'd fucked up both.

His hand touched his face and he felt his nose, crooked and broken since the accident. It was a permanent reminder of his fall from grace that mocked him every time he saw his own reflection. In an instant, he was recalling happier times. He had been so driven back then, a successful businessman who had owned his own roofing company. One moment's lack of concentration, one foot wrong, and the whole facade came crashing down.

He regained consciousness in a hospital bed, a day or so after falling from a roof, his wife by his bedside. But then he had six months in traction, followed by endless physio. They saved his life, but for what? His business had gone belly-up and he could no longer do the only job he knew. After his discharge, he moped around the house, watching daytime TV with a bottle to relieve the boredom. But the escape it provided soon became his reality. When his wife and kids left he hardly noticed and it wasn't long until the bank foreclosed on the mortgage. He remembered the day they came to evict him, but that's only because of the brief separation from his alcohol. He sobered up enough to find somewhere to crash, then the drowning continued.

At the thought of drowning, he pulled himself up and leaned over the high handrail to stare at the murky waters flowing below. It was the middle of the night and he was on the Goodwill Bridge with the rumble of the traffic on the Pacific Highway passing over his head. The reflection of the lights from Southbank was a blurred smudge on the water over in the distance. He often found himself here in a moment of lucidity. It wasn't far from the City Botanic Gardens that offered many hidden sleeping places. At this secluded spot on the bridge, he would contemplate his downfall and wish he had the courage to take one more leap. Feel the air rush by his face one more time, without the chance of waking up in a hospital ward. Do it right this time and avoid all the pain, all the heartache. But he knew he would once again wake up all alone under a bush, or on a park bench and restart his search for more grog.

As he watched the water swirl and bubble, he thought he heard a noise behind him. He tried to turn to see what it was, but someone scooped up his feet and lifted his legs high in the air. His old friend gravity did the rest.

As he fell, he didn't cry out. He was grateful to his saviour. Whoever it was that gave him the push had managed to release him. They had achieved in one swift movement what he'd been trying to do for years. Rather than fear or sadness, he embraced the darkness that clouded round his vision as he felt his head collide with the concrete support of the bridge.

His ruptured skull was devoid of any consciousness by the time his limp form entered the water. No fanfare marked his departure from this world. Even the Brisbane River swallowed his body with only the faintest splash.

16

VERBAL

I'd slept a couple of hours in the afternoon, but despite the sea breeze, the daytime heat was intense and I woke in a pool of sweat. Since I was cycling in, I waited until I arrived at station before having a shower. I now stood in front of the changing room mirror, washed but not refreshed and shattered before the shift even began. Weary blue eyes within a pale face were staring back at me. A rub of gel supported my spiky brown hair; if only I could use the same stuff for the rest of my body. "God, I hate night shifts."

I went to put my phone in my pocket and realised I'd missed a call from Detective Giallo. It had to be about Ivy, I glanced at my watch, 6:50 PM. It was unlikely he'd still be at work, but to show willing, I called the number anyway. Giallo's recorded voice kicked in on the fourth ring, so I left a message to call me the following afternoon as I'd be sleeping off a night shift.

I walked into the deserted corridor and bent down to retrieve my stuff from a cupboard when Maxine burst in from the plant room. "Hi Jon, the vehicle's all checked. We just need your drugs and kitbag then we're ready to roll. I hope you got some sleep, 'cos the day crews have been hammered. All the hospitals are ramped. We're in for a long night."

I kept my head behind the cupboard door until I'd composed myself, trying to sound light-hearted, but failing. "I thought I was working with Scotty tonight."

"He's thrown a sickie, I hope he's all right, not sure what the story is. They called me about midday to see if I could cover the shift and when I heard it was with you, I jumped at the chance. I've got so many questions to ask, but now you've arrived I'll get us logged on. Here, have a pager."

She handed me the device, spun around and was gone. I leant against the cupboard and slowly banged my head on the door. I had a vague recollection of Scotty mentioning something about calling in sick if he couldn't arrange a shift-swap, but getting a night off mid-roster was like having sex with an echidna: fucking impossible. However, it wasn't fair to hate him too much; he hadn't rostered me with Maxine. I had a desperate feeling that tonight would be one of the longest in my career. I hoped it'd be just run-of-the-mill jobs. At least Magneto was off sick.

I sighed and peered at my feet, but before my depression had time to solidify, the pager went off. "Great."

I looked at the screen: Please proceed to the Prince Charles to relieve a day crew.

"Even better. Ramped before I've signed out my drugs."

I drove the short distance to the hospital from the station, while Max prattled on beside me about nothing in particular. I didn't need to respond, she seemed happy to listen to her own voice. She held her mousey brown hair up in a bun at the back of her head, which always reminded me of the ones that Princess Leia wore; either that or a Danish pastry. She'd pulled each of the individual follicles so tight from her hairline it looked as if she was trying to achieve a face-lift. I'm guessing her age was somewhere in the mid-forties, but she'd aged well and was still an attractive woman. She would certainly represent a good catch, so long as you were stone deaf.

I had to park some distance from the entrance due to the number of ambulances outside and we made our way into the lion's den. About five stretchers were lined up perpendicular to one wall, each complete with a patient and an attending paramedic. Six patients were also seated in chairs against the opposite wall and a few paramedics were trying to type on their Toughbooks, despite having nothing to sit on. Another crew was at the triage desk and Mitchy, the Senior Operations Manager, was centre stage ranting at them. "Didn't you get the page? We're flat strap here struggling to find beds for the ones who're already here and you guys bring in another. What's your excuse? Why didn't you call Comms?"

The focus of his attention was Dave Morley, a Pommie friend of mine from Liverpool. He let Mitchy blow off steam while he slouched against the end of the stretcher and waited for him to stop. "Ave ya finished der mate? Diss lady 'ere was discharged only two hours ago after abdominal surgery conducted at this 'ere 'ospital. When she got 'ome, she discovered her wound was bleedin', so the ward told 'er to come back in. She ain't stoppin' in the ED, so you can nip down dat corridor, go to the bog an' put ya knickers back on de right way."

Mitchy gave his customary confused look, which was justified given Dave's accent, but then he turned to me. We hadn't seen each other since he lodged a complaint with my Station Officer.

"I hope you're here to transfer a patient out."

"Nope. I heard there was a party and thought I'd gatecrash. Dave here said it was OK."

"What?"

"We're here to take over from a day crew. Have you got a problem with that, or would you like to lodge another complaint?"

He pointed a finger at me. "D'you have any idea how high you are on the radar?"

I smiled back at him. "Ping."

He gave me a stare, but then took out his phone and walked off holding it to his ear. I turned to Dave and we both grinned, tapping our fists together.

"How've ya bin der, Jono? 'Aven't seen ya in ages."

"That's 'cos I always see you first, ya Pommie bastard."

He laughed, but the triage nurse interrupted our reunion and sent him off up to the ward with his patient. "Catch ya later, Jono."

I walked over to the ramped crews. "G'day everyone, is there a special on here today or something?"

I received a generalised "Hi Jono", but they all looked tired and bored.

"Well, which lucky crew wants to go home? Comms have sent us to relieve one of you and if you don't move quick, Max here may take that instruction literally and whip out a catheter."

A paramedic from Northgate responded. "I've heard they'll catheterise us anyway, so we don't have to waste time taking toilet breaks. We didn't get a feed all day and our shift ended fifteen minutes ago."

"I have one bid for a seven o'clock finish, can anyone beat seven?"

A Charlies crew piped up. "We're a six o'clock finish. C'mon Jono, you gotta give it to us."

"I have a six o'clock, going once…"

"We're a six finish as well, but we still have to drive back to Narangba."

"Sold, to the northern crew."

The others groaned, but it was all good-natured. "If you give Max a handover and a copy of your paperwork, you can make a run for it. Who're you working with?"

"Lily. She'll be in the write-up room with her feet up."

"I'll go help her swap our stretcher over."

"Cheers, thanks Jono."

"No worries."

After helping the other crew depart, I returned to find Max standing next to our newly inherited patient. She was an elderly woman with curly grey hair that reminded me of Ivy's. She was clutching onto a vomit bag as if it was a winning lotto ticket and she had both eyes screwed tight shut, accentuating the myriad wrinkles that made up her face.

"What is it Max, gastro?"

"Yes! This is Mabel, she's…"

"You good to hold the fort, Max?" I interrupted what would no doubt be an exhaustive handover. I knew she meant well, but to be honest, I didn't have the energy to care.

She looked surprised. "Why, where are you going?"

"I'm off to get a coffee. Do you want anything?"

"Oh. No thanks, I'm fine."

I walked out of the triage area and made my way to the hospital canteen, but was dismayed to find the cafe closed. I had to settle for some crappy tea in a polystyrene cup and returned drink in hand. The nursing staff had found beds for two of the ramped patients and we were now next in the queue, assuming that no one brought in a more deserving customer.

I leant against the central post and took a sip of my drink, glancing over at Max, who was making strange facial expressions. After some confusion, I realised she wanted me to look at the patients on the seats behind me. I turned and my heart sank. Slouching on a plastic chair with her head lolled forward so her straggling hair hung down like a mouldy shower curtain, was the unmistakable form of Psycho Sammy.

Samantha Macfarlane was in her early twenties, fat, fair and fugly. She no doubt had psychiatric issues, but most revolved around attention-seeking behaviour. She lived somewhere near Toowong and would often call triple zero claiming someone she knew had either taken an overdose, self-harmed, or was threatening suicide. When the ambulance arrived, she would deny all knowledge until the crew made to leave. Then she'd admit it was her who called and reveal that she'd been self-harming, or something similar. To put it another way, she was a total pain in the arse.

Unfortunately, when the city hospitals refused to give her the attention she craved, she would catch a bus to the northern suburbs and try her scam with us. The problem was that she would keep calling all night, in and out of the emergency departments more than most of the paramedics.

I looked at Max, closed my eyes and shook my head. The way things were shaping up, I just knew we were destined to deal with Sammy later.

Eventually the hospital secured a bed for Mabel and we said our farewells. As soon as we hit the clear button, our pagers buzzed.

I fired up the engine. "Gonna be one of those nights. What they got for us now? Oh for Chrissake! An RFDS!"

"Y'know, I like the odd RFDS. I get to have a chat with the patient and there's little paperwork and no stress involved."

"Well, I can't agree with you there. I just don't see why they need to use front line emergency ambulances to ferry patients to and from the airport. If they're sick, the nurse or a doctor travels with them and we just drive the bus. And when they're not too bad, why can't a PTS truck take them, or a taxi?"

"I suppose it's a waste of an ICP."

"Personally, I think it's a waste of an ACP."

We made our way through the suburbs to the airport, getting a wonderful view of the light-encrusted skyscrapers of the city from the overpass on the East-West arterial. In the distance, the parallel humpbacks of the Gateway Bridges were visible, looking like a giant buckled Scalextric track.

Max chatted away beside me and I made the odd non-committal grunt, but I'd zoned out before leaving the hospital grounds. My mind had wandered to the conversation with Scotty about Amber. I don't know whether it was the time of night or the sensory overload provided by Max, but it dawned on me that he was right. I was being a fool and what's more, I'd come up with a plan.

"What're you so amused about?"

"Huh?"

"Just then. You looked like you'd scored a date with Miranda Kerr."

"Oh, something like that. Did you hear that Ivy Watson won't be bothering us anymore?"

"Really? Has she moved down South?"

"In a matter of speaking. She arrested in an ambulance yesterday, I had to back them up."

"No way! What happened?"

I spent the rest of the trip telling the story of Ivy's last triple zero call. Max was still asking questions as the pilot opened the security gate to allow us onto the apron. He waited for me to lower my window. "You here for Jacobs?"

I lent forward and checked the MDT. "Yep. In from Roma and off to the Camilla."

"The Camilla? We've got him going to the Holy Spirit."

"That's right, it's what we call it. You know, the bit on the side of Prince Charles."

"Very funny."

Without even a smile, he nodded and strolled back towards his plane, a small twin turboprop being refuelled by a tanker. I manoeuvred the ambulance and parked a safe distance from the left wing tip to avoid his wrath. Pilots tended to be protective of their flying machines, with good reason. We offloaded the stretcher and rolled it next to the plane where we waited for the nurse to appear. A welcome cooling breeze blew in from the sea, across the flat expanse of the airport, spoilt by the pungent smell of aviation fuel.

The nurse popped her head out of the door in the fuselage. "Good evening all. Bernard here is a walker. If you could position your stretcher at the bottom of the steps, he'll be able to get on, but he must lie on his side."

"Righto."

She disappeared inside and a portly grey-haired man in his seventies stepped out, wearing a hospital gown. He eased himself down the stairs and climbed onto the stretcher with obvious discomfort.

"Hi Bernard, I'm Max. Just a few seat belts for your safety. Jon's behind the wheel and he's a frustrated rally driver. How was the flight?"

"Not too bad, considering."

"Considering?"

He looked bemused. "Considering I'm here to go to hospital."

Max blundered on. "Well, better than travelling all the way from Roma in an ambulance."

"To be quite frank, I'd rather have stayed at home."

"Good point, but these things can't be helped. What are you here for?"

He gave Max a look that a lord may reserve for an annoying peasant. "I have an anal fistula. Can we please go now?"

As Max wheeled the stretcher away, I looked up at the nurse who had reappeared and gave a wince. "Guess he's not too happy with his ailment. Do we need to top up his pain relief?"

She leant forward and spoke in a hushed voice. "He's had plenty of analgesia. I think he's just a grumpy old bastard. Hardly said two words the whole flight. Anyway, all his obs are fine and here's his paperwork. Hey, what do the yellow ones mean?"

She was looking at my epaulettes and I realised the staff of the Royal Flying Doctor Service were not used to seeing ICPs. I gave my standard answer to those that bothered to ask. "What, these? They show I'm a urine specialist. The red ones are trauma experts. They deal with the blood and I just wander around taking the piss."

She laughed as I waved a goodbye and walked over to help Max load Bernard into the ambulance.

We dropped off an ungrateful Bernard at the Holy Spirit and Max's verbal diarrhoea flowed like a rip in an overloaded incontinence pad. I guess she needed to make up for lost time.

The trip to hospital was conducted in an awkward silence after Bernard told her to shut up because she was giving him a headache. I thought of doing the same, but knew if she tried to remain quiet for much longer she'd explode.

Max pressed the buttons to clear the case and I started to drive back to station, but Comms had different ideas. The MDT beeped, followed by our pagers. "So, what wonders await us now?"

Max read out the details. "It's a 2A. Call's come in from the police about a woman at the taxi rank of the Chermside Westfield who says her sister has taken an overdose."

My shoulders sagged and I let my foot slip off the accelerator so the ambulance made a similar deflated gesture. "Great. I knew it. When you pointed her out in triage, I just knew we'd be dealing with her later."

"Who? Wait. You don't mean Sammy?"

"The one and only. Psycho Sammy, it's her standard MO. Crazy bitch'll have everyone fussing over her. She won't be pleased to see me though. She knows I don't put up with her bullshit."

With a backing track supplied by Max's voice, I drove through the hospital grounds, past the ambulance station and out onto Hamilton Road. It was just over a kilometre from the emergency department entrance to where Sammy had called, so it must have been a cheap taxi ride. I can't imagine she walked there. After stopping at the lights, we crossed the Gympie and entered the car park of the shopping centre.

I pulled up in the alley near to the Police Beat to avoid entering the parking barriers and climbed out of the cab, catching a strong whiff of refuse from an industrial bin. Despite being after ten, plenty of people were still milling around. At least the swarms of rainbow lorikeets that flock to the nearby trees had the sense to settle down for the night.

I wandered towards the taxi rank, but Max looked confused. "Don't we need to bring any of the kit?"

"Not unless you've got a taser. Should we see if the cops will oblige?"

She smirked and I pulled on a pair of gloves while walking over to the scene. Nearing, I could see the sedentary shape of Sammy adorning one of the bench seats, illuminated by the strip lights above. She was surrounded by a posse of Westfield security personnel, four cops and a blonde woman in her thirties whose body language suggested frustration. I had instant empathy with her. Spotting our approach, she strode in our direction. A dusting of makeup covered her face and her dark roots revealed her hair colour came from a bottle. She was wearing a charcoal suit with a cream blouse and a strained smile. She greeted us with a deep sigh and a longer than necessary look at the grey concrete ceiling.

"Hi guys. I'm sorry we had to call you out, but this lady here seems convinced her sister took an overdose and ran off into Gillhooleys. We've been in there three times and can't find anyone matching her description."

While she was talking, I glanced at her name badge. "Thanks Amanda, I'll stop you there. This... er... 'lady' is well known to us. Samantha often thinks one of her relatives is in dire need of assistance, but it's her who needs the help."

Amanda closed her eyes and her head sank forward. She looked like a Duracell bunny competitor as its battery ran out of power. But a second or two later she stood tall, eyes shot open and she completed her professional guise with a broad smile. "Of course. Great. Well, thanks so much for coming. I guess we can leave her with you then?"

"Not a problem. Many thanks for your assistance. I think we've got enough people here now to deal with the situation."

She nodded, smiled again and made a hasty retreat. I then

turned my attention to Sammy, who I noticed had been glaring at me as soon as I stepped into the fluorescent lights.

"Hi Sammy, what's your latest story?"

Her glare intensified. "It's me sister. I think she's taken an overdose and she ran off into that pub over there."

"What of?"

"Eh?"

"What's she overdosed on?"

"Her tablets, y'cockhead!"

One of the police officers chastised her. "There's no need for that language, he's just asking a few questions."

I nodded my thanks. "What tablets does she take?"

"Eh? I dunno. How am I supposed to know that?"

"Sammy, you don't have a sister, do you?"

"Yes I do!"

"How old is she?"

She paused. "Twenty-five."

"What's her date of birth?"

"Er… the third of April… nineteen… ninety… no, hold on eighty… nine?"

"Mental arithmetic's never been your strong point, has it Sammy?"

"You callin' me mental?"

"No. It's an expression. Mental arithmetic. It means doing sums in your head."

"There's nothing wrong with me head!"

She pursed her lips, folded her arms and turned her body away from me, sulking like a five-year-old. I gave her a little time before continuing. "If you have a sister, Sammy, she's not here is she?"

Her mouth puckered like she'd just chewed on a lemon and she twisted further towards the back of the bench. I tried again. "Sammy, the security staff may be needed elsewhere.

Can we at least call off the search so we can focus all our attention on you?"

No response.

"Can I call off the search?"

She made a slight nod of her head and I gave a thumbs up to the security detail. "Thank you gentlemen. I think the search is now over."

They nodded and wandered off towards the main entrance, shaking their heads. I turned back to our patient. "So, Sammy, what can we do for you tonight?"

"Nuffin."

"So why the call?"

"I've been cuttin' meself and I took an overdose, but I ain't goin' to no hospital."

She unfolded her arms and pulled up the sleeve of her left arm to reveal several scratch marks on the inside of her forearm. A hatch pattern of criss-crossed scar tissue covered her pudgy white skin, reminding me of 'The Thing' from 'The Fantastic Four'. She had a significant history of self-harm, but tonight's effort was just for show. I'd had worse cuts from twisting the top off a stubbie, but I played along.

"So what have you taken and how did you make those marks?"

"I've had about twenty Panadol an' I used a piece of glass in me handbag."

If she had overdosed on paracetamol, there wasn't a rush to treat her, but if she was carrying a 'sharp', then that endangered me. I looked at one cop standing with his feet wide apart, thumbs tucked into the armholes of his stab vest. He gave me an unimpressed expression. "D'you want me to search her bag?"

"If you wouldn't mind, thanks."

"Excuse me Ma'am, but could you please hand over your bag?"

She did so with minimal fuss and he crouched down, tipping the contents onto the pavement. Among the usual items of phone, fags and fuck knows what, there were two pieces of broken glass. He picked them up with a black-gloved hand and threw them in a nearby bin.

I smiled at our patient. "Any other sharps, Sammy?"

"No. Other than your fuckin' cock. I bet it's built like a tiny little needle!"

She fell about laughing at her joke and I had to admit, it was quick for her. The cop looked set to reprimand her again, but I dissuaded him with a subtle hand gesture. I can imagine that some men might get upset by such insults, but verbal abuse is part of a paramedic's territory. You need a thick skin and if you're easily offended, you're in the wrong job.

"Well, I'm glad to say that's something you'll never find out. But back to you. Where's the Panadol box?"

"Dunno, I chucked it."

"When did you take them?"

"Just before I called."

"So the empty packet will be in that bin?"

One of the cops shot me a look of dismay, but Sammy covered her story. "I threw it in the back of a passing ute."

"Right." I let out a sigh. "OK Sammy, well we'll need to do some assessments on you, so come on over to our ambulance."

"I'm not goin' to no fuckin' hospital!"

"Sammy, I saw you about an hour ago up at the Prince Charles. Why the sudden change of mind?"

"Those fuckers left me on a seat for ages. I'm not goin' back there."

"Hey, at least you got a seat. Max and I had to stand."

She looked confused, so I thought I'd chance my luck. "If you won't go to Charlies, does that mean you'll come with us if we take you to the Royal?"

"What is it you don't understand, needle dick? I'm not fuckin' goin' nowhere. You can't make me go. I know my rights!"

"Sammy, you told me you overdosed on paracetamol and you've been self-harming in a public place. That behaviour demonstrates you pose an imminent risk to your own health. Therefore, under the Mental Health Act and the Ambulance Service Act, I am well within my rights to use any means necessary to transport you to a medical facility for further assessment."

"No you fuckin' can't!" She turned to one of the cops. "He can't, can he?"

The policeman nodded. "Yes he can."

"OK, Sammy, you've got one of three options." I counted them off on my fingers to emphasise each point. "One, you can accompany us to the ambulance of your own free will. Two, these police officers cuff you and escort you to the ambulance, with force if you resist. Or three, these officers hold you down while I sedate you and then we put your semi-conscious body in our ambulance. It's your choice, but please note that the outcome of all three options is that you end up going to hospital."

With a sour look and a shake of her head, she dragged her weight off the bench. "You're all fuckin' wankers the lot of ya!"

She grabbed her handbag, which the cop had refilled, and waddled off. "Which way's the fuckin' ambulance?"

"Keep going, you can't miss it. Max'll show you the way."

We all wandered down the walkway and I pressed the remote to unlock the doors. Sammy climbed in the back and sat on the captain's chair followed by Max. "Do you mind if I get a set of obs, Sammy?"

"Knock yourself out, just keep needle dick away from me."

"Hey, I'll go nowhere near you if you behave, Sammy. You OK in the back, Max?"

"No worries. Sammy and I'll have a nice little chat on the way in."

Despite all her verbal abuse and attention-seeking behaviour, I couldn't help feel a pang of sympathy for Sammy. If she wasn't suicidal now, I wondered what she'd feel like after fifteen minutes with Max.

I was still outside the vehicle, so I turned to the police officers. "Thanks guys, I think we should be able to handle things from here. If she kicks off, I'll take great pleasure in sedating her."

They nodded their thanks. "No worries, mate. I was hoping she'd go for your option two, the one requiring force."

"If that's the case, any trouble and I'll call 'LR'. That way you can 'restrain' her for us."

An ambulance crew making a Law Required call was guaranteed a swift response from the police. It was a good excuse for any nearby cops to drive with lights and sirens. He grinned, but pointed to his chest where he kept his recording device. "I'm sure you'll do what's best for your patient."

I smiled back. "Always do, officer, always do."

"Don't doubt it. Take it easy."

I reached in and threw my gloves in the bin, handed the Toughbook to Max and slammed the side door. As I was walking around the cab, my phone rang. "Detective Giallo, I've just been with some of your colleagues. Working late aren't you? I thought you'd have knocked off by now."

"You should know the law never sleeps."

"So that's why coppers always look so tired."

"Too true. I've just got back from dealing with a floater they fished out of the Brisbane River. Looks like he was a homeless guy, probably why the bull sharks only took a few bites. Anyway, as I'm wide awake, I figured I'd give you a shout regarding your death in care yesterday. Strike while the iron's hot, as it were. Can you spare a couple of minutes for a few questions?"

I thought of Sammy trapped in the back with Max. "Fire away, take as long as you want."

"OK. I'll have to get you in for a formal statement, but how well did you know the deceased?"

"Ivy? Shit, most paramedics on the Northside know her only too well, or should I say knew her. She was a regular. Had an ambulance out at least twice a week, usually for chest pain. I guess no one wanted to risk leaving her at home, in case she was having a heart attack. As a result, we all spent some time with her travelling to hospital."

"Did she seem the sort who would experiment with drugs?"

"Not anything like Viagra. But that drug can be prescribed for reasons other than the obvious."

"Yes, I understand it's also used for…" There was a pause while I assume he referred to his notes. "… Pulmonary hypertension. The issue is that she had an envelope in her handbag containing a shipping receipt for the drugs. They were sent to her address from an overseas company, so she wasn't prescribed them from any doctor in Brisbane."

"Well, there goes my theory. However, there's one thing I can tell you about Ivy. When they were handing out brains, she got bored and wandered off for a smoke. She was pretty simple and could've been easily led, or overheard something and grabbed the wrong end of the stick. She may have bought the tablets because someone told her that Viagra made you more popular. But on that note, I'm not sure how she could have ordered them from overseas, her reading was still at the kindergarten level. She must've had help, but as far as I'm aware, she didn't have many friends."

"Mmm. Just two more questions. Did she mention she was taking any new tablets and did you see her put the pill bottle in her bag?"

"Sorry, can't help you with those, I was called as backup after she arrested. I spotted the pills on the floor of the ambulance, they appeared to have rolled out of her bag. But by the time I got there, Ivy was in no state to talk. You'll have to contact the initial crew for that kind of stuff."

"OK, I'll let you get back to work. I've got to be up bright and early for tomorrow's autopsy. Are you able to come in sometime to give your statement?"

"I'm back on shift this Wednesday, if that's OK?"

"Anytime next week should be fine, I don't think this one'll be going anywhere. Thanks for the chat."

"No worries. I'll see you next week."

I disconnected the phone as I climbed into the driver's seat and was greeted by Sammy shouting from the back. "Hey, needle dick, does this bitch ever shut up?"

When one hospital ramps the others often follow suit. So, after passing through triage at the Royal, we found ourselves third in line for a bed. Even though Sammy was just sitting on a seat and not taking up our stretcher, we still had to stay with her until we could handover to a nurse. This was because I'd placed her under an Emergency Examination Order, a legal document that bound her to remain in the hospital for at least six hours. The intention is to protect 'at risk' patients, but I have to admit, my concern for her well-being was not the overriding reason. By keeping her at the Royal she wouldn't be bothering any more crews tonight.

I put my brain in park and avoided talking to either Sammy or Max by pretending to read something on my phone. We didn't have long to wait and once free from Sammy I sorted out the ambulance while Max finished the paperwork.

When I walked into the write-up room, Gerry from Roma Street greeted me. "Hey hey, look who it is. Poison Ivy! Heard you dispatched our old friend Ms Watson."

He stood and reached out his arm. "Let me shake your hand for providing the people of Brisbane with such a wonderful service."

I took his hand. "Thank you, thank you, but I can't accept any responsibility for the act. She was already dead when I got there."

"I heard you gave her the GTN that caused her to arrest."

"Well, that goes to show how much bullshit the rumour mill churns out. No, I was called to backup the crew, who'll remain nameless seeing as the whole case is now under investigation."

"I don't fucking doubt it! The B-CAS investigates officers for spending too long in the dunnie. I'm sure the shit must have hit the fan when a regular croaked in the back."

"Hit the fan and every other electrical appliance. She's the forth regular I know of to pop their clogs in the last week. Come to think of it, didn't you go to what was left of Mad Marcus?"

"Only found the top of his head." He shrugged. "Couldn't see the point of looking for anything else. Mind you, if you're keeping a tally of regulars, you can make that five. D'you hear about the body floating in the river this arvo?"

"Some homeless guy, wasn't it?"

"Not any old homeless guy, that was Dan, Dan the Outdoorsman."

"No shit!"

"His demise'll certainly reduce the calls to the Botanical Gardens for an unconscious male in the middle of the night. It's a crying shame we've lost three outstanding pillars of the community in Marcus, Ivy and Dan. I hope they rest in peace. At least we can now!"

"You're all heart, Gerry."

"Anyway, good to see you, Jono. We'd better clear, we've been here ages."

"No change there then."

Soon, I was left alone with Max as she worked away on the Toughbook. Unfortunately, she didn't type as fast as she talked. I closed my eyes for what I thought was a few seconds only to open them to see Dr Cansfield-Clarke standing in front of me.

"Were you the one who brought in Samantha Macfarlane?"

My defences were up. "Yes, how can I help?"

"Why on earth did you issue her with an EEO? I'm sure you're well aware this woman habitually claims to have taken overdoses, but in the last…" He looked at the large file he was carrying, "… eighty-seven admissions, her blood tests have never shown anything other than normal levels."

"Yes, but you still ran a tox screen each time, didn't you, just in case?"

"And I'll do that again, but because of you, she'll be here for six hours."

I tried to keep my voice calm, though I could feel my blood pressure rising. "She'd been self-harming and claimed to have taken an overdose. I assessed her as posing an imminent risk to her own health, which is enough justification for an EEO."

I watched as an artery throbbed on his left temple. "Oh

please! Use some discretion when treating time-wasters like her. You're an Intensive Care Paramedic for God's sake! Assess your patient appropriately and only issue EEOs when they're absolutely necessary!"

He spun round and stormed off and I turned to Max who was now looking like a poster child for PTSD.

"Best pass me that Toughbook, Max. The paperwork for this one'll still have to stand up after it's been poked more times than a geriatric hooker."

17

GROSS

Everything had been prepped for the morning's slice and dice session in the main mortuary room of the John Tong Centre. The rows of stainless-steel instruments gleamed in the fluorescent strip lights and all the players were gloved and gowned awaiting the virtuoso.

Dave, the mortuary technician, was the first to break the listless silence. "So here we are again. Seems like only yesterday we were all gathered around another unfortunate corpse."

Detective Giallo was sitting on a bench sipping a takeaway cup of coffee. "I may be half asleep, but I'm sure it was about two weeks ago."

"Wow, doesn't time fly by when you're having fun."

"You really are weird, Dave. So, is my favourite pathologist on today?"

"If you mean Dr Beecham, yes Hil's on."

"Do you know what mood's she in?"

"The usual. But at least she wasn't on call last night, so she shouldn't be too frosty." He let out a snort from his oversized nose. "When she's on form, the centre saves a fortune on refrigeration."

Giallo took a sip of coffee. "I don't doubt that. Mind you, I reckon I could thaw that heart of hers."

Dave grinned. "Oh Christ. Don't tell me you've seen that smile of hers. I'm sure it's not her heart you're interested in warming up."

"Thanks for that. Anyway, I'm still waiting to hear the outcome of the lab reports from Rosie Brennan. Is it worth broaching the subject?"

"Give it a go, we can all watch with amusement if she rips you a new one."

"Your concern is underwhelming."

The morgue fell back into silence. Centre stage was Ivy's naked form, laid out on a steel autopsy table with a clear plastic endotracheal tube left protruding from her mouth. A large-bore cannula was still inserted in her right forearm. Her untimely demise was about thirty-six hours ago, which was the longest she'd been without a cigarette since her teenage years.

As her death had been pronounced in hospital, there were no signs of decomposition. Her body had been chilled at the first opportunity and so now she appeared to be sleeping in the buff, albeit rather pale and lying on a metal table.

Harry Meyham had taken all the external shots he needed and was jotting down notes after checking his camera equipment. "Hey Gee, I hear you're responsible for the next autopsy. Are they short of detectives on the Northside?"

Giallo smiled. "Just the luck of the draw. I was down to investigate this one when they found the floater yesterday. In the wrong place at the wrong time. Story of my life."

"I've heard he's in a mess after the bullies took a few bites."

"Yep. Some bits are missing, but we could still ID him. He's a derro that used to hang out around the City Botanical Gardens."

He paused for more coffee. "I have to admit, we were lucky. One of the beat cops who helped recover the body recognised him. We've even got CCTV footage of him staggering along William Street late Wednesday night. It's looking like a slam-dunk. I had the river police take samples of what looked like blood on a concrete supports of the Goodwill Bridge. Turns out it was blood, so if it matches his DNA, we've got a time, location and probable cause."

"Not bad for a day's work."

"What d'you expect when you're dealing with the best of the best."

Harry looked up over his glasses with raised eyebrows and then went back to his paperwork. "So, what's the story with this old dear then?"

"Silly chook thought she'd try taking Viagra."

"No way. Wait… and that killed her?"

"Yep. Apparently, the little blue pills interacted with one of her meds. Caused her to arrest."

"Holy crap! Bet they don't advertise that side effect."

"Actually they do, or at least it's mentioned in the drug info sheet, but Ivy here couldn't read all that well. Hey, Harry, you seem a bit worried about the dangers of Viagra. Anything we should know?"

"What? Oh… No, nothing to worry about there mate. There's still enough lead left in my pencil."

"Just can't get your missus interested in sketching anymore?"

There was laughter from everyone in the room who had a pulse. Harry shook his head. "Hilarious, Gee. Sounds like your coffee's kicking in. But as you brought up my other half, why the hell would a woman in her fifties be taking Viagra?"

Giallo took another sip of his drink. "That, my friend, is why I'm here. I've got to work out whether someone was to blame, or if it was just death by misadventure. I'm tending towards the latter, as by all accounts she was one or two stubbies short of a six pack, but you never know. By far the biggest issue is that she died in care."

"What, the hospital wasn't able to revive her?"

"Not quite. She arrested in the back of an ambulance, so it could get messy. One saving grace is the lack of any living relatives. Well, any that give a shit about her. But that might change if they get wind of a potential litigation payout."

"Christ. So everyone's covering their arses."

"With big iron-clad chastity knickers."

Just at that point the pathologist swept into the room carrying a folder of documents. She gave Giallo a glare. "I hope that comment wasn't directed towards me, Detective Giallo?"

Gee winced. "Certainly not, Dr Beecham. We were discussing the best policy for dealing with teenage daughters."

She continued to stare at him like a Taipan considering whether to strike a bandicoot. "Really? I hadn't taken you as a family man."

"You have me there, Doc. My comment was pure conjecture. I've so far avoided the complexities of married life, but I'm sure you don't want to waste your time discussing my failings."

"Now there's the understatement of the year." She turned her attention to Dave. "I presume everything's ready?"

"We're all good to go."

And without further ado, the dismemberment of Ivy began.

Two and a half hours later, Dr Beecham was once again sitting at her venerable computer typing notes, when Giallo appeared at the doorway.

She looked up. "What's with you this month, Detective Giallo? Are you trying to fill up my morgue for any reason? I'm sure you're well aware that I'm not someone you should vex lightly."

"It's nothing to do with me, Doc. I think I'm on the flotsam and jetsam watch. All the low acuity stuff seems to wash up on my desk, quite literally with Mr Wheatley. I must have annoyed the brass."

Dr Beecham raised her eyebrows. "You don't say."

"I know. Hard to believe, isn't it, such a personable bloke like myself."

"Mmm…"

"Anyway, what's the chances I could get your first impressions on dear old Ivy?"

Her shoulders sagged and she stared at him for a few seconds before sighing. "In my opinion, Ms Watson died of a cardiac arrest, which from the paramedic's paperwork, was almost certainly brought on by the administration of glycerine trinitrate to a patient taking sildenafil."

As she spoke, she rested her elbows on the table and touched the tips of her long slender fingers together. "The two drugs have a synergistic effect, dramatically lowering a patient's blood pressure. That, combined with the damage decades of smoking had wrought on her cardiovascular system, meant she was ill-equipped to recover from such a catastrophic event. And I haven't even mentioned the advanced state of her lung disease." She paused and tilted her head. "Food for thought, Detective Giallo?"

He looked up from his notebook and smiled. "I'll take that under advisement."

"Anyway, it's not surprising that despite the sustained efforts of the medical staff, their attempts to revive her were futile. As to the amount of sildenafil in her system, I don't think I need to remind you about the wait for lab reports."

"On that note, has anything come back from the Rosie Brennan case?"

She reached over to a file on top of her in tray. "You're in luck. The findings arrived yesterday, but so far I haven't had a chance to give them more than a cursory look. The only thing of note was the level of opiates in her blood was high, even for an addict like Ms Brennan. But, as I'm sure you're aware, unusually pure batches of heroin sometimes do the rounds and catch out unsuspecting users."

"Yes, there were another couple of deaths recorded around that time, but I wasn't the investigating officer. I guess there's no quality control on illegal drugs. Junkies just don't know what purity they're buying and most of them don't care." He paused to make a note. "Any idea when you'll be ready to start the next case?"

She looked at her watch. "Give me half an hour, let's say eleven o'clock. Plenty of time for you to have a smoke."

Giallo smiled. "I've been cutting back. I was hoping you'd notice my smell's not so bad."

The newly stitched Y-shaped incision that ran the length of Ivy's torso disappeared from view as Dave slid her body inside one of the morgue's horizontal cold chambers. The interest in her remains ended with a faint click and Dave was already looking along the row of doors for the next customer. He closed an eye, rubbed his diminutive chin, then grabbed a handle and pulled. The chamber opened to reveal a crumpled black plastic body bag. "Bingo!"

Detective Giallo was leaning against the opposite wall and shook his head at Dave's behaviour. It was already 11:25 AM with no sign of Dr Beecham. Why was it that doctors always thought their time was more important than anyone else's?

Harry helped Dave transfer the bag over to a table and then retrieved his camera.

Dave paused as he reached for the zip. "Y'all ready for this?"

Giallo shrugged. "I was there when they fished him out. Can't imagine he's got much worse."

"Yes, but the smell's had time to build inside this plastic."

With that Dave pulled down the zip in a single flourishing move to reveal the naked mutilated form of Daniel Wheatley. In doing so, he unleashed the stench like an angry Kraken, thrashing pungent tentacles in all directions to seize the senses of those present. However, the real abomination was the sight of the body itself. His arms were raised, as if fending someone off, but both hands were missing. The right one severed at the wrist, while the left arm was amputated midway up the forearm. The crushed ends of the ulna and radius protruding through the mangled pale flesh. A huge semi-circle of muscle had been excised from his right thigh, the jagged serrated pattern along the edges testament to the razor-sharp teeth that had torn into his leg.

And then there was his face.

A bed of long damp straggly hair framed his head, which lolled at a bizarre angle, his neck broken. All vestiges of colour had drained from his skin, which was bloated and wrinkled from its time in the water. His lips and eyelids were swollen tight shut as if left in a grimace from the moment he lost his nose. But the hole in the centre of his face was nothing compared to the rent in the side of his skull. Here the ripped tissues and shattered bone afforded a clear view of Daniel's pulverised brain.

"Someone's gonna have their work cut out if his rellies want an open casket."

Giallo was wrinkling his face at the smell. "There's not much fear of that. I'm sure he's destined for the cheapest crem."

Harry took photos and lent in to take a close-up. "I wonder how he lost his nose."

"Perhaps he was picking it when the shark bit his hand off."

Harry stifled a laugh. "I thought Dave was the sick one, Gee."

"I'm sure you'll tell me if I ever offend you, eh Dave. By the way, why did you put him back in the bag after removing his clothes?"

Dave shrugged. "Oh… yes, well, he had a few, er… passengers. His hair was full of lice and I didn't want them escaping."

"You mean to say they were still alive?"

"Yep. They can survive a couple of days under water, so that may help with your timeline."

"Why didn't the freezer kill them?"

"We only freeze the bodies with no ID. As you'd determined his name and his autopsy was imminent, he just went into cold storage at 4°C. You know, like a nice Chardonnay."

"Only you could come up with an analogy like that." Giallo thought for a moment. "Were there any fleas?"

"Probably, but I didn't see any. They can only hold their breath for about a day, though."

Harry was finishing the external photo record when Dr Beecham burst in. "Right, if everything's ready, let's get started."

Giallo made a show of looking at his watch, but said nothing.

As per usual, the pathologist began with a verbal description of Mr Wheatley, but after a few minutes, Giallo interrupted her flow. "Did anyone see that?"

Dr Beecham frowned at him. "See what?"

"His right eye just moved."

"Detective Giallo, I think you must be mis…"

"Look! It did it again!"

This time they were all watching when his right eyelids jiggled as if he was in REM sleep.

"What the…"

Dr Beecham grabbed a pair of forceps from the tray. "Get the camera ready." She then leant forward and prised apart his eyelids.

As the opening enlarged, a small snake-like fish slithered out from the socket and disappeared into the torn hole of his nasal cavity. Harry let off a series of flashes, capturing the moment for posterity.

"Ah fuck, that was gross."

"Detective Giallo! Do I need to remind you that our voices are being recorded."

He collected himself. "I apologise, Dr Beecham. Let the record state that the sight of a fish exiting the corpse's eye socket and entering his nose physically and mentally repulsed me. However, I think my initial comment was more succinct."

She stared at him before turning to Dave. "Can you get a specimen jar ready?"

Then, using the forceps, she clamped the tail of the fish and retrieved it from its hiding place, dropping the squirming animal into the pot that Dave held forward.

Dave held it up to his eyeline. "Mind if I keep it as a pet?"

"Yes I do mind! Fix it, bag it and get back here!"

"Yessir... Er, ma'am."

Later, in the pathologist's office, Giallo came straight to the point. "So, in your opinion, which I realise is preliminary and without the aid of any lab reports, did he drown, or was he dead when he hit the water?"

Dr Beecham closed her eyes and when they opened, she seemed to be seeking divine intervention from some ingredient of her tuna salad. She settled for stabbing her fork into a cherry tomato before answering. "There are no autopsy findings pathognomonic for drowning."

Giallo looked blank.

"I mean to say, that some pathological changes are characteristic of drowning, but the diagnosis is one of exclusion."

Giallo still looked blank, but she continued. "This time of year, the temperature of the Brisbane River is about 20°C. That means if a person drowned, it would take somewhere between three to seven days for the body to float back up to the surface, before it could then wash up. Mr Wheatley was found within 24 hours of his last sighting.

"As you know, white foam was absent from his lungs, they were not oedematous or waterlogged and I found no water in his stomach. That means he either drowned with a closed glottis, which sometimes happens, or he wasn't breathing, nor struggling to breathe, when he entered the river."

She waved her fork around as she spoke, its movement

accentuated by the bright red cherry tomato. "Now if he fell in head first and was unconscious or dead, the air would be trapped in his lungs and would cause his body to float.

"Regarding his cranial insult, postmortem head injuries are common in bodies found in water, as corpses almost always lie with the head hanging down. It's therefore the most likely body area to come in contact with the river bottom. However, in this case, Mr Wheatley didn't have time to sink and refloat, so the injury must have happened prior to, or during his entry into the water. It's also not consistent with any damage caused by a boat."

She seemed about to eat the tomato, but then continued. "Now all of this information coupled with your last sighting, along with blood found low down on a bridge, leads me to postulate that Mr Wheatley fell from the bridge, striking his head on the concrete pillar on the way down. The resulting impact caused massive blunt force trauma to his cranium and fractured his neck in three places. The undoubted cause of death. If the blow didn't kill him, he would certainly be unconscious when entering the water and either way, unable to strive for a breath, or right himself. With air in his lungs, his body would have floated on or near the surface and washed ashore under the influence of the prevailing currents."

She ate the tomato. "None of that, however, can help you with the question you need to answer."

Giallo looked up. "Which is?"

"Did he fall or was he pushed? And unless you have a witness, or video footage of the event, that conundrum is likely to go unanswered."

"Thanks for that, Doc. You know, you could have just said he died due to the fall."

She smiled at him. "You asked for my opinion."

"Right."

Giallo got up to leave. "One last question. Do you think there's any relevance to the shark bites?"

She gave him a pitying look. "My dear Detective Giallo, the Brisbane River is teeming with bull sharks. The only thing that surprises me is that they left anything of Mr Wheatley for us to work with."

18

OYSTER

Amber's loose hair thrashed around in all directions as it was buffeted by the wind whipping over the bow and into the cockpit. Despite hanging on with both hands to the grab rail, she'd been laughing from the pure exhilaration since leaving Sandgate. The sea in the bay was a little choppy for the crossing to Moreton Island and once again, I negotiated our way up another rolling wave. At the crest, I launched the boat into the air, the engine whining its objection, before we crashed down in a cloud of spray. Then the prop dug in hurling us forward.

It was difficult to be heard over the combined howl of the motor and the wind. "Had enough yet?"

She threw her head back and laughed. "Not a chance! More, more! Go faster!"

"Some women are never satisfied."

I opened the throttle further as we flew up the next wave. Eventually, the lee of the island placated the sea's petulance and once in its shelter I turned north towards Tangalooma. I stayed on the plane, with only the prop in the water, until we were in sight of the resort and then eased back on the revs letting the hull relax into the sea.

"Now that's what I call fun! Can we do it again?" Amber's eyes were wide with glee and she looked like a child on Christmas morning. But the skimpy black bikini she was wearing bore stunning testament to the fact she was all woman.

"Well, we have to get back at some point, but seeing as we're here I'll let you in on the itinerary. First, I thought we'd do a bit of snorkelling on the wrecks, followed by a picnic on the beach. After that I hoped to collect some new critters for my tank from the seagrass beds, before heading home."

"Guess I'll have to wait for the return journey. Sounds like you've got the day all planned out."

"You'd be disappointed if I hadn't."

"True."

She pulled herself up on the top edge of the windshield and craned her slender neck to take in the view through her oversized sunnies. Low, undulating tree-covered hills sloped down to the golden beach, which disappeared off into the distance until it became a fine yellow line that seemed to underscore the island's beauty. Two-toned turquoise waters lapped the shore, the wide darker margin caused by the thick carpet of fringing seagrass. Some areas of the land appeared to have rips in the verdant cloak and the resultant sloping landslides revealed Moreton was nothing more than a huge sand dune. It was an island paradise just over an hour from Brisbane's bustling city centre.

"Wow. This place is amazing. I can't believe I've never been here before. Born and bred in Brissie, but a virgin to Moreton. Wish I could've taken you up on your last invite. It's so beautiful."

I bit my tongue and stopped myself before I made some

wise-arse comment about her virginity. I was determined nothing would spoil today, especially me. "It's my little retreat when the city wears me down. Takes me back to my childhood on Maggie Island."

She smiled. "My family holidays were always camping trips to Carnarvon Gorge. I think it was my Dad's attempt to get back to nature. No towns, no mobile phones and hardly any people. I'd often go for walks on my own and not see another soul for the day. Just trees and wildlife. A crazy white girl, alone laughing with the Kookaburras. It was bliss. Hey, are those the wrecks you mentioned up ahead?"

"Yep."

A few hundred metres along the beach, the orange-rusted carcasses of several ships jutted out of the water, foaming white around their bases. She took in the sight as we approached. "How'd they all sink in the one spot? Is there a reef here or something?"

"You haven't heard of the Mermaid of Moreton? The beautiful temptress who lured mariners to their doom by her enchanting soulful songs?"

She looked at me over the top of her sunnies. "You're full of shit."

"OK, so they were old barges that were sunk to form a safe harbour, but that's far too boring a story."

"You should work on that Mermaid of Moreton tale, it has a certain ring to it. I'm sure that's how legends start. Anyway, we're not likely to meet any sharks around here, are we?"

I was glad I was wearing my sunnies to hide my lying eyes. "Ha, sharks. As if! Why do you ask?"

"Oh, well, ever since 'Jaws' I've always been wary of swimming in the sea."

I gave her my most reassuring smile. "Don't worry. There's

nothing to be afraid of over here. What's more, I'll be right with you the whole time."

"Aar, my personal knight in shining armour."

As it was a Monday, there were only a couple of boats near the wrecks and the beach was deserted. After positioning the boat, I clicked the throttle into neutral and climbed onto the bow to drop the anchor. Once set, I returned to the cockpit and cut the ignition. A glorious calm greeted us, broken only by the lapping of the water and the distant cry of a whistling kite. I sat back in my chair, taking a moment to drink in the peaceful setting and my sunnies afforded a surreptitious sideways look at Amber. Her beautiful tanned body was draped over the seat, with her bikini leaving little to the imagination. I felt a stirring in my anatomy and took remedial action.

"Right, time to get wet. Man overboard!"

I threw my sunnies and cap on the dash and jumped over the side, creating a huge splash that dampened my ardour. As I surfaced, Amber was leaning over the side. "You're crazy!"

"It's a prerequisite of my job."

I pulled up on the gunwale and gave her a long kiss, before dropping back into the water. I then duck-dived under the boat and came up on the other side, to be greeted by a wonderful view of Amber's bottom as she bent over to search for me.

"Wow, now there's a sight to behold."

"Wha'?"

She spun round, picked up my hat and threw it at me, laughing. I launched myself up and caught the missile, before crashing back with a splash. "Gotta be faster than that."

Back on board, I stood dripping water onto the deck. Amber shook her head. "Look at you, you're all wet."

"That was the general idea. I was going to snorkel in this stuff, anyway. Are you ready for a swim?"

"Ready as I'll ever be."

"I'll get the gear out."

I retrieved the bag from under the helm and pulled out the masks and fins. "You might want to wear a T-shirt, it's easy to get sunburnt while snorkelling."

I thought it best not to mention it would protect against marine stingers. She was looking anxious enough as it was, so I attempted to distract her thoughts while she donned her gear. "Hey, did I tell you that tomorrow I've got to give a statement to the cops about Ivy? Do you think I should mention our theory that there's someone bumping off regulars?"

"Our theory? I thought you had it down as a new government policy."

"Yes, but now the tally is five."

"Five? I thought Ivy made four."

"Didn't I tell you about Dan the Outdoorsman? He was the body they fished out of the Brisbane River."

"Really? Well perhaps you need to wait until it's six or seven before alerting the authorities." She shook her head and laughed. "What am I saying, they're regulars. At least double figures!"

"Sounds like your MC-squared has been influencing you. I had a run-in with him for EEOing Psycho Sammy. You were right, he's a total prick."

"He creeps me out."

"More than snorkelling?"

"We'll see. But I'd rather be here than at work, any day."

"OK. Let's do it. Hold on to your mask."

We were now sitting on the gunwale and I reached out and gave her hand a squeeze. I nodded and we both rolled backwards into the sea. I felt my back hit the surface and a myriad of bubbles fizzed around my view. Once I resurfaced, all I could hear was Amber letting out a squeal. "Are you OK?"

"Look at all the fish! There's hundreds of them!"

I breathed a sigh of relief. At least her fear of sharks appeared to be water soluble. "That school there's mainly Sergeant Majors. They're just the welcoming committee. Come on, I'll take you for a tour."

I held her hand and guided her around the wrecks, pointing out the marine life and naming the things I knew. At one point, a large mottled-brown fish swam from under some ironwork, the slow sinuous movement of its body graceful and elegant in its relaxed simplicity.

"Look, down there."

"Oh wow!"

Amber dived down to get closer and we followed it across the sand to the next wreck, where its elaborate camouflage allowed it to blend in to its new hiding place. Back on the surface, Amber spat out her snorkel. "Oh my God! That was amazing! What was it?"

"It's a Wobbegong. See, not all sharks are scary."

"Sharks?"

"Yep, you just swam alongside a two metre carpet shark. They're pretty docile, so there was nothing to worry about. Are you good to carry on?"

"You bet, this is great!"

We took our time circling round the remaining wrecks and made our way back to the boat. On the return, I'd been keeping my eye out for something on the bottom. Spotting one, I called out to Amber. "Hey Babe, wait here a sec, I've got to get you a present."

As I duck-dived down, I retrieved an item from my pocket and pushed it into the gap between the two shells of an oyster. The animal snapped shut and I took out my knife and cut the bivalve from the rock.

At the surface, I handed it to her. "It's an oyster. I thought you might like to look for a pearl."

"Yeah, right. What're the chances of that?"

"You never know your luck."

Swimming back to the boat, I jumped on board and helped Amber in. "Come on, let's see if you're lucky."

She sat on the side and placed the shell on the stern bench. "So how do we open it?"

I used my knife to cut the adductor muscle holding the two halves together. Then, using the tip, I flipped the top half away revealing a glistening diamond engagement ring. Amber stared open-mouthed.

I picked up the oyster and with my heart thumping, bent down on one knee, lifting the ring on its marine platter. "I know this may seem crazy, seeing as we've not been going out for long, but Amber Shaw, will you do me the honour of marrying me?"

Amber appeared transfixed, as if my opening of the oyster had frozen her in time. Even the water lapping on the boat stopped. My mind raced and panic built. Had I just screwed things up?

She moved her hand up to cover her mouth, but remained silent, staring at the ring. An eternity seemed to pass. "Are you going to say anything?"

She looked confused and turned both her palms up. "How did you get the ring in the oyster?"

"I meant about my proposal."

"Oh that." A wide smile spread across her face and her eyes twinkled. "Yes, yes, of course I will!"

She launched herself from the side, nearly bowling me over with her embrace and before we kissed, I managed to say, "Thank Christ for that. It'd be an awkward picnic if you said no."

19

HELIUM

Wally sat in front of his TV without really watching it. He'd been flicking the channels, but at 8:10 PM, there was a distinct lack of semi-naked women to watch. The subtitled movies on SBS hadn't even started. He thought about surfing for some porn on his computer, but decided that could wait until later.

He had the TV's volume turned up, partly due to his developing deafness, but mainly to annoy his neighbours. Mind you, they were unlikely to be in. The warden was throwing a bingo night and most of the residents were out for the evening. He could do with the company, but even he had to draw the line somewhere. Spending time with a bunch of old wrinklies who smelt of piss, playing a crappy game for some crappy prizes just didn't do it for him.

There was a light knock behind him.

He turned to look at the closed door. Strange. It could be the warden coming to drag out the stragglers. He waited to see if he was hearing things, but the knock came again. With a sigh, he pushed himself out of his threadbare armchair. "Yes, who is it?"

There was a muffled voice and he could pick up only a word or two. But Wally had so few visitors, even the warden would be a welcome guest. He shrugged and opened the door.

A well-dressed man stood in the darkened doorway. For some reason the outside lights were all on the blink and the only illumination seeped out from around Wally's silhouette. The man was carrying a large leather briefcase in his left hand, while his right held forward an identity card, attached to a lanyard embossed with the words 'Queensland Health'.

Wally looked at the man's face. "No need for the ID, I recognise you. What do you want?"

The man spoke in a pleasant, quiet voice. "Well, I've been asked to make a few house calls to select patients and you're a special case, Wally. Is it all right if I call you Wally?"

"You just did, didn't you?"

"Do you mind if I come in? I'd like to chat about your frequent emergency admissions."

"I'm not a well man, I have…"

"I know, Wally, you have many serious medical conditions and I want to discuss them with you and make arrangements whereby you can receive the most appropriate help."

Talking about his ailments was Wally's favourite pastime, other than watching pornography. He smiled and stepped to the side, holding open the door. "Be my guest, come on in."

The man walked into the small living room and Wally picked up the remote to silence the TV.

"Oh, no need to switch it off, we can sit at the kitchen table, if that's OK. I promise I won't take much of your time."

Wally shrugged. "Suit yourself."

As they entered the kitchen, the man made a beeline for the kettle. "Would you like a brew? You have tea, white with lots of sugar, if I remember rightly."

Before Wally could object, the visitor was busying himself

boiling water and getting two mugs out of the cupboard. Once again, he shrugged and sat down at the table. "Don't mind if I do."

"So, Wally. It's been noted that you're coming to the local emergency departments on an almost daily basis. I know we have records of what you've been admitted for, but I was wondering if you could tell me which of your illnesses are troubling you the most."

For Wally, this was like a shaft of light descending from the heavens. A medical professional in his own home, willing to listen to his needs with no other distractions: pure gold.

He groomed his moustache with one hand and began to detail his regular bouts of chest pain, followed by the issues with his digestive system, urinary system, backache, rheumatism, deafness, dermatitis… the list went on. Wally had long since finished his tea, while the man sipped at his, sitting opposite and nodding as he jotted down notes.

Far from paying attention to Wally's ramblings, the man was whiling away the time, contemplating the pharmacology of the sleeping pill, nitrazepam. How benzodiazepines enhanced the action of the GABA neurotransmitter within the central nervous system, causing their trademark sedative and hypnotic effects.

Suddenly, Wally realised how exhausted he had become. Fatigue engulfed his body like a white blood cell surrounding a microbe. He was even slurring his words.

"I… I'm sorry. I'm gonna haff to ask you to leave. I need to go to sleep now. Wha' wash your name again?"

"Don't you remember? You're tired. Come on Wally, I'll help you to bed."

Wally had the vaguest feeling of unease, but was too exhausted to construct a tangible thought process. He accepted the offer of assistance and allowed the man to guide him to his bedroom.

Once there, he lay on his bed and let the darkness surround him like a shroud.

After a few moments, the man checked Wally's reflexes. Once happy with the level of sedation, he retrieved a large plastic bag from his briefcase along with a length of tubing and a small cylinder.

He placed the bag over Wally's head and flushed the air out using a steady flow of gas from the helium bottle. Within minutes, Wally asphyxiated in his sleep. He checked for a pulse and used a stethoscope to listen for heart and lung sounds.

Wally was dead.

Next the man set about creating his forensic camouflage. Finding Wally's box of prescribed sleeping pills in the bathroom cabinet he used his victim's lifeless fingers to push out all the remaining tablets, dropping them in the briefcase. He then left the empty strip and box on the table next to the mug Wally had drunk from.

He washed and put away the other mug and retrieved the second tea bag from the bin. The plastic film painted on his fingertips meant he was sure he had left no prints.

Returning to the bedroom, he once again picked up Wally's hands and used them to touch all the equipment that made up the aptly named 'exit bag'.

Finally, he turned his focus to Wally's computer, sitting on a desk in the bedroom's corner. He tapped the mouse and the screen jumped into life without the need for a password. He smiled, sat down and typed out a brief suicide note.

As he was writing the last line he heard the drumming of rain on the tiled roof of Wally's home and looked up. "Right on time."

He had a final look around the apartment and reached into his bag, pulling out a compact black umbrella. Opening the door slightly, he checked the coast was clear then disappeared into the night.

20

COINCIDENCE

Amber and I spent a wonderful time on Moreton and the next day we chilled around her house near Samford. She lived in an old high-set wooden Queenslander on acreage, nestled amongst the gumtrees at the edge of the forest. A fortunate hand-me-down from her grandmother's will. One advantage of being an only child of an only child. It was a tranquil place, when you got used to the cicadas, and it was Amber's sanctuary from the stresses of the city. All the trees may have reminded her of those childhood camping trips, but it was too far from the sea for my liking.

It also meant I had an hour's cycle to work, so when I arrived I was grateful for the soothing massage of the water and found it difficult to drag myself out of the shower. But although my muscles were complaining, it was a satisfying ache and I was in a good mood to start the day.

The sight of five ambos strewn about the crew room greeted me. The night shift were curled up on the La-Z-Boys, two others were having some sort of breakfast and Scotty was at the computer.

"Morning all, ready to save a life? Ready to pluck some poor soul from the jaws of death?"

A croaky voice replied from under a hospital issue white blanket. "Ready to go home after dealing with wankers all night. Why are you in such a chirpy mood? Your usual whinging is at least quieter."

"Just cycled twenty K's and full of the joys of summer."

A grumble came from the other La-Z-Boy. "Probably got laid while we were out ferrying tossers."

"You're all so cynical."

I turned to the computer desk. "Am I with you again, Scotty?"

"Yes, boss. Vehicle's all checked, just need your kit."

"On it."

I caught myself humming a tune as I signed out my drugs and smiled as I thought of the reason: Amber. I would have to tell Scotty my news, but I wasn't ready for a general announcement. The rumour mill would see to that.

When I returned to the crew room, I discovered that Boardie had arrived early and was spoiling for a fight.

"Ah, Jon, is that your pushbike in the plant room?"

I wandered over to the cupboards to make a drink. "Seeing as I'm the only one here who cycles to work, I reckon you're onto something there."

"Right. Well, it's too close to the fire hose reel. You have to move it."

I jiggled a tea bag in the hot water from the urn. "Do you really think if the place is burning down anyone would find it difficult to move a pushbike, especially a bunch of firies?"

"That's not the point. It's a Workplace Health and Safety violation and it represents a hazard."

"You wouldn't know the exact distance it needs to be from the fire hose?"

"Just lean it up against the other wall in future. Oh and Jon, have you done your vehicle checklist? I never seem to find any with your name on them. You shouldn't need to be reminded it's B-CAS policy to submit a form for each and every one of your shifts?"

I was determined that Boardie's petty bureaucracy wouldn't sour my mood. As he had picked the time and location for his latest dig, it was only fair I put on a show for the assembled audience.

"I tell you what, Boardie, you tell me what you do with the forms and I'll fill one out for you."

"What?"

"Tell me what happens to the forms and I'll complete one."

He looked flustered. His ears flushed as the background chatter died down. "What I do with the forms is not the point, you need to fill one out."

"Just so we're clear, I'm not refusing to do one. I just want you to say what you do with them."

"I shred them, but that's irrelevant. You have to complete one. It's policy."

"Well, for the record, I haven't been breaking policy, I've been cutting out the middleman: when I found nothing wrong with the ambulance I shredded my own form. However, as you've now explained to everyone what happens to them, I'll get one filled out." I called down the corridor. "Scotty?"

"Yep?"

"Can you do one of those vehicle forms for us?"

"No worries. Already done, boss."

"Anything wrong with the car?"

"No boss."

I turned back to Boardie. "Do you want me to shred it, or should I leave it for you to do?"

He glared at me. "You have a serious attitude problem."

He waited for a response, but I returned his stare and took a sip from my tea.

I guess he decided to cut his losses, as he shook his head and walked off, closing his door with a louder than usual click.

Scotty grinned at me. "You shouldn't keep winding him up like that. You know he'll screw you over in the end."

"All part of the fun and anyway, he's fortunate I was in a good mood."

By some miracle, our pagers remained silent when we logged on, so I took the opportunity to arrange a meeting with Detective Giallo to record my statement. As he was in, we jumped in the ambulance for the trip over to the Carseldine cop shop.

Leaving the station, we drove down Hamilton Road as I called up Comms. "967, out local. I have to make a statement to the police."

"Roger that Alpha 967."

I turned to Scotty. "Did the copper get you to do one?"

"Yep. Did mine yesterday. You know how you were going on about regulars dying, did you hear about Wally?"

"No. Don't tell me that old fraud's dead as well?"

"Yep."

"What, really? How?"

"Suicide."

"You're shitting me!"

"Fair dinkum. He took an overdose of his sleeping pills and asphyxiated himself using helium."

"Seems a bit high tech for Wally."

"I thought that, but Jan was called to it. She was giving us all the details yesterday at the station, so we Googled 'helium suicide'. Apparently, it's the new way to pop your clogs, there's even 'How to' manuals on the internet. There wasn't any doubt about the circumstances, he left a suicide note up on his computer screen."

"Hey, if it wasn't for the fact he's now the sixth regular to die in two weeks, I'd be breakin' out the bubbly. But am I the only one who's suspicious about the pattern?"

"OK, so you might've got me thinking, but, c'mon, the deaths can't be anything more than a coincidence. And, to be honest, I'm not that sure I care enough to worry about it, boss."

"Really?"

"Well, look... take that place for example." He pointed to a caravan park we were passing. Carseldine Meadows was infamous among both ambulance and police officers for its ability to spawn frequent low-quality call-outs. "There's you worrying about the death of six regulars when most ambos in Brisbane would happily drop a tactical nuke on that festering bunch of trailer trash."

I laughed. "You've got a point, but at least with all of them in the same place you know you're going to a crap job - unless it's an assault. I've been to some good stabbings there."

"Perhaps that's the answer. Lock the gates until one super loser remains. Sorta like a Mad Max Thunderdome with caravans and alcohol."

"Nice analogy, Scotty. You should run it by the Premier, see what he thinks."

I gave up on the subject, although Wally's suicide had got me spooked. Why would an attention-seeking hypochondriac pervert commit suicide in such a private and convoluted way? It didn't feel right. Mind you, neither did the increasing body count. Surely it wasn't all a coincidence?

We soon drew to a halt in the car park of the police station and I left Scotty phone-surfing in the cab, while I went to find

Detective Giallo. I was buzzed in at the door and shown through to his office space.

Giallo had his feet up on a desk and was drinking black coffee from a stained and chipped mug, while flipping through emails on his computer. The smell of tobacco hung around him like a force field.

"Good to see you're easing yourself into the morning. Had enough nicotine for the day?"

He smiled. "I remember when the haze of cigarette smoke in a police department was so bad you were hard pushed to see the next desk, but now we have to go outside for a durrie. Just means we're forced to binge smoke. Anyway, you ready to give this statement?"

"As I'll ever be."

I pulled over a nearby wheelie chair as he swung his legs under the desk and opened up a Word template on the screen. He entered my details and I recited my statement as Giallo typed away.

After about fifteen minutes, he printed out two copies and I signed one for each of us. "Right, that's about it. You can go back to watching morning TV from your recliner."

"As if. I'm not a firie you know."

Although I realised this was my cue to leave, I remained in the seat. Having just recalled the circumstances of Ivy's death only underscored my unease regarding Wally's demise. Perhaps this was the perfect opportunity to voice my concerns?

Giallo picked up on my indecision. He lent back in his chair and reached for his coffee. "C'mon, out with it. I'm all ears."

I sighed. "Off the record?"

"Can you see a notebook?"

"It's just a feeling I've got. I'm concerned about a pattern I've noticed." I shrugged. "Six of our local regular patients have died in the last couple of weeks. Ivy was one, but before her, there was BB, who was found dead in an alley; Shirley from anaphylaxis after a bee sting; Marcus was hit by a train; Dan fell from a bridge; and now Wally, who committed suicide with helium, of all things. It doesn't feel right to me."

Giallo looked at me over his coffee and I couldn't decipher his expression. However, I had to admit that listening to myself putting words to my thoughts sounded rather silly.

"So what you're trying to tell me is that six of your former patients have died in the last fortnight in circumstances that were not suspicious and the only link, other than yourself, is that they had often presented to the local emergency departments via ambulance."

"Well..."

"Presumably, they all had at least one or two physical or psychological medical problems?"

"Well... er... yes."

He rubbed his chin and I could hear a slight rasp from his layer of stubble. "So rather than some mastermind serial killer who can hide his tracks and commit murders in different ways so the deaths are easily explained, maybe your pattern is... a coincidence?"

I sat back feeling foolish. "Well, when you put it like that it does sound unlikely. I was just surprised by the number of them dying. Anyway, I thought detectives didn't believe in coincidences."

He gave me a quizzical look. "I think you'll find that's Harry Bosch. This is reality, Jon, not a fictional novel. I'm investigating at least two of those deaths and so far I've uncovered nothing that would convince the Chief to divert further resources my way. You ambos work on one job at a time, whereas us detectives have to multitask. You should see my pending workload."

"But why was Ivy on Viagra? She's never taken it before."

He sighed and sipped his coffee. "What's the chances you could get someone to dose themselves up on a drug so it interacts with another to cause them to arrest? Seems a long shot with so many variables."

"A doctor could do it."

"So now your serial killer is a doctor who's not only happy to defile his Hippocratic Oath, but will risk a life behind bars to help clear the time-wasters from the Emergency Department?"

I shook my head. "I guess it does sound... far-fetched."

"Do you know how many serial killers have been caught and convicted in Australian history?"

"No, but from your tone I'm guessing it's not many."

"Less than thirty in over two hundred years. Not bad for a nation based on a bunch of convicts."

I must have looked crestfallen, because he changed tack as he stood up. "Look, thanks for voicing your concerns, but until you have some evidence rather than an uneasy feeling, there's no way I can justify spending time on reviewing the cases."

He held out his hand and I shook it as I made a hasty retreat, mumbling a goodbye.

"You're quiet boss. What's up?"

We were on Gympie Road, crawling back to station through the rush-hour traffic and I was deep in thought, regretting having said anything to Detective Giallo. I'd been a fool. I made a mental note never to mention any suspicions I may have to a copper, until I had tangible proof to report. But six regulars dying seemed wrong. I guess cops didn't appreciate the "gut feel" concept unless it was from their own belly. On the other hand, my story did sound ridiculous.

"Hello, anyone in there?"

"Huh? Oh, sorry Scotty, just mulling over something the copper said."

"You didn't mention your tally of dead regulars, did you?"

"Is it that obvious?"

"Let me guess, he made you look like a dickhead?"

"Sometimes you're too perceptive for your own good."

"Hey, I agree it's weird, but they're all such varied deaths. As I said before, it can't be anything more than a coincidence."

"That's about what he said. Anyway, enough of that. I wanted to be the first to tell you I took your advice."

He looked across at me. "What? You've stopped wearing your Superman jocks?"

"No, you cockhead, about Amber."

"Shit. I gave you advice about her?"

"Yes, I think your actual words were 'seal the deal'. So I did. We're now engaged."

"Holy fuck! Well done mate! You've bagged a winner there, congratulations!"

He reached over to shake my hand and just missed sideswiping a truck in the next lane. "Eye's on the road Scotty! But thanks and thanks for the advice."

"Shit. If I'd known she'd say yes, I would've kept my mouth shut. Can't imagine what she sees in you. Have you got a big cock or something?"

"What? You don't think my dashing good looks and lightning wit are enough?"

He paused, then turned my way. "Nah! You'd still need to have a big cock."

The beeping of the pagers and MDT cut through our laughter. "Knew it was too good to last. What've we got, boss?"

"Looks like Magneto's lost his touch. It's a 2A in Lutwyche for a 30-year-old bloke with groin pain. Y'know, I get that when I don't wear my Superman jocks, perhaps this guy's got a big cock as well."

Our latest patient's pain was likely caused by a urinary tract infection, or an STD, something he could have driven to see his GP about. If he had a car and hadn't spent all his money on illicit drugs. Outside his apartment block the distant outline of the Royal was clearly visible, but I couldn't be bothered arguing. I directed him to the Captain's chair and he sat for the five minute journey, only to be triaged direct to the waiting room.

Scotty wandered out the door, while I did a quick circuit of the ED to see if Amber was around. At one point I spotted MC-squared and went in the opposite direction, the less contact I had with him the better. But as I walked away, a familiar voice called out from the cubicle on my left.

"Hey, are you lost, needle dick?"

Sammy cackled at her joke, but before I could respond, Amber appeared by my side.

"Oh, so you two know each other well, then? You never told me your relationship was that intimate, Jon."

I smiled at my new fiancée. "Very funny. It's Sammy's pet name for me as I'm now her favourite taxi driver. What're you in for today, Sammy? Self-harm, overdose, suicidal ideation?"

"Nah. Fuck all on TV."

"Well, at least you're being honest."

I turned to Amber. "I'll be in the write-up room if you're free."

"Got to check on Sammy first, but I'll be there in a bit."

She gave me a heart-melting smile, but Sammy ruined the

moment. "This your girlfriend, needle dick? Don't tell me you're two-timing me?"

I gave Amber a wink as I left. "Oh Sammy, you know our relationship wouldn't amount to much, after all, I could never satisfy you."

Sammy's laughter faded as I made my way to the write-up room, where I found Scotty talking to Ed and Jan. "Hey, what's up team? All we need now is Boardie and we can have one of his useless station meetings."

Jan leant forward and pointed a finger at me. "Don't get me started on that wanker. You won't believe the grilling he gave me over the water damage to 967. I thought he was going to stroke out. He's rostered me with you tomorrow night as punishment, so there'll be no more hosing of ambulances, d'you hear?"

I held up my hands in defence. "Hey, didn't I give you the 'plausible deniability' excuse?"

She shook her head. "I think that was my idea."

"Anyway, what's this about you winning the ambo lottery and getting to fill out a ROLE form for Wally?"

Her eyes lit up. "Recognised life extinct and danced a little jig in his bedroom. At least the sad old tosser was still wearing his trousers."

"What did his suicide note say?"

She looked surprised. "You know about that? Well, it mentioned something about the attitude of an ambo named Jon driving him to despair, but I can't remember much else."

"Great, he finally took my hints. No, seriously did it seem… genuine?"

"Genuine? I guess so, why wouldn't it be?"

Scotty pipped up. "Oh he reckons some serial killer's bopping off our regulars. Wally was the sixth one to die in the last two weeks."

Jan screwed up her face. "Sixth? Y'know, it was me who suggested a serial killer when the count was only two, but I was joking."

Ed laughed. "What's the interest in it, Jono? Did someone steal your idea, or did you want to join them in their quest?"

Jan shook her head. "No, he wants to track them down so he can give them a list of managers to target."

I put my hands on my hips. "Am I the only ambo with the slightest bit of moral fibre? Surely our regulars don't deserve to be murdered?"

The three of my colleagues paused in comical contemplation. Ed broke the silence. "Murder is too strong a word. You could use 'euthanasia'?"

"Perhaps 'justifiable homicide', boss?"

Jan wagged a finger. "Social self-defence?"

"Fuck it, I give up!"

An arm snaked around my waist. "What're you all laughing about?"

Before I could answer Scotty leapt forward. "C'mon, Amber, let's see the ring."

Jan looked surprised. "Ring, what ring?"

Amber held out her left hand to show off her sparkling new diamond.

"Shit, I bet that set you back a bit, boss."

"Ha, don't you believe anything he says. The cheap bastard found it in an oyster!"

21

SNAPPED

It was another glorious Queensland day and I eased myself into the morning, sitting on my deck, people-watching as I sipped on a cup of freshly brewed black coffee. Joggers passed by with their headphone cords swinging, some walked their dogs and others strolled along the esplanade, as the seagulls flocked and swirled like white confetti.

The guy with groin pain had set the tone for yesterday's shift and after saying goodbye to Amber, the jobs never rose above minor ailments or GP taxi runs. Even so, we ended up finishing two hours late and Amber decided to go back to her place after clocking off at the Royal. She had another shift today and with me working tonight, we'd have hardly seen each other. Having a partner that works rolling shifts screws with your social life, especially when it's both of you.

I debated whether to take my boat out for a spin, but didn't have the energy, so I pottered about the house, cooking up meals I could freeze and use for decent shift food. I attempted to get to sleep, but the day was pushing the mercury and I only dozed between bouts of profuse sweating. So, despite the relaxed start, I woke tired, grumpy, and regretted even trying to get my head down.

The cycle in didn't improve my mood, with a dickhead in a Commodore feeling it necessary to blast his horn for no reason, before cutting across me in a screeching left turn. I slammed on my brakes and hurled abuse his way, giving him the obligatory one finger wave, but his actions had sent my heart racing. I was still hyped when I walked into the station and needed to rant at anyone who'd listen.

"What is it with some drivers who think they own the road? Do they have a special licence that says I've spent more on my set of wheels so everyone else can get the fuck out of my way?"

Jan was standing in the hallway leaning against the notice board and had been talking to a couple of paramedics sitting in front of the computers. "Good evening to you too, Jon. What's sparked you off this time?"

I related the incident with the Commodore, but received little sympathy.

"What did you expect? You will insist on riding a pushbike. That poor driver probably got distracted by your hairy legs."

"Thanks Jan, I can always count on you for your support."

"I wouldn't think you need anyone's support with lycras like that."

Laughter erupted and I cut my losses, exiting to the changing room. "With wit that sharp, Jan, you can use your tongue to cannulate our patients tonight."

Our first job ended up taking us into the Royal, with predictable consequences. The last place any ambo wanted to be on a Saturday night is anywhere near the city centre. If they're not drunk, they're mad, and if it's not one of those, then it's both. As soon as we cleared from the hospital, Comms gave us a Code One in The Valley for an unconscious female at the NightSafe, a rest and recovery venue for night-time revellers.

"Great. A pisshead at the Chaplain's digs. I thought that place was established to avoid having to call an ambulance."

"You really are in a foul mood tonight. Shouldn't you be full of the joys of life and love now you're engaged? Oh, and when were you going to tell me about that?"

I looked across at Jan from the attendant's seat, the light from the oncoming cars was illuminating her face in brief pulses. But she kept her eyes locked on the road and I couldn't gauge her expression.

"Don't be too put out, Jan. You were only the second ambo to find out, I'd told Scotty less than an hour before. Anyway, what's it to you, are you shitty I'm off the market, or something?"

"Ha! In your dreams. Just thought you boys were keeping me out of the loop."

Although intrigued by her lack of eye contact, I dropped the subject as we were approaching the address. "Right. Game faces on, we've got a seriously ill patient to deal with."

Jan pulled into the China Town Mall and drove part way up, parking outside the entrance to the NightSafe. We jumped out and put on our gloves, grabbing the kit before walking in. To my surprise, the boss fella himself met us, Senior Chaplain Gary Bartholomew, who was already wearing his purple shirt ready for his night shift wandering the streets. He wore his black straight hair with a severe side parting and lines of concern etched his gaunt pale face.

"G'day Chappy, what you got for us?"

"Hi… Jon and… Jan isn't it?

I nodded in response. It never ceased to amaze me how he could remember our names. Even so, I glanced to check that, like me, Jan wasn't wearing her name badge.

"Thanks for coming, I'm a little worried about this teenager who came in about half an hour ago. She claimed her drink was spiked, though she just appeared drunk. Now we can't wake her. As you can see, we've put her in the recovery position."

He had led us over to one of the low camp beds where the figure of a plump girl in her late teens lay on her side, her upper arm hanging down off the bed. Her skin was pink and well perfused, and her chest undulated in a normal breathing pattern. I crouched down beside her and held her wrist, feeling a good radial pulse. It was at that point I caught sight of her face and doubted her drink had been spiked. When this unfortunate individual fell out of the ugly tree, she'd hit every branch on the way down, then bounced back up and took a few more passes through the foliage. She had a face like a dropped pie.

Just to check my suspicions, I slipped my hand down to the tip of her fingers and dug my nail into one of her nail beds, while staring at her closed lids. There was a telltale flicker at the corner of both eyes.

"Well, I don't think she's had her drink spiked, Chappy."

"Really? How can you tell?"

I shrugged. "Date-rape drugs don't come cheap and…"

I got a wide-eyed stare from Jan and decided not to go there.

"… I know, let me demonstrate."

I rolled her onto her back and picked up one of her hands, holding it high above her face. I then let go and we all watched her hand's trajectory divert enough so it landed just above her head.

The Chaplain's forehead crumpled in confusion. "So?"

"If she was unconscious, her hand would've hit her face. Do we know her name?"

"Yes, Mandy Sykes. Her ID says she's from Tingalpa."

I spoke in a loud voice, as I administered a sternal rub. "Hey, Mandy, wakey wakey, time to stop bothering these good people and come along with us."

She made more slight facial grimaces, but still feigned unconsciousness. I lent in close to her ear so she could hear my whisper. "Look, Mandy, we both know that you can hear me. I'll give you one more rub on your chest and I want you to wake up. Otherwise I'm going to drive you to Nambour hospital and you'll have to pay a fortune to get a taxi home from there."

I gave her a moment to contemplate her options then once again rubbed her sternum. Within seconds she groaned and opened her eyes. "Gerroff me!"

The Chappy's expressive face was the picture of surprise. "Wow. What did you say to her?"

"Just a few words of encouragement. They call me the dog whisperer."

Jan closed her eyes and shook her head, while the Chappy looked confused. "Er… are you going to take her up to the Royal?"

"Will do, she'll need blood tests to refute her drink-spiking claim, so I guess we'll be on our way. Come on Mandy, shift your butt, you know the deal."

Pushing up from her arms, she raised her torso off the bed, then swung her legs round, keeping her head bent to avoid any eye contact. "I feel sick."

"That's one of the downside of drinking too much."

I produced a plastic emesis bag and opened it with a rustling flourish. "Here's your very own party bag to keep as a souvenir of your ambulance experience. Please use it wisely as Jan hates it when I have to clean up vomit. Just out of interest, how much have you had to drink?"

"'Bout nine vodka Red Bulls."

"It's always the ninth drink that's spiked. Have you noticed that, Jan?"

She gave me another one of her looks and gathered up the kit.

"Right Mandy, let's get out of here."

I hooked my arm under her left armpit and marched her from the NightSafe, saying our farewells to the Chappy and his volunteers. Once in the ambulance, I guided her to the stretcher and she flopped on her side, clutching the vomit bag under her chin.

Jan had climbed in the driver's seat. "Good to go?"

"As I'll ever be. Le Royale with cheese, s'il vous plaît."

We delivered our pickled cargo to the RBH and were ramped behind three other crews. "Christ, I'll be glad when the government solves the bed-blocking issue. Wasn't that an election promise: no more hospital ramping from the start of 2013?"

An ambo from Northgate responded. "Can't see how they'll manage that in the next few weeks. It's been getting worse over the past year."

"Come on, it's easy. They'll just change the name to something like 'Access Block'. Then they can report there's no more ramping."

People nodded and I dumped my Toughbook on a nearby counter. The conversation died and most went back to the inevitable phone surfing, so I typed up the last job. I'd almost finished my paperwork when I turned to discover MC-squared was standing at the foot of our stretcher, reading through Mandy's triage notes.

He looked up from the paperwork. "Ah, it's you again. Well at least you're consistent with the calibre of patient you bring in. Ever thought of leaving any of them at home?"

He waited for a response, tapping the clipboard on his hand, but I somehow kept my cool and just locked eyes with him. Seconds passed and he let out a little snort, tossed the notes onto Mandy's legs and walked off. I could feel my blood pressure pounding in my ears and looked over to find Jan, arms crossed, smiling at me.

"Glad to see I can amuse you."

She leant forward as if examining my face. "Open your mouth, let me look."

"Why?"

"Thought you must've drawn blood, biting your tongue that hard."

I was not in the mood to be wound up any further and I had to rein in my temper. After all, it wasn't Jan who'd been twisting the knife. "Hilarious. Can you check out my sides while you're at it? I think they might've split from laughing."

She raised her eyebrows, but before she could respond, a nurse beckoned and we wheeled Mandy down to her waiting bed.

The rest of the night did little to help my mood. Comms seemed determined to work us like a two-bit whore. Clearing from a job led to an immediate dispatch, without the slightest hint of a break.

It had gone 3:00 AM and the tiredness was soaking

through my bones like water into a sponge. I was now in the driver's seat and we were trundling out along Moggill Road, heading towards Kenmore for someone who had woke with a headache. I was envious. At least waking with a headache meant you'd been sleeping.

The soporific combination of the streetlights and gentle twist of the road caused me to blink a few times and I had to shake my head to stay awake. I glanced across at Jan to find she had somehow dozed off with her face pressed against the cool glass of the side window. I had a fleeting idea to press the window's power button, but the sudden beeping of the MDT woke her from her slumber.

"Wha…?"

"C'mon sleeping beauty, time for action. Sounds like they're diverting us."

"Alpha 962?"

"Go ahead Comms."

"You're being diverted to backup a single officer, Alpha 725. They're responding primary to an unconscious 26-year-old female, query overdose. All units Code One."

I plugged in the address to the satnav, flipped on the lights and threw a U-turn. "Christ, the RRV must have been on top of the job. We're less than five minutes away."

Jan reached up for the gloves. "Great, that's all I need. Two ICPs on scene. One's enough of a pain in the arse."

"I feel as if I should defend myself, but I know what you mean. Two people calling the shots can get confusing."

"I was thinking more like two arseholes who act like they know everything, but we'll go with your take on it."

"You're all heart."

Our flashing lights reflected off street signs, windows and parked cars as we sped towards our destination in silence, both inside and outside the cab. As we turned into the road, I could see the rapid response vehicle up ahead, a few hundred metres on the right with hazards blinking. I pulled up behind and checked the number of the address. "Unit five of eighty-seven. Guess that'll be that lovely shithole of an apartment block in front of us."

"I think the phrase you're looking for is 'a renovator's delight'. Do we need anything?"

"We'd better. You know what ICPs are like with carrying stuff."

"Too true."

We took the response kit and the monitor and made our way to the unit. A brief look at the numbers on the ground floor flats confirmed Ambo's Law was in play.

"It's on the third floor. Why is the job always on the top floor?"

We trudged up six flights of stairs that had the faint aroma of stale urine mingled with burnt marijuana and walked through the open door of number five.

"Hello? Anyone home?"

A voice came from somewhere in the bowels of the flat. "Through here."

The beeping sound of a pulse oximeter guided our path, as we lugged our equipment through a seedy-looking kitchen. In the back bedroom, we were greeted by the sight of Liam Fraser placing ECG dots on a slumped obese woman lying on her bed. Brown stains marked her hands and brown vomit caked her shirt and doona, while the adjacent wall was decorated with similar splatter patterns.

"G'day Liam, what you doing away from your desk?"

He looked up as we entered and the contrast between his tanned skin and white teeth made his smile appear to gleam. "Hi Jon, you got here quick. I took the opportunity of some overtime tonight. Anyway, this woman's GCS 8. I've given her a good sternal rub and her best response was eyes opening to pain, incomprehensible sounds and she's only withdrawing from painful stimuli. So two, two and four makes eight."

He gave us a thorough handover and took a breath. "There's a bottle of diet pills on the desk there and it looks like she's been substituting the contents with those black crystals. It looks like an intentional overdose with whatever that is."

"Black crystals? Any ideas?"

"Not a clue, mate. Never seen the stuff before."

I looked over at the desk while Jan went to help Liam. The pill bottle was open and several capsules were scattered next to it, some pulled apart and empty. I tipped one out from the jar and separated the two halves, catching the contents in my gloved hand. Black crystals. They were familiar, but I couldn't quite place them. Then, as I turned back to the patient, I saw her brown stained hands and it clicked.

I spotted a glass of water next to her bed. "Hey, guys, I reckon I know what it is."

I walked over and tipped the crystals into the liquid. An instant vivid pink swirling cloud formed as each particle dissolved on impact with the liquid.

Jan looked up. "Impressive, Sherlock. What is it?"

"They're Condy's Crystals."

I got two blank faces. "Potassium permanganate. I've used it to sterilise my aquarium, bloody stuff stained my hands brown, like hers. I'm pretty sure it's a powerful oxidising agent. Nasty shit if you can work out a way of swallowing enough. Guess that's why she's put it in the capsules."

"So do either of you ICPs carry anything that'll fix her?"

"As far as I'm aware, nothing fixes it. Unless they find someway of replacing all her internal organs in the next day or two, she won't make it out of ICU."

Jan looked surprised. "So this discussion is all academic and the only thing we can do is get her to hospital?"

"Point taken, I'll go get the stairchair."

I grabbed our gear and returned to the ambulance, readying the stretcher and retrieving the stairchair, along with a couple of sheets. I then made my way back up to the room, where Jan appeared to have lost some of her composure.

She spoke as soon as I entered. "Jon, have you seen who this is?"

I had to admit on my previous visit I'd only given the patient a cursory glance. I walked in and inspected her brown vomit stained face.

"Holy shit, it's Sammy!"

Liam looked up. "You know her?"

I couldn't resist a dig. "Most of us who work on road know her. She's one of our regular psych patients. In fact, she was giving me abuse at the Royal only yesterday. What the fuck!"

"Well, whoever she is, we'd better get going. As I expected, her ECG was sinus tach. I've got a line in, but you can put a bag of fluid up once she's in the truck. I think it's a case of man-handling her onto the stairchair, then strapping her in for the ride down."

I nodded. Despite being shocked by the revelation I concentrated enough to throw the sheets on the chair before wrapping Sammy in them once she was on the seat. We clicked all the straps in place and Liam and I manoeuvred her down the stairs. The tractor treads on the back of the chair made the job a lot easier than it used to be; at least now we didn't have to carry our patient down six flights.

Once in the ambulance, Jan hooked up all the monitoring while I loaded the stairchair. Liam called to us from outside. "I'll go get my gear and lock her place up. I'll meet you at the Royal, presuming they don't give me another job. Here's the bottle of those tablets and the code summary from my monitor. I'll give the Royal a call on my way in. See you up there."

"Cheers Liam."

He left and I handed over the stuff he gave me to Jan. "You happy in the back?"

"Don't think either of us can do much for her. Should I give her an anti-emetic?"

"Hey, you could sacrifice a goat while dancing naked around a stone altar. Nothing we do will make the slightest difference to her outcome."

"Right. Thanks for the insight. Can you at least pass the Toughbook? I'll get the paperwork started."

Despite her inevitable prognosis, I still opted to drive in Code One, but at this time of the morning, the roads were clear. My mind was reeling. "Another regular down. That's seven now, are you not remotely suspicious, Jan?"

"I wouldn't have thought of it if you hadn't been keeping a tally."

"But this one. Sammy? Potassium permanganate? Does that sound likely to you? It would take some serious Googling to come up with that as a suicide option. And putting the crystals in capsules to ensure they get in the stomach rather than burning your mouth. Now that's ingenious. Far too smart for Sammy! She never wanted to commit suicide, she just craved the attention from all the fuss."

As I thought about it, I was getting more and more wound up. "You know she was at the Royal yesterday. What's the betting someone gave her those capsules already made up. You can see it: here, take these diet pills, they'll help with your self-esteem. Silly cow probably took a handful before going to bed."

"Jon, calm down, you're ranting. You have no proof."

"Granted, but the only person able to convince a patient to

take some tablets would have to be a doctor and the one I suspect was on yesterday. We'll see what the pompous fucker says when we bring in Sammy."

"Don't go there, Jon. It will only end in tears. Chill out, you're worrying me."

I took a deep breath. "And there speaks the voice of reason."

It was not long before I was reversing into the ambulance bay at the Royal. I jumped out, flung the back doors open and offloaded Sammy on the stretcher, while Jan followed behind carrying the attached monitor.

"Any changes?"

"No, she groaned a few times, but most people do that when you're driving."

"Do you want to do the handover?"

"No way! This one's all yours. I don't think I'll remember potassium per... thingy, anyway."

"No worries."

I punched in the access code and the triage nurse waved us through. "Is this the GCS 8 we got a call about?"

"Yep."

"Go straight through, they're waiting for you in resus 2. Have you got any details?"

"Yes, we all know her. It's Samantha Macfarlane. She was only here yesterday; her file's probably still in the ED."

"Oh Christ, looks like she's really done something this time."

"And then some!"

We walked round the corner and up to the staff gathered around the second cubicle. As we wheeled her next to the bed,

I noticed MC-squared walking over from the central fishbowl. Just what I needed!

As soon as our patient was transferred, I started my handover in a loud monotone. "This is Sammy, a 26-year-old woman found collapsed in her flat at 3:35 this morning. She appears to have taken an unknown quantity of these diet pills…" I held up the bottle. "… which have had their contents replaced with what I think is potassium permanganate. On our arrival, she had been vomiting this brown liquid, but there were no indications she'd aspirated any. Her GCS has remained at eight: eyes two, voice two, motor four, but other than her heart rate being 110, all other obs have been within normal limits.

"As I'm sure you'll be aware, Sammy has an extensive psych history, which includes self-harming, but other than that, I don't think she has any other ailments or allergies."

The nurses attached their own monitoring, while one of the junior doctors looked my way. "Was there anyone else on scene?"

"No and there was no obvious suicide note either."

"So who called you guys?"

"Haven't a clue, the unit block was a dump. Someone may have found her, but didn't want to get involved, other than making the call. It sometimes happens."

He nodded. "Thanks for that."

I turned to leave and almost bowled over MC-squared, who leant towards me and said in a quiet voice, "Glad to see you've brought us a real patient."

Something inside my head snapped. Looking back, this was the precise moment my whole life unravelled. If I could rewind everything to this exact point and force myself to walk away, I would do it in a heartbeat. But I can't. And I didn't.

Instead, I stood my ground. "I beg your pardon?"

People looked towards us, but MC-squared just stared at me. So I carried on.

"Have you not bothered to check who this patient is? This is Sammy, you know, the one you burled me out for when I put her on an EEO last week for suicidal ideation."

More heads turned our way, including Liam who had arrived and was waving something at me. But I ignored him as MC-squared was still staring at me with a supercilious grin.

"It seems mighty strange that she was here yesterday and somehow gets hold of diet pills filled with a toxic chemical with no known antidote."

"And your point is?"

Jan made her way over towards me, shaking her head, but she was too late - I was on a roll.

"She'll be the seventh regular to die in the last fortnight, perhaps someone here has tired of dealing with their repeat customers. Perhaps that someone sees them as a drain on resources. Perhaps they think it's for the greater good. Perhaps that someone's you!"

His eyes opened wide and the blood vessel on his temple throbbed. "I don't like what you're insinuating!"

Jan finally reached me, grabbing my shoulder and dragging me away.

"Sorry Doc, we've had a long night, he's delirious, I'll get him out of here."

As she bundled me from resus she hissed in my ear, "Shut the fuck up and keep walking, you stupid bastard!"

She stopped her frogmarch only when we were outside next to our ambulance and swung me around so that my back slammed against the cab door.

"What the fuck's wrong with you? I get it, you're pissed off with the system. But why d'you have to drag me into your self-destructive bullshit!"

I was lost for words. Her nostrils flared and she looked like she was about to cry. I did what I always do when taken off guard - resorted to humour. "You know, you look really attractive when you're angry."

She shook her head and closed her eyes, but when she opened them she was looking at the ground. "Fuck. And all he can come up with is a lame-arse joke. Do you realise how much shit you're in? You just accused a consultant of being a serial killer. In front of all his staff!"

She shook her head again, but this time looked me in the eyes. "Make yourself scarce. Stay in the cab while I sort the vehicle out and do the paperwork."

She pointed to the hospital. "Don't go back in there for anything and let's hope to God our next job takes us someplace else."

She stormed off and I lent my head on the cab door, looking up at the stars. The night air was cool and refreshing and I replayed the resus scene over and over in my mind. Had MC-squared just goaded me into that outburst? Had he just played me?

Liam, who had come out to look for me, interrupted my thoughts. "What the hell was that all about?"

"Ha! Don't you start, I've just had a lecture from Jan."

"Mate, you can't say shit like that to a doctor, I'll be seeing you up in the HMO's office when his complaint comes in. What were you on about, anyway?"

"Oh, I've noticed that several of our regulars have been dying off and I'm getting suspicious, that's all. I don't like coincidences."

"Well you were right about one thing."

"What?"

"I was trying to catch your attention in there. When I went

back up to her flat, I found an open bottle of Condy's Crystals. It'd fallen under the desk."

"So Sammy could've made up those tablets at home. Shit! I thought someone had given them to her. Damn! There goes the proof I needed. I guess I'll just have to wait until the deaths reach double figures, then at least I'll have convinced my girlfriend." I realised what I'd said. "Huh, listen to me. Girlfriend. She's now my fiancée. That's going to take a bit of getting used to."

"Fiancée? You and Amber? Since when?"

"Only a few days ago, but with the way the rumour mill works, it'll soon be common knowledge."

"Well, congratulations mate! She's a real looker, no idea what she sees in you."

"Thanks, that's becoming a recurrent theme. Lucky my ego's big enough to stand up for itself."

Jan reappeared by my side. "I thought a big ego was a prerequisite for an ICP?"

Liam laughed. "On that note, I'd better be off. Take care out there. No doubt I'll see you soon. Mark my word, that Doc won't let you get away with what you did in there."

22

CONTRITION

I woke late on Sunday afternoon after cycling home and crawling into bed when most sane people were having a lie-in. As consciousness washed over me like a rising tide, I developed that hangover feeling. The one where you're not sure what it was you did, but as fast as the amnesia dissipates, the regrets coalesce.

And like a hangover, the previous night's memories came back in a series of caffeine-fuelled flashbacks. I sipped my coffee and winced as I remembered each thing I'd said, but that was nothing compared to the shock I got when I checked my work email.

In amongst the myriad of messages regarding road closures, special events and training bulletins, the one from the Regional Executive Officer stood out like a night shift's morning glory. My cursor drifted over to the title and I hesitated before double-clicking the mouse button. The text was brief and to the point. My presence was required for a 9:30 AM meeting on Tuesday to discuss the matter of a formal complaint.

"Christ, that was quick!"

And it's a Sunday. Someone can pull strings!

As a result, I found myself two days later carrying a briefcase and walking through the automatic glass doors into the Emergency Services Building in Kedron. I caught sight of myself in the reflection, all spruced up in my dress uniform: light teal shirt, dark teal tie and pants, with a gold caduceus on each shoulder and one on my chest. At least I looked the part, I'd even polished my shoes.

Walking into the small lobby, I was greeted by my Station Officer who was smiling like he'd scored the last shrimp on the barbie. "G'day Boardie, fancy meeting you here. Did you get an invite as my manager?"

"Yes, but to be honest, I wouldn't miss this for the world."

"You're all heart. Is it just the two of us then?"

"Are you not in the union?"

"No. Haven't been since the last award settlement."

"I guess I'm your only representative then."

"Great." I had a sinking feeling. Boardie looked like a kid waiting to meet Santa. "What d'you reckon they'll do? I can't imagine they can sack me for pissing off a doctor."

"I wouldn't bank on it. They could ping you for bringing the Service into disrepute, which, of course, is an instant dismissal."

"You're loving this, aren't you?"

"Every second. I've no idea how you've evaded this for so long, but I have tried to warn you."

"Are you wearing your 'I told you so' T-shirt under that fancy uniform?"

"You can't continuously thumb your nose at the powers that be and expect to get away with it forever."

"You could tone down your smile. The disciplinary panel will have to wear sunnies if you keep beaming like that."

He shook his head and looked away and we lapsed into an awkward silence. Anything he could add was unlikely to make me feel any better, so I made a show of studying the large Aboriginal painting that adorned one wall of the lobby. A huge multi-coloured snake worked its way across a sunburnt landscape. Despite my current predicament, I began wondering which Dreamtime story the artwork depicted. It was an embarrassing realisation that I knew so little about my homeland's indigenous culture. Here I was, my career in jeopardy due to my concerns over regulars dying and most of what I knew about sixty-thousand years of civilisation was from my interaction with another regular, Mr Wendal. He was such a negative stereotype that I resolved there and then to redress the imbalance in my knowledge.

Reality returned with a bump, as Liam appeared beside Boardie. "Morning Darren, Jon."

He nodded towards me. "Told you I'd be seeing you soon."

"I don't think either of us thought it would be this soon. Any clue on who's pulling the strings?"

"Don't know what you're talking about, mate. I'm sure it's just a coincidence that your friend from the Royal was at med school with Dr O'Driscoll. But I guess you weren't to know that."

"Oh shit!"

"Oh shit indeed. Come on, they're all waiting for you."

He turned and walked past the security desk to the internal staircase and we followed, Boardie moving with more spring in his step than I could manage. On the next landing, he showed us into a meeting room, but as Boardie entered, Liam stopped me. "Look, Jon, I just want you to know I put in a good word for you. I told them that when you had your meltdown, you didn't know about the bottle of Condy's Crystals in the room.

As far as you were aware, someone other than Sammy had tampered with the tablets."

"Thanks, Liam. Did they accept it?"

"Haven't a clue." He shrugged. "Hey, I tried."

I nodded my thanks and walked into the shark tank.

An over-sized polished wooden table that could have seated twenty took up most of the space. But today just three people were one side and Boardie had taken a seat opposite them. I joined him and Liam sat with the others. There were brief formalities, but the faces before me all maintained their stern expressions.

The Regional Executive Officer, Lawrence Denning, was a hulk of a man. He was a product of the days when Ambulance Officers were selected for their capacity to lift patients; a time when 'load and go' was one of the few treatment pathways. His ruddy complexion and bald head bore a few scars from skin cancer excisions and two over-bushy grey eyebrows shaded his eyes. He had his arms folded in front of him and he sat bolt upright next to the Head Medical Officer, Dr O'Driscoll. She was wearing a smart grey suit with a white blouse and her ID badge hung around her neck from a bright green lanyard. As I sat down, one of her blue-eyed stares skewered me. She had the unnerving ability to make you feel guilty even if you weren't on trial. But today I was.

Next to her was Raymond Chinn, a Clinical Practice Coordinator for the Brisbane region. He had the dark straight hair and aesthetic features that often accompanied an Asian-Caucasian mix. But his genetics had also saddled him with a diminutive stature, made even more obvious sitting alongside his colleagues. He was renowned for his Napoleon complex and I wondered whether his size was the reason he left road work and went into education as soon as he attained his ICP qualification.

Looking at the panel assigned to determine my fate, I couldn't escape the irony that it was the HMO who spent most of her time working the frontline.

The REO began the formal proceedings. "Well, Jon, as I'm sure we're all aware, I've called this meeting to discuss the very serious matter of an accusation you made against a member of the hospital staff at the Royal…"

"With all due respect, sir, I apologise for the interruption, but…"

As I spoke, his eyebrows shot up his forehead like two hairy caterpillars jumping away from a bird. I reached into my briefcase and retrieved a sealed envelope along with four loose A4 sheets.

"… I've prepared a written apology I would like, with your approval, to be submitted to Dr Cansfield-Clarke. I fully accept that this does not absolve me for my unacceptable behaviour, but I would like to start this meeting from a position of contrition for my actions. As I mention in the letter before you, any accusations or implications I made towards Dr Cansfield-Clarke were totally unfounded and I am sincerely sorry for any offence I caused."

All four faces were staring at me, but no one spoke. Then, one by one, they looked down and read my letter. Although I thought I knew how the B-CAS worked and suspected my fate was already sealed, it was Amber's influence in play here. She urged me, for once in my life, to be conciliatory and not to go on the offensive. We'd almost had our first argument, but my feelings for her weakened my usual belligerence and forced me to listen. Now, observing the assembled panel, I had to admit the ploy appeared to have them wrong-footed. Out of the corner of my eye, I could see Boardie giving me a strange disheartened look.

Eventually they all finished and glanced among each other,

uncertain which of them should take the lead. It was the Big 'O' who stepped up to the challenge.

"Well, this…," she waved the sheet, "… will go some way to repairing the damage you've caused to the reputation of the Brisbane City Ambulance Service and inter-departmental relations. But I must ask, what on earth were you thinking? Obviously, I wasn't there, but from what Martin said, you seemed to accuse him of murdering his patients."

I sighed and looked down. "I have no justifiable excuse. Over the past few weeks I've noticed that several of our regular patients have died and was concerned about the developing pattern. When I ended up at another regular who'd been fatally poisoned, I lost it. I thought someone had supplied the tablets. But I was unaware the poison was in her flat and she'd deliberately taken an overdose. To be honest, when it came to my outburst, I don't remember what I said. It had been a very long night and, as I've already mentioned, I simply lost it."

Liam broke the silence that followed. "Have you voiced your concerns to the police?"

"As a matter of fact, I talked to a detective I know. He assured me there was nothing suspicious about any of the deaths, but I should call him if I found any evidence. I thought I'd done just that with this latest poisoning. But I was wrong."

Another long pause followed, which the HMO broke. "Well, as this incident does not appear to reflect an error in your clinical judgement…"

Raymond Chinn interrupted. "Er… there is the issue of an ICP driving in Code One and leaving an ACP in the back. If the patient was compromised enough to warrant a Code One transport, surely…"

His sentence came to a stuttering end when he received a frosty glare from Dr O'Driscoll. "As I was saying, because your clinical judgement has not been called into question, I don't deem it appropriate for you to lose your ICP status. However, I think there needs to be some form of disciplinary procedure."

She turned to the REO, who took his cue. "I agree. We cannot have paramedics, especially ICPs, causing such inter-departmental friction. The B-CAS has to demonstrate action on this matter. I move to suspend you, without pay, for two weeks, effective immediately. On your return, Darren here is charged with monitoring your behaviour for the next six months. Any issues he brings to me during that time I will deal with very harshly. Am I making myself absolutely clear."

I nodded. "Yes, sir."

He exchanged glances with the other three. "That'll be all."

I picked up my briefcase and left the building, giving the Dreamtime painting a nod on the way out. Thanks to Amber, I still had a job and now I had two weeks to reflect on my life's direction.

Or so I thought.

23

AWAKENING

"Oh, shit!"

I awoke with a start in the dead of night. A niggling unease had somehow solidified into a sharp recollection and like a surgical blade, the memory had sliced through the amorphous veil obscuring my vision. Now I could appreciate all the implications of that single event.

Amber stirred. "What's up, you had a nightmare, babe?"

"If only! Oh shit!"

She sat up and flipped on the bedside light. "What's wrong, Jon? You're scaring me."

"It's the tablet. I took it from the bottle!"

"What tablet?"

"The diet pill I broke open. I took it from the bottle."

"Are you awake? You're not making any sense."

I swung my legs down and sat on the side of the bed, my head in my hands. "Oh shit, oh shit, oh shit!"

Amber curled her warm naked body round mine to comfort me. "Calm down, Jon. Tell me what's wrong."

"When we were in Sammy's room, I took a capsule from

the bottle of diet pills and broke it open. I recognised the black crystals and that's how I worked out she'd taken potassium permanganate. Right?"

"Yes. So?"

"If you took the trouble to open a capsule and replace the contents with a poison, why would you put it back in the bottle of untampered tablets? How would you know which ones you'd changed?"

"But…"

"And what's the chances of me picking out the only tampered one?"

"Well… She might've changed them all…"

"Why would she bother to do that? Why change a pot of a hundred tablets when you only need a few to kill yourself?"

"That presumes she knew the lethal dose."

"She knew enough about the poison to use capsules to prevent it burning her mouth. That's what stops people killing themselves with this stuff. Usually you can't swallow enough because of the oral burns."

"So what's your point?"

"I think you're right."

"About what?"

"All the tablets in the bottle were changed, but it wasn't Sammy who did it."

"I think you've been down that route, but go on."

"Say she was given a full bottle of poisoned capsules, marked as diet pills to ensure she took an overdose. That'll explain why, when I picked one out of the bottle it had the crystals in it."

"And?"

"There were no spilt crystals on the desk."

This time Amber didn't respond, she just looked at me with her brow furrowed.

"When I saw Sammy's desk there were opened capsules, but no sign of any crystals and no bottle of potassium permanganate. You'd need a steady hand to load all those capsules without spilling a single crumb."

Amber was now sitting cross-legged on the bed, her elbows on her knees and her chin in her hands. "I'm listening."

"I've got a feeling we walked in too early."

"What do you mean?"

"I think the scene was being set. All he needed to do was switch the tampered diet pills with a normal bottle and tip the Condy's Crystals on the desk. But we were too close when we got the job."

"What are you saying... Liam?"

"There's no record of who called the job in. It could've been him. I even said at the time that he had to be on top of the address to get dispatched before us."

"But Liam... the ICP?"

"Think about it. His role is auditing jobs. He not only sees who the repeat callers are, but has access to all their medical history and contact details. He can drive around day or night on his own in a marked-up car with no one asking any questions."

"But why?"

"That's the bit I'm stuck on. I've just accused a doctor of doing the same thing with no more a motive than clearing time-wasters from his department. But I recognise there has to be more to it than that."

"But Jon, it's all ifs, buts and maybes. You still have no evidence."

"Yes, but I've now got a starting point. That bottle of diet pills. If the one that's held by the police has just normal capsules, the odds are stacked against me picking the only tampered one. That suggests that Liam switched the bottles.

And I'm betting that the cops found crystals on the desk. Liam was on his own when he went back to the flat to lock up, which is when he supposedly 'found' the Condy's Crystals bottle."

She sighed. "It's still all circumstantial, Jon. How's about you focusing on our future and just let this whole thing go. Or have you forgotten we have the small issue of a wedding to plan?"

I smiled and leant back to kiss her. "How could I forget that, babe? You're the most important thing in my life, but surely you can let me make a few enquiries."

She held out a hand and stroked my face. "OK, but please don't go accusing anyone else until you have something more concrete."

"Don't worry, I've learnt my lesson. From now on, slow and steady is the name of the game."

Little did I realise I was playing the wrong game.

24

CLOUDS

Amber was working the next few days and decided she'd stay at her own place tonight. After my midnight revelation, neither of us got much sleep and she snuck out about six, so I slept in.

I woke around 11:00 AM and after eating brunch, tried a few times to contact Detective Giallo, but each attempt diverted to his voicemail. I gave up and left a message for him to call me back.

Without being able to pursue my only lead, I was at a loss for what to do. If Liam was a murderer, then all the recent fuss over Sammy would convince him to lie low, at least for a while. On the other hand, what were my options anyway? I could hardly stake out all the remaining regulars on the off-chance one was the next target. And as for blowing the whistle, I guess I'd already tried that.

I decided to do what I always do when I want to clear my head - go fishing. But it was now too late to set off, so I spent the rest of the afternoon prepping my boat to take her out at the crack of dawn.

Once everything was ready, I chilled out with a beer or two watching telly and crashed early, setting my alarm for 5:00 AM. Looking back, it's amazing how normal a day it was.

The next morning I woke before the alarm. My phone beeped at 4:45 AM, signalling a text. I fumbled about retrieving the device, before trying to focus on the illuminated screen. It was a cryptic message from Amber. I rolled over on my back, shook my head and read it a second time:

```
Jon U need 2 come 2 my place now!
    I cant cover 4U any more!
```

"What?"

I hit the call button, but after the standard number of rings the line went dead. I tried again, but got the same response.

"Weird."

I then called her landline, but it was engaged. Perhaps she was trying to call me. I waited a few minutes, but nothing happened, so I sent a text:

```
What's up??
```

A reply came within a few seconds:

```
We need 2 talk face 2 face
```

I sighed. "What the hell?" But typed:

```
On my way
```

I threw on a T-shirt, pair of shorts and cap, then grabbed my sunnies and keys, kicking on some thongs on the way to my ute. As I pulled out onto the esplanade, the sun had already clawed above the horizon. The fiery ball had painted a distant layer of stratus clouds a vivid pink and set the whole sky alight with a crimson glow.

"Huh, red sky in the morning, shepherd's warning."

Even at this hour, the traffic was building on the highway, but I made my way over to Samford in about thirty minutes. I had the stereo on and the window down, so by the time I was bumping down Amber's long driveway, I was wide awake.

And so were my Spidey senses. They tingled as soon as I saw her house. Something was wrong, but I couldn't quite place it.

I rolled to a stop in front of the building and the cloud of dust from her unsealed drive caught up and enveloped my ute. Floating particles glinted in the rays of early morning sunlight that filtered through the trees. The specs alighted on the windscreen and bonnet, but my attention was transfixed on the balcony. There wasn't a sound; even the cicadas were holding their breath.

Opening my door caused a metallic creak, which seemed to rip through the silence, but there was no response. I stepped from the cab, gripping the window frame. "Amber!"

Nothing.

I noticed her bright green Toyota Yaris was still in its usual place and my heart rate increased a notch or two. I shouted her name again. It came out more like a question, but the house just stared back.

I had a fleeting thought: was this some sort of joke? I pulled out my phone and checked for any new messages. Nothing. On a whim, I called her number. It took a few seconds to connect and then a distant tune came from inside the house, mirroring the tone from my handset. Well, she was here, or at least her mobile was. I called out her name again as I walked up the stairs to the veranda, but the only sound was the creaking timber and Amber's muffled ringtone.

I hit disconnect then reached out and opened the fly-screen door. The hinges made their characteristic grinding whine, as I used my other hand to turn the handle. It was unlocked. I pushed the door open and called her name again. There was now a pleading tone to my voice.

I stepped into the living room and sucked in a breath. It looked like there had been a scuffle. The antique lamp-stand she had so proudly brought back from Vinnies was lying on its side, the stained-glass shade in pieces on the polished wooden floor. Broken crockery and books littered the room, as if someone had been throwing them around. In a few rapid steps, I passed through her kitchen and ran down the short corridor to her closed bedroom. I called her name again before flinging open the door.

"Amber... No!"

I couldn't breathe. I felt as if the air had become clay and was clogging my lungs. My limbs turned to ice, my heart to stone. There before me, on the bed where we had made love so many times, was Amber's naked body, the handle of a knife protruding from her motionless chest.

My legs buckled and I fell to my knees. There was a primeval wail being torn from some injured beast and I only had a vague realisation it was coming from me. One look at her pale skin and the position of the blade, I knew she was gone. No need for a pulse check, no point in CPR. No one could fix her. No one could bring her back. If I'd been here to witness the stabbing, there would've been nothing I could've done, except cradle her in my arms. She was dead.

My body collapsed forward, my forehead touching the smooth floorboards. I toppled over and curled into a foetal position. I could feel nothing, my senses were numb, my mind overwhelmed. Then the grief rolled over me like a freight train, magnified by my brother's death and the suppressed emotions from dealing with the tragedies of countless strangers.

I'm not sure how long I lay there, but when I came round my eyes were stinging and the side of my head was wet from the pool of tears on the floor. I somehow picked myself up and sat next to Amber. Grasping her limp left hand in mine, I lifted it to my face, pressing her cool skin against my cheek. The nails she had painted only a few days ago glistened in stark contrast to her pale fingers.

I leant forward and kissed her lips, but the jump for joy was now replaced by a cold iron fist clamped around my heart.

I sat up with a deep sigh and reached out to close the lids of her staring lifeless eyes. Anger was starting to usurp my grief and the embers of a burning rage ignited inside me. I gripped the hand I was still holding, closed my eyes and spoke between clenched teeth. "I promise you Amber, I'll get the bastard who did this!"

As I lay her hand back on the bed, I noticed her engagement ring was missing. Was this a robbery? The thought snapped me back to reality and I dialed triple zero for the police. As the connection went through, I looked at the wound in her chest and gasped. The handle was jet-black ebony. There were two silver rings embedded in the wood. And a small iridescent fish motif shone in the light from the window.

It was a work of art.

My work of art.

My Sujihiki.

My Japanese chef's knife.

A voice interrupted my thoughts.

"What?"

"Which emergency service do you require?"

My mind was now spinning like water down a drain. There were cuts to both her forearms, defensive wounds, but on Amber's upper chest, next to the small pool of blood around the hilt of the blade was a red smear. I hadn't registered it before, but it was in the shape of a letter. A single capital letter 'J'.

Blood tipped the index finger of her right hand.

"Are you there, sir? Which emergency service do you require?"

"I'll get back to you."

I disconnected and shot to my feet. The choking cloud of utter despair began to recede, fear was clearing the fog. I was standing in a crime scene where everything pointed to me as the prime suspect. I flipped to my texts, rereading my wake-up call.

```
Jon U need 2 come 2 my place now!
    I cant cover 4U any more!
```

What did it mean? I was now certain it had not come from Amber. I looked around the room for anything out of place, anything that shouldn't be here. Furniture and clothes were disturbed, giving the impression a fight had continued into here from the living room. And then my eyes latched onto the end of a metal tin about the size of a shoebox, half covered by the bedclothes. The box belonged on top of my fridge at home. It was where I kept my receipts.

I pulled it out and flipped open the hinged lid. Instead of the usual mess of shopper dockets and scraps of paper, there were about forty boxes of morphine sulphate. Around two hundred vials, identical to the ones we keep in the safe at the ambulance station. Some packs had been ripped open and the picture was completed with a few needles and syringes.

"Shit!"

Before I had time to comprehend the implications, there was a crunch of tyres and a purr of an approaching engine. I put down the box and moved back into the living room, where I had a view of the driveway. For the second time that morning I dropped to my knees, but this was no collapse, it was a defensive crouch. A police car had pulled up behind my ute.

If they caught me here and now, there wasn't a jury in the world that would find me anything other than guilty. Despite having just discovered my fiancée's body, years of focusing while witnessing trauma took control. It was an essential attribute of a good paramedic: emotional detachment.

I knew I'd have to deal with my anguish over Amber at a later date, but now I needed to think and act without the hindrance of personal feelings.

Staying low and treading carefully I stole over to the front door then waited for the officers to close their patrol car. The double thud masked any sound of me slipping the bolt.

I crept through to the back door and locked that before making my way to the central corridor. There I stood, with my back against the wall, wedged out of sight in a corner with my heart thumping so loud they surely could count my pulse.

The stairs creaked as the two policemen walked up to the veranda.

Then there was silence.

I held my breath as a bead of sweat trickled down my face, taking the same path the tears had made minutes before. Although expected, the bang on the door made me jump. From my hiding place I could hear the officers talking.

"So what was this job again?"

"Domestic disturbance. Someone reported an argument, raised voices, stuff smashing, y'know, the usual shit. They got concerned when they heard a woman scream."

"Caller must have good hearing. We're in the middle of bloody nowhere here."

"Well, it's probably bullshit, but we've got to check things out."

There was another loud knock.

"Police. Open up."

"They must be in, there's two cars."

There was a creak from the fly screen and the door handle rattle.

"Looks like you're right, it's bolted from the inside."

"They could've left out the back door."

There were three more bangs. "Police! Open up!"

"I'll go check the back."

During their conversation, I'd formulated a plan and this was my cue. Under the cover of his receding footsteps, I crept into the back room and used my mobile to call the B-CAS Metropolitan Ambulance Coordinator. A bored voice answered the phone. "MAC, Drew."

I whispered into the phone. "It's Dave. I'm at the Samford Ambulance Station. Someone's trying to break in."

"Sorry, can't hear you. What d'you say?"

I hissed as loud as I dare. "LR, LR, law required, Samford Ambulance Station. Someone's breaking in. I need the cops here now!"

"Oh, shit! No worries, mate. Hang tight, I'm putting the call through."

I hung up and held my breath. The other officer was coming up the back stairs. In a matter of seconds he would discover both doors were locked from the inside.

A radio crackled. "Unit 452?"

"452, go ahead."

"LR call from Samford Ambulance Station. You're the

closest resource, please respond. I'll be sending you backup from the city."

"Roger that, on our way."

Both officers ran down the steps and the engine of their patrol car roared into life. Edging along the corridor, I saw them disappear in a cloud of dust down the driveway.

I had bought myself some time, but not much. They'd return as soon as they discovered the call was a hoax, so I had to move. I ran into the back room and retrieved my spare cycling gear from the chest of drawers and threw it in a small rucksack. Hesitating as I passed Amber's door, I had to stop myself from looking in. The images I already had in my mind would haunt me for the rest of my life.

I grabbed her phone from the kitchen side and wrote a quick note:

Mum, I had an argument with Jon and have gone away for a few days to get my head straight. Back soon. Love you, Amber xxx.

I picked up her keys and unbolted the back door, locking it from the outside. Sticking the note in the doorjamb, I trapped it in place with the fly screen. It was not foolproof and had no chance of standing the test of time, but it might cause the cops to think twice before breaking in.

I ran over to where Amber kept her bike, grabbed it and her helmet and threw them in the back of my ute, covering them with a tarp. Once done, I jumped in the cab and drove off down the driveway, watching in the rear-view as my own cloud of dust obscured Amber's house.

25

BREADCRUMBS

I tore out of the driveway and swung sharp right onto Samford Road, my tyres squealing as they struggled to grip on the dirt-covered tarmac. The police would have turned left to get to the ambulance station, but then I remembered there was a backup car coming from the city and so checked my speed.

"Calm, Jon, calm!"

I beat a fist on the steering wheel, trying to stay focused. The last thing I wanted was to be booked for speeding. I felt a wave of nausea and fear bubbling up inside me like a shaken soft drink. My vision blurred, ribs ached and fingers began tingling. I realised I was hyperventilating and needed to pull over to control my breathing. Turning into a short siding, I stopped amongst the trees, out of sight of the main road, and held my face in my hands.

"Fuuuuuuck!"

I screamed the expletive in a prolonged yell, exhaling for as long as I could before holding my breath. And when my chest began to burn and stars flashed before my eyes, I sucked in a lungful of air.

Hold. Exhale. Hold. Inhale. Hold.

Once the symptoms subsided, I dropped my hands in my lap and stared out the windscreen. What had just happened? What had I done? The planted evidence might have pointed to me, but fleeing the scene had sealed my fate. Or had it? Could I go back? Claim I was unconscious and didn't hear the police? Phone in the murder myself? Then I remembered my triple zero call. Damn!

I could turn myself in, but what would be the point in that? Whoever framed me was not only a cold-blooded killer, but they had murdered numerous people without leaving any evidence. I was certain the case against me would be watertight. No. Running was my only option. If I wanted to catch this bastard, I needed to be free to lay a trap in Brisbane. But who was I kidding? In a matter of hours I'd be public enemy number one, my face plastered on every billboard!

My mind kept flipping between panic and rational problem solving.

I somehow had to make the cops think I'd fled the city, forcing them to concentrate their search elsewhere. It was why I'd grabbed my cycle stuff and Amber's bike; at some point I would ditch my ute and return under pedal power. Although the clothes were bright, people turned a blind eye to them and a helmet with sunnies made a useful disguise.

But where the hell would I go?

A movement in the trees ahead of me caused my sightless eyes to focus. A Kookaburra was sat on a low branch, head cocked to one side looking at me. After a moment's deliberation, it ruffled its feathers, lifted its beak skywards and let out a raucous call.

My mouth dropped open.

What had Amber said on our boat trip? She was a crazy white girl, alone laughing with the Kookaburras! Her camping holidays in Carnarvon Gorge. No towns, no mobiles and not another soul! It was only a few months back the police captured a man in New South Wales wanted for murder. He'd made the news after evading arrest for over seven years by living rough in a National Park. I could make it look like I was doing the same in Central Queensland, all I needed to do was leave a trail for the cops to follow!

The bird had fallen silent and we were once again staring at one another. Was Amber still trying to influence me? Trying to help from the other side? I'd never believed in the paranormal, but the implication she was dead ate through my frail mental shield like acid through limestone. Once again clay filled my lungs, frost spread though my body and tears burnt my cheeks.

Gripping the steering wheel, I clenched my teeth and closed my eyes, forcing down the emotional glue seeping out of my soul, miring me to the spot, preventing me from action. I needed a clear head to avenge her death and I needed to get moving. Now.

I pulled out of the siding and used my driver training as a form of meditation, scanning the road ahead from bonnet to limit point. I checked my mirrors and vocalised a running commentary on all potential upcoming hazards and warning signs. It was enough to occupy my mind, stave off the inevitable thoughts of Amber.

As I passed through Keperra, I spotted a BCF sign and turned off into the shopping centre, pulling up outside the camping store I realised the place was deserted and checked my watch.

"Shit!"

It had just gone 6:00 AM. So much had happened in the last hour. Far too much. More than I could bear. I shook my head and read the opening times on the front door. There was another two-and-a-half hours before they opened.

"Fuck!"

I pulled out my phone and searched for the company's website. They had a store in Toowoomba that was about two hours drive away. I guess that fitted my plan. It was on the way to Carnarvon Gorge, but I needed cash. Closing down my bank accounts would be one of the first things the police would do.

Driving over to a nearby auto-teller, I withdrew five thousand dollars, then did the same from Amber's account, using the card she kept with her mobile. Her name embossed on the plastic made me stop. I couldn't believe she was gone. The fermenting despair once again bubbled up like lava in a volcano. Ready to erupt. Ready to explode. Ready to destroy everything.

I closed my eyes and gritted my teeth, giving me time to regain the composure to embark on this ordeal. And amid my mental storm there was one thought I clung to, a Jesus line whipping about in the maelstrom: if they caught me, Amber's murderer would escape and that could never be.

Looking down, I removed my sunnies, rubbed my face and then looked straight towards the security camera. At least the trail would start with a good mug shot for the cops to use.

I returned to my ute, but froze as a siren came from the main road. My whole body tensed for action, but the sound passed, heading for Samford. It was the police backup from the city. My hoax must be still viable as they hadn't been stood down. Then another thought struck me: perhaps they were going to Amber's place. Too soon, surely? I lowered myself in my seat and stuffed the cash in the rucksack before driving to the servo to fill my tank. I had a long journey ahead of me and didn't want to stop again.

As I was standing by the pump, a beat-up combi van pulled

up beside me, complete with hand-painted marijuana leaves and peace signs emblazoned on each side. The hippy that climbed out wasn't old enough to be conceived in the sixties, let alone remember them. His long straight hair hung down to his waist and a brightly coloured bandana held it off his face, but his bloodshot eyes looked like they needed the shade.

To my dismay, he strolled over, his right arm draped across his body as he scratched his left shoulder. "Hey man, d'you know where the fuck I am? I got lost comin' through the city."

Having to chat with a dope head was not part of my plan, I glanced at him and went back to pumping fuel. "Keperra."

"Right… right… right… Any chance you can give me some directions, man? I've no map and won't have nothin' to do with no satnav. The government uses all those fuckin' satellites to spy on your every move. Don't have a mobile either. No one's free if they have one of those things, man. There was this dude I knew…"

It sounded like he was launching into a full-on conspiracy theory, but his concerns had sparked an idea. "Where you going?"

"What? Oh, Cairns."

"Cairns? Shit, you've a few Ks to go."

"Gonna visit some friends up at Kuranda."

"That figures. Have you at least got a pen and paper in your van? I'll draw you a map to the highway."

"Cheers, man, that's awesome."

We walked over to his wheeled home and he pulled open the side door to dig through his assorted belongings. After a while, he presented me with a chewed pencil and a piece of cardboard ripped from a cornflakes box. "Best I can do."

I opened the passenger door and leant on the grubby seat to draw the directions. "You need to get back onto Samford

Road there and turn right. Follow that until you get to the set of lights at Enoggera train station and turn left..."

As I drew and explained the route, I could see my hands shaking. Despite my relaxed voice and demeanour, my underlying nervous system was shot to pieces. It was all part of that swan philosophy, years of creating a front for the patient's benefit. But now the skill was keeping me stable. At least on the surface. The hippy nodded as if he was taking it all in, but while he listened, I slid my phone under his seat. If he was right and Big Brother was watching, my signal would be tracking in the wrong direction.

"... then take the signs for the M1. After that, stay on the highway and drive about another two thousand kilometres north."

"Easy as. Thanks, man!"

He smiled, showing off his crystal-meth-sculpted teeth and we parted company. I had a slight pang of guilt and hoped he wasn't using when the cops caught up with him.

I paid for the fuel, got back in my ute and switched off Amber's phone, taking out the SIM card. I then turned down Settlement Road and made my way through the traffic to the Ipswich Motorway.

I can't recall the number of times an anxious patient has blamed a panic attack on their work life. "I have a very stressful job, you know."

I've always asked them their profession, hoping that one day someone would say 'air traffic controller', or 'bomb disposal expert'. But they never do. Invariably I'd give them a withering look when they replied: concierge, or IT consultant. "You should try being a paramedic."

But now I realised, until this point in my life, I hadn't truly experienced stress. Sitting behind the wheel of my ute, boxed in by bored commuters, buses and delivery vans, my heart rate never dropped below a hundred. Sweat soaked my clothes and my blood pressure was high enough to give a giraffe a headache.

Eventually, I made it onto the Warrego Highway, where the vehicles thinned and I was at least able to travel somewhere near the speed limit. Despite that, it was still 9:15 AM when I pulled into the Toowoomba BCF carpark. The initial city traffic had delayed my journey by over an hour and I must have lost a few kilos in perspiration.

The whole way I'd been flipping radio channels, listening for any news bulletins, but Amber's murder hadn't hit the media. The police may have kept a lid on the story and were searching for me now, but I still needed to buy some camping equipment and food to make my disappearance plausible.

I parked my ute nose-in under a tree to hide the rego, grabbed some cash and got out, dropping the tailgate to obscure the back number plate. I stood by the cab and examined the front of the shop. Was the dope head right about Big Brother? Had they already caught him? Could they have accessed the last website viewed on my phone? Shit! I should have cleared the memory before dumping it.

The coast looked clear, but for all I knew, a SWAT team might be hiding down the fishing tackle aisle. I pulled the peak of my cap down a notch and drew a deep breath. Here goes nothing.

The sun beat down as I walked across the carpark to the automatic doors, my heart once again thumping in my chest. As the glass slid open, my eyes had to adjust to the darkness. But rather than a multitude of heavily armed police training their weapons on me, I was greeted by a bored woman in her twenties sitting at the checkout. She was chewing gum with the same look of concentration that a cow has when chewing the cud. She gave me a disinterested glance then swivelled on her chair, facing the other way.

I went through the turnstile and walked around the shop, looking for the camping section, when one of the sales staff approached me. He was pushing forty with a wispy brown beard and a sagging midriff. The name tag pinned to his white shirt read 'Nathan'. "G'day, sir, how can I help?"

I mustered up a broad smile. "Today, Nathan, is your lucky day. I've had an argument with my missus and want to go walkabout for a while, but all I have is what I'm wearing. So, I need just about everything."

"Excellent! No worries, I'll have you decked out better than Bear Grylls in no time."

True to his word, Nathan had been like a whirlwind, producing gear and equipment as if he'd been planning to do the same himself. In less than an hour, I was dumping my purchases in the back of the ute. While in the shop, I'd taken the opportunity to study a map of Carnarvon Gorge. The only guaranteed standing water in the area was the nearby Lake Nuga Nuga, so that was where I was heading.

Before leaving Toowoomba, I picked up some provisions at a large supermarket, ensuring I spent time in front of a security camera, as I'd done in the camping store. It was a risky balancing act. I needed to drop enough breadcrumbs for the police to follow, but not leave myself open to being caught in the process.

After topping up the ute, I was once again back on the Warrego Highway, sitting on the speed limit as I headed out west. There was no news on the radio and I settled into an uneasy routine, changing channels and searching the dusty horizon for any signs of a roadblock.

I've lived in Australia all my life, but it's easy to forget how vast the country is. Towns passed by slower than the hours - Dalby, Chinchilla, Miles, Yuleba. And the monotony of the gum-studded red landscape tried hard to sap my concentration, my mind yearning to think of Amber. But I knew I had to stay focused. There would be time to mourn later, but not now. Now I had to keep putting out those spot fires of feelings that kept sparking into life and think like a Vulcan. Logical. Without emotion.

I turned my thoughts to planning my next move. How would I catch Liam? Was it Liam? Who else could it be? Liam was there in the meeting when I mentioned informing the police. He asked me about them! And then it dawned on me. Outside the hospital, after my rant with the doctor. I'd also told him I'd discussed the murders with Amber.

"Shit! Shit! Shit!"

I hit the steering wheel with the heel of my hand, causing my ute to swerve. An oncoming truck blasted its air horn and the sound pulled me back in line. "Focus, Jono, focus. Nothing can change what's already happened. You just need to get the bastard!"

I steadied my breathing, tried to calm myself and forced my mind to work on creating a plan. I'd have to catch him in the act, but how? Could I use a regular patient as bait? Which one? How? Then a recollection of the Dreamtime painting in the Emergency Services Building came to mind and I knew who I could use. One thing I had noticed was the train track running parallel with the road. That would be my way back to the city. Back to find Amber's killer.

It was just before 2:00 PM when I reached Roma and

turned right onto the Carnarvon Highway, heading north. The term 'highway' was a bit of a grand description, which was now a single carriageway, with dirt less than a metre from the white edge line. But at least it was sealed and I could still keep up a good speed. I now left behind the comforting sight of the train track and knew that getting back to Roma would be under my own steam.

Ten minutes outside Injune I reached over to grab another water bottle and looked up to find a police car driving towards me. Although my muscles screamed for action, I somehow kept the wheels straight and my foot steady on the accelerator. Like on a Code One drive, my eyes darted from side to side, looking for escape routes, but then I picked up movement inside the cab. My vision shot to the driver, arms ready to swerve left, only to see the officer had raised his hand in a greeting. In a reflex action, I returned the gesture, as I've done thousands of times from an ambulance and we passed each other, speeding away in opposite directions.

I stared in my rearview until the squad car disappeared in the rippling heat haze, then realised my chest was burning. Gasping, I inhaled a deep lung full of air, the first since spotting the cop, and let out a long sigh. At least it seemed the police were yet to release a BOLO for me; either that or the Be On the Look Out order hadn't reached this far west.

I kept expecting to see flashing lights tearing up behind me, so the right-hand turn-off for the Arcadia Valley Road came as some relief. If the cop started chasing me, he was more likely to follow the main highway.

After the first few hundred metres, the surface turned to loose gravel and I had to temper my speed. But even travelling at sixty, my tyres left a plume of dust like a big orange smoke signal for any would-be tracker. There was nothing I could do about it, other than keep going. The sooner I ditched the ute and gave the impression I'd gone bush, the safer I'd be.

I finally stopped at an intersection and my trailing dust cloud caught up and surrounded me. The particles alighted on the windscreen and bonnet like ash from a funeral pyre. In an instant I was sitting in front of Amber's house looking up at the veranda, before all this nightmare began. Could I have done anything different? If I'd been quicker could I have saved her? If I'd stayed at home would I be in this mess? My last question caused a wave of guilt for being so selfish and I shook away the thought in disgust.

After an hour and a half of travelling along a washboard road, my nerves were not the only things frayed. The corrugated surface had rattled every bone in my body, with my arms and shoulders aching from holding the wheel for so long. I'd passed just a few remote homesteads, with most of the landscape looking stripped. The natural tree cover of this area had been cleared to provide for agricultural land.

I checked the handheld GPS Nathan had sold me. I didn't want to set off down some farmer's driveway. The device took a minute to pick up the satellites, but then confirmed my location and I turned down Lake Nuga Nuga access road.

As my destination came into view, my heart sank. The idea was to submerge my ute in the lake, making it difficult to find and slow the inevitable manhunt. But the wide expanse of lily-covered water suggested I'd be hard pressed to hide a skateboard. Gentle sloping banks eased into a marshy foreshore, but the most surprising sight was the dead trees. Ancient denuded trunks thrust out of the surface, littering the lake like some scene from Hiroshima. If I managed to get my ute to travel in deeper, the trees were likely to halt its progress.

I retrieved my newly purchased binoculars and scoped the perimeter, looking for any signs of life. There were plenty of birds wading the edges, or roosting in shrubs, even some pelicans were working the waters, but no campers.

The incongruous sight of those stark black and white seabirds made me think of my last fishing trip. The freedom their flight represented seemed like a lifetime away. I closed my eyes and rested my forehead on the steering wheel. An unbearable wave of fatigue and despair buffeted my body and I lost the tenuous grip I had on my emotions. Images of Amber flooded my mind and before I knew it, tears were streaming down my face, making patterns in the dust on the dashboard.

It was like a massive snarling demon had cornered me, pinning me to the spot by the enormity of the fight ahead. But what choice did I have? Lie down and be captured, be charged with Amber's murder? Or press on and try to slay the beast?

I don't know how long I cried, but when I read my watch it was 5:23 PM. I'd been on the road for over ten hours to get to this point and I wasn't giving up now. My ute was equipped with a snorkel; if I found an area that looked deep enough and was free from trees, the plan may still work.

I started driving around the lake, but the access track soon ended, making the going much slower and more challenging. At a few points, I had to drive some distance from the waterfront. So, each time, I stopped and used a camp shovel to bury some of my provisions, wrapped in pieces cut from my tarp. I tried to hide them well, but even if the stores were discovered, they would look like food caches and lend credibility to my deception. It was just one more breadcrumb for the trail and a lead the cops would have to waste time staking out in case I returned.

At last, I came across a bay that had fewer tree trunks and appeared deeper than what I'd seen so far. It would have to do, the light was fading fast and it would soon be dark. I positioned my ute in what I thought was the best line, then offloaded the camping gear, my rucksack and Amber's bike. With all the food hidden, the next job was to destroy the tent and things I didn't need. It was a long ride back to Roma and I didn't want to carry any extra weight, but couldn't afford anyone finding this stuff. It would ruin my cover. I set about collecting firewood and then walked inland some way before building a campfire. Now all I could do was wait for nightfall to hide the smoke.

Like the sunrise that seemed so long ago, the vivid blue of the day transitioned into a deep blood-red sky that made the lake with its eerie lifeless trees appear like an artist's depiction of hell on earth. My hell on earth!

Once the sun had completed its death throes and yielded to the star-studded dark, I flipped on my headlamp and lit my fire. After ten minutes, I had a good blaze going and then item by item, burned all the camping gear. I watched as flames flared around the plastics, releasing acrid black fumes, before melting into a bubbling mass. Visions of Amber's face danced in the orange and yellow light, but rather than dispel the images I took some comfort in them. I was starting to accept what had happened, but felt the weight of the inevitable sadness to follow.

Under her watchful gaze I used a stick to fish out any metal items and piled them together. Zips, D-rings, tent pegs, buckles. I let each one cool, then threw it in the lake. It was time-consuming work, but I imagined that when they found the ute, this place would be crawling with police, SOCOs and sniffer dogs.

Eventually, there was nothing left that bore any resemblance to camping equipment, just several lumps of molten plastic. I poured water on them and threw them as far into the lake as I could, before putting out the fire.

Now it was time for my ute.

I'd bought the car when I moved down from Townsville and since then the two of us had travelled well over a hundred thousand kilometres together. She'd been part of my life for so many years, but I reached into the cab, used a rock to jam the accelerator and flipped her into drive without a second thought.

The wheels spun a little as she jumped forward, then gained speed across the scrubby ground before hitting the marshy shore. With the four-wheel drive engaged, a slew of mud sprayed up behind her as she slammed into the lake with a huge splash. Water lapped over the bonnet, but she kept going, the snorkel preventing the air intake from being inundated. As the cab filled, her momentum slowed and she came to a standstill with the white roof glinting in the beam of my headlamp, standing proud among the lily pads.

"Shit!"

But I shouldn't have doubted her. I could still hear the engine running and mud was churning up around the sides. The spinning wheels dug down through the silt of the lakebed and ever so slowly the roof of my faithful old ute disappeared out of sight. As if in a last farewell, a splutter of water shot in the air when the snorkel went under and then all the swirling stopped. Insects resumed their repetitive songs and the lily pads drifted back into place as if the lake had become my ally.

I turned and looked at my belongings - a bike, a rucksack and a new pair of walking boots. Now all I had to do was get back to Brisbane.

26

FACE

Lacing my boots, I put the rucksack on my chest and hefted the bike up onto my back. I'd been careful not to let the tyres touch the ground when retrieving it from the ute and hoped I could carry it as far as the Carnarvon Highway. Any tracks there would be less of an issue.

I checked my watch, 8:24 PM.

My headlamp carved out a cone of light in front of me as I stared into the darkness. I closed my eyes and Amber's face was there to greet me.

Smiling.

Beckoning.

I had to be strong. I was doing this for her memory. To catch her killer. To bring him to justice. Strong was too weak a word. I had to be dedicated, committed, focused. Steadfast. Nothing else would do. With a nod, I set off north into the national park proper, making sure my shoes left good prints in the mud.

As expected, it was tough work. Amber's cross-bike was

light, but cumbersome and I wasn't walking on any obvious tracks, so I had to place each step with care. I'd already stumbled through several huge spider webs, but my greatest fear was treading on a brown snake. Out here, a bite from one of those would be fatal.

At 10:30 PM, I came across a rocky outcrop and checked the GPS. I decided it was far enough to give the impression I was fleeing into the park, plus I was tiring and still had a long way to go. I took off my boots, switched back to my thongs and walked on the rocks for a while, before plotting a course for Carnarvon Creek.

About an hour later, I crossed the shallow waters where the Moolayember and Carnarvon Creeks merged and followed the banks of the latter. This waterway meandered across open farmland, all the way to the gorge, and was intersected by the highway. Unfortunately for me, that was still about 15 kilometres away. I had a short break and drank some water, before setting off again, avoiding soft ground and using my headlamp to guide me.

It was about 4:00 AM by the time I stumbled across the road. I'd been walking in a semi-trance for the last few hours, following my visions of Amber. When I stopped, my muscles screamed from the self-inflicted abuse. I sought refuge under the bridge and sat down with my back against the cold concrete support. My entire being craved sleep, but I knew there was less than two hours of darkness left. I had to make the most of the cover.

After eating an energy bar, I changed into my cycling gear and fitted the headlamp to my helmet. Stuffing everything else into the rucksack, I carried the bike the last few metres up to the sealed road. Once there, I threw my leg over and clipped my shoe onto the pedal. Taking a long hard look down the bitumen as far as my light allowed, I zeroed the cycle computer and set off with a grunt.

The change from carrying the bike to riding it was a welcome relief and the cool night air whipping over my skin was refreshing. I'd calculated that if I could maintain an average speed of over twenty kilometres per hour, it would still take me ten hours to reach Roma. And that was with no breaks.

The sky to my left grew lighter as I travelled south and soon I switched off the headlamp. I put my mind in park and got into the zone, pumping away at the pedals and trying to keep the average speed display on the bike computer as high as possible. There was little traffic on the road, but I still received some verbal abuse and a horn blast from a couple of drivers as they hurtled past. It was surprising to discover that even out Woop Woop the same battle lines were drawn between cars and cyclists.

I'd been riding for over six hours when I approached the outskirts of Injune. My water had run out and the heat of the day was intense. Sweat poured from my body and I had to replenish my fluids, or risk suffering heat exhaustion. I also needed to stock up on water before pushing on to Roma. But how could I keep a low profile? What if my face was plastered across the newspapers? A cyclist in the city goes unnoticed, but out here? I stuck out like a roo with a swollen scrotum.

I thought of a cover story and checked my GPS. Remembering that most of the shops were on the highway, I took a side road off to the right before entering the main drag. Circling round past the racecourse, I came out to the south and when I finally cycled into town, it appeared I was heading north.

I stopped and leant my bike up outside a newsagent, before

walking into the store, still wearing my helmet and sunnies. A stout man behind the counter looked up from his newspaper and gave me a nod. "G'day mate. You picked a hot one to use ya treadly."

From the look on his face, I suspected he was taking the piss, but I couldn't afford to rise to the bait. "You're not wrong there! I've a mate waiting for me up the highway at the 200 K mark from Roma, but I got delayed leaving and didn't bank on the heat."

"Two hundred Ks? Jesus, you must have a few loose in the top paddock!"

"I like to call it dedication. Where's your water bottles?"

"Over there."

He pointed to the fridge in the corner and went back to reading his paper. I walked towards the drinks, using the opportunity to check out the front cover of the newspapers in the stand. It took all my nerve to keep moving when staring back at me was my own face. It was a grainy shot taken from the auto-teller. The banner headline was a single word: 'WANTED'.

Holy shit! Perhaps posing for that camera wasn't such a bright idea. I bought the water and said my goodbyes to the disinterested shop attendant, before downing about a litre. I then refilled the bike's bottles and set off north along the highway. This time I used tracks to the east of the town to circle back and, once on the main road, hit the pedals with a renewed vigour.

If my picture was in today's newspapers, then the story must have broke sometime yesterday, so I had to be on my guard. My muscles ached and tiredness fogged my brain, but the thought of being caught kept the pedals spinning.

It was nearing three in the afternoon when I rode into Roma and I made my way straight to the station. I was guessing there'd only be a few trains a day going to Brisbane, so I was hoping I hadn't missed the last one.

Cycling down several roads lined with bottle trees, I followed my GPS to a green and cream station building, shaded by two large palms. Dismounting, I pushed my bike up the ramp access. After eleven hours in the saddle, it was a strange feeling to be walking again.

The place seemed deserted and I wandered out onto the platform. I must have missed the train. Down one end an old man brushed the concrete at a rate that was slower than any accumulating dust. He wore a wide-brimmed straw hat and dirty blue dungarees. I propped my bike against the wall and walked over to join him.

"G'day mate, have I missed the last train to Brisbane?"

He paused from his work with a quizzical look.

"Nope. Far as I know, no one's plannin' on stoppin' 'em."

His speech was as slow as his brushing.

"Right. When's the next one then?"

"Next one? We only get two through here a week."

"Two a week! Is there one today?"

"Yep. Guess you're in luck. Mind, you'll have to wait another eight hours or so. The Westlander stops here at 11:35 tonight. Takes 'bout twelve hours to get to the city from here."

He rested his chin on his hands, which were now on the top of the broom handle. "Course, that's if you've booked yourself a ticket. You have booked a ticket, right?"

"Can't I just buy one here?"

"Nope. No ticket office. Hasn't been one here for years. Not much point when there's only two trains a week." He paused looking down at the platform. "S'pose it's four really, if you count the return journeys."

I could feel exasperation building inside me, but tried to keep it out of my voice. "So how do I get a ticket?"

"You gotta book a seat or a sleeper."

"Can I do that in Roma?"

He looked taken aback. "Course you can, this ain't the back o' beyond, y'know!"

I gritted my teeth and managed a smile. "Sorry, I didn't mean to offend you. Where can I book a ticket?"

His expression was one of incredulity. Why did he have to deal with such a stupid city boy? "At the travel agents on Arthur Street, of course."

I humoured him. "Huh, where else? Thanks for that. Don't suppose you could give me directions?"

He shook his head in pity. "Turn left out the station, then turn right at the T junction. It's up on the left next to the IGA."

"Cheers, mate."

I walked away, but turned back when I thought of something else. "You know those sleepers you mentioned, are they single berth?"

"Nope. Most are triples, but they've got doubles in first class."

"Thanks again. Sorry to have bothered you."

He mumbled a reply as he returned to his brushing. "No worries."

I followed his directions and found the little travel agent in a matter of minutes. Keeping my disguise in place when talking to the old man was easy, but wearing a cycle helmet and sunnies while ordering a ticket in a shop was likely to cause more suspicion than it was worth.

In a moment of inspiration, I grabbed Amber's phone out of my rucksack and, while still straddling my bike, I clattered open the door.

"Am I too late to buy tickets for today's train?"

The startled woman behind the desk stared at me open mouthed. "Er… no… I don't think so. I'll check the availability."

I then put the phone against my ear, obscuring more of my face and discarded the bike outside, walking into the shop. "Yer babe, I'm here now. They're checking for availability. Yer, I know, I know. I'll sort it, don't worry. OK, stay on the phone. They shouldn't be too long." I turned my back on the woman as I spoke.

"Er, excuse me, sir. What tickets do you require?"

I glanced at her over my shoulder. "Have you got any twin sleepers left?"

Then said back to the phone, "That's what you want, right, babe? Uh hu… Yu… Yu… I know…"

"Sir? You're in luck, there's one left on tonight's service. How would you like to pay for that?"

"It'll have to be cash. The missus has my cards."

I carried on talking to myself and handed over just short of four hundred dollars when asked to pay. I then waited for the ticket, thanked the woman and dashed out. She'd no doubt remember me as a rude bastard, but it was unlikely she could describe my face.

With eight hours to kill, I decided that the train station was my best option. There was a phone near the entrance, so I ordered two pizzas and had them delivered there. The old boy was still brushing the platform and I walked to the other end, sitting down on a bench to wait for my food. I wasn't sure which feeling was the most pressing. Hunger or fatigue.

I somehow stayed awake long enough to eat a pizza, but I must have fallen asleep afterwards. It was dusk when I awoke, still sitting up on the bench, cap over my face, an uneaten pizza boxed beside me and the air filled with the sound of approaching sirens.

27

WAKE UP

The wailing noise got louder as I sat glued to the bench, action mired by indecision; mental wheels spinning like the tyres of my ute in the lake. I peered ahead of me into the gloom. I could grab the bike, jump off the platform and run across the track. There was open ground on the other side. But then where? What next? How did they find me? How did I screw up?

I somehow regained control of my muscles and launched myself off the seat, just as I realised the sirens were dwindling. I tried to disguise my sudden move by reaching my arms up into a stretch and stole a glance along the platform, but my subterfuge was unnecessary. I was all alone.

I flopped back down on the bench and gripped the wooden edge with both hands, digging my nails into the hard surface. The sweat covering my body had nothing to do with the balmy evening, but at least my heart was slowing.

How was I going to pull this off? The sound of a siren had been enough to cause a panic attack and here I was preparing to travel back into the lion's den. Back into the territory of a few thousand police officers. Back into the field of view of a few million prying eyes. I couldn't afford to let my guard down. I had to keep my focus on the endgame: to catch Amber's killer.

Amber... Once again, a sea of despair welled up inside me, threatening to drown me in grief. I closed my eyes, gritted my teeth, held my breath, hoping the pressure would stop the rising tide.

An age passed and I had to release the air, opening my eyes to find my knuckles white on the seat edge, with pain spreading through the muscles of my hands. Whatever I did, it seemed to work; the feeling had subsided and I could at least think now. I looked at my watch, 7:30 PM. Four more hours!

I ate the second pizza and guzzled down a bottle of coke, trying to formulate a plan, trying to stay awake. Whether it was the caffeine, or maybe just a sugar high, an embryo of an idea developed within my addled brain. I whiled away the hours, inspecting and prodding it from every angle, adding in what-ifs and fallback options. By the time the train pulled into the station, my idea had grown a spine, limb buds and had a functioning heart.

I woke to see jet-black hair strewn across the pillow next to me. Early morning light filtered in through the closed curtains, bathing Amber's naked body in a warm glow, painting golden highlights on the curves of her shoulders and hips. She was lying on her side, facing away from me, the bedclothes rolled up in a pile in front of her.

Her chest moved in a light rhythmical pattern and I could hear the gentle passage of air from her nose as she exhaled. Although she was sleeping, I couldn't resist the desire to touch her, feel the warmth of her smooth, tanned skin. I reached out and stroked her body. Slow. Tender. From the nape of her neck down to the small of her back. My hand then travelled further, lingering, caressing the rounded shape of her buttocks, feeling my arousal build, my need for her rising.

Her breathing changed as she regained consciousness and she wriggled under my touch. She rolled over to face me, her mouth forming a beautiful smile as she flicked a strand of hair from her face. Her eyes locked on mine, pupils dilated, amusement playing in her laughter lines.

She reached out her hand and stroked the side of my face, the smile dancing on her lips. Then she moved her hand to the back of my head and pulled me towards her. But it wasn't a loving move, more a violent grab. As I stared at her, bewildered, her eyes turned black and tears of blood trickled down her cheeks. I screamed in horror as the skin of her face peeled away, revealing the white blood-smeared bone beneath. As I struggled to free myself from her vice-like grip, her skeletal jaw dropped down and she bellowed, "Wake up!"

My eyes snapped open and I looked about in panic and confusion. I was on the lower of two bunk beds in a small cubicle of a room. There was a sink below a window covered by a blind, which was leaking light through the slats. The opposite wall housed a door that rattled as someone pounded on it.

"Wake up! Brisbane Roma Street. This is the end of the line!"

My memory flooded back in a huge wave of emotion and nausea. I leapt up and vomited in the sink.

The disembodied voice came again. "Are you OK in there?"

I turned the tap on and splashed water on my face, before grabbing a towel. "Yer, mate. I'm all good. I'll be out in a few minutes."

"You sure?"

I took a deep breath. "Yes. No worries."

"OK. Well, we need you out of there as soon as possible."

"Will do."

I sat back on the bed and held my face in the towel for a minute or two. I just hoped that nightmare was not how I'd remember Amber. Perhaps my subconscious was trying to kick my arse into gear.

I threw on my cycling clothes and gathered everything else into my rucksack. I then donned my cap and sunnies and checked the mirror. Stubble was forming on my chin, but it was not enough to disguise the line of my jaw. I'd have to keep my head down while in areas like the train station as I was certain there'd be CCTV surveillance.

I tapped the peak of my cap and nodded to my reflection. "OK, Sherlock, let's do this."

Easing the lock, I peered out along the corridor. The guard had left, as had the other travellers, and so I made my way to the exit and swung open the door. Despite my sunnies, my eyes took a few seconds to adjust to the bright sunlight and there before me was a mass of people gathered like a press conference. I caught my breath, but to my relief, they were just milling about on the platform and none paid me any attention.

I dropped my chin to my chest and strode off in the direction of the guard van. After collecting my bike, I replaced my cap with my helmet and walked down the stairs to get to street level. People were everywhere. I'd been in the main concourse of Roma Street Station so many times before, both in uniform and in civvies, but now I was a wanted man, a fugitive. My pulse was racing and I kept near the left wall so the stream of humanity only flowed past one side. I was making good progress when the sight of a billboard caused my heart to stop.

Plastered over it were several copies of the Courier Mail, the front page of which was my B-CAS ID photo. Once again, there was a single word headline: REWARD!

Recovering from the initial shock, I threw some coins in the vending machine and grabbed a copy. Then, lifting the bike on my shoulder, I exited through the turnstiles with the bored security guard not even glancing in my direction. Within minutes air was rushing by as I cycled over to the Parklands to read the article.

A solitary crow glided across a skyscraper backdrop, sunrays glinting off its black body creating a silver sheen that only seemed to emphasise the heat of the day. With a flap of its wings, it alighted on a street light and gave a loud caw for no apparent reason.

I looked up from my newspaper to the sound of the bird's feet clattering along its metal perch. Was it trying to get a better look at me? It cawed again and dropped down, landing on a nearby picnic table with a flurry of taffeta feathers.

Fixing me with an unblinking stare, it let out a caw between guttural clucks.

I spoke to it in a low voice. "Just my luck, spotted by a crow. Guess you must be after the reward? Here, this is the best I can do."

I threw it the remains of my last muesli bar and the bird used its large beak to grab the prize, before flying off across the expanse of grass.

I'd reread the article several times, but couldn't believe it. Three days after Amber's murder and the police were still focused on Brisbane! Why would they withhold search information? Surely they wanted people looking in the right area?

The false lead up the Bruce Highway courtesy of the hippy had got a mention, but nothing else. Had I covered my tracks to Carnarvon too well? Then the by-line caught my attention - Michelle Ludkowski. How did I know that name? Michelle Ludkowski?

Recollection dawned on me and with it the start of a crazy idea that was so outrageous it just might work.

28

BREAK IN

Michelle Ludkowski pressed a button on her remote and the garage door retreated upwards. It had been another long day and the anonymous reward donated in the hunt for Jonothan Byrne resulted in her phone ringing off the hook. Why did she have to talk to all the nutjobs just because she wrote the article? She had to pass on to the cops any of the leads that were halfway credible, but there had been precious few of those. She needed a glass of wine, either that or a bottle.

As she drove into the garage, she noticed her father's car was missing. Then remembered he was off out to a charity fundraiser at the Customs House. Good. She could do with a quiet evening in, curled up on the sofa with a trashy romance novel. There was even a tub of Häagen Dazs in the freezer.

She got out of the car and went through into the hallway, walking straight for the security panel on the wall as a shrill beeping sound echoed throughout the house. There were a few letters waiting for her on the elegant mahogany console table and she opened an envelope as she wandered into the kitchen. Kicking off her shoes, she stooped down to rub her heel, then froze as she straightened up.

A man was sitting on a stool next to the central island, wearing shorts, T-shirt and a pair of thongs. His back was resting against the stonework surface and he stared at her as he took a swig from a bottle of beer. She recognised him instantly. It was Jonothan Byrne.

She eyed me like the crow in the park, but I doubted I could buy her off with a piece of muesli bar. I waved the beer in her direction. "Hi Michelle. Hope you don't mind, I helped myself."

She didn't move, just stared. Was she going to bolt? I picked up a Ventolin puffer I'd found on the kitchen bench and threw it in her direction. She caught it out of instinct.

"Take a shot, you look as if you need it. We don't want you having another asthma attack, do we?"

Without taking her eyes off me, she double tapped the puffer almost as a reflex action, and inhaled. Despite that, she still took a minute to find her voice and I realised I was hearing it for the first time. It was a pleasant alto with a slight hint of an accent; from her name, I was guessing Polish.

"How did you get in here?"

"I'm a paramedic. Every now and again we have to break into houses."

"But the security system?"

"They rarely put motion detectors in kitchens. Too much heat. So, if you're going to leave a window open, don't make it in the kitchen."

"My father will be back any minute!"

"No, he won't. I saw him leaving in his Jag about an hour

ago, wearing a dinner jacket. It's Saturday night. I reckon we've got the evening to ourselves."

She reached into her pocket and snatched out her phone. "I'm calling the cops!"

"What? And miss out on the story of a lifetime? I thought you were an investigative journalist."

She paused as she looked up from her mobile.

"I save lives for a living, Michelle, you of all people should recognise that. I didn't murder Amber, but I know who did. And what's more, he's a serial killer."

She continued to stare at me for what seemed like an age, her phone raised in her hand. But she hadn't dialled the number. Then, as if in slow motion, she put it back in her pocket and walked over to the fridge. Taking out a beer, she circled around the island and sat down on the opposite side.

"Go on. I'm listening."

29

GUT INSTINCT

Detective Giallo looped a dark blue tie round his head and slipped the knot up to his neck. He then folded the collar down on his short-sleeved checked shirt and used his fingers to comb back his hair. He was standing outside the Chief Inspector's office having read the front page of the 'Sunday Mail'. It had made him choke on his Weet-Bix. The small headline was squeezed in alongside the main cover story, something about a radio DJ's telephone prank. But when his mobile displayed a summons from the Chief his despondency was confirmed. There was nothing funny about that call.

He knocked on the door and received a gruff, "C'min."

Giallo entered to find the Chief sitting behind his desk, with his chin resting on his interleaved fingers. He was a fat man in his late fifties who could sweat even in an air-conditioned office. Despite only being 9:00 AM, discoloured patches were already blossoming from both armpits.

The newspaper was laid out in front of him, open to the article that set about berating the efforts of the police force to date. With 'minimal effort' one of their journalists had unearthed a trail leading out west and Jonothan Byrne was said to have 'gone bush'.

"I presume you've read this."

He flicked the newspaper with obvious disdain.

"Yessir."

He shook his head and his jowls wobbled. "I trusted your gut instinct! You convinced me he'd remained in Brisbane. You said you knew this guy! You said the hippy with the phone proved he was leading us away from Brisbane! You said he'd want to clear his name! Now we look like fucking cockheads!"

His voice was getting louder with each sentence and his face redder. Giallo hoped he wouldn't stroke out in front of him.

"Just so you're aware, Giallo, I've pulled back the teams you had surveilling his associates and established a Task Force to go out west. I can't believe I was so stupid as to be taken in by your bullshit!"

"But sir, the crime scene. It didn't add up."

The Chief glared at his detective. "How so? It was an open-and-shut case. How much more evidence did you need, for Chrissake?"

"That's just it. Most murders you've at least got to look for clues. But this one? I've never been to a crime scene with so much evidence against a suspect. It didn't sit right with me."

The Chief stared at him and his face seemed to take on a slight purple hue. He shot to his feet, his fists resting on the desk and leant forward towards Giallo.

"Sit right? Sit right! He's as guilty as a puppy sitting right next to a pile of shit! Now get out of my sight!"

"Yessir."

Giallo turned and went to leave his office, but paused when the Chief called out. "And Giallo…"

"Yessir?"
"Lose the tie. You look like a jerk."

30

SUNBURN

As it turned out, Michelle had been easier to buy than the crow. She had required nothing tangible, just a promise of an exclusive story. I guess she figured that either way, guilty or innocent, there was a bestseller in it for her. All she had to do was pervert the course of justice ever so slightly. It was a no-brainer for an ambitious journo and I'd banked on her having flexible morals. But in her defence, she may have thought she owed me the benefit of the doubt. I had saved her life only a week ago.

I spent the night cycling the streets of Brisbane, looking for my quarry. But as dawn broke and St John's Cathedral bells rang out, I gave up and made my way to the Maccas at Kangaroo Point. At least on the Southside I was less likely to bump into any ambos who knew me.

I had to fight to keep my eyes open, but years of night shifts had trained my body to accept similar diurnal abuse. Over a massive breakfast in a concealed booth, I read Michelle's article with some trepidation. Way to go, girlfriend!

Now the police would be champing at the bit, but with any luck about seven hundred kilometres west of here.

After eating my fill, I cycled over to the Captain Burke Park and lay down on the grass in the shade of the Story Bridge, among the other Sunday-morning leisure seekers. Looking up at the huge iron superstructure spanning the Brisbane River, I couldn't help but feel inconsequential; trivial in the grand scheme of things. Here I was, my world turned upside down, but like the cars crossing the bridge, life just seemed to carry on.

Amber smiled at me. I was lying on a picnic rug and we'd finished eating my latest alfresco offering: barbecued jerk chicken with fresh mango salsa. She was wearing a floral dress and sitting next to me holding a glass of sparkling wine, watching the bubbles rush to the surface to escape the liquid. Her dark hair hung down like a black satin curtain and the sun shone through the strands, tracing patterns across my face.

I felt so content, replete, basking in the glow of this beautiful woman. She moved her head to one side and I had to hold up a hand to shield my eyes, but the gentle warmth became an intense heat. I raised my arms only to find my skin bubbling; the blisters bursting as they smouldered. A scream echoed from my lips as I looked at her in confusion. But she just winked back, blowing a kiss that only served to fan the flames engulfing my body.

I woke with a start and blinked at the intensity of the light. I'd slept for so long I was no longer in the bridge's shade and was now lying in full sunlight. Shit, I hoped Amber wasn't going to make a habit of warnings like that. Soon I'd be too scared to sleep.

Shaking my head, I climbed back onto my bike. There were a few things I had to get organised before tonight's search.

It was Monday night and Scotty was about to drink a beer in front of the TV when he heard the characteristic sound of his classic Camaro's engine roar into life. She was his pride and joy and he kept her in a dedicated garage to the side of his house. He'd only take her out for a drive when the forecast predicted clear skies. Mud wasn't allowed anywhere near her polished pristine paintwork.

"What the fuck!"

He sprinted down the stairs, grabbing the baseball bat from behind the door, and ran to the garage. The roller door was open, but the car was just sitting there, the engine ticking over. He raised his weapon.

"Hello... Anyone there?"

He made his way inside and used one hand to feel for the switch, flipping it down. The fluorescent strip light on the ceiling remained dark.

"Shit!"

Peering around the gloom, he couldn't see anyone hiding in the shadows. He bent down and looked through the open car window, but the seats were empty. Leaning through the gap he reached in to turn on the lights.

A low voice came from the back seat. "I wouldn't do that if I was you."

"Jesus!"

Scotty recoiled in fright and belted the back of his head on the doorjamb. "Fuck!"

The voice hissed out again. "Keep the noise down, Scotty, they might be watching your house."

He used the bat like a crutch and bent over it, rubbing the back of his head. "That you, boss? I was wondering when you'd show up. So sorry to hear about Amber, mate. You do know you're in a world of shit, though, don't you?"

"Yes. D'you believe what they're saying?"

"Fuck no! I might've had my doubts if it'd been one of the brass stabbed to death. But Amber? Not a fucking chance. Hey, I saw the way your face would change when she called, or when her name was mentioned. You and her were the real deal, man. Fuck, I'm so sorry for you."

He had opened the door and was now sitting on the driver's seat, with his legs out the car, still rubbing his head. "And as to you having a morphine stash, that's a crock of shit. Most shifts you're like an ADHD kid on crack, even before your caffeine. I just couldn't work out why you ran."

"Thanks, mate. I ran because… the real murderer had done such a good frame job on me I felt I didn't have a choice. Bit difficult to prove your innocence when you're locked behind bars. Anyway, d'you want to take this museum piece out for a spin so we can talk face-to-face, lying on this back seat is fucking uncomfortable."

"What? Drive her at night? That's a big ask, boss!"

"Well, if the cops are watching your place, they might get suspicious that you're talking to yourself in the garage. And if they find me here, you'll be up for harbouring a known fugitive."

"Good point, I'll go lock the house."

"Oh, and Scotty, bring some beers, would ya?"

He was back in a minute or two and I heard the clink of a six-pack being dumped in the footwell. He revved the engine, pulled out of the driveway and headed off down the road.

"Keep an eye out for anyone tailing you."

"Already on it, boss. I'll cut through a few estates, then

head out to the Bunyaville Reserve. There won't be a soul out there this time of night."

"Sounds good. And Scotty, thanks."

"No worries, boss. You've really been fucked over. Guess you were right about your serial killer. Got any ideas who it is?"

I twisted round to get comfortable. "Yes, but the last person I told ended up with a knife in her chest. So, if you don't mind, I'll keep my suspicions to myself."

"I'm fine with that, boss."

We fell into silence as he made a series of turns, in and out of side streets. "Pretty sure no one's following us, I'll head off to the reserve now. By the way, how d'you start my girl?"

"You shouldn't keep a spare key under the wheel arch. Far too obvious."

"Fair call."

I laughed. "Bet you thought your car had transformed into the real Bumble Bee!"

"I've told you before, it's not fucking Bumble Bee; that was a 1967 Camaro. Mine's a 1970s model. Totally different."

"Right. Silly me."

After a while the road surface became bumpy and he pulled over to a stop, switching off the engine. "Here we are boss, no one's around. You can get out now."

He climbed from the car and flipped the seat forward to let me out. I unfolded my aching body from the back and stepped into the night. The air was full of the smell of eucalypts.

"Jesus, boss! What the fuck have you done with your hair?"

"Clippers and bleach. I had to do something, my face is plastered everywhere."

"Yes, but did you have to choose a look like a sunburnt Sisqo!"

"Enough of your bullshit, where are those stubbies?"

He broke off two beers and handed me a bottle.

I reached into the car and retrieved my rucksack, pulling out an old brown overcoat I'd bought from Vinnies. I laid it on the ground and poured the beer over it.

Scotty stared at me. "If I'd known you'd do that, I'd have brought the can of Fosters someone left in my fridge."

I smirked, turned my back on him and urinated over the coat.

"What the fuck are you doing?"

"Believe me Scotty, you don't want to know."

I shook off the last few drops and picked up the coat, hanging it out on a nearby tree.

"Right, that shouldn't take too long to dry."

He sighed. "So what can you tell me?"

"Well, I need you to get a few things, before I can set a trap. The general idea is to catch the bastard in the act. But I have to warn you, if it doesn't work out, you could face prison time for helping me."

He gave a slight nod. "I know the risks. But I'm doing this for both you and for Amber. She didn't deserve to die like that." He handed me another beer and raised his bottle towards me. "To Amber. May she rest in peace once we've caught this fucker."

Over the past few days I'd somehow bolted a lid on my emotions, encasing them in mental concrete so I could focus on the task in hand. But now, seeing Scotty and talking about Amber for the first time since her murder, I could feel the cracks spreading.

I had to grit my teeth and looked down at the muddy track for a second, while I buried my anguish deeper into my subconscious. I knew the grief of losing Amber would be something I'd have to deal with later and shutting it down like this was not wise. But I had to catch the killer and clear my name.

In a heartbeat I'd regained control and looked my friend in the eyes. Twisting the top off my beer, I clinked the bottles together. "I'll drink to that."

31

SITUS INVERSUS

Detective Giallo was sitting at his desk chewing on the end of a pencil and wondering whether anyone would notice if he ducked out for another smoke. It was only an hour since the last one, but boredom had that effect on him. So much for cutting down to impress that pathologist. After his meeting with the Chief, he'd been dropped from the Byrne's Task Force and he found himself investigating an assault at Carseldine Meadows. There were now six similar cases from the same caravan park arranged in front of him. A series of grub versus grub battles that not even the combatants cared about. The Chief was making his point, loud and clear.

He threw the pencil at his computer screen and stood up from his wheelie chair, causing it to fly backwards into a filing cabinet. The clang reverberated around the large open-plan office and everyone turned to look in his direction. He shrugged an apology and wandered out the building to the designated smoking area. The latest nicotine hit was just dissolving into his bloodstream when his mobile rang.

He raised an eyebrow when he saw the caller ID and

pressed 'accept'. "Dr Beecham, how nice to hear from you. Is this call work related, or personal?"

"In your dreams, Detective Giallo. I thought you might be interested in a hearing a theory I had about the Amber Shaw case, but I'm regretting contravening the recognised protocols."

He smiled at how easy it was to rile her. "Please, Doctor, I didn't intend to make any insinuation and apologise for being less than formal. What do you have for me?"

He remembered her smile and imagined her long fingers drumming on the desk as she paused before answering. "Well, you know how during the autopsy I discovered Ms Shaw had dextrocardia?"

"That's the switched heart thing, right?"

"Yes. And I mentioned at the time that it was actually situs inversus totalis. As in, all her internal organs were transposed."

He sighed, recalling the gruesome spectacle in the morgue and that niggling crumb of guilt that bothered him ever since. Could her murder have anything to do with Byrne's crazy serial killer story? Mind you, he was off the case now and his frustration at being sidelined caused him to take another drag on his cigarette. "Oh, I remember. She was one in a million."

The pathologist took his comment literally. "Mmm, not quite Detective. It's rare but not unheard of. From recollection, the frequency is 1 in 10,000, so for Brisbane there should be around two hundred individuals with the condition."

"Really?"

"Yes. Anyway, the reason I'm calling is that I remember being surprised she had enough time to draw the 'J' in her blood. The blade sliced through her aorta. With her heart still pumping, she would have been unconscious in seconds and dead in less than a minute."

"But it wouldn't take long to trace out a single letter and she must've intended to write more than that."

"True, but with only seconds before hypoxia rendered her unconscious, the killer would see his victim writing in her own blood. Why would he let her do that? Now, if Ms Shaw had a normal body configuration without dextrocardia, the blade would have punctured the left ventricle, impairing the heart, but paradoxically slowing her inevitable death."

"So, what you're trying to say is that if she had her heart in the right place, she would've had time to write the J after the killer left."

"Precisely. But as we now know, that wasn't possible."

"Which means the killer wrote in her blood?"

There was a pause before she answered. "Detective Giallo, my job is to determine the facts, yours is to interpret the implications."

He pictured her smiling and resolved to find out more about this frosty pathologist. "Right. Thanks for the heads-up, Doc. Just one thing, is there any way the killer could've known she had... dextrocardia?"

"Well, unless she had a chest X-ray or an ECG, even Ms Shaw may not have known."

32

BAIT

The previous night, I'd stumbled across the subject of my search by accident, curled up fast asleep next to an industrial garbage bin. He was clutching a box of cask wine like a father holding a baby and I wasn't sure which smelt worse, the man or the refuse.

A day later, he was back slumbering in his foetid lair and I was in an alleyway on the opposite side of the road, standing beside my bike. Now, with everything in place, it was time to bait my trap. I took out the phone Scotty had given me and hit three numbers. Zero. Zero. Zero.

Within five minutes, an ambulance arrived with lights flashing, but thankfully no siren. It was past midnight. From my secluded vantage point, I could see the ambos wander over to the alley, white light from the roof of the truck illuminating the scene.

I recognised one as Gerry Seabrook and could just about hear their conversation.

"There he is, by the bin. Jesus, is that stink from him or the rubbish? Oh, shit!"

"What?"

"It's Mr fucking Wendal."

"Who?"

"Don't worry, he's a regular. If we're in luck, he'll tell us to fuck off."

Gerry bent down and gave the sleeping man a shove.

"C'mon Mr Wendal, wakey-wakey. It's the ambulance."

He reached towards his chest. "C'mon, wakey..."

A slurred shriek echoed out. "Fuck off ya cunt! Can't ya let a black fella sleep, ya fucka!"

"Now, now. There's no need to be like that. We had a call from someone who thought you were unconscious or dead."

"Well, I'm neither, am I? Now fuck off!"

Gerry turned to his colleague. "I do believe this gentleman doesn't require our services. Perhaps we should comply with his wishes and fuck off. You know what they say, the customer's always right."

They walked away, but as an afterthought Gerry called back. "Do us a favour, Mr Wendal. Pull your legs in. I'd hate for us or the cops to come and disturb you again."

He grumbled another expletive, but dragged his legs out of sight and the ambos got into the cab and drove off. As he passed by, I caught a glimpse of Gerry talking into the mic and the normality of it struck me. That could've been me only a few days ago.

With the loss of the ambulance's halogen lights, the early morning scene returned to muted tones, courtesy of the sodium glow from a solitary street lamp. Distant sounds drifted over from the traffic passing through The Valley, but otherwise all was quiet. All was still.

I retreated deeper into my hiding place and locked up my bike. Trying not to make a sound, I changed into my homeless clothes: newly scuffed walking boots, thin trousers, soiled T-shirt, tatty old deer-stalker hat, and a pair of heavy-framed glasses. I then put a dab of Vick's inside each nostril, before pulling out the overcoat from its sealed plastic bag and throwing it on.

With my disguise complete, I took a swig from the box of cask wine, dribbling most down my front, picked up my rucksack and lurched out into the street. I staggered across the deserted road before stumbling headlong into Mr Wendal's alley, clattering against the bin and collapsing onto a pile of garbage bags.

Mr Wendal woke. "Wah the fuck! Gerroutta 'ere, ya fucka!"

I lay as still as I could manage with my face in some foul-smelling slime, while Mr Wendal continued to protest about his latest sleep-time intruder. "Dis is my spot. I was 'ere first, na fuck off ya cunt!"

With a surprising amount of power, he swung out a well-aimed boot that crunched into my leg just below my knee. The pain was so intense it caused my eyes to water, but other than letting out a slight whimper, I maintained my overall comatose demeanour.

He landed another couple of less effective kicks, before deciding I was too much effort. After what felt like a lifetime, I stole a cautious look and could make out his foetal form, once again curled up behind the bin. Five minutes later, he was snoring away, so I dragged myself further into the alley and sat up with my back to the wall.

Whatever it was I'd fallen into was still adhering to my cheek and was smeared across my glasses. I took them off and used my sleeve to wipe the slime from my face. Whether I spread some into my mouth, or it was the smell combined with that of my coat, I'm not sure, but a wave of nausea hit me causing me to spew.

As I spat into the pool of mucus and bile next to me, I

recalled a similar experience in the train and my mind flashed up that first Amber nightmare. But not the evocative preamble, just the horrific part. It was over in an instant, but when I looked down, tears were mingling with the vomit on the concrete.

Somehow I stopped myself from wiping my eyes and screwed them up, leaning back against the wall and letting the tears roll down my face. I thought I'd been holding it together, trying to seal my feelings down deeper with every hour that passed. I only hoped I could catch the killer before the inevitable happened and I lost myself in a wormhole of psychotic grief.

The stomach acid was burning my gums and tongue, creating an awful taste. Looking about, I grabbed my box of goon and took a big slug, swilling it around my mouth. I was about to spit it out when I realised Mr Wendal was watching me.

I swallowed the mouthful and clutched the cask close to my chest. His eyes never left mine, nor blinked, as he rose cross-legged amongst the garbage. We both sat there, transfixed. A Mexican standoff over a box of cheap Australian wine.

Mr Wendal was the first to speak. "Ya wanna stay 'ere t'night, ya gonna have t'share dat, brudda."

"S'mine!" I held the box tighter.

"No need to fight, brudda. I's only wanna nightcap."

He produced a tattered old enamel cup from a bag he'd been lying on and waggled it towards me. "No need fo' tings t' get nasty. Just a friendly drink wid ya black brudda?"

I switched my eyes from his to the cup and back a few times.

"C'mon, brudda, just 'alf a cup?"

I nodded. "Half now, an' a fullun in mornin' if you leave me the fuck alone."

He grinned at me, the dim light glinting off the saliva coating his few remaining crooked teeth. "Deal!"

He held out his cup further and I filled it half way, not forgetting to add a shake to my hands. Once he realised that was all he was getting, he withdrew his trophy and cradled it below his nose, inhaling deep as if to enjoy the bouquet. Then with a flick of his wrist, the wine was gone. He wiped his face with the back of his hand and dropped the cup back in his bag. "Tanks fo' dat, brudda. Sweet dreams, I'll see ya at breakfast."

He grinned again, gave me a nod and returned to his position behind the bin. As he was no doubt watching, I took another slug from my cask and moved deeper into the alley, away from my vomit. I curled up on my rucksack, with a hand through the handle of the wine box and pretended to sleep.

Mr Wendal's snoring soon broke the silence and I sat up to watch over his sleeping body. I reached into my bag to retrieve a caffeine tablet, but the search only found my newspaper cutting. Lifting it out, I traced the edge of the dark outline in the dim light. I didn't need to be able to see to recall every detail of her face. I allowed myself a moment's indulgence, a few seconds of false intimacy created by the touch of her image, then returned the picture to my bag. The nights would be long from now on, but I had to stay vigilant during the hours of darkness. After all, if I was the serial killer that's when I would stage a non-suspicious death.

I raised my eyes to the heavens. One by one, the stars disappeared and now there was a blue wash permeating through the stratosphere, like pale ink spreading through blotting paper. The light was also improving in the alley, allowing me to see more detail on the exoskeletons of the cockroaches whose activities I'd followed throughout the night. The insects sensed the day's arrival and soon it was only the adventurous or foolhardy ones left, working through the garbage for that last morsel before their enforced rest.

With the break of dawn, I decided to follow the roaches' lead and get some sleep. There was no cover for Liam to strike now and Mr Wendal wouldn't leave the alley without claiming his free drink. I looked at my watch for the thousandth time that night, 5:20 AM, but on this occasion I realised my error. The homeless rarely wear watches; there's little point in marking time when you're on the street. I slipped it from my wrist and dropped it in my bag, curling up as best I could and closing my eyes. Here's hoping Mr Wendal was a late riser.

I woke with my boot being kicked and an enamel cup tapping on the concrete below my nose.

"C'mon, sleepy head. I needs me breakfast."

"Wha'?"

"Ya mightn't 'member, but ya made a deal wid me lass night. Ya owes me a cup o' grog, brudda. Na pay up!"

I rubbed my face and sat up straight, clutching my bag and sneaking a glimpse at my watch in the opening. It was still only 6:00 AM; feigning a hangover was real easy.

I poured him a mug-full of wine, but unlike last night, this time he sipped it, as if savouring the first shot of coffee before venturing out to work. I let my head loll down, but didn't sleep. The ball was now rolling and I couldn't afford to lose track of my bait.

When he'd finished, he tapped his cup on the pavement and threw it in his bag before standing up. "Well, tanks for dat, brudda. I'm off now, yet anudda day beckons."

He paused and looked at me. "Kunaatha, as my mob says."

With a nod, he turned and walked out of the alley, pausing as the early morning light illuminated one side of his body. He seemed to consider both directions with his hands on his hips, then shrugged his shoulders and set off away from the sun. As soon as he left, I jumped up, grabbed my stuff and crept to the entrance.

He was strolling along the pavement with his small bag slung over his shoulder, heading towards the Parklands. After checking the coast was clear, I slunk across the street, changed into my cycle gear and unlocked my bike. Within a few minutes I'd found Mr Wendal and spent the rest of the day, tailing him at a discrete distance, resting when I could.

That night I stumbled into his alleyway and offered him the same deal. He was sitting with his back to the bin and eyed me with suspicion. "Nah, fuck off!"

I'd already sat down further in the alley. "OK. Full cup now and another in the morning."

He stared at me for some time, with his head to the side, then broke the silence. "Why, brudda? Whatcha want wid me?"

I took a guzzle from my topped-up box of wine and shrugged. "I don't like sleepin' alone. These streets at night... they scare me. I may be wrong, but I kinda think two sets of eyes and ears are better than one."

He continued to stare at me, the look penetrating deep into my soul. It was unnerving. Then he let out a cackle and retrieved his cup, tapping it on the ground, before waving it at me.

"Fine by me. I rely on me smell for safety. Stinkin' like I do can 'ave its advantage." He winked at me. "Evva 'eard o' anyone messin' wid a skunk?"

He had a point, but unfortunately he was wrong.

33

WASH

Time marched by with mind-numbing boredom. Following an alcoholic homeless man gave me a whole new perspective on a wasted life. I often wished I could get as shit-faced as him, just to zone out for a while.

Every couple of days I would hide across from his latest sleeping place and call an ambulance. Sometimes he stayed. Other times they transported him and he scored a bed for the night. When he did go, I hung around the streets near the Royal in my cycle gear, waiting for him to leave, or be kicked out. It was a dangerous time for me. Despite my growing beard, there were too many ambos coming and going and I had to be careful.

Sometimes I'd grab a little sleep when he was dozing in a park, after he'd downed a bag of goon. However, I always set my alarm for an hour and lay with my head on my backpack so it would wake me. But this was only a morning luxury. If I lost him, which happened a couple of times, it gave me the rest of the day to track him down.

This evening we were hunkered down in a small side

street, which was open at both ends. I felt exposed, more vulnerable, but Mr Wendal had been far too drunk to care. I debated calling an ambulance, but he'd only been discharged a few hours ago and had been binging ever since. In hindsight, it would've been safer if I had.

It was gone 2:00 AM when I heard a bottle smash in a nearby road followed by the sound of laughter. I huddled closer to the wall as the silhouettes of three men appeared at the intersection. Light glinted through the brown glass of a beer bottle as one of them lent back for a final swig before lobbing the stubbie high in the air. It burst on the bitumen with a popping shatter.

"Wait up, I need a piss."

One man staggered down our side road and I cringed when the shout came. "Hey, guys! Look what I found. A fuckin' Abbo! Jesus he stinks!"

"C'mon, Brad leave the poor fucker alone."

"Will do, soon as I've given him a wash."

He began urinating on Mr Wendal, who leapt up and pushed him away. "Fuck off ya cunt!"

Brad stumbled backwards falling on the road, but the third man, who was yet to speak, appeared beside Mr Wendal. There was a loud smack of white on black skin as a fist drove into the side of his head, causing him to collapse to the floor like a bundle of dirty laundry.

Brad was back on his feet. "Right! This little coon's gonna get a good kicking!"

But before he could swing his foot, a scruffy walking boot impacted his knee with enough force to buckle his leg. He cried out in agony and his mate swung round to see what had happened, only to find his vision filled with stars as the bridge of his nose exploded under the impact of my head-butt.

The two of them were now writhing on the road as I faced

the one who remained at the intersection. He raised his palms, shaking his head as he backed away and ran.

I turned to Mr Wendal who held out a hand while rubbing his jaw with the other. Reaching down, I pulled him up.

"Tanks for dat, brudda." He retrieved his bag. "Guess yous was right. Ma smell don't always work. C'mon, wees best fuck off."

34

PUSHBIKE

Detective Giallo was so engrossed in the files on his desk he was unaware of his approaching colleague, Adam Addis. "Ivy Watson? Wasn't that the death in care a week or two back? What you still doing with that, thought it was done and dusted. Hasn't the Chief been assigning you every shit case that curls out the arse of Carseldine Meadows. Like big steaming turds of 'don't fuck up'."

Giallo swept up the paperwork in a single pile and threw it in a drawer, turning to look at the other detective. He was in his late twenties with a blonde crew cut and was wearing a tailored suit and tie. He already looked like management, but just hadn't attained the rank. Yet. The only thing holding him back was his propensity for gossip.

"Thanks for that vivid description, Double A. It seems the harder I try to flush those Meadows jobs down, more keep floating up. But no, I was reviewing some recent cases relating to Jonothan Byrne. What's the latest from the Task Force?"

Detective Addis smiled and tapped the hilt of his holstered

gun. "I could tell you, but I'd have to shoot you. Either that or the Chief'll have me shot."

"C'mon. If you end up in a shoot-out with the Chief, at least you'll have a bigger target."

"Ha! You're not wrong there."

He sat down on the nearby chair and sidled over closer, craning his neck back and forth. "In all honesty, we're pushing shit uphill out there. They've found his ute buried in some fucking swamp and a few food stashes, but all the sightings are hampered by the mobile coverage. Y'know, like, there isn't any. Some pissed-up redneck spots something suspicious and reports it when he returns to semi-civilisation three days later. The next thing you know, there's twenty cops chasing a bullshit lead that's already days old."

"Mmm… Sounds as if our man couldn't have planned it better."

"What you thinking, Gee? You still believe he's in the city?"

"Careful, talk like that will have the Chief coming after you with all his guns blazing." Giallo shrugged and chewed the end of his pencil. "I don't have any evidence to back up my suspicions."

"Right. Well, I was on my way to the latest Task Force briefing, so I'd better be off. Another thirty minutes of my life is about to be wasted. I have to say, investigating scrotes from Carseldine Meadows is starting to look appealing."

"Be careful what you wish for, mate."

He laughed and wandered off to the meeting room, leaving Detective Giallo to stare at his desk drawer. The phone interrupted his thoughts.

"Hi Gee, it's Melissa from reception. Got a Mr Shaw on the line enquiring about his daughter's property. Are you able to take the call, the Byrne's Task Force are all tied up in a meeting?"

He sighed. "Yer, go ahead Mel, put him on. You owe me one."

"Thanks Gee, connecting him now."

"G'day Mr Shaw, I'm Detective Frank Giallo. How can I help?"

The sound on the other end of the line was that of a broken man. It's often said how parents should never have to bury their children, but that sentiment had found a physical embodiment in the voice of Amber Shaw's father.

"Hello Detective. I understand that you're no doubt busy, but we're trying to sort out Amber's things and wondered when you'd be returning the items you collected."

Melissa owed him more than one for this. "Ah, well, unfortunately as the investigation is still ongoing, any secured property will be held as evidence, often until after the court case has finished."

"I understand. That's what I suspected. Anyway, sorry to bother you, Detective."

"Not a problem, Mr Shaw. And I'm so sorry for your loss. Please let me assure you we're doing everything we can to track down the person responsible for your daughter's murder."

"Thank you, Detective. But I'm not sure you're chasing after the right man… Amber felt so… secure with Jon, but I've already told you folks that. I guess you know what you're doing…"

His voice trailed off, but he stayed on the line and Giallo was reluctant to hang up while still listening to the man's breathing. He could sense the sorrow oozing through the speaker. A body on autopilot. A mind lost in grief. In the distance there was the chirping of cicadas. "Erm... Is there anything else I can help you with, sir?"

"What?"

"Can I help you with anything else, sir?"

"Oh... no. I'm standing outside her house now. I... I just don't know where to start..." He sighed and Giallo could picture him on the dusty driveway, directionless and despondent. His distracted voice returned. "Huh... her pushbike's gone. Was that another thing you guys took?"

"Her pushbike?"

"Yes. She always kept it up against the shed, but it's not there. Can't imagine why you'd need that as evidence."

"Right... Well, I'm not sure either, sir, but I'll see what I can find out for you."

"OK. Goodbye."

The line went dead and left Detective Giallo staring into space. He replaced the receiver as his free hand drummed on the desk. A minute passed and he grabbed the phone. "Hey, Robbie, it's Gee."

"G'day, Gee, what can I do for you?"

"Can you check the evidence log for the Shaw murder?"

"No worries, mate, it's all on the computer. Just give me a sec to bring it up. What you looking for?"

"Can you tell me if they collected a pushbike from the scene?"

"A pushbike? Hold on."

There was the tapping sound of a keyboard. "Nope. Nothing like that. Can't imagine why it would be relevant, she was stabbed in her bedroom."

"True. It was just a thought."

"No worries, mate."

"Oh, Robbie?"

"Yep?"

"Am I able to see that surveillance video from the Toowoomba BCF? The one from the car park that showed a view of Byrne's ute?"

"C'mon Gee, I know you're not on the case, mate. You won't be able to sign it out. The Chief'll have my balls if I let you take it."

"Yes, but you've got a computer there in the evidence store that can play the file. No one has to sign it out if you happen to be watching it when I swing by."

"I'll put the kettle on."

"I'll bring some cookies."

35

CHARITY

It was Christmas Eve and hoards of people were out on the streets, with tinsel and fake santas adorning every bar and shop window. But I was far from being in a festive mood.

We were back in the original alleyway and I was once again playing with the roaches to the sound of snoring when I heard approaching footsteps. My body tensed, ready for action, as the beam from a flashlight illuminated the industrial bin, then travelled around to rest on Mr Wendal's legs. Was this Liam or another drunken assault? I readied my trap, but froze when I realised there were two voices.

"Got someone over here."

"Righto, be with you in a minute."

A young man in his twenties knelt down next to Mr Wendal and placed the flashlight on the ground so its initial harsh light was now only a dim glow. He was wearing a fluorescent yellow vest along with a radio and for a split second my heart went into overdrive. Had I just been cornered by the police? But then I realised he had no sidearm.

There was a sound from outside the alley and he turned to

reveal STREETWATCH stencilled across his back. I relaxed a little, it was one of the Chaplain's volunteers. He had woke a disgruntled Mr Wendal, who responded in his usual way.

"Wha' tha fuck!"

"G'day, sir, my name's Simon. I'm here to check you're OK and see if I can help you in any way?"

"Ya cudda helped me by not fuckin' wakin' me, ya fucka! Na piss off unless ya wanna boot in ya smilin' fuckin' face!"

"Come on, sir, there's no need to be like that. We're just here to spread some Christmas cheer and provide you with a blanket and some food."

He looked dumbfounded. "Well, why tha fuck d'ya not say soona?"

As they were talking, another man entered the alley with a small parcel. I caught my breath. In the dim light, I could make out the shape of the Chaplain himself. With his photographic memory, if he saw my face I was screwed.

Without making a sound, I pulled down the peak of my hat and tried to melt into the garbage bags, but as Simon stood he grabbed the flashlight and swung it my way.

"Oh, sorry sir, I didn't realise there was anyone else here. Can I offer you...?"

I tensed my body and curled my fists, arching my back so I rose out of the garbage. In a swift move I was standing, still hunched over, fists clenched and head down. With all the menacing undertones I could muster I spat out a growl. "Put that light out and leave. Now!"

He dropped the torch beam, but stood his ground. "Oh, come on, sir. We're only handing out Christmas presents."

"I don't want none of no charity!"

"But..."

The Chaplain placed a hand on the younger man's shoulder. "Our job is done here. I think it's best we do as he says."

The two of them retreated from the alley and left me listening to Mr Wendal rummaging through his goodies. He'd already wrapped the blanket round his shoulders and was tucking into a bar of chocolate when he began chuckling.

I relaxed and turned to him. "What?"

"Guess ya dunna like do-gooders, brudda. Ya certainly scared da shit outta me!"

"Funny. You don't smell any worse."

He looked at me for a while, then his lined face crinkled into a beaming smile. I couldn't help but smile back and there, amidst the squalor, we both laughed. Between guffaws, I retrieved my box of wine. "C'mon, get out your cup. Let's celebrate Christmas properly!"

36

TWO AND TWO

It was three in the morning and my body was aching, both physically and mentally. I was losing count of the days and suffering from sleep deprivation, as well as a continuous junk food diet. Liam would have to make a move soon, because I couldn't keep this up for much longer. I passed the time watching the roaches, most of which I now knew on a first name basis. I tried to avoid thinking. When I let my mind wander, all roads led to Amber. Wasn't it Tolkien who wrote 'Not all those who wander are lost'? I certainly was.

I sighed and took another caffeine pill, then saw the cone of light from a vehicle's headlights stop near the alley's entrance. The lights switched off. Was this it? Had he finally come? I held my breath and strained my ears, listening for the slightest sound. I could hear the unmistakable footfalls of someone trying in vain to creep closer and my blood ran cold.

Then a whisper broke the silence. "Pssst! Boss, you there?"

Shit, it was Scotty. I peeled myself off the pavement, every bone creaking from lying for hours on the unforgiving concrete and made my way past the snoring Mr Wendal, out into the night.

Scotty had walked back towards his less conspicuous everyday car, a bright red Ford Falcon V8, complete with racing stripes and a spoiler. He seemed nervous and was avoiding eye contact.

"Hey Scotty, what's up. How d'you find me?"

"That was easy. I can track the phone I gave you. I guess that solar charger works well. Look, I had to warn you about what I saw today."

"Go on."

"The cops are pulling over cyclists and checking their IDs. There's been nothing in the news, it's all low-key, but they must be on to you."

"Shit! That'll make things difficult from now on. I'll have to ditch the bike. Thanks for the heads-up, but why didn't you just text me a warning?"

Then the reason he was behaving so sheepish stepped out of the passenger side of his car. "Hi Jon."

I hissed at my friend. "Holy fuck Scotty, what have you done?"

"I'm sorry boss, she insisted. I needed help from someone, for when I was on shift, and she's been distraught ever since all this went down. She managed to get the truth out of me. C'mon, you know what she's like."

Jan walked over to us, her arms folded. She was wearing black jeans, a dark T-shirt and her face was a picture of concern. Forcing herself to smile, she tilted her head to one side. "Stop blaming Scotty, Jon. It wasn't his fault. He started behaving weird at work and I put two and two together."

"Well that makes me feel a whole lot better. So what you're saying is that if the cops are watching Scotty I'm screwed? Look, I didn't want to get anyone else involved. This is serious shit. At the very least you're now both risking a prison sentence for simply talking to me."

She sighed and dropped her hands to her sides, palms towards me. "It was my decision, I'm a big girl, Jon. I know the risks, I've entered into this with my eyes wide open. I know I doubted you when you had that rant at the doctor and for that I'm sorry. It's why I needed to see you, face-to-face. All I can say now, is that you have two people working with you on this. We both believe in you. You're innocent and we need to catch this bastard before he hurts anyone else."

She walked towards me with her arms open, faltered for a second then closed the gap and gave me a hug that squeezed the air from my lungs. I shut my eyes and tried so hard not to cry. A cauldron of emotions boiled within me.

The mere touch of another person after weeks of isolation.

The knowledge I was not alone in my fight.

The smell of female perfume.

The loss of Amber.

Tears were inevitable.

After a while I somehow stemmed the flow. "You have nothing to apologise for, Jan. And thanks for your support. You don't know how much it means to me."

She nodded and backed away, wiping her eyes, but then screwed up her face. "Jesus, Jon, you fucking stink!"

I had to grin. "Hey, that's something I learned from Mr Wendal. It's safer on da streets if ya stink like a skunk!"

37

GHOSTER

"What is it, Giallo?"

"It won't take long, sir."

"Better not, I'm on my way out. The wife's insisted on me going to some goddam New Year's Eve party. So make it quick."

Giallo rubbed the collar of his chequered shirt as he approached the Chief's desk. "Well, it's about the Jonothan Byrne case."

The Chief's head snapped up causing his jowls to quiver and his face took on the look of a cane toad drinking vinegar. "I thought I'd made myself clear about your involvement with that case."

"Clear, sir. Very clear. It's just that I might have stumbled on some relevant information that could be important."

He sat back and folded his arms. "Stumbled, eh? Go on, but this better be good."

Giallo remained standing as he delivered his pitch. "Well, as I've mentioned in the past, just before the Shaw murder, Byrne approached me with his crazy story of a serial killer targeting ambulance regulars. He thought the culprit could be a doctor and, as you know, was suspended for accusing one."

"I haven't got time for this, Giallo."

"Please hear me out, sir. So, with him accused of murder, I got to thinking perhaps his story wasn't so crazy. But if it wasn't a doctor, what about another ambo? It would make more sense. So I ran a check of all the on-road staff currently working for B-CAS."

The Chief's face turned a darker shade and he shook his head. "How much time have you wasted on this! Every ambo has to have police checks done before being employed."

"True, sir, but that just reveals criminal activity. I was checking for death certificates."

"Death certificates?"

"I was looking for a ghoster and I found one." He placed one of the sheets he was carrying in front of the Chief and tapped the photograph. "This man was a young office clerk when he died in New York on the eleventh of September 2001."

The Chief frowned. "The World Trade Centre?"

Giallo nodded. "He was born in Australia, but grew up in America. However, his parents never knew of his death as they died a few years earlier in a fire. No one to miss him and a death certificate in another country. Very difficult to trace and perfect fodder for a fake ID. Unless you're looking for it."

"You seem to have been doing a lot of stumbling. So who is he?"

Giallo placed a second page on the desk. "This is the man going by that name. I ran his face through our databases, but only found mentions of his exemplary ambulance career. So I used the youngest picture I could find and fed that into a search engine. Came up with this."

He handed over another sheet and the Chief picked up the

printout. The news article read 'Ambulance last to arrive' and described an horrific crash that claimed the lives of three family members in Brisbane's CBD. The photographs of those killed were inset over an image of a mangled car. He lifted the photograph and compared the two. "I'll grant you they're similar, but isn't that the brother who died."

"Yes, sir. He was an identical twin."

The Chief nodded, then looked up at Giallo. "So?"

"Well, this young man was studying law and the joint heir to a fortune when his whole family were killed because the nearest ambulance was dealing with a derro. I'd say that's a strong motive. He could've done anything, but a year or so later he goes overseas and disappears. This is presumably when he took on his new identity, assuming one with the same first name. After that he returns and studies to become an ambo down in Sydney. He let's years pass before he transfers to Queensland, working his way up to a position where he has access to patient records and can operate on his own. Which gives him both opportunity and means."

The Chief sat staring at him, face impassive, hands on the desk in front of him. "Go on."

"Regulars and ambulance time-wasters start dying in numbers, but Byrne banging on about a serial killer threatens to undo his master plan. So he frames Byrne for the murder of his girlfriend and we're left chasing the wrong guy."

The Chief lent back in his chair and sighed, crossing his arms. "Just great, Giallo. This is nothing more than your fucking gut instinct again, isn't it? OK, so we can pull in this ambo for identity fraud, but have you considered he may've just done that to start afresh? That crash wiped out his whole fucking family. He may've returned to Brisbane to help prevent others suffering the same fate. Christ, I can't believe I've wasted more time listening to your crap."

"Whether or not you accept my theory, sir, I know where Byrne is hiding."

"Is this more bullshit?"

"No, Chief." Giallo handed over his last piece of paper. "This was a report I came across in my inbox. A homeless man in the CBD assaulted two men a few days before Christmas. The only reason it ended up on my desk was that one of the injured scrotes lives in Carseldine Meadows, which appears to be my current area of focus."

The Chief glared at him and snatched the page from his hand. As he read, Giallo continued. "In their statement, they described two homeless men. The assailant, who appeared from nowhere, took down both of them and was the same height and build as Byrne. He was also wearing walking boots, like the ones that made the tracks found at Lake Nuga Nuga. One of them got a good look at the boot, seeing as the man used it to shatter his knee. The other homeless guy involved matches the description of Mr Wendal, a prolific ambulance abuser, especially over the last few weeks." He paused for a breath and let the information sink in. "Sir, I think Byrne is using Mr Wendal as bait to draw out the killer. We just need to find him and we'll find Byrne."

The Chief looked up after reading the report and glared at Giallo. "Why the fuck didn't you give me this at the start?"

"I'm sure Byrne is innocent, sir. I didn't think you'd listen to my theory if I just told you how to find him."

After a while his glare eased and he rubbed his face with a pudgy hand. "You're the one who phoned in that anonymous tip regarding Byrne being sighted on a bike in the city, aren't you?"

"I know nothing about that, sir. I've had all my Carseldine Meadows cases to work through. So, are you going to mobilise the Task Force on this?"

He stood, throwing his suit jacket over his shoulder and sidled out from behind his desk. Giallo was treated to a waft of stale sweat as his boss lumbered past him on the way to the door. "It can wait 'til tomorrow."

"Tomorrow, sir? If I'm right, Byrne has no idea who he's up against. If this guy is a serial killer, he's a mission-orientated psychopath who's been planning his revenge for over a decade."

The Chief turned and looked back at his detective. "If you're wrong, Giallo, I'll have you doing traffic duty somewhere out Woop Woop for the rest of your career. But even if you're right, it'll still have to wait. I don't know if it's escaped your notice, but it's gone six o'clock on New Year's Eve. We've simply got no spare coppers to comb the streets of the city for your Mr Wendal. Now, I'm late for that fucking party. Make sure you close my door when you leave."

38

ROACHES

The pubs and clubs of The Valley were brimming with people prepared to pay the inflated prices for drinks so they could join in with the festivities. But the homeless don't celebrate New Year, it's just another night sleeping rough. Another night exposed to the elements. Another night of discomfort and fear.

Mr Wendal had crashed early, perhaps because the extra human traffic on the streets would make it difficult to find a secluded alleyway. But when I joined him, he was still awake.

"G'day, brudda. Ya not out celebratin' wid ya white folk?"

"My folk? They're all dead. What 'bout you?"

"Dunno. Haven't bin back home fo' years, brudda."

I have to admit that it hadn't crossed my mind he was from anywhere other than Brisbane, or at least nearby. I sat down opposite him. "So where d'you call home?"

"Up north. Mornin'ton Island. I'm one of da few remainin' Lardil people."

"Mornington! Shit, that is north."

I flicked away a cockroach that was exploring my trouser leg. "So what made you come to Brisbane?"

"Bin 'ere since '92. I fucked up, brudda. Da grog made me do summat bad. Real bad. Got kicked off da island. I went walkabout an' ended up 'ere, just when dat fuckin' song was on da radio. Mr Wendal. Da name stuck. Kinda suited me. Don't deserve anytin' betta dan what I's got now.

He'd been looking down while he told his story, but on finishing he turned his head to one side to look at me. "So, what d'ya want wiv me den, Jono?"

I froze. "What did you call me?"

"Jono, ain't it. Jonothan Byrne. Dey t'ink ya killed dat pretty nurse. Ain't she da one in dat paper clippin' ya keep lookin' at?"

I stared at him. "How long have you known?"

"Ya bin to me loads of time in ya amb'lance. Always a smart-arse, but least ya were never cruel. I recognised ya when ya came back dat second night. What, were ya hopin'? I thought all white fellas look da same?"

He cackled at his own joke.

My mind was in free fall. Spinning like a novice jumper left to fend for himself. I had assumed this man was a stupid drunk and it had been me that was the fool all along. How many other things had I miscalculated? Where else had I screwed up?

"You could've turned me in. You could've claimed the reward they're offering."

He shrugged. "What da fuck would I do wiv all dat cash, brudda? Be dead in days, no doubt 'bout dat. Nah. Man's business is just dat, his business."

"So, d'you think I killed her?"

"Dunno. Why should I care? I's just can't work out what ya want wid me."

"Company?"

He laughed. "Bullshit, brudda! If ya won't tell us, den dat's cool. After alls, I's owes ya one. Ya saved me from dat beatin'."

"Well, let's get something straight. You don't owe me anything, except maybe a few boxes of wine."

He laughed and the sound of his enamel cup tapping on the concrete rang out around the alley. I shook my head and filled the container. "Happy New Year, Mr Wendal!"

"Sames to you, brudda!"

The light from the full moon created a silhouette of her face. The celestial body seemed oversized in the pitch-black night sky, her head creating its own lunar eclipse as her naked form swayed astride mine. We were lying in a desert landscape, the eerie glow casting muted shadows among the dunes and short scrubby foliage. I felt the gravel-like sand scratching my back as her body pushed down on mine.

She leant forward, her hands on my chest, her nails digging into my skin. She smiled at me, then dragged the tip of her tongue around her mouth, wetting her lips, her hips moving faster. Deeper. She reached down, holding my head between her hands, curving over and pressing her mouth to mine in a hungry kiss. As her tongue parted my lips, fireworks exploded in the sky and something scraped at my teeth. Amber's tongue was not warm and moist, but dry and scaly. Things moved about within my mouth, pushing out my cheeks, clawing over my tongue and down into my throat. I began to choke as she rose above me, her body thrusting hard as she wiped away the cockroaches streaming from her mouth.

I awoke with a sharp intake of breath. Flashes of light from the midnight fireworks display lit up the alley and I could see a figure squatting by the bundle of rags that was Mr Wendal.

The man tensed and his head shot up, looking straight at me, but his face was obscured by what looked like a small pair of binoculars attached to a headband.

He was wearing a green paramedic uniform and as he stood I could make out a syringe in his hand. He stared at me for a moment then chuckled. "Well, well, well. Look what I've found."

I grabbed my box of wine and pushed myself up into a seated position.

"Ha, nice try, Jon. You can dispense with the charade, I know you're no wino. I can see you clear as day through these night-vision goggles, but, hey, with all these fireworks I don't really need them."

He reached up and pulled the contraption from his head and even without his glasses, I recognised him in an instant. My mouth dropped open, mind racing, and I could only think of one word. "You?"

39

A DISTANT MEMORY

In his frantic state, the young man spots an ambulance in the distance. It is stationary on the other side of the river, over at Southbank. He waves his arms in a frenzy, shouting and screaming at the top of his voice. But they cannot hear him.

He pulls out his phone as he runs back to his brother.

"There's an ambulance across the river. It's only a minute or two away. I'm calling now to get them to send it."

His brother nods with the slightest of movements. "It's OK… just hold my hand."

He gives his brother's hand a squeeze as he waits to be connected to the ambulance call taker.

"Hello caller, what's your emergency?"

"Look, I'm at the crash on Elizabeth and William Streets intersection, Brisbane CBD. My brother is critically injured and we're waiting on an ambulance, but I've seen one across the river. Can you send it?"

"Er… Hold on, sir. I'll check your location."

"Hurry!"

There is a pause on the line while she reviews her screens.

"I'm sorry, sir, but that crew is dealing with another patient. We've *already dispatched an ambulance to your location and it'll be there as soon as possible."*

"That'll be too fucking late!"

"There's no need to swear."

"Fuck you!"

He throws his phone on the ground and it shatters, the pieces of plastic and glass mingle with those on the road from the BMW.

His brother looks at him. "Bad connection?"

"Can't you ever be serious?"

"Only when... money's involved."

He shakes his head and sits down next to his twin. Still holding his brother's hand, he uses his other to stroke his hair and, as an afterthought, he feels his neck for a pulse.

"At least your heart rate has slowed."

He let's out a weak laugh. "Not a... good sign... Bro. Means I'm... decompensating... not enough blood... in the system." His eyes flicker. "No time left... hey... these last few years... at Uni, an' all... I've missed you... so much... You know I love you... Right?"

"Don't talk like that! Help's on its way. Just hold on!"

"Don't worry... It's too late... Have to go now... Catch you... on the flip side... Darren."

His hand goes limp and the eyes that were focused on his face, dilate and stare past him.

The young man lets out a wail. "Noooooo!"

One of the firies comes over and checks his brother's pulse. He kneels by his side and starts pressing on his chest. Between compressions he calls to a colleague to come over and help.

The young man staggers to his feet and surveys the scene, his new suit crumpled and stained. He stands alone. Isolated. The single survivor of a family reunion that became a massacre.

Some firies are draping a tarp over the bodies of his parents, while two more perform CPR on his dead brother. His head feels as if it's smothered in cotton wool. Detached. Like he's watching a movie scene with the volume turned low. Then he hears the building sound of another siren.

Eventually the ambulance comes to a halt beside the wreck and he walks over to the driver's side, flinging open the door. "Where the fuck have you been?"

The ambo slides down from his seat, on the defensive. He is slim with close-cropped hair and a craggy, sullen face. He looks at what he thinks is another rude bystander.

"Got here as quick as we could, mate. Had a long way to go. Guess if people in the city keep calling ambulances for crap, there's none left for the real jobs."

The other ambo, a female officer, grabs the bags and dashes to where the firies are working on the body. She calls back. "Vic, I need you over here. Now!"

He glares at the young man. "I have to go."

He attempts to push past, but the man stands firm. "You're too fucking late!"

"Get out of my way, or I'll have you arrested!"

The young man stares at the ambo for a few seconds with a pale expressionless face, then steps aside. Vic pushes past him and walks over to the scene. He grabs the bag-valve mask from the oxygen kit and goes to place it on the patient's face, only to see a mirror image of the man he's just threatened to arrest.

40

PLAN B

My Station Officer, Darren Boardman, was enjoying my confused surprise. He smiled as he toyed with the syringe, while Mr Wendal snored away in the background.

"So, who did you think was providing this service? Obviously not me."

"But Sammy... the jar of potassium? How was it not Liam?"

"Liam? You mean Liam Fraser? Well, you can credit him if you wish, but here I am with a syringe in my hand. As to Samantha's suicide, I just had to swap the bottle of pills over in the ED. Your little rant got everyone flustered. No one took any notice of another ambo wandering through."

I regained some of my composure. "I guess it doesn't really matter, does it? I've caught you in the act, what was it this time. Adrenaline?"

"No. Already used that before, with varying results. But, no, I tend to use insulin on the homeless ones, especially this one. You see, I needed something the authorities could find if they needed a push in the right direction."

"What do you mean?"

"You still don't get it, do you? Even when you worked out what was going on, you could've saved yourself by turning a blind eye."

"But you're murdering people!"

"Murder's such a divisive a word. I'm just taking out the trash. These lowlifes are risking the wellbeing of good ordinary people by their repeated abuse of the ambulance service. I'm doing society a favour. I should be up for a medal, or a commendation."

"But why you? You don't strike me as the vigilante type. Something or someone must have fucked you up good and proper."

For a split second his arrogant smile faded, then it was back. "You're right, I guess there was a trigger point. Something you should relate to, Jon. Didn't you lose your brother to cancer? Myeloma, if I recall. Nasty disease. I lost my brother because some homeless regular needed a bed for the night. There are too many losers and not enough ambulances. I'm just doing my bit to redress the balance."

"So why kill Amber?"

He smiled and nodded. "I wondered when you'd bring her up. Well, how should I put it?" He shrugged his shoulders. "I don't want to get caught." He shook his head and wagged a blue-gloved finger at me. "You know, Jon, I spent years developing this… enterprise. D'you think I'd embark on something so risky without establishing a few… contingencies? I guess that's where you, my dear friend, come in. You were always my Plan B. My scapegoat."

He shrugged again and leant against the wall, folding his arms. He looked like he was enjoying his diatribe. "You see, I required an ICP that management were unlikely to defend, someone who bucked the system, someone who was a permanent thorn in their side, someone like you. And most of the time you'd fire up without needing a push from me. You were my sacrificial lamb I could throw to the wolves if the heat became too intense."

The popping sound of fireworks was followed by more light in the alley, illuminating Boardie's face, like Dracula bathed by lightning in a low-budget movie.

"Jon, you have no idea the level of shit you're in. I've thought of every single detail." He nodded at Mr Wendal, who was no longer snoring. "Even this poor bastard's death will be pinned on you. The police now know that you're back in Brisbane and you can hardly deny you were here."

He smirked before continuing. "Did you think it was a coincidence you knew and had treated all those losers I freed from their tawdry existences? If the police bother to look into the deaths, which is still unlikely, they'll discover you could be implicated for each and every one. And d'you want to know the clincher?"

He smiled at me, waiting for an answer, so I obliged. "What?"

"You, my friend, killed your only alibi."

"What d'you mean? Amber? You murdered her, you sick fuck!"

"Ha! Well, yes, I guess if you insist on being pedantic, I may have carried out the deed. But it was your incessant blathering about a serial killer that caused her death. You're as much to blame as if you had plunged that fancy kitchen knife into her chest. And what a shame to defile such a wonderful, naked body like hers. Sleeping there, she looked so... peaceful. So... desirable."

I had planned on keeping him talking, but his last comment stung too deep. Without thinking, I launched myself in his direction, but he was ready for my lunge. He moved to the side and I sailed past, crashing into a pile of garbage. When I turned to face him, he had dropped the syringe and whipped out a multitool from his belt, the ten-centimetre blade now pointing towards me.

"So, was that your big plan? A citizen's arrest? Let's see, a suspected murderer apprehends and accuses a well-respected B-CAS manager? C'mon Jon, who's going to believe you?"

Before I could respond, there was a ring from the mobile phone in my overcoat, signifying a text message. To Boardie's surprise, I held up my hand and reached in my pocket. "Excuse me a minute, I need to check this."

I looked at the screen:

```
Gr8 pics and sound, boss. Uploading well.
    Cops informed. U got the fucker!
```

I smiled at Boardie and some of his confidence seemed to ebb away. "Something amusing you, Jon?"

"Oh well, you know how I always love an opportunity to stick it to management? See that wine box over there? Give it a wave. Apart from half bag of goon inside, there's an infrared GoPro camera hooked up to a mobile phone. A video of our whole conversation is going live on YouTube. Smile, you're now viral you twisted bastard!"

Boardie straightened up and shook his head, his smile gone. Without breaking eye contact with me, he flipped the knife up, so it spun before landing back in his hand. He did it again, as if tossing a coin.

"Well, Jon. Congratulations. Looks like you've forced me to implement Plan C."

The knife spun up again, but this time he caught the handle and drove the knife down, as he dropped into a squat. With stunning accuracy, the blade plunged into the side of Mr

Wendal's neck, piercing his carotid as he let out a gurgling scream.

"No!" I leapt over to the homeless man, as Boardie pulled out the knife and stepped back. A jet of blood sprayed out across the alley and over my chest. I grabbed his neck and held my hand tight over the puncture wound, as Mr Wendal clawed at his neck, writhing in pain and surprise.

Boardie leant over the two of us as he cleaned the blade with a crisp white handkerchief. "Now here's your moral dilemma, Jon. Do you remain here and try to save the life of this piece of shit, or do you chase after me and apprehend your serial killer? You can't do both."

Blood was oozing between my fingers as Mr Wendal stared at me wide-eyed. "Stay still don't fight me!"

Boardie strolled away down the alley, his voice trailing off as he departed. "I've got a feeling you're going to let me walk free. I hope you've thought about the hundreds I might yet kill. Is this one life worth so many others? But hey, don't stress it. Your decision's only streaming worldwide. So long Jon, until we meet again…"

A pool of blood was forming under Mr Wendal's head. I needed to get more pressure on the wound before he bled out. I searched for anything to use as a bandage and then looked at my free hand covered in grime. The wine box was some distance away.

"Shit!"

Holding his neck with one hand, I dragged him over to the box, sat down and pulled him onto my lap. He was kicking and screaming, so I wrapped my legs around his body to pin him down. Grabbing the cardboard box, I ripped the silver foil out, causing the camera to fall on the floor, then tore a hole in the bag. While gripping it in my teeth, I shoved my hand inside, washing my fingers in the wine as best I could. I then bent over and looked Mr Wendal in the eyes.

"This'll hurt, but I'm trying to save your life."

"Wha' da fuck?"

As I released my hand holding his neck, a spurt of blood shot out before I thrust my alcohol-soaked index finger into the hole left by the knife.

"Ahhhh!"

I could feel the pulsing vessel and bunched up the rest of my hand, pressing down hard.

"Geroff, geroff!"

"Stay still, brother! You've got another carotid, I just need to stop this one bleeding!"

His body stopped fighting and his eyes locked on mine. When he spoke, the words were full of disappointment. Or was it hate?

"Ya no brudda o' mine. I heard everythin' that fucka said. All doze nights, ya been callin' da ambulance on me. Waitin' for 'im. Ya used me, ya cunt! Ya used me as bait. You's as bad as him, ya fucka!"

In the distance there was the growing sound of sirens. The flow of blood from Mr Wendal's neck had slowed and he still had a strong pulse. My finger would have to stay in place until the surgeons had a chance to repair his neck, but he would survive this ordeal. Survive, so he could serve out his self-imposed life sentence. Survive to return to his prison on the streets of Brisbane.

I lay back to avoid having to look in his reproachful eyes. The last of the fireworks were splashing their sparks across the blackened night's sky and all I could think of was Amber. I'd not forgotten the promise I made her, but catching Boardie would have to wait. The moral dilemma he'd posed had been based on his own twisted paradigm. For me, there was no question. I had to save Mr Wendal, it was instinctive, it was in my genes. And Amber would never have forgiven me if I'd abandoned him.

But then again, who was I to criticise someone's morals? Without a second thought, I'd used this man in my arms as bait to lure out a killer. I'd have to live with the guilt of that. Live with the loss of Amber. Live with all the associated mental trauma that was no doubt heading my way.

I'd seen enough people dealing with grief. Had to break bad news more times than I care to remember, watching as the sorrow flooded out from every pore of those left behind. And as with all paramedics, I just flipped a switch inside, maintained my detachment and relied on a warped sense of humour to cope with the stresses of my job.

The sirens had become deafening, echoing off the narrow walls of the alley. Then they stopped. Red and blue lights swirled round the confined space as engines roared, tyres screeched and voices called out.

Gerry's face appeared above me.

"G'day Jono. Fancy meeting you here."

He sounded his usual flippant self, but I could tell he was rattled. "Good to see you too, Gerry. I'm fine, I just can't move my hand. Mr Wendal's got a knife wound to his neck."

"Shit mate, I know! We've been watching it. Fuck, everyone's been watching it. We didn't know where you were until Scotty called it in."

Faces I knew floated by in a blur. Scotty, Jan, Liam, Dr O'Driscoll. Even Detective Giallo appeared. They were interspersed with visions of Amber and I was unsure which were real, which were hallucinations. At one point I found myself in an ambulance, my finger still deep in Mr Wendal's neck, his glare as sustained as his silence. I blinked and looked around my former office, once so familiar and now so strange.

It was then I realised my true dilemma.

With all my new emotional baggage, could I return to my old life? Did I want to return? Could I go back to dealing with other people's emergencies? Moping up the grief of strangers. Did I have enough capacity to absorb more woes, or was my cup overflowing? Could I remain detached? Professional? Or would I just lose myself in the process?

Only time would tell.

ACKNOWLEDGMENTS

Like it takes a village to raise a child, I have discovered that writing requires a supportive team of people to nurture an embryonic idea until it becomes a fully fledged book. I would therefore like to thank the following people for their support and feedback during the many formative years of this novel: Amie, Damo, Gaye Franks, Glenn Davies, Ian Coombe, Issy, John Bathurst and Lisa King. A special mention must go to Qbone Kenobe, who can somehow annotate while reading at a blistering speed, Vicki Nelson, with her razor-sharp insights and Petra Johnson, whose comments and use of emojis in BetaBooks did more than encourage me to continue on this quest. Also, many thanks to Lynnette Cameron, who had the unenviable task of editing the first draft, and Gordon Wise, whose astute comments revamped the book and spawned my short story series.

And last, but by no means least, I must thank the two most influential and important women in my life. My ever-supportive mother, who not only put me on the planet and taught me to write, but insisted on bankrolling the first print run of *Dead Regular*. And my lovely wife, my harshest critic and most ardent fan, who first suggested I write a book as a coping mechanism to deal with the stresses of my shifts. By reading and re-reading my many drafts, as well as coping with my moods and typing absences, she helped mould the story to what it is now. To her I owe so much on so many levels. Thank you.

ABOUT THE AUTHOR

Harry Colfer is the pseudonym of an experienced paramedic who lives and works in Brisbane, Australia. Although his stories are totally fictional, his writing style is very realistic and he maintains a healthy level of paranoia with respect to his anonymity.

To date he has published twenty short stories in the *Ambo Tales From The Frontline* series and plans to write another twelve, one for each of the thirty-two AMPDS codes, the system used worldwide to categorise emergency calls.

He has also written *Beneath Contempt,* the sequel to *Dead Regular*, which will be available in 2021. If you wish, you can turn the page to read the first chapter.

www.HARRYCOLFER.com

facebook.com/harry.colfer.1
twitter.com/Harry_Colfer
instagram.com/harrycolfer
amazon.com/author/harrycolfer

BENEATH CONTEMPT

JONO BOOK 2

1

AMBER NECTAR

I gazed at a bead of condensation as it formed on my glass, like sweat on the forehead of a dying man. Moonlight sparkled off its curved border, as it grew in size, gaining weight. Eventually, it overpowered its own inertia and began trickling down the smooth surface, picking up momentum by consuming other droplets. As I watched, it occurred to me that the drop was a metaphor for life. We spend so much energy rushing about meeting others, but for what purpose? In the end, every individual just fades away, like the drop now lost within the ring of water around the edge of my drink.

I reached out and picked up the tumbler on my second attempt, tipping it back to drain all the rum, the ice from my thermos long having melted. The liquid burned my throat as I swallowed and I stared at the glowing full moon through the distorted lens formed by the thick base of my glass.

It didn't seem to matter what shit happened in your life. The moon. The stars. The world. They all just carried on as they'd been doing for countless millennia. I slammed the glass down almost missing the little rickety camping table next to my deck chair and toppled over my bottle of Bundaberg Rum.

"Aahshit."

I lurched forward, grabbing for the bottle by my feet, but was relieved to discover I'd had the foresight to replace the cap. Refilling my glass, I snatched up the new measure and held it up to the star-scattered sky, toasting the moon. "Here's to life just carryin' on, ya heartless bastard."

I threw back the drink, but this time kept it in my mouth for a while, bathing my tongue in the velvet liquid. Parting my lips, I sucked the warm night air over the rum so my lungs received an intoxicating hit from the evaporated alcohol. I then swallowed it down and went to refill my glass when I noticed the silver-edged silhouette of a figure, standing on the beach near the dark water's edge.

It was a woman in her early thirties with long black hair, wearing a light flowing dress that billowed around her shapely legs in the gentle sea breeze. As she approached, I could see the sad look in her eyes marred her beauty and I knew her bare feet would leave no footprints on the sand. I knew because I'd looked so many times before. I sighed and poured myself another drink.

"I's wondering when you'd show up. Glad yous could join me for our annivers'ry."

She came closer and stood about a metre or so away from me with her arms folded. I could almost touch her, smell her perfume. Despite the darkness, I could see every detail of her face, all the features I loved so much. The woman before me was Amber Shaw.

She shook her head with pity and smiled at me. "You need to stop your drinking, Jon."

"Ha." I took a swig from my tumbler. "Now ain't that the truth."

I dared not take my eyes away from her or even blink, in case reality returned and she disappeared, leaving me alone again.

"You know my shrink says you're just an hallooshination. A mental construct to help me cope with my post-traumatic stresh."

"And what do you think, Jon?"

I smiled and raised my glass. "I thinks I drink to catch another glimpse of you. I drink to pretend that you're real again. Jusht for a while. You see, I miss you so much. I'm lost..."

Tears streamed down my face, but I kept my eyes open so I wouldn't lose her again. She leant forward and kissed my wet cheeks, stroking my head before standing up.

"I will always be with you, Jon. We had something special. But you need to move on now. You've spent too long wallowing in self-pity and being here in this place isn't helping. You've got too much time to think."

She looked back at the waves rolling in and then at the sparse vegetation, as a gust of wind caused her hair to fly around. "You must leave this island and return to Brisbane. Restart your life and face your demons. And what's more, you need to do it now."

I laughed, but there was no humour in the sound. "Jusht my luck to get counselled by my own mental construct. How warped is that?"

I reached for another drink, but she snatched the bottle from my grasp. "I think you've had enough. What you need, Jon, is a wake-up call."

With that, she lifted the bottle and swung it into the side of my head causing pain to explode throughout my skull. A new constellation appeared across my vision and the last thing

I saw before I blacked out was Amber throwing the bottle into the sea.

Consciousness came to me wielding a sledgehammer to pound my brain as I opened my right eye a fraction. I was lying on a combination of rock and sand on the upper part of the beach, looking out at the water lapping the shore. But the weak morning sun was too much for my optic nerve and the light forced me to retreat inside my skull. Despite the unforgiving mattress, I tried to go back to sleep, but someone kicked the sole of my boot.

"C'mon Jono. Up ya get, rise and shine. Looks like you fell out your deck chair last night and belted your head, eh. Hope you don't need patchin' up, seein' as you're on shift at twelve. You know the island needs you and I'm sure you don't want Albert treating you, eh."

I pushed myself up into a sitting position and rubbed my face, but instantly regretted it. A mixture of sand and congealed blood encrusted my right temple and I winced as I made a fingertip exploration of my newfound injury. I attempted to speak, but it felt like a roo had taken a crap in my mouth.

Screwing up my face, I squinted at the man whose tall lean body blotted out the rising sun, but the image was still too bright and I had to look away. Nevertheless, I knew who'd delivered my wake-up call. "What time's it, Charlie?"

"Time you were gettin' up for work, eh. I can't keep draggin' your sorry arse back to town every time you start your run of shifts."

He squatted down in front of me with amusement playing on his dark-skinned face and he rubbed his broad nose as if to conceal a smile. "I knew I'd find you here, my friend. You were seen leavin' town with your table and chair, eh."

"Well, aren't you the tracker?"

"Ha. Thought I'd get you this time, but what a surprise - you stink of booze, but no sign of a bottle. How d'you do it, Jono? One of these days I'm gonna catch you and you'll be up for a big fine, eh. You know Mornington's a dry island."

"Can't you give a guy a break. I think someone assaulted me."

He laughed. It was a warm sound that echoed from deep inside his belly. With a flick of his hand, he knocked his wide-brimmed Akubra to the back of his head and scratched the exposed wavy black hair. "Assaulted, out here? The only thing that assaulted you was gravity, eh. That and about four million mozzies. You look like you've come down with the measles. I'm surprised they didn't drink you dry, eh."

He looked out at the flat calm waters of the bay. Our two figures cast long shadows down the beach in the morning's golden glow. "Mind you, you're lucky a croc didn't drag you off. You must have a death wish sleepin' rough out here, eh."

"I just came to watch the sunset, didn't intend to stay the night."

"You never do. Now, get your butt in my car, so I can drive you back to your digs, eh. You need to clean yourself up before anyone sees you. You're a smart man, Jono. Why d'you insist on being so dumb?"

"It's a talent I have."

He stood and held out his hand to pull me up and I accepted the offer, although being upright seemed to invigorate the sadist with the sledgehammer. Charlie chuckled on seeing my face and then folded up my table and chair, throwing them into the tray of his marked-up dual cab police ute.

I climbed into the passenger seat and used the vanity mirror on the sun visor to check out my head. It was a small laceration that looked more from a rock than a bottle. Alcohol often caused my dreams to merge with reality.

Charlie swung himself in beside me. "You'll live, more's the pity. If we lose you, they may have to send us a real ambo, eh."

He started the engine and negotiated his way off the beach before bumping back along the dirt track towards the island's only town, Gununa. As the dust swirled up behind his car, he chuckled to himself. "How long does it take you to walk out here with that table and chair? It must be ten Ks or more."

"'Bout two hours. It can be relaxing."

"Ever thought of gettin' yourself a pushie?"

I tensed at the mere suggestion. I hadn't used a pushbike for about a year, ever since that night.

"You OK? You look like you've seen a ghost, eh."

"You don't know the half of it. No, mate, I'm OK. Just one of my flashbacks."

He glanced over at me, then stared at the road ahead. "You know, Jono, you were really fucked over last year, eh. You've got every right to be screwed up, but you'll get through it. I know you will, eh. Just hang on in there, mate."

I sighed. "Thanks, Charlie. And thanks for coming out to get me. I owe you one."

"What, another? Guess you're lucky I'm not countin', eh."

He flashed me a wide grin and we continued in silence for the rest of the trip. We soon pulled up outside my place within the hospital compound. It was one of the two dongas assigned for the island's paramedics and it's where I'd lived for the past eight months. I waited for the dust trail to settle before getting out.

"Thanks again Charlie, I'll catch you later."

"Just make sure you show up on time, Albert'll give you shit if you're late, eh."

I grabbed my gear from the back and gave a wave as I walked away, but Charlie called out, "Oh and Jono, call me when you have a clear head. I've been doin' some detective work and I think I've found your man."

I stopped in my tracks and turned to him. "What man?"

"Mr Wendal, of course."

Printed in Poland
by Amazon Fulfillment
Poland Sp. z o.o., Wrocław